SPECIAL
INTENTIONS

SPECIAL
INTENTIONS
Mary Pat Kelly

N E W
ISLAND
BOOKS

Dublin

Special Intentions
is first published in 1997
in Ireland by
New Island Books,
2 Brookside,
Dundrum Road,
Dublin 14,
Ireland.

ISBN 1 874597 71 5

New Island Books receives financial assistance from
The Arts Council (An Chomhairle Ealaíon),
Dublin, Ireland.

Cover design by Jon Berkeley
Typeset by Yellowstone
Printed in Ireland by Colour Books, Ltd.

ACKNOWLEDGEMENTS

While this is a work of fiction, there are a number of real Sisters I would like to thank: Sister Ruth Eileen Dwyer, Sister Bernice Kuper, Sister Alexa Suelzer, Sister Barbara Doherty, Sister Virginia Marie Cashin, Sister Mary Olive O'Connell, Sister Marcella O'Malley, Sister Marie Denise Sullivan, as well as Ellen Howard, Cathy Lucas, Marilyn Marshall, Sylvia Fromme, our band and my students. For their assistance in preparing the manuscript I am grateful to Ann Morea, Lucia Sciorsi, Joyce Nolan, Elliot Willensky and Eddie Panian @ fordham.com — their help was crucial, as they know.

Thank you to The Group and to Rabbi Bernard Cohen, Doris, Jeffrey, Seth and Micah.

Writing this book was a long process and I appreciate the help of Martin Scorsese, Mardik Martin and the Marys — Mary Gordon, Mary Maher, Mary Sheerin, Mary Cummins and Mary Bringle. Thank you to Frank Price for his encouragement, to Majorie Haskell for her empathy and to Roberta Sorvino for everything. Without Maeve Binchy's support and postcards I would never have finished. Philip Nolan, Frances O'Rourke and Aidan McNamara were crucial in the publication and I am very grateful to Sharon Plunkett for representing *Special Intentions* so well.

Special thanks to my mother and all my family, immediate and extended. I am very grateful to my sister Margaret Kelly for her belief in me. My husband Martin knows my gratitude and I dedicate this to him.

Also by Mary Pat Kelly

Martin Scorsese - The First Decade
Martin Scorsese: A Journey
Proudly We Served: The Men of the USS Mason
Home Away From Home: The Yanks in Ireland
Good To Go: The Rescue of Scott O'Grady from Bosnia

For Martin, with love

THE PROLOGUE

A double rainbow arched from the big church to the Plaza Fountain where all of us, nuns and ex-nuns, who had gathered to celebrate the 150th Anniversary of the foundation of the Sisters of the Redemption were saying our last goodbyes.

I looked up at the twin streams of colour, pink, yellow and an almost lime green: a sign — but of what? The rain had been gift enough, drizzling away the Indiana humidity I remembered so well. I used to wring the sweat out of my black wool serge habit every night. Only a handful of nuns wore habits now. Most were in regular clothes and with the earlier days of adjustment, when polyester and extra short haircuts marked nuns, past, you really couldn't tell who was in and who was out. Reverend Mother wore Gloria Vanderbilt jeans and Mexican silver earrings. There was a very real possibility, she had told us, that religious life, as it had been known in the Church for a millennium, was over for women. She wasn't too disturbed. "The Spirit blows where it will," she said.

The breeze was picking up now. The oppressive afternoon was turning into a sweet-smelling evening. Mother, or the General Superior as she was now called, gave us a crowd estimate: "More than 800 of us worshipped together in the Big Church today, 542 former members and 273 Sisters of the Redemption."

There had been 1,500 in the community when I arrived; fifty-four other girls entered with me. There were fifty-two in the band ahead and seventy-six in the band behind. This year, the order had no new candidates, although next year they expected three. The average age in the community was sixty-eight. Most of us ex-nuns were in our late thirties, forties, and fifties. Only three from my band were still in the order. One ran a clinic for Aids babies, one taught in Guatemala and the third administered a parish in southern Illinois. "We rent a priest on Sunday," she told us. "The laity does everything else." That was me now, I was the laity.

The Superior General had personally invited every ex-member back for the celebration. My letter had been forwarded four times. I'd been nervous about coming back. The convent and I had not parted on the best terms and under certain conditions, I could still get riled about my six years as a nun. But when we'd arrived, 'Welcome Home' banners lined the avenue and a painted sign said, 'Benedicamus Domino'. Mother further eased the tension when she said how proud the order was of those who witnessed to God's presence in the world. "You are our fruit," she said.

"What were we doing here?" asked the former Sister Nicole as we drank beer sitting on the steps of St. Anne's chapel. "I'm not sure," I said. But one thing I did know: somehow that six-year experience defined me whether I liked it or not. I told Nicole, "Last summer I was doing research for a book and tail hooked onto an aircraft carrier. There I was taking my helmet and lifejacket off and this marine comes up and says 'Welcome aboard, Sister Margaret Mary'."

"How did he know?", asked Nicole.

"He didn't, he was just joking," I explained. "Something about my name or my face, and of course I ended up walking along the flight deck hearing everyone's confession." She laughed. "It's not funny," I said. "When I worked in Hollywood and tried to be decadent, I ended up advising on religious movies and arranging exorcisms for houses in some of the more notorious canyons. They called me 'theologian to the stars'."

"No wonder you came back," said Nicole.

"No, I came back to prove to myself that those six years in the convent were just a brief segment on a rich and diverse journey."

"Did it work?"

"Nope."

And now, at the very end of the celebration, the rainbow, this excessive technicolour effect. A sign, that young nun that was me would have said, "Of what?"

That it's time to tell the story.

1

FIELD DAY

I almost crashed bang into the Oscar Meyer Wienermobile the day I announced I was entering the convent. The huge motorised hot dog, with Oscar himself wearing a tall white chef's hat at the wheel, was making a very wide turn into the parking lot of Ladyhill School for Girls and I was heading right for it. My bike picked up speed as I coasted down the steep hill that gave our school its name — along with Mary the Mother of God, of course. But my bike was old and the brakes were shot and now it was hurtling down because I had not ridden it regularly since I was twelve years old. It was too uncool. But today was Field Day, the day when the four hundred students of the Sisters of the Redemption allowed themselves to be free from cool. We put our hair in pigtails, dotted freckles on our faces with eyebrow pencil and pedalled to school singing "My Little Runaway, Run Run Run Run Runaway".

We spent the last day of every academic year running relay races, pole vaulting, hitting softballs and generally having a good time being 'simple' before picnicking on the frankfurters Oscar dispensed from some secret place deep within the Wienermobile. Then at the proper moment, the members of the senior class would sit down in a circle under the giant oak tree that had been decorated with toilet paper at the centre of the campus. The girls who planned to enter the convent would announce their decision to the rest of us. It was the highlight. This year I would be one of them.

"Sorry, Oscar," I yelled at the unnerved little man as I swerved around him, bumped on to the grass and finally slid to a stop. Yes, today I would take the irrevocable step and tell the world, at least my world, that I was becoming a nun.

In 1962, on the North Side of Catholic Chicago — which had the largest parochial school system of any diocese in the world — entering the convent was not considered that unusual. Nuns themselves were very familiar to us. We'd been taught by them all our lives, had loved some and hated some; but while we spent a large number of our waking hours with them, after school they left us for a world that was a mystery. This wasn't such a big deal, since many things we accepted were a mystery. That's what you were told when you said you didn't really understand papal infallibility or transubstantiation, or why unbaptized babies could never get out of limbo. It's a mystery, they'd say.

Take birth control. OK, I knew it was against natural law but what exactly was it? When I was ten, I asked a babysitter — because she was Protestant and therefore, I thought, more open about sex — what birth control was. "Mechanical interference with intercourse," she said. Unfortunately, that didn't help much because I didn't know what intercourse was. Mechanical interference, I could picture that. An apparatus that was a cross between an iron lung and the machine that pitches baseballs back, somehow stopping the conception of children (the primary end of marriage). No wonder it was a sin.

We knew nuns — and we didn't know them. When I say we could predict our sixth-grade teacher Sister Julianna's mood for the day by whether she jangled her rosary beads during the opening prayer, but still wondered if she went to the bathroom, I'm not exaggerating. By high school we were more sophisticated. One girl even said Sister Anna Rita was menopausal. Still, we wondered what the nuns wore to bed.

Priests, now they were different. Every parish sponsored socials with priests at them as chaperones. They were dances — 'Stag 25 cents, Drag (with a date), 75 cents' — and they varied in quality depending on things such as how dark the gym could be or how current the records were. An easygoing priest was a big plus. St. Ignatius' dances were always good, St. A's (Athanasius) not bad, Queen's (Queen of All Saints) getting better. Everyone at the socials came from one of six Catholic high schools, the boys from Gonzaga, St. Peter's and St. John's, the girls from Ladyhill, Mercy and St. Mary's. This was where we met each other, in church basements and parish halls with priests in attendance.

But nuns were gone into that other world of mystery. Still, they were with us, camped out in our minds and consciences. So while we were typical teens at the end of that whole 1950's world, cruising in convertibles, screaming for the home team and twisting to Chubby Checker, we never missed Mass on Sunday. And when we parked in the forest preserves, our kisses were closed-mouthed and calculated. Kissing was OK, it was arousing the boy that was wrong. So I'd often simply stop and ask, "Are you, you know . . . ?" "No," he'd say, "No, No, No, No, No, it's OK." And we'd start again, carefully, because one touch of the tongue could send you to hell just as surely as if you gave up your faith to Chinese Communists who were shoving bamboo splinters under your fingernails. No, the nuns were never very far away. Wait until I tell people I'm going to be one of them.

Last year when the Ladyhill nuns-to-be had made their announcements, they just blurted the news out. People couldn't hear them. There was a lot of — "Who?" "What did she say?" — and it was very unsatisfactory. No drama at all. So today I had brought a big black chiffon scarf with me. I had my best friend Janet tell the class that she would start handing the scarf around the circle and anyone entering could take it and stand up and tell us where they were going. It worked perfectly. The other classes clustered around our circle. Every eye was on the scarf as it moved from hand to hand. Sally Murphy couldn't get rid of it fast enough, but Jennifer Nolan held on until people started squealing and then she handed it to Donna Kennedy, who did stand up. There were gasps of surprise and applause. She was joining a missionary order. It moved along the circle, Nancy Beigle stood up. Big deal, we all knew that she'd be a Carmelite anyway. Soon Sharon Kelly, Marilyn McGuire, Carol Sweeney, Ginny Devlin, Joyce Breslin, Cathy O'Grady, Suzanne Whelan, Jackie Anderson and Susie O'Neill were all joining the Sisters of Redemption. Eleven vocations. We were going for a Ladyhill record.

Last of all, I stood up. Everybody started screaming when I said, "I'll be going to Linton, Indiana to be a Sister of the Redemption." I actually heard, "No, no, I can't believe it." People ran up to me, hugging me and crying. I felt pandemonious and wonderful. I had struggled for months against my vocation and giving in felt wonderful. It was the right thing to do. I wanted my life to count for something. What a send-off — and this was just the beginning. I had a whole summer of farewell appearances ahead.

It did take me all of June, July and August to say my goodbyes. First, much to my surprise, I had acquired two simultaneous boyfriends. One was my age, just graduated from high school, and the other a year older and at the University of Notre Dame. They were nice boys, fun. We'd always go out with another couple, to movies, miniature golf, my dances, their dances, and since Dan lived ninety miles away from Paul and was home mostly during vacations and summer, it worked. They were official dates and both knew the ground rules: "Are you . . . ?" "No, No, No, No".

But there were other boys in my life, or rather in Janet's and my life. Janet had been my best friend since the day I moved into Kilbourn Avenue on September 3rd, 1954. We walked to Queen of All Saints Grammar School together every day, spent every school afternoon babysitting for her younger brother or my little sisters and brother. Doing it together made it fun. We trained the kids to play together while we read books and talked.

"What more can you possibly have to say to each other ?" my father would ask after I had walked her home across the street, she had walked me back and I had gone half way back again with her. I would finally come home and immediately go to the phone. "Less words were spoken at the Yalta conference," he'd mutter.

My Dad liked conversations to be brief and to the point. "Summarise," he'd tell us, when we'd begin some long explanation. But Janet and me — summarise? Impossible. Mostly we discussed boys. At twelve we had a joint crush on Johnny Riordan on the corner. We'd wait in my yard until we heard the rattle of his dog's chain which meant Johnny was taking Zippy for a walk down the alley. That first clink started our hearts beating. We waited and then casually carried a paper bag to the garbage cans just as he arrived at my gate.

"Hi, Johnny."

"Hello. Come on Zippy."

He spoke to us. Us — we never wanted him to prefer one over the other, just an encounter we could analyse for two or three weeks.

In a way that pattern continued. Like me, Janet had her official boyfriends. We dated them on Fridays — casual — and Saturdays — nylons and flats. Neither of us would ever accept a date for Saturday after Wednesday or call a boy or be ready when he came to pick us up. Those were the rules in Sauganash, our neighbourhood, a suburban-style enclave within Chicago proper. We also had a group of friends we'd known since grade school, two other girls our age, Annie and Susie, and four boys two years older than we were. At first, these boys (yes, Johnny was one) merely said hello to us when we happened to show up at their baseball games or walk by their houses seven or eight times in an evening. But in the last two years they seemed to seek us out. Janet and I would be sitting on my stoop listening to Ella Fitzgerald, Tommy's rattletrap car would happen by and we'd be off on some adventure. Not a date, but a trip to the beach along Lake Michigan maybe, or a raid on the Amy Joy Donut shop. There'd be stunts — like jumping out of the car at a stop light and getting in the opposite doors. My father was not impressed. "That crew wouldn't pay a quarter to see an earthquake." But that was the point. Boys who paid for us were dates and were governed by the rituals but The Group, well, was The Group.

Strangely enough, the person who I most dreaded saying goodbye to was one of the group, Kevin, my friend, my pal who I never dreamed of kissing. Now lately we had gone a few places alone together — a concert at Ravinia, the outdoor music theatre, and a dance at his fraternity. "He just needed someone to go with, I guess" I told Janet.

Of course she and I had liked each of the four boys at one time, and so had Annie and Susie, but we said nothing. The Group meant too much to risk the perils of pairing off. At the heart of our activities were the serious discussions — politics, the Church, Africa and India — whatever was in the news. We also sang together, which really flaunted all the rules of cool. And the boys in the group liked it when one of us girls excelled, getting high marks in exams or athletic awards at school, achievements which seemed to make the dates ill at ease. They also liked it when we had adventures. When Janet and I used our school paper press passes to get into the front row at a campaign rally for Senator John F. Kennedy in Glenview, it became a story the guys in the group made us tell over and over.

"Maggie actually crawled under the tables right up to the stage," Janet would say.

"Yes, I knelt right below him and kept touching his toe the whole time he was speaking." Janet and I demonstrated how we had jumped to the car and told them we couldn't stop jumping for an hour afterwards.

"He's everything we thought and more," we told the group. But our regular boyfriends only listened to the story once.

And now tonight I was meeting Kevin alone at Queen of All Saints playground to explain to him exactly why I was becoming a nun. And I knew no theatrical gesture nor any of the lines I'd practised all summer for relatives and my parents' friends would work with Kevin.

The car radio played Johnny Mathis' 'Chances Are' as I went back and forth on the same swings we had played on since grade school. I leaned back, looking at the stars. Kevin sat next to me on the see-saw.

"Are you sure, Maggie? How do you know?" he asked.

"Kevin, it's just that I've always thought about it. I don't want to live just an ordinary life. I want to do things for people — important things. I'm not going to be a nun like we had. I'm going to be in the slums working for what's right."

"Yeah, but you don't have to be a nun for that."

"If you're going to throw your whole self into it you do, Kevin. Besides, I think this is God's will for me and even if it seems hard it's what I should do and then I'll be happy."

"But how do you know?"

"I just feel it. You know, until May I'd forgotten about the whole thing, but then, Suzanne told me she was going and I spent a lot of time with her and Sister Patrice talking about how Suzanne could get her parents to let her. And I thought, here I was — my parents probably wouldn't even really object. I mean, you know they're in the Christian Family Movement. Well, anyway, I just couldn't put the whole thing out of my mind. And one night a couple of weeks ago I was sitting with Suzanne and just to try it out I said, 'Suzanne, I'm going'. And I felt so happy and so relieved I knew it must be right. I'm finally in step with things." There, I had flung enough words at him surely.

Kevin didn't say any of the things I thought he would. He just kissed me. "I wish you weren't going," he said. "I understand how you feel. I thought about joining the Jesuits last year, but I didn't really feel I had the call; but if you do, you should follow it. At first I couldn't really believe you were serious. I thought you might have said you were to kind of force my hand."

What??? (The nerve, the colossal unmitigated gall). "I guess I just didn't want to believe it." (That was better.) "But now I think it's probably just as well that you're going."

(Wait a minute. What kind of thing is that to say?)

"Because, Maggie, the way I feel I'd want to make plans for us that we're just too young for."

I didn't hear the rest. Shock had set in. He was serious. Marriage wasn't even in my vocabulary. I was on the brink of an adventure. Get married at seventeen? Did he think I was some hoody girl with no future who needed a husband to make her important? In the movies marriage always came at the end. I wasn't ready for the end. Maybe I was getting out just in time.

2

ENTRANCE DAY

The night before I was to leave I was in the bedroom Brigid and I shared, packing with the help of most of my immediate family.

"Mother, I know those nuns. When they say 36" x 12" x 15", they mean it."

"Maggie, we are never going to get all this stuff into this trunk. We've got a bigger one in the basement. Use that one."

"I can't. It's the wrong size and it's not black, plus it has all those daisy decals on it."

"So the daisies will be nice — a little different."

"Mother, they do not want things different. They want them the same."

My mother had been colliding with the Catholic school system's obsession with uniformity since I was in first grade when, desperate for a ribbon, she had cut half of the sash off my sister's blue cotton dress, pinned it in my hair and sent me off to the May Crowning. My partner in the procession wouldn't walk with me because, as she put it, "That's no ribbon. It doesn't shine. Sister said a blue RIBBON."

To tell the truth, I secretly felt my mother was right and that the difference between white synthetic blouses and white cotton blouses or knee socks and anklets was not worth all the fuss the nuns made. But I was afraid to admit my doubts to my mother or we'd be going to school with plaid blouses under our blue serge uniform jumpers. Still, the nuns liked my mother because she'd drive them places, talk to them about the same things she talked to her friend Mrs. Murphy about and insist on stopping for milk shakes on the way home. So once we were known in a school, they'd look the other way. My mother said that if the nuns had six kids to get ready for school every morning, they wouldn't be so concerned that our milk money be in separate envelopes, each containing the exact amount. "Here Maggie, you go to the Principal's office and give Sister one cheque for all of you." Mom, please!

I remember one typical early morning. We were all running around. "Where are my shoes, Mom?" "Who took my books?" "I can't find my homework." "Mom, I need seventy-five cents for the Mission Crusade." Then Michele (third grade at the time) said, "Mom, I have to bring in a baby picture of me. We're guessing who's who from their baby pictures today."

At this point my mother was feeding six-month-old Patrick with one hand and helping Laurie comb her hair with the other.

"Here," she said to me. Then I was feeding Patrick and combing out Laurie's hair. She was back in a minute and gave Michele the picture.

"Mom," said Michele, "this is Brigid!"

"I know, but don't say anything and no one will know. You all looked alike as babies anyway."

As we walked to school together Michele was very nervous. "What if somebody like Elizabeth Ducy says, 'Sister, that doesn't look like Michele Lynch. It looks like

Brigid Lynch'?" But on the way home she was all smiles. "As I walked up to pin my picture on the board, I dropped it at Elizabeth Ducy's desk. Of course she looked. And then when it came time to guess, she was waving her hand like crazy. 'Sister, Sister. I know that one — Michele Lynch.' " Terror struck again when Brigid's class had a similar contest and Brigid took the same picture. But Brigid told her not to worry. If anyone from Michele's class even noticed, they'd think Brigid had taken Michele's picture. Brigid didn't care. She would even have taken my brother Patrick's picture.

So do you wonder why I was getting a little nervous as my mother pointed out the arbitrariness, and in some cases stupidity, of some of the "List of Necessary Items for Postulants Entering September, 1962." I had no milk shakes to balance bringing white cotton briefs when the list said white cotton trunk-style underpants. "They'll check, Mom."

But it was hard to be serious with Brigid, fifteen, modelling one of my convent undershirts over her blue jeans while Michele, thirteen, was running around in the black petticoat. Laurie, ten, twirled around in the voluminous nightgown and Sally, nine, pulled on the black lisle stockings and then tried to walk in the grandmotherly shoes. My father and Patrick, five, came in to find a giggling chaos.

"I thought the Holy Spirit swept down and carried a few nuns off to the convent on a fiery cloud," said my father. Patrick just asked, "Do you have to go?" He needed me to play with. I could make a swing into a rocket ship. I was the NASA Controller. "10, 9, 8, 7, 6, 5, 4, 3, 2, 1. BLAST OFF. We have lift off Ladies and Gentleman, Astronaut

Patrick Lynch is going into orbit. Apollo 9 is in outer space."

We all loved Patrick. You couldn't help it. We fought over who got to take care of him or take him to school on family days. We brought him to our friends' houses. From the time he was a tiny baby we'd kept him up when our parents were out. There he was at six months, wrapped up in his blanket, lying right between Brigid and me on my Mom and Dad's bed watching TV with us. At two he learned to run to his crib when he heard the key in the front door. "What an angel," my Mom would say while Patrick feigned sleep, "never any trouble." Even now he was trying to help, pushing on piles and jumping up and down on the towels so we could close the trunk. "We have to finish!" my Mom said. "It's ten o'clock, you kids should be in bed!"

"Brigid, help," I pleaded. In a flash, she had all the clothes packed and somehow got the lid down. "Great — thanks everybody," I said. They were all looking at me, and I at them, my family. Sally and Laura, so close, so different in personality. How many bubble baths had I given them? How many times had I set their hair in pink rubber curlers, helped them with their times tables? I remembered Michele as an infant coming home from the hospital; I was four years old, whispering her name — "Michele, Michele, I'm your big sister." And Brigid, she was a friend now. We actually doubled on dates. I could count on her. She rescued my entire senior science project by redoing the logarithm table.

I was leaving my family in twelve hours. Was I nuts? How could I? That evening, everything seemed precious. All the fights about whose socks were whose and my mother's unreasonably early deadlines and my father's

24

"Look me straight in the eye and tell me again how the car ran out of gas after you changed the flat tyre," disappeared.

I can't do it. I won't be able to go. But I have to, I'm signed up. I have a vocation and there's no way around it.

"Mom, I'm going to meet Janet," I said and ran out of the house.

We found the group and started riding around. "We'll go to Minnesota so you can say goodbye to Kevin," Tommy said. I'll skip the part about how I finally got Tommy turned back towards Chicago at 3 a.m. and about us driving up just as my father was getting into the car in his pyjamas to search the neighbourhood. Nor will I give the details of my mother's remarks, which ended with "Don't talk to me now or I will say something I may always regret." I won't go into how Brigid spent three hours straightening her drawers to stay out of the way after she heard my mother tell my father, "Don't take her off to our medical insurance. They'll send her back within a week."

The next morning was tearful. I stood with Janet saying goodbye as her father loaded her things into their station wagon for her journey to college. I saw her record player, portable radio, hair dryer, records and stacks of books. Her clothes were in plastic dry cleaners bags hanging on a rod across the back. She wore a madras shirtwaist. So did I.

"Goodbye, Maggie, I'll write to you all the time. I'll come to visit you and . . . "

"Tell me all about the Notre Dame guys . . . Have fun. Cheer hard at the games."

She nodded.

Across the street my father was loading our station wagon: one trunk without daisy decals and a black naugahyde suitcase.

Janet got into her car and they drove off. Two cars pulled up in front of our house. Michele's and Brigid's car pools had arrived to take them to school. I stood with them. We didn't cry because Cindy Malloy was driving one of the cars and she would have had a big story about the Lynch sisters weeping circulating around Ladyhill by lunchtime. They each got into their cars, and I waved them down the block. Then Sally and Laurie started out for their school. They walked backwards waving until they got to Iona St. and turned away for school. Finally, only Patrick and my great-aunt Rose were left to say goodbye at 6026 North Kilbourn. I expected never to see the house again. There were no home visits for Sisters of the Redemption in 1962. No more water skiing, or Indiana sand dunes. No raids on Amy Joy's Donut Palace, no summer evenings sitting on the stoop waiting for the boys to happen by. No more Notre Dame University weekends, or three-hour phone conversations with Janet, no more going to the Birdhouse to hear Cannonball Adderley — no more music or records.

But I won't think about that. I'll think about the Charlie Brown *Peanuts* books Kevin had given me, my picture of John Kennedy and Pope John, of Teilhard de Chardin's *Phenomenon of Man* and how I'd fix up a little nook in my room where I would read and write and meditate. OK, I'd be homesick but I'd see the family when they were allowed to visit me in three months. And there was the Ladyhill contingent. Sharon and Susie, Joyce and Marilyn and Carol and Ginny and Suzanne and Cathy and Jackie — we'd be together. But it was so hard to go. Had all the nuns felt this way? Impossible.

The tears I'd been holding back broke through on Edens Expressway and I cried for the next 175 miles. My mother kept turning around asking if I were alright. "Yes, fine," I'd say and continue crying. "I'm doing the right thing," I'd say to myself, "I'm doing the right thing," as the last urban bits of Chicago disappeared and the Dan Ryan became a country highway. The fields of high corn and waving wheat went by in a watery blur. Finally, dehydration set in and I stopped crying in time to see the turn-off for Our Lady of the Hills.

The road swept into the college and the Motherhouse of the Hills. Two iron gates, tall and ornate, opened onto a wide main drive. Well-proportioned stone buildings sat back in the trees with full-skirted lawns around them. This part of the campus was for the regular college girls. Five hundred of them came to the Hills for a good Catholic liberal arts education. Like many Midwestern colleges, the original buildings were about 100 years old. A grand art deco dorm and auditorium had been added in the Twenties and a new library and science building had come courtesy of the baby boom and government funds. But when we turned and went over a stone bridge, all the buildings were old. We passed a church that reminded me of the medieval French cathedrals we'd studied in art appreciation and a grotto that looked like the one in *The Song of Bernadette*. The trees seemed ancient — all thick trunks and spreading branches. There were a lot of them, pines, oaks, sycamores and maples that bordered the road or clustered together to form a grove. Their shade looked very inviting because it was hot and humid in that particular Indiana way that takes no prisoners. I looked at the trunk filled with layers of underwear, all meant to be worn at one time under the postulant's heavy black pleated calf length skirt, the sturdy black cotton blouse, and the black cape. I was already sweating in my madras shirtwaist. I couldn't imagine assembling all that, let alone wearing it.

"Well, what do you think, Maggie?" asked my mother.

"It's nice, I guess."

"You know," said Dad, "it's not too late to change your mind." Change my mind, I thought, how can I change my mind after six going away parties? Change my mind after my big announcement at Field Day! What would people . . .

"Don't worry about what people would think," my mother said. Will she be able to read my mind even after I'm a nun? I wondered. She patted my shoulder. "There's a lot of life you don't really know and maybe you should wait."

Things I don't know? I thought, now wait a minute — I'm not some stay-at-home type who has no experience. . .

"Maggie," she said again, "are you listening?"

"Mother, I've got to do what I feel is right. And this is it."

"OK," she sighed.

We pulled up to the Novitiate. This was the first modern building on this side of the campus. It was shaped like a Y, built from red brick, stainless steel and glass. "I hope this place is air conditioned," said my Dad. It wasn't — except for the chapel. In a way that made it harder. You'd be nice and cool during prayers and Mass and then bam, walk into that encompassing humidity. I always thought of a fly swimming in a bowl of cold water that suddenly turns into hot oatmeal.

Dad switched off the engine. A novice in a white veil came up. "Hello, I'm Sister Ann Martin. You're the Lynches and I'm your guardian angel." I was sure my dad would have a remark for that one. But he was good and just smiled and raised one eyebrow. Sister Ann Martin smiled.

Her face was tanned very brown against the white linen. Good, we must get out in the sun. "Do you have your letter?" Sister Ann Martin asked. I fished in my purse and pulled out the 'Letter of Instructions' I had received.

Here it was. I scanned the letter. Had I forgotten anything? When the printed sheet headed 'The Conditions for Admission to the Novitiate of the Sisters of the Redemption' had arrived, Janet and I had laughed through every phrase.

> *Applicants should be sound in mind and body without any notable deformity, and of a constitution sufficiently strong for the duties of the religious life.*

"How noticeable are your deformities?" said Janet.

> *They should be of legitimate birth, of irreproachable character, and of a family free from blemish or reproach.*

Blemish, reproach. "Oh, oh," I said.

> *They should also be free from hereditary diseases, from a family history of insanity, epilepsy, emotional instability, and so on.*

> *They should be sincere and earnest in the desire of giving themselves to God, and determined to serve Him in the duties of their calling with great fidelity to the Rules of the Order, and with entire submission to the direction of Superiors.*

"When did you ever entirely submit to anything?" she asked.

They should present certificates of baptism and confirmation, their parents' Church marriage certificate, a letter of recommendation from their pastor or confessor, and a certificate of health.

As a rule, they should not be older than twenty-eight years of age.

No dowry is required, but applicants are expected to bring what money they can to defray at least the expenses of their noviceship. The applicant is asked to state any difficulty in regard to this.

They should be perfectly free, having no one depending on them, and no debts.

An applicant who has been a member of another Community cannot be admitted.

I could still hear Janet giggling about the dowry and she had a comment for every article of clothing on the list.

Sister Ann Martin reached over and took the papers from me. "Good," she said. "Now, would you like to make a visit with your parents?"

"A visit?"

"In the Chapel."

"Oh," I said, "no, I think we . . . "

"It's customary," she said.

"Oh. OK . . . "

So we knelt together, Mom and Dad and I, in the modern chapel. Sun poured over the blond wooden pews and the brown marble of the walls and the green veined floor. It was all very new, very cool, very calming. Dear God, I'm here, please help me. Don't let me start crying again. Please bless them all especially Patrick. I had wanted to kiss Patrick and cry over him a little when I left, but he didn't like wet kisses and tears would have scared him.

Sister Ann Martin cleared her throat and stood up. We three did the same and followed her from the Chapel into the hall where a sign said 'Reception Area'. Under it, two young novices sat at a wooden table. Again, white veils and the white linen covering their necks contrasted with their sunburnt faces. How are these nuns getting these tans? I wondered. Not with iodine and baby oil surely. "Welcome to your new home," said the blue-eyed novice, with a slight southern accent and a big smile. "And what is your name?"

"I'm Margaret Mary Lynch from . . . "

"Margaret Mary," I heard from across the room. "It's so good to see you, so good to have you here."

"Kathy!" Kathy Feeney, who'd graduated from Ladyhill last year, rushed toward me. Her long black skirt billowed behind her. When she hugged me, I smelled the starch in her white collar and the scent of ironed wool I always associated with all nuns.

"You look great in the habit, Kathy, but it seems so funny to see you like . . ."

"Like a nun? Well, I've been in the habit almost a month now. Covers the weight I gained as a postulant. Watch the apple pie, Margaret Mary."

"Mom and Dad, you remember Kathy . . . er Sister . . ."

"Sister Jacinta."

Kathy hadn't changed. Still talked and moved fast. I felt relieved. "I like the name, Kathy," I said.

"Hello, Mr. and Mrs. Lynch," she said quickly and to me, "Thanks, I like it, though it wasn't my first choice.

You'd better start thinking about names yourself. February's name day, and . . ."

"Jacinta," Sister Ann Martin interrupted, "Margaret Mary hasn't even signed in yet. Here, Margaret Mary, write your name and the time, 3:24 p.m."

I bent over and signed my name under a list of about thirty names. In the hall behind me, other parents and daughters were going into the Chapel and then lining up behind us at the table. I felt a slight push from behind. I hurried with my last name and then turned to see who had shoved me. I couldn't believe it. I mean, who would expect to see a bleached blonde with a duck tail haircut in the Novitiate!

Kathy was talking again. "Margaret, sorry I couldn't be your guardian angel. I've got Anna Sophia," she pointed to the blonde. "But you'll like Sister Ann Martin. She's OK even though she's older and from the college."

"Thanks a lot," Sister Ann Martin said. She turned to my parents. "Mr. and Mrs. Lynch, if you drive Margaret Mary's trunk around to the back someone will be on the dock to take it. Good, you've got your suitcase, Margaret. We'll get her dressed and meet you back here in a few minutes."

My parents exchanged a look and walked out the front.

"But . . ." I began, moving to follow them. Sister Jacinta put her hand on my arm to stop me.

"They'll be right back. It's better to distract them for a minute because you see they're not allowed upstairs in your cubicle. Ann Martin will take you to change. See, it's hard to tell parents they can't come up if they ask. You know some want to see where you sleep, but seculars can only be in the Chapel and parlours and if they ask, then. . . "

"Seculars? My parents?" I thought as I followed Ann Martin upstairs.

On the third floor of the Novitiate the halls were so quiet it seemed right when Ann Martin dropped her voice to a whisper.

"Your cubicle section is down here."

"OK," I whispered back.

She opened a door and we stepped into what looked like a large railroad car. Curtained openings lined each side of a narrow aisle. Through the curtain was a compartment with a white iron bed covered with a white cotton spread and a chair, that was all. Pink steel walls separated my space from that of the six others in the section. Ann Martin opened a door in the wall and showed me a narrow closet with four shelves and three drawers.

"I'll explain how you arrange your shelves later, but now let's hurry with your uniform," she said. "Your parents are waiting."

I swung the black suitcase up on the bed. She shook her head and pointed to the white speckled chair. "Never anything on the bed. Including you. No sitting."

"OK." Why? I wondered. My mother thought it was bad luck to put a hat on the bed. But to sit . . . ?

"Breaks down the mattress," she explained.

I moved the suitcase onto the chair and took out the heavy black pleated skirt, the cape, the black blouse and the black slip or petticoat and spread them on the bed. "OK?" I asked.

"For now. I'll show you how to lay out your clothes later. OK, put your undershirt on, the blouse and the skirt and then I'll help you with the cape and the collar and cuffs."

She stepped out of the little room and pulled the curtain. I looked around the enclosure. Four sides of pink steel. "The new Novitiate is very modern," Sister Ann Marilyn at Ladyhill had said, "Everyone has her own room. Not like in my day, when we slept in huge dormitories — fifty beds to a dorm, with curtains between. Heaven help you if the novice next to you snored!"

"Margaret Mary, come on," Sister Ann Martin hissed.

I pulled off my madras shirtwaist and took the nylons off the garters of my pant girdle and replaced them with the black hose.

"Hand me out your dress," Ann Martin whispered.

"I'm going to give it to my mother, for my sister. My Mom wears the same size too," I whispered back. "We all shared . . . "

"Your dress," she said firmly, "goes to the clothing room."

"OK, here."

She took it.

"I'm ready, " I said loudly. "Oh, sorry," I whispered.

She came in, and looked me up and down.

"I'll help you press the skirt later. Permanent pleats supposedly, but look at the wrinkles."

I thought they were razor sharp.

"The blouse is nice. Better made than ours were. They changed uniform companies."

She appraised the uniform in a soft voice as she deftly pinned the white cuffs on to the sleeves, pulling each pin from a pincushion attached to the black ribbon that hung from her waist.

"Handy," she said, showing me the thin circle rimmed with straight pins. "You've got one too. With your pocket downstairs. I'll show you later. Alright, Sister Margaret Mary, let's go to the parlour and say goodbye to your parents."

"All these floors shine so," I said to Sister Ann Martin, as we walked down the stairs.

"You'll be polishing them soon enough," she replied.

My mother and father waited with five other sets of parents in the parlour. Postulants had been arriving since early morning, Sister Ann Martin told me, and almost everyone was here.

They got up when they saw me in the doorway.

"Not too fashionable, Mom, but it fits," I said.

My mother reached out and straightened my collar. It wouldn't move. "Pinned on," I explained. Well, I guess this is it!! What do I say now? "I'll see you in two months, Mom, Dad. It'll go fast."

This is not forever. I'm only 175 miles away.

"Give my love to the kids."

First my dad. He hugged me. "Goodbye, Margaret Mary." And then my mother. The three of us clung together for a moment. Slowly I became aware of the other parents and postulants and of the novices hurrying silently past in the hall and Sister Ann Martin twirling her pin cushion, impatient. It was time for them to go.

Now Sister Ann Martin took over. "Goodbye Mr. and Mrs. Lynch," she said. "I hope I'll see you again." She ushered all three of us to the door.

"Goodbye, goodbye." She and I walked my parents down the outside steps and stopped. I waved at them as they got into the car. I waved again when the motor started. I wanted to stand there waving as they pulled away, but Ann Martin said "Come on. Best thing is to get busy and we've got a lot to do." And so we turned away and went up the steps.

There was a plaque next to the door. It said, 'Those who instruct the many to justice shall shine like stars for all eternity.' Dan. 1:25. 'Instruct the many to justice' — yes, I liked that — I must remember why I'm here. 'Shine like stars' — 'Anyone who leaves Father and Mother for my sake' . . . OK. I get it. I took a breath and went in.

Ann Martin led me down the stairs into a basement. Even here the terrazzo floor gleamed (nuns are even cleaner than I had thought before). A long corridor held fifty-five identical trunks lined up side by side. Over each was a name card. I found Sister Margaret Mary (Lynch) easily enough — very nicely printed, but it seemed the 'Sister' was done in even blacker printing than the rest. In front of each trunk a postulant and her guardian angel novice unpacked while checking each item against the list. Sister Ann Martin opened my trunk to begin the process. She looked at the solid mass and then at me.

"Yeah, well it is packed tight, but we had a little trouble closing the lid so . . ."

"Oh well," she said yanking the first layer, "that manila envelope contains your name tags, Sister."

Sister? Already? I picked up the envelope; sure enough there was five feet of 'Sister Margaret Mary 98', 'Sister Margaret Mary 98'.

"You sew one of these on all your underwear and handkerchiefs so you'll get them back from the laundry."

"I didn't bring handkerchiefs. I have some Kleenex — and there's always toilet paper, hah — hah." She didn't laugh.

"We use handkerchiefs. I can get you some from the no-number box."

"The what?"

"The box for clothes that come back from the laundry without a number."

"Then why bother to . . . " She looked at me. I stopped.

"You'll sew the tags on at recreation."

"When's that?"

"An hour after dinner, that's what we call the noon meal and an hour after supper."

"What do we do?"

"Different things. Sometimes we take walks, sometimes just sit around the recreation room and talk, but then you're supposed to be 'profitably busy'."

"In other words, sew on numbers."

As we talked she separated the contents of my trunk according to the list's directives. The underwear and nightgowns passed. Other things did not. I watched the discard pile grow. The Jean Naté talcum, the bottle of peroxide to keep up my 'highlights', the raspberry coloured gym shoes I'd brought — all were rejected.

"But the list didn't specify any particular colour for gym shoes," I said.

"The list assumed black or white."

I started to object but stopped when I looked up and saw Sister Marie Charles, the Mistress of Novices, coming down the hall. Small and delicate, her habit seemed to flow around her like black chiffon. She walked along welcoming everyone. Very nice, but definitely in charge. With her was a younger nun, aged about forty. She was much more 'of the flesh'. Her round smiling face had none of the ascetic planes that gave Sister Marie Charles her other-worldly looks. They reached us just as Sister Ann Martin got to my books and my two framed pictures, one of Pope John XXIII, and the other of John Kennedy.

"Welcome, Sister Margaret Mary," said Sister Marie Charles.

"Thank you."

"Thank you, Sister."

"Oh, you're welcome."

"No Sister, we use 'sister' after 'Thank you' and 'Please' etcetera."

"Oh. OK. I mean. Certainly, um, Sister."

Sister Ann Martin jumped in. "Sister Margaret Mary, may I introduce you to Sister Mary Francine, your Mistress of Postulants." That was the jolly-looking one's name. She smiled at me.

Sister Marie Charles looked down at my pile. "I see you have quite a few books. Well, Sister, you need only have brought one book for Spiritual Reading and the New Testament."

"I read quickly — Sister — so I brought some extras."

She started to go through the pile, giving Sister Ann Martin Instructions. She read out the title, *You're a Good Man, Charlie Brown*. "This can go to the village school — second grade."

"But, Sister, really Peanuts is philosophy in a way.   It's . . ."

Sister Ann Martin gave me a look, and I stopped as Sister Marie Charles picked up the next books.

"Portrait of the Artist as a Young Man, Dr. Zhivago, and three Agatha Christies, Sister?"

"Yes, well I like to read before I go to sleep, and . . .

"Sister Margaret Mary, novels are not acceptable and we never read in our cubicles." We don't? I couldn't believe it. Not read? I ended every day of my life reading in bed.

"Send these to the college library and give the detective fiction to the infirmary, Sister Ann Martin." She picked up my Pope John Paul XXIII and John Kennedy pictures. "And Sister Margaret Mary, I'm afraid we have no framed pictures in our cubicles."

"But, Sister, it's Pope John and President Kennedy." I had typed out quotes from the inaugural address and Pope John's speeches and put them around the pictures. "I think these two are the essence of what we are trying to bring to . . . "

"Very nice, Sister. They are certainly great men, but we only have a crucifix in our rooms."

Sister Ann Martin gave me another of her looks so I stopped. Then Sister Marie Charles picked up my *Phenomenon of Man* by Teilhard de Chardin. Finally, a point for me.

"Ah, Father Chardin's book," she said.

"Yes, isn't it exciting," I said, "I read through it once but didn't understand it all. Now I'll have time to really study it. Did you read the article in *Time,* when he was on the cover?"

"We don't read *Time Magazine,* Sister."

"Oh well," I said, "I guess it is superficial but it shows that even non-Catholics are opening up to the Church. Look how the whole world loves Pope John! They're writing about the Council in *The New Yorker* and of course, John

Kennedy helps. And with Teilhard's stuff about converging in love and harmony, well it all . . . "

I trailed off; even I can't keep babbling on when there's absolutely no response. Sister Ann Martin seemed distinctly uncomfortable. Sister Mary Francine smiled but said nothing.

"Well, Sister Margaret Mary," Sister Marie Charles said, "your enthusiasm is commendable, but I am not sure Father Chardin's work is proper reading for a postulant. I have not read his books, but Father Jakowski, our chaplain, has, and I will consult him. I will take the book and inform you of his decision."

As she spoke, I'd started twisting the medal around my neck. When I saw Sister Marie Charles looking, I stopped. "Sorry, Sister, a nervous habit."

"It's lovely. Gold?"

"Yes Sister, a gift from my uncles, two priests and . . . "

"We don't wear gold, Sister."

"But, Sister, I . . . "

Sister Ann Martin tugged hard on my cape. "Shut up," she hissed.

Sister Marie Charles moved on to the postulant next to me.

"Sister Anna Sophia Thurler" her card said — the one with the Elvis haircut.

This should be good, I thought.

Jacinta began to introduce Sister Marie Charles but her postulant broke in.

"Please Sister, I'm not Anna Sophia — nobody calls me that, ever. I'm Nancy or Nan — always have been."

"We don't use nicknames here, Sister Anna Sophia."

"But it's not a nickname — I used it in school, on my driver's licence."

"Well, you won't need your driver's licence here, Sister."

That was a joke. I knew, because the novices laughed and Sister Mary Francine chuckled.

"But, Sister, could you drop the Sophia at least . . ."

"There are so many Anns and Annas, Nance," Jacinta explained. Now Sister Marie Charles picked up a guitar from Anna's trunk.

"You play?"

Well, that will go, I thought. And I bet she does a great Elvis impersonation. We at Ladyhill had progressed to folk singers.

"That's very good," Sister Marie Charles said.

What???

"Music adds so much to recreation."

I gave Ann Martin a look. *She* can keep a guitar and I can't keep my medal!! Call that fair?

"Of course the guitar will be common property of all the postulants while you're here."

Sister Mary Francine spoke up. "Sister Marie Charles, I wonder if maybe this Sister's name couldn't be considered common property too."

I didn't get that. Neither did Sister Marie Charles.

"Her official name would remain Sister Anna Sophia but in the Novitiate we would call her Sister Nancy."

Interesting logic, I thought. Sister Marie Charles looked at Sister Mary Francine for a moment.

"I have no objection, Sister. Welcome to the community, Sister Nancy."

This might be *my* chance.

"Excuse me, Sister Marie Charles, I'm always called Maggie . . ."

She turned to me.

"Margaret Mary is a lovely name," she said. "Welcome to the community, Sister Margaret Mary."

They moved on.

I sat down on the floor next to my discard pile and looked up at Sister Ann Martin.

"Well," she said, "you can take those pictures out of their frames, fold them and put them in here." She handed me a small prayer book, black with 'The Little Office of the Blessed Mother' stamped on the front in gold. "There are lots of spiritual reading books in the library," she added. "I have a good one now for spiritual reading about the Little Flower."

I'm afraid I didn't listen much as she told me about St. Therese always smiling at this nun she couldn't stand until the nun asked St. Therese why she liked her so much and so on. I was thinking about Kevin and my Charlie Brown books and poor John Kennedy flattened into the Little Office of the Blessed Virgin Mary. Shine like stars, huh.

"Wait a minute, I'll be right back," she said. I watched her white veil depart, no wrinkles at all. That's incredible, I thought, don't novices lean back?

"She took some of your stuff?" Sister Anna Sophia Thurler, now 'Nancy' again, said.

"Yeah."

"Mine, too. I brought a bunch of albums. But 'no secular music, Sister'."

"Oh yeah," I said. "What did you bring, Elvis' greatest hits?"

She just stared at me.

"Sorry," I said. "That sounded snotty, I guess."

"Yeah, it did!"

"Well at least you got to keep your guitar. Where are you from?" I asked, although I'd already placed her accent as inner city Chicago. She's from Redemption, I thought.

"I'm from Redemption," she said.

Redemption High School was on the West Side. Once it had been the premier school of the order but the neighbourhood had changed and now — well, now, you drove through the West Side with your doors locked.

"And what high school are you from? No, let me guess — Ladyhill, right?" she said.

"Yeah — but how did you know?"

"Just a guess," she said. "How many came from Ladyhill?"

"Ten," I said proudly, "Ten out of 110. And how many from Redemption?"

"Two others — two out of 250."

"Well," I said, a little embarrassed. I didn't want to show off too much about Ladyhill. Everyone knew we had the best academic standing of all the high schools of the Sisters of the Redemption. "Eighty-seven point two percent of our young women go on to college," our principal said on every occasion.

Just then Sister Ann Martin strode back. She picked up the raspberry gym shoes from the discard pile and handed them to me. "Here, Sister Marie Charles said you may wear these until you can get black ones from home. Otherwise you'd have to miss a gym night," she said.

"Horrors," said Nancy. "Miss a gym night!"

"A lot of us enjoy the gym, Sister Nancy," Sister Ann Martin said.

"I'd love to go," I said quickly. Nancy took the tennis shoes from me.

"You really thought you could have shocking pink tennis shoes?" she asked.

"They're raspberry, and I do have them for a while."

I took my medal off and handed it to Ann Martin. She took an envelope from her pocket, slipped the medal into it and put it in my trunk.

Nancy watched.

"Our own personal treasure chests, locked up contraband waiting to go home with us if we don't make it," she said.

I looked at Ann Martin.

"It's not that you're *expected* to leave. But you know this year is like a test — you look us over and we do the same," she said.

"Yeah," said Nancy, "we could get kicked out."

"Not me," I said.

With that a siren went off.

"What's that — an air raid?" I asked.

"No," Ann Martin laughed. "That's the bell."

Bells at the new Novitiate were electric. While the church tower clock chimed the hours for the older sisters, across the road, here the call to prayer or work shrieked with raw insistence.

Ann Martin stood up and brushed dust, invisible to the naked eye, from her long black wool skirt.

"Prayers — it's five to five — we've got five minutes to get to Chapel."

Ann Martin handed me a small black book. She flipped the pages to 'Vespers'.

"This is the Little Office. We chant Lauds in the morning, Vespers at this time and Compline at night."

"Come on, we have to hurry," Jacinta said. "Take your office books, your rosaries and your spiritual reading book."

"But I don't have a book," I said. "She took mine."

"Here, how about this," said Nancy, "I brought these two."

She handed me a book called *Love Does Such Things* by Father Gregory O.S.B.

"Thanks," I said, and grabbed it. It wasn't Chardin but . . .

The novices almost pulled us along. "Come on."

We dashed up the stairs from the basement corridor to the entrance hall in front of the chapel. Four or five other novice-postulant pairs were sliding to a halt in front of the chapel too. The novices shifted into instant composure as they entered. Each one placed her finger carefully in the Holy Water font, blessed herself and moved silently to her place. They look so complete somehow. I don't want to be a nun, I thought, I want to be a novice. Ann Martin directed me to the middle row. I found my name scotch taped on a prie-dieu, 'Sister Margaret Mary'. Well, I thought as I knelt down, they certainly are efficient here. Everywhere I went there was a labelled place for me.

"In the name of the Father and of the Son and of the Holy Ghost." Sister Marie Charles started the Rosary. I fished in my enormous pocket to get my beads. Ann Martin seemed to consider the pocket, a big black cotton pouch sewed onto a black grosgrain ribbon which tied around my waist, the essential garment. "Everything you need's in here — a pen, notebook, handkerchief, rosary and of course, your pincushion," she'd said. I could feel that round black circle against my leg. Pins and handkerchief. Two items I'd never had much use for. I glanced at the postulant who was my prie-dieu partner. She said her Rosary with her eyes closed. Very pious. "Hail Mary full of grace the Lord is with thee," we said. "Blessed art thou among women and blessed is the fruit of thy womb, Jesus."

Familiar words. In fact I learned the facts of life when I was ten because I asked my mother what 'fruit of thy womb' meant. She'd been loading the dishwasher and stopped and said, "I guess this is as good a time as any."

"The First Joyful Mystery," Sister Marie Charles announced. "The Annunciation." All the voices blended in one rhythm.

Glory be to the Father ...

"The Second Joyful Mystery, the Visitation."

Our Father ...

My family will visit in November. Just two and a half months away, only ten weeks.

Hail Mary, full of grace ...'

Now wait. I should try not to be distracted. I'll concentrate on the mystery. Visitation. Mary visits Elizabeth, "the babe in my womb leapt." Patrick will start kindergarten Monday. I'll miss his first day at school.

Holy Mary ...

Oh Holy Mary help me.

Glory be to the Father, and to the Son . . .

I read Nancy's book for twenty minutes, and prayers were over. Not so bad, I thought, that went fast and I even felt . . . I heard movement from behind me. The novices filed out of the Chapel. I looked at the other postulants. No one knew what to do. Then I heard, click. I knew that click. It had signalled me forward at processions, halted my row at the 9 a.m. Children's Mass, told me when to stop (one click), genuflect (two clicks), stand up (three clicks) and process out (four clicks) at First Communion, Confirmation and Graduation.

Click, click, click. The postulants stood. Click, click. We genuflected. Click, click, click, click. We turned and filed out of the Chapel. The novices don't have to tell us everything, I thought, as our black uniformed line followed their white veiled one. At the door of the refectory, indecision struck again. Each of the 106 novices waited with bowed head behind her chair at her place. But where did we go? "Find your guardian angel." Sister Mary Francine had come up behind us. I headed for Ann Martin, Nancy came behind me. Sure enough there was *Sister Margaret Mary*, lettered in gothic calligraphy on a white celluloid strip sealed in a plastic ring. A napkin ring! The only person I'd ever seen use one was my grandfather.

We all said grace. But no one sat down.

"Benedicamus Domino," Sister Marie Charles said.

"Deo Gratias," the novices replied.

With a great scraping of chairs we all sat. Now the refectory sounded like the Ladyhill cafeteria, as the novices shifted from religious silence to teenage chatter.

"Why the Latin?" I asked.

"Sister Mary Francine will tell you about that," Ann Martin said.

"Oh goody — bacon, lettuce and tomato sandwiches for supper. I'll bet we have ice cream for dessert in honour of the new postulants!" Jacinta said.

"Our main meal — dinner — is at noon," Ann Martin told Nancy and me. "Supper is a light meal."

"Right," Jacinta chimed in, "See, it's almost seven hours from rising to noon so that's when you're really hungry. Then six hours from dinner to supper, but only two-and-a-half hours from supper to bedtime so it wouldn't make sense to eat too much. It's sandwiches because of you. Sometimes we just have cereal and I just can't get used to eating cornflakes at 6p.m."

"Cornflakes for dinner?" I said. "That sounds . . ."

"For supper," Ann Martin said. "Jacinta!"

"I'm only telling them . . ."

Sister Jacinta's words trailed off as Sister Ann Martin stared at her.

I rushed in to reassure them. "Don't worry about us," I said. "We . . ." But now Nancy interrupted me.

"What — are there secrets or something?"

"No secrets, Sister Nancy," Ann Martin said. "We just get you settled and tell you about the Novitiate routine. Sister Mary Francine will explain the other things at Instructions. You'll have Instructions every morning at 8:15 — after your employment."

"Your employment is your cleaning job in the Novitiate or in the Motherhouse," said Sister Jacinta. "Big House, we call it — like Big Church."

She glanced at Sister Ann Martin. "See, I can give information correctly," her look said. Sister Ann Martin nodded and Sister Jacinta continued. "Most employments are easy except for infirmary trays, but you wouldn't get that, only Canonicals do."

"Canonicals?" I asked.

"Yeah — that's us — First year novices. We don't go to school this year — Canon law says one year has to be cloistered." Jacinta paused: had she said too much? No, Sister Ann Martin chewed away at her bacon, lettuce and tomato sandwich and Nancy and I were listening calmly.

"So we end doing most of the hardest work." Sister Ann Martin looked up. "The second year novices," Sister Jacinta hurried on, "go to school — they're scholastic novices. But postulants get easy employments. You won't even have to serve in the refectory for the first few months. Unless you get the Big House lavs. Those toilets don't work and the old nuns can't control their . . ."

"Jacinta! No one wants to hear about the Big House lavatories at supper!" said Ann Martin.

"Sorry, A.M."

I noticed that as we talked both novices dropped the 'Sister' and shortened their names.

"We rise at five-fifteen, except Sundays, when we sleep until six," Jacinta went on. "You have a half hour to get ready. Morning prayers at a quarter to six, meditation from six to six thirty. Then Mass, and breakfast's at seven."

"Ice cream, anyone?" Ann Martin interrupted. Our server, a novice with a polka-dotted apron around her habit, set a bowl of chocolate and vanilla ice cream on the table. She carried two other bowls. One she balanced on her wrist and the other she had wedged somehow between her fingers.

"How does she do that?" I asked as the server moved away.

"Practice," Ann Martin said. "You'll learn."

"I will?" I said looking over at Sister Jacinta busy eating ice cream. "I mean, I *will*."

I took the ice cream and heaped some chocolate into my bowl. After dinner, no, after supper, we returned to the basement and the unpacking. I found Suzanne and Kath, and the other girls from Ladyhill. They introduced me to their novice guardian angels. I knew the three novices, who graduated from Marywood last year.

"We're all going on a picnic tomorrow, Maggie," Suzanne said.

"It's fun," Sister Jacinta said. "We each make our own sandwiches and then go for a long walk and picnic in the woods beyond the dairy."

"A dairy, with cows and all?" I asked.

"Oh, yes," Sister Jacinta said. "A prize herd, I'm told. The workmen keep the barns immaculate."

"Any calves?"

"I presume so," she answered me.

"Great!" I said. "My sister Brigid will be thrilled to see them. She loves animals. And my little brother Patrick, he's five, will love the calves. I'll take them on the visit. I . . . ."

Sister Ann Martin stopped me with a look, "Not good to talk about family now. Makes people homesick."

"Oh, OK," I said, "Sorry. It's going to be hard not to talk . . ."

"You'll enjoy the picnic, Maggie. We bring cokes along too and let them cool in the stream. We'll probably take the whole afternoon," Sister Jacinta rattled on.

Nancy picked up her guitar and started to tune it. She hadn't said much.

Suzanne was talking to her new friend, Kathleen Ann, from the Academy in Washington, D.C. Her father was a congressman.

Nancy strummed a few chords.

> *If I had a hammer, I'd hammer in the mor-or-ning . . .*

She sang into the crowded corridor. Her clear voice had husky undertones that made it easy to follow. And follow we did.

> *I'd hammer in the evening, all over this land,*

the postulants sang. Jacinta smiled and Ann Martin nodded.

> *I'd hammer out danger, I'd hammer out warning, I'd hammer out love between my brothers and my sisters.*

The novices stood silent.

"Don't you know this song? Peter, Paul and Mary," I explained. Nancy smiled at them, encouraging. Sorry, Sister Anna Sophia, I thought, for thinking you were your haircut. After the second verse the novices caught on and sang along. As we started the final chorus, the electric bell rang. The novices stopped immediately. Our postulant "all over the land" faded into silence.

"Sisters." Sister Mary Francine's voice. "Now begins profound silence. We do not talk or make eye contact with any of our sisters until after breakfast tomorrow morning. I will explain the reason for this to the postulants in their Instructions. Please postulants, in consideration of your sister novices, observe this profound silence strictly. Good-night, Sisters."

"Good-night, Sister," the novices replied.

Sister Ann Martin and Sister Jacinta walked away with their eyes down. Nancy put her guitar down. A string twanged, echoing through the hall. One giggle escaped me but I suppressed the second one.

When we walked into the chapel the novices were chanting the night office, Compline. I thought of the monks and nuns who'd sung the same psalms for centuries and centuries. I was joining now, I was one of them. The campus was quiet and dark and here we were in this little lighted space listening and watching. The novices bowed at certain passages, their white veils dipping in unison. No one missed a beat.

> *Much have they oppressed me from my youth,*
> *let Israel say.*

Then the other side answering.

> *Much have they oppressed me from my youth,*
> *yet they have not prevailed against me.*

A novice in the back stood and intoned:

> *Out of the depths I have cried to You, O Lord.*

Then they picked it up:

Lord, hear my voice.

I found out later that this was the 'De Profundis'. We said it after every meal. It was also the prayer for the dead and since there was an infirmary attached to the Motherhouse where the old nuns came home to die, I came to know the words well. But they were new to me tonight.

> *If you, O Lord, mark iniquities, Lord who can stand? But with You is forgiveness and plentiful redemption.*

Well, that was encouraging. My mind started to wonder what iniquities this group could be worried about. Then my side was saying:

> *My soul waits for the Lord, more than sentinels wait for the dawn.*

The other side agreed:

> *More than sentinels wait for the dawn, let Israel wait for the Lord.*

Then the novice right behind me stood up. She really had a nice voice and she kind of syncopated her line:

> *Lord, my heart is not exalted.*

This must be a favourite psalm, I thought, because the other side picked up the beat too, swinging out the words:

> *O Lord, my heart is not proud, nor are my eyes haughty. I busy not myself with great things, nor with things too sublime for me.*

They were right — I didn't even have to worry about what to wear tomorrow.

> *Nay, rather I have stilled and quieted my soul.*
> *Like a weaned child, so is my soul within me.*
> *Oh, Israel, hope in the Lord both now and*
> *forever.*

Then the whole chapel stood up, we postulants just a few seconds behind the rest.

> *Now, Lord, you may dismiss your servant*
> *according to your Word, in Peace.*

I did feel like my soul was stilled and quieted as I walked out with all the rest. There were strange juxtapositions in this world. 'If I had a hammer' full blast, then 'Goodnight, Sister', plain chant and this monastic quiet.

Upstairs the silence continued, even though 150 girls were taking showers, rinsing out nylons (made of cotton!) and brushing their teeth. Over each sink and individual shower, three names were taped. I found 'S. Margaret Mary' and waited. Other showers were free but I somehow knew that taking just any one was not done. But the toilets were unassigned. Nature triumphing over grace.

I looked down at myself. I finally knew what nuns wore to bed. I had it on: a long white cotton nightgown, a black robe and black shoe style slippers (no mules the list said). The novices added nightcaps to the outfit. These were made of two half circles of white linen sewn up the back. I guess the idea was to cover your hair even at night. And while some caps were pulled tightly so that nothing showed, most of the novices wore their caps more or less perched on the crowns of their heads. Some had the brims turned back, others left the side ribbons untied.

Nancy and I stood together waiting for our showers, trying not to make eye contact. I'd look at her to see if she were looking at me and then we'd both look down at the floor. Profound silence turned what could have been a giant slumber party into a smooth, almost military, operation where the only sounds came from the water of the sinks and the showers and slippers along the floors.

Back in my cubicle I put away the cigar box that contained my soap dish, toothbrush, glass and toothpaste. For the first time in my life I positively knew no one else was going to use my toothbrush. I stood at my window and looked out at the acres and acres of farmland, orchards and woods that the Order owned. Sunset colours lingered in the sky. As a kid I'd always hated to go to bed in the summer when it was still light. Well, I'll just sit here on the window-sill and watch the stars appear. By nine o'clock everything was quiet. Some one threw the central switch and all the lights went out. No more movement until the 5.15 a.m. rising bell. Outside the fields settled into darkness. The silence was palpable. "Now have I stilled and quieted my soul. Like a weaned child on its mother's lap, so is my soul within me."

OK, I didn't like giving up my books and pictures and what difference did it make what my medal was made of? I valued it not because it was gold but because Uncle Frank and Uncle Chuck gave it to me. But, I thought as a breeze came across the fields and into my room, I knew there would be rules. Concentrate on the chanting, this peace. They'd been in business a long time. Give them the benefit of the doubt. I yawned. It'd been a long day and I'd not had too much sleep last night. Mom and Dad and . . . No, best not to think of that. I'm here now. Who did Marie Charles remind me of? Helen Hayes, yes, Helen Hayes in

Anastasia. The Grand Duchess. What if I had run into her in the hall, night-capped and black robed? I smiled to myself. The bed was just a few feet from the window-sill. I dived toward it and hit the mattress square in the middle.

Bang. Profound Silence shattered as I and my mattress went right through the bed frame and hit the ground. I screamed. Lights flashed on. Three novices ran in, not guarding their eyes. Damn. Why didn't they have a box spring instead of those coils?

'Nay, I have stilled and quieted my soul.'

Well, almost.

3

INSTRUCTIONS

"You're the postulant who fell through her bed, right?" That question came from twenty different laughing novices next morning.

"Yeah, ha, ha, that was me."

"Yes, I'm the one . . . No. I didn't jump on the bed actually, just hit it wrong I guess, ha, ha!"

And to Sister Mary Francine, "No, my bed is fine now, Sister, thank you. The novice in our section fixed it. I'm fine too, thank you. I'm sorry if I disturbed anyone. Excuse me, Sister. Thank you, Sister."

"If one more person mentions that goddamn bed," I told Nancy as we sat in our basement study hall waiting for Instructions to begin, "I will scream."

"Forget it."

"Easy for you to say, Nancy, your bed held up."

Sister Mary Francine was entering the room — almost. She paused at the door. We stood. She smiled, gestured us to sit down and then she came in.

"Sisters, a few days ago you were in the world. Now you are religious women. God called you and the Order has affirmed your vocation by accepting you as postulants in the Sisters of the Redemption. Not all that apply are accepted, you know. 'You have not chosen me but I have chosen you,' Jesus told His apostles. He says the same to you today. His choice is mysterious. From thousands of young Catholic women, He chose you. He wishes to use *your* particular talents, *your* young strength as an instrument of His Love."

I sat up straighter and folded my hands before me on the desk.

"We all know the great needs of the world. Both our Holy Pope John and our President John Kennedy ask us to remember the poor, to share our abundance with the needy. Sisters, it is not easy to give. Oh, to give material things is not hard, but to give of yourselves, your time, talents, and very life, that is the challenge. Let me assure you, however, Sisters, when you learn to give unselfishly, great rewards await you. Not only in this life but for all eternity.

"You have all experienced profound silence and seen, I hope, how essential quiet is for communication with God." Sister Mary Francine paused. "Now, Sisters, I have something to tell you that you will perhaps find difficult to accept. Not only do we keep silence during the night, but except for two daily hours of recreation and when duty demands, we also keep silence during the day."

There was a shocked intake of breath from the postulants. Around me various voices said "You mean we never talk?"

"Silence??? Sister, you can't mean all the time!"

I raised my hand, and stood up without waiting to be called on. "But, Sister, this isn't a contemplative order. The nuns at Ladyhill talked to us. We're an active order, right and . . ."

Sister Mary Francine said, "Exactly, Sister. We are an active order with a great many duties to perform. But our first responsibility is to God, to pray always. There is no place in our life for idle talk. You will find, Sisters, that the habit of silence you develop in the Novitiate will stand you in good stead your whole life. It will be a tranquil pool into which you may dip during the frantic life you will lead as a teacher on your missions."

Now she looked right at me. "You know, Sisters, the postulant year is a testing ground. You observe us and we observe you. Not all of you, frankly, will make it. However, those whom God has chosen, He will give the grace to follow their vocation. The ability to keep silence is one sign of a true vocation."

She still smiled, still seemed friendly but I heard the challenge in her words. I sat down. "Do you understand, Sisters?"

"Yes, Sister," we answered.

She spoke briskly now. "It is customary to ask my permission to leave the building, to go to your cubicle, to the sewing room, or to the Novitiate library. You need not ask permission to visit the Chapel or attend class." Thanks, I thought. "Also, Sisters, because of the scarcity of equipment, permission is necessary to iron or wash your uniforms. I certainly want you to present a neat appearance, but excess concern can lead to vanity. Of course, Sisters, if there is an emergency, for example, if I am not available and you must attend to sanitary needs you may interpret permission, that is, take care of your hygienic task and tell me at your first opportunity."

I rubbed my hand over my forehead and re-crossed my ankles.

"Now, mail. Every Saturday the letters that have come for you that week will be passed to your study hall desk.

You will write your family letter on Saturday also. Sister Myrna and I will read outgoing and incoming mail."

"What, read our mail?" My hand went up, then down.

"Let me explain," she continued. "As your spiritual adviser, I need to be aware of your thoughts and feelings in order to help you. I also wish to know of any disturbing outside influences. Also, Sisters," she smiled, "an educated woman uses correct form and punctuation in letter writing, so I can assist you there. We have found that letters from teenage friends are an undue distraction, so they are returned to the sender. Since our life and that of the world differ so much, continued communication becomes strained on both sides. And Sisters, make your letters home cheerful, that is what pleases your family. They know you miss them. Do not make them feel worse by indulging your quite natural homesickness. Offer it to Christ, don't burden your dear families."

She paused looking at each of us. "Now my postulants, I know you have much to absorb. You need time to understand the wisdom represented by these practices. Remember the Church has been forming religious women for over a thousand years and you came to us only yesterday," she smiled. "I do not expect you to perform the practices of religious life perfectly all at once. I do expect a willing heart, however. But why else would you have come to us if not to try with all your strength, if not to give your best?"

She turned to leave. "It's usual to stand, Sisters, when your Superior enters or leaves the room." We stood. "Now, I don't want you to rise when I come to the recreation room. The novices do that for Sister Marie Charles, but I don't require that of you. Oh, that reminds me, Sisters, you have adjusted so nicely, I think your novice guardian angels can return to their own affairs. Henceforth, we will not mix with the novices except for Sunday evening recreation and on gym and swim nights."

She walked to the door. We sat down. She turned and came back. We stood. Another nun followed Sister Mary Francine in. "Sisters, most of you have met my assistant, Sister Myrna. She has your class schedules and will pass them out now. You may be seated."

Sister Myrna handed a pile of forms to the first person in each row who passed the papers to the postulant behind her. But Sister Mary Francine had one more announcement.

"Will Sisters Margaret Mary, Suzanne, Marilyn, Kathleen Ann, Elizabeth Ann, and Florence please come to my office now."

I heard Sister Myrna begin as we followed Sister Mary Francine to her office. "Now, Sisters," she said to the remaining postulants, "most of you will have the same class schedules. You are all elementary education majors and therefore . . ."

As the rest of us filed out, Sister Mary Francine stepped aside to let the line enter her office. "Sister Margaret Mary." Sister Mary Francine stopped me at the doorway, "I know you are overwhelmed right now." She patted my shoulder. "Trust us, Sister, and try. I only ask that you try. Sincere effort brings understanding. Rely on the great faith that led you here."

I nodded and tried to smile up at her.

"You feel confident of your vocation, don't you, Sister Margaret Mary?"

"Er yes, Sister. I wonder about some of the rules, but I don't doubt my vocation."

"God gave you the grace to leave those you loved in order to pursue a greater love. He will give you the grace to follow the precepts of the religious life. Don't get stuck in the details."

The other postulants waiting inside her office were straining to hear.

"Sister, I don't want to take time now, the others are ..."

"Sister Margaret Mary, they will wait if you wish to ask me anything."

"No, no. That's OK — thanks." I eased past her and took my place in the line next to Suzanne.

"Give her a lot of good advice?"

"Shut up," I muttered between clenched teeth.

"Sisters," Sister Mary Francine said as she sat down behind her desk. "The religious life is not easy. It requires courage to do God's will, real courage. Secular writers speak of 'the courage to be'. Becoming a full and authentic person is a struggle. I am always fascinated at the correlation between some of the best modern psychologists and classic spiritual authors. Terminology differs of course. But take Erich Fromm's statement of a mature relationship, 'I need you because I *love* you not I love you because I *need* you.' Doesn't that echo Mother Taddeus' precept? 'Only the Father's love can satisfy His children's needs'?"

This is encouraging, I thought. Modern psychologists, good. I bet if she *really* read Charlie Brown, she'd see that Schulz's philosophy is quite profound and . . .

Movement outside the ground floor window caught my attention. I saw the shoes and skirt bottoms of the Canonical novices flash by as they hurried to their Canonical employments. Sister Ann Martin cleaned the second floor of the infirmary. She changed the patients' beds, emptied bed pans, and served their dinner trays. Sister Jacinta washed the big house lavs. I suppose the classic spiritual authors fit housework in somewhere too.

"But, I digress. Let me congratulate you, Sisters. Because of your excellent high school records and high scores on the College Entrance Examination Board tests, you have been chosen to be secondary school teachers. You will have some of your classes with the college girls at the main campus. The other postulants — elementary education majors — will have their classes in this building."

She paused, waiting for a response.

"Thank you, Sister," we gushed. Suzanne, Marilyn, and I were from Ladyhill; Kathleen Ann was from the order's Academy in Washington; Elizabeth Ann from their expensive boarding school in Indianapolis; and Florence had finished two years in the college as an art major. Only one hadn't gone to one of the order's three college preparatory high schools. Sister Mary Francine opened a black loose-leaf notebook.

"Now, Sisters, the vast majority of our 200 schools are elementary schools, therefore, our fundamental need is for good grade schoolteachers. However, our fifteen secondary schools must be served. We need sisters of superior intelligence, who can be trained to teach more demanding subjects. You have been chosen for an important work."

"Excuse me, Sister, but is that fair? I mean, shouldn't the others have a choice? Won't they think that we . . ." I began. Sister Mary Francine lifted one finger.

"Rejoice in the gifts God has given you and seek to use those gifts in his service, do not underestimate the spirit of generosity within your sister postulants. Each one knows her own capacity. Remember your courses will be in the college and demand much work. When you're studying while the others take extra recreation, then," she laughed, "you may consider what's fair." Now we laughed. I thought of Nancy. I didn't doubt her generosity of spirit but the thought of explaining this 'chosen for talent' bit to her made me very nervous.

Sister Mary Francine read from the notebook, "Sister Suzanne," she looked up, "your teachers suggested French as your major. Does that suit you?"

"Oh yes, I'd love to study French!" Suzanne said.

"Perhaps a trip to France sometime, Sister, to the original Motherhouse." Another page was turned. "Sister Marilyn, your high school preference was science. I see you won many awards. Which of the sciences particularly interest you?"

"Biology, Sister."

"Excellent, Sister Marilyn. We have a lot of high school biology classes who need teachers," Sister Mary Francine said and turned the page.

"Now, Sister Kathleen Ann, I know music is your main interest. Such a fine record. Concert performance already, I see, and quite a bit of study at the conservatory. Excellent, Sister. What instruments?"

"Oh, piano, Sister, piano and violin," Sister Kathleen said. "I performed both at my senior recital and I played Brahms and Beethoven's Concerto in . . ."

Sister Mary Francine raised her finger. "Very, very good, Sister. Our music department is excellent as you know. Sister Cecile will be delighted with such an enthusiastic pupil."

"Now, Sister Elizabeth Ann, Sister Janet Marie wrote me that you are a budding historian." Elizabeth Ann shifted her stocky body and pulled her cape down over her stomach and smiled. I knew her. We shared a sink and shower with Sister Linda, the other girl from Nancy's high school. The last two nights, Elizabeth Ann made Linda and me wait fifteen minutes for the shower.

"I wouldn't have minded so much," Linda said, "if I could have brushed my teeth while she showered, but her stockings were soaking in the sink!"

"I know and then she didn't rinse the sink out, and left rings and rings of black all over." I had noted the J.P. Stevens labels on her towels, too. And she's supposed to be from such an exclusive school! My towels were Royal Fieldcrest from Saks.

"I don't care if she is supposed to be smart," Linda went on. "I think she's a fat, pimply-faced inconsiderate slob. I'm going to ask Sister Mary Francine to take her off our shower and sink. She lets the water overflow the stall."

"She is a mess, but I don't like the idea of tattling," I'd said. "I'd take her stockings out of the sink, but I don't want to touch them."

Sister Mary Francine continued, "You will be a history major, Sister Elizabeth Ann, with a speciality in . . ."

"Medieval history, Sister Mary Francine," Elizabeth Anne said, "especially the papacy in the middle ages. It's amazing how the Popes . . ."

"Yes, I'm sure, Sister," Sister Mary Francine interrupted. "I know you will do well, after all, you are a National Merit Scholar as is Sister Margaret Mary."

Elizabeth Ann flashed her yellow teeth at me. I forced a small smile back. Sister Mary Francine found my page in her book. "Congratulations to you, Sister Margaret Mary, on your National Merit Award." The others shifted in their places. "I think an English major would be very good for you, Sister."

"Well, that would be nice but I'd like to major in journalism and I think the journalism department here is excellent and so is the the college newspaper. I thought . .."

"Sister Margaret Mary, that's very nice but the order needs English teachers. I understand that you are quite interested in literature. Sister Marie Charles mentioned that you brought novels with you. While indiscriminate reading is not recommended, I wouldn't object to any assigned readings, of course, even fiction."

"I do like to read, Sister," I said, "but I like to write and I'm interested in current affairs."

"Oh, we do encourage writing. In fact, all postulants take Freshman Composition taught by one of our Junior sisters. Sister Joseph Jeanne, who, I seem to recall, published poems in the college literary magazine before she entered. You will have many occasions to write, Sister," she concluded, turning my page. "And, if you wish to take one or two journalism courses, I think we can arrange that," she smiled. "The community publishes a yearly magazine. Perhaps someday something of yours will be published there. But we need English teachers now."

"Now, Sister Florence." On to the next. There was my future neatly arranged. "You will continue with your art studies at the college. Sister Teresa speaks highly of your talent."

"Thank you, Sister."

At that point someone was knocking on the steel frame of Sister Mary Francine's door. It was Nancy. "Excuse me,

Sister." She stepped over the threshold and stood in front of me.

"Sister Nancy." Sister Mary Francine lowered her voice to what I already recognised as her stern tone.

Nancy didn't let her continue. "Sister — I want to major in English! Sister Ava told me she wrote to you."

"Yes, I received her letter. But Sister," she paused, "your grades . . ."

Nancy pressed her clenched fists into the black pleats of her skirt. "I would study hard, Sister," she clipped her words. "I could do it."

I couldn't believe her nerve. But Sister Mary Francine took it in stride. "The Chairman of our English Department, Sister Marie Brian, requires a great deal of her English majors. She did her graduate work at Oxford University." She paused. "I don't know if you . . ."

"Sister Mary Francine," I said, "sorry for to interrupt, but couldn't I, er, help Sister Nancy. I mean we'll probably have the same classes and I could, I mean, not that I know anymore but . . . I . . . well." I glanced at Nancy. She didn't look at me.

Sister Mary Francine flipped her notebook pages. "The advanced courses don't start until scholastic year," she said slowly, "and the real work comes as upper classmen during your two Juniorate years. Perhaps you could begin on a probationary basis, Sister Nancy."

Nancy nodded.

"And then if your grades merit it . . ."

"Fine, Sister," Nancy said.

Sister Mary Francine stood up and handed us each half-sheets of paper. "Here are the class schedules."

"Your minds are gifts from our Lord. Use them humbly, but remember, intellectual preparation will only be part of your work here. Your spiritual development will always be of prime importance. Intellectual pride has destroyed many of the Church's greatest thinkers."

And psychologists?

"Good morning, Sisters." She nodded and smiled. Dismissed. We walked into the empty study hall. Suzanne, Kathleen Ann and the others grabbed their notebooks and left. The rest of the postulants were upstairs at their first class. According to my schedule, three of my classes — Psychology, Theology, and English Composition — were in the Novitiate and two — Chemistry and Art Appreciation — were in the college. *All* classes for elementary education majors were in the Novitiate.

"This seems unfair . . ." I began to Nancy after the others left.

"Silence time now, Sister Margaret Mary," said Elizabeth Ann from across the study hall. She waddled over to our desks, a thick loose leaf notebook with coloured separators clutched against her chest. "We should be getting to Chemistry. I'll be happy to help you too, Sister Nancy."

"Thanks," Nancy said.

"I'm glad we're in class together," she whispered to us. "No one else came from my high school so I don't know anybody. Well, let's go," she beamed.

"Why don't you go ahead," I began. Her face fell. The new girl who didn't know anyone. I'd been that at three different grade schools but at Ladyhill, I'd found my niche. I belonged. I didn't have to be glad when someone, anyone, talked to me and — God, this was the *convent*.

Charity and simple *humanity* and the courage to be —
what the hell.

"Wait, Elizabeth Ann, I'll meet you and Nancy at the
door." Elizabeth Ann's beam returned. "I have to go to the
bathroom. If I use the lav down here I can perform at least
this hygienic task sans permission." Nancy giggled and
Elizabeth Ann guffawed.

And so it started. New rules, new classes, new friends.
I had questions, was uneasy about some things, but I hadn't
expected a Caribbean cruise. It was supposed to be hard. I
could handle it. You'll help me, right, God? I mean that was
the deal!

I thought I was doing pretty well those first weeks.
Made it to Chapel on time, stayed awake during meditation.
I got an A on my first quiz in English class and polished the
third floor terrazzo hall with a gigantic machine that was
fun to wheel around. Yes, I was homesick but so was
everyone else. And we were busy — walking, talking,
singing during recreation. I found that dividing the days
into pieces made them go quickly. I tried to communicate
something of this new life in my letters home but by the
time I did four drafts and eliminated incorrect punctuation
and general mess, the life went out of them. Plus, it was
hard to explain that I had begun to find strolling through
the cemetery, speculating about Sister Zina or Sister
Clotilde — one who died at twenty-five, the other who
lived to ninety — interesting.

There was always something to look forward to, like a
feast day when we would talk at dinner or have ice cream.
In October, there was a nice little run of celebrations:
October 2nd, Guardian Angels, the 3rd, St. Therese the
Little Flower, and the 4th, St. Francis of Assisi. Our first
real challenge arose on our fifth Saturday. Sister Myrna

posted the list of new weekly employments. Nancy and I were listed to be the first postulant servers.

"That's all we need," I said. "Have you watched those novices whip around the refectory, carrying three bowls at once? We can't do that!"

"I guess Sister Mary Francine thinks we can," Nancy said glumly.

Our serving ordeal started that night. As the novice head server tied long gingham aprons around our waists, she rattled off fast but explicit instructions. "Take three of each dish, one for each of your services. Balance one on your first three fingers between your thumb and little finger. Like this. Put the second on your wrist and the third in your other hand."

It took three tries before we achieved a precarious balance.

"I can do it with empty plates," I said to Nancy. "But what happens when they're full?"

At supper we managed — barely. But we recreated — talked — at the meal, thanks to St. Teresa of Avila, and that made it easier. I dreaded breakfast, the most solemn of all our meals. Though a novice read from a spiritual book at all meals, at breakfast she began with the death roll.

"Sister Mary Bartholomew. Entered community September nineteen hundred and two, departed this life on November fifth, nineteen hundred forty-seven."

The number of deaths sometime reached ten or twelve. I felt as if I were about to join that list as Nancy and I followed the novices from the Chapel a few minutes before the rest of the Novitiate. Profound silence lasted until 8 a.m. so the novices didn't talk to or look at Nancy and me as we awkwardly pinned on aprons and slipped into gingham sleeves. By the time we dressed, the novices had finished setting water, milk and bowls of cereal on their service. Slow and steady wins the race, I thought, as I filled three stainless steel pitchers with water and placed them on the table. I speeded up when on my next pass through, I saw three lonely pitchers of milk. Mine. Nancy walked ahead of me, then stopped. "What's that noise?" she said.

"What?" I kept moving. Then I heard it — an ominous tap, tap, tap. It was me. "Hard heels," I said. "It's my hard heels."

The postulant's list specified that rubber heels be put on our shoes. I did that. But there are two kinds of rubber heels — hard rubber and soft rubber. Mario, the shoemaker on Peterson, favoured hard rubber because it was more practical. However, the nuns wanted soft, more silent rubber.

"When these wear out we will replace them with the correct heels," Sister Mary Francine had said. But that was weeks, months away. The refectory would be silent except for the drone of the reader's voice and my heels. Now I could hear the novices coming from the Chapel and not only weren't my tables ready, but when I walked the sound of my heels reverberated throughout the dining room. I ran back to the kitchen on my toes. There I found two novices rushing three pitchers of cream and bowls of Rice Krispies onto my services. "Thanks," I said. They didn't look up. Sister Ann Marie, the head server, grabbed my arm and pulled me into the kitchen just as Sister Marie Charles entered the refectory. The long silent line of novices and postulants, each with her head bowed and eyes lowered, followed. But this solemn phalanx no longer impressed me. I knew they were all longing for that first cup of coffee and wondering if we'd have banana bread.

The line dissolved. Sister Marie Charles led grace from the head table, and then, carefully lifting their chairs, the Novitiate sat down.

"Sister Zoe entered community September nineteen hundred and twelve, departed this life . . . " The rising sun split the clouds and light poured through the refectory windows. Outside,the cows moved to their pasture. All was pastoral, peaceful — and then I came out with butter for my tables. Tap, tap, tap. Oh no. The sound echoed, re-echoed louder. I tiptoed back to the kitchen.

Sister Ann Marie signalled me vigorously. Time to bring out the fruit.

Each plate had five pears on it. Five of the most misshapen pieces of fruit I'd ever seen. I somehow got my three plates loaded. I willed the pears not to roll as I slid along to my tables. Made it. The plates of flat banana bread were a snap. Sister Ann Marie assigned me to pour the tea. Only three people in the Novitiate drank tea. No problem. Now if I could clear my services. I began breathing normally as I whisked away empty cereal bowls and bread plates. Then I went to get the empty fruit plates, but they weren't empty. Each held two bumpy pears. No wonder they'd been left. I took a breath and picked up the plates. Balancing carefully, I moved past the head table toward the kitchen. "Such a grasp of the meditative state is unusual except . . . " the reader was saying. Then the pears slipped. As they skittered across the plates, I lost my balance. My heels cracked down on the terrazzo floor as I juggled the plates, moving across the floor unsteadily. I clasped all three plates to my aproned breast trying to catch the pears in my lap by bringing one knee up and contorting my body into a basket. For one second I thought I had them and then — Bam — three plates and six pears hit the floor. The unbreakable plates smashed, the pears rolled, and every black-clad shoulder in the place shook with silent laughter. Every shoulder but two.

I knelt down to pick up the pieces of plate and then had to crawl past chairs and tables after the fruit that slid along the over-waxed floor at an astounding speed. One pear rolled all the way to the head table and stopped at Sister Marie Charles' small, soft rubber-heeled shoe. As I reached under the tablecloth to retrieve it, I glanced up. Sister Marie Charles was not guarding her eyes. They were staring into mine. Oh, oh. She looked at me the way I had looked at the intractable pears. I couldn't look away. The preliminaries were over. I was not going to fit in here easily. But I wasn't about to give up this soon. I had a vocation. There's supposed to be a place for me here. And I was trying.

I wanted to say, "Sister, it was just the pears." But it wasn't. And she knew it.

4

NEW NAMES

I avoided Sister Marie Charles during the next weeks and stayed in the postulant's world of the Novitiate basement. I passed her in the hall once. She nodded and I thought I heard her sigh but that would be breaking silence, so I'm probably wrong. Anyway, our first family visit was coming and that's all I could think about. It would be one week before my eighteenth birthday.

I was awake long before the 6 a.m. rising bell that Sunday. The regular schedule — prayers, meditation, Mass, breakfast, High Mass at the Big Church — seemed endless. Finally it was time — 10 a.m.! At 10:01 I was pacing the study hall floor. Where were they? Nancy and I stood on top of our desks peering out of the ground floor windows. "Those are my Dad's legs!" Nancy yelled. She jumped down and headed for the door. She stopped. "Where is that novice?"

Families presented themselves at the door and a novice then came and called us to the visiting room. "I'll meet her halfway," Nancy said as she took off. "Have a good visit! You look great — very clean!" Yes, I was. It took a great communal effort, but my cuffs and my collar were white and stiff. A perfect crease cut the middle of my best cape. The pleats of my skirt hung straight and sharp. I was ready. And now it was 10:15! We could only visit until 12 noon, then again from 1:30 to 4:30. So every second was precious. They said they'd leave on Saturday, so they're here. Why don't they come? To think I saw them every single day and never really appreciated it! *Mom.*

"Sister Margaret Mary." A novice stood in the study hall door. "Visitors." I raced past her and up the stairs. Two and a half seconds later I was hugging them all at once — a scene in the front hall. Laurie and Sally looked almost like teenagers in their pleated skirts, and sweaters with matching knee socks. Patrick seemed older too, in a navy blue blazer and long grey pants. Brigid and Michele were dressed as if they were going to church in nylons and heels. My mother with a grey pillbox hat and my Dad in his pin-stripe suit had that air of official parenthood they assumed at graduations or fundraising card parties.

Gosh. Coming to see me had become a formal occasion like going to see Great Aunt Rose on her birthday.

"We'd better move out of the hall," I said. "I have so much to tell you, so much I want to hear. Let's go in the parlour."

But other families crowded the parlours. I waved at Nancy, then Suzanne and the others — I'd say hello to their parents later.

But now, "Let's go out!"

It was a little cold, but I'd got used to walking around as a form of entertainment. So there we were, tramping around the grove. I was trying to tell them about school and picnics and prayer and find out about everything they were doing at the same time. On top of that I kept thinking of Sister Mary Francine's final instructions. There were don'ts. "Don't eat in front of your family. Don't let pictures be taken. Don't go into the college area. Don't open any packages they bring." And do's. "Do be cheerful. Do make them comfortable. Do have fun."

Well, after an hour they were freezing. The basement auditorium had been opened for the overflow and so we pulled eight steel chairs into a circle and prepared to, well, I guess recreate. But at home we never just sat like this to talk — it just happened around the kitchen table or when my mom was putting her make-up on.

In a very short time we ran out of things to say. We sat staring at each other. Oh please don't let them be bored, I thought.

"Let's do it now, Mom, please," Laurie asked my mother.

"Well, it's early, but I guess so. Maggie, we have your birthday cake in the car and some presents. I thought this afternoon but since we, well, seem to have time . . ." my mother said. Laurie and Sally were up and on their way out.

"I don't know, Mom. There's this, uh, rule. See we can't eat in front of people or open packages. I'm sorry, I know it sounds stupid, but Sister told us especially . . ." I stopped and kicked at the leg of my chair. "I can't have my picture taken or take you to the college either. I'm sorry, I . . ."

Brigid and Michele looked at each other while Laurie and Sally sat down deflated.

"Mom, I . . ." I began.

"Margaret Mary, don't worry, we understand. I'll leave the cake . . ." she said.

"Wait a minute, let's go into the car!" my father suggested. "You can do that, can't you?"

I thought for a minute. "I can't *drive* in the car but as long as it doesn't move, I guess I can sit in it!" I said.

We piled into our station wagon, as we had so many times before, and there in the empty parking lot under the bare branches of the Novitiate trees, we celebrated my eighteenth birthday.

> *Happy Birthday to you, Happy Birthday to you,*
> *Happy Birthday dear Sister (giggles) Margaret*
> *Mary,*
> *Happy Birthday to you!*

I didn't eat the cake or open the presents wrapped in birthday paper, but I blew out all eighteen candles with one breath.

At noon, I had to leave for my dinner in the Novitiate and they went to lunch. That afternoon, I bent the rules and took my sisters and Patrick to one of the real points of interest — the crypt where the foundress was buried. It was deep underneath the big church at the end of a long dark corridor. A perfect place to tell them about the faceless nun who roamed the halls at night. And there she was! Sally screamed. We laughed. I took Patrick, all by himself, to the cemetery and showed him the graves of the nun nurses who had served in the Civil War, World War I and World War II. I embellished their war records somewhat, had them returning enemy fire, but Patrick loved a good story and he somehow got the idea the battles had been fought right here. Good. I want him to see this as a place of adventure.

Finally we all walked to the cow barns to pet the calves. Four o'clock tolled. "Next time we'll climb up into the church tower and ring that bell," I promised frantically. "Next time. Next time," we all said as the last half-hour disappeared.

"February 8th, I'll see you February 8th. Only three months!" I said as I kissed each of them. The last minutes were lost in a flurry of families leaving.

We had ice cream at supper. "Always do on visiting days," Jacinta told me. "Helps to cheer everybody up."

After the family visit, two postulants left.

"Maybe they were asked to leave," I said to Nancy at recreation a few weeks later.

"Nah, probably just homesick. Seeing their families again broke them. But to quit after only two months. Geez."

"I know," I said. "You spend your whole life wondering if you have a vocation and then leave after only two months?"

"Did you really spend your whole life wondering if you had a vocation?"

"Well, yeah, kind of," I said.

"Oh, you were one of those nunny little kids."

"I wouldn't say that," I snapped. "I'm not here because I want to be you know — I happen to have a vocation!"

"Relax. Relax," she said.

"I am happy here — most of the time — so I guess I made the right choice."

"Yeah," Nancy said reflectively, "but I could be happy a lot of places."

As we talked I rocked back and forth on the stainless steel 'S' legs of the red vinyl chair in the recreation circle. We were inside. It was too cold out, even for nuns. Sister Mary Francine motioned to me. "Sister Margaret Mary, that is not lady-like." I stopped rocking but continued talking to Nancy. She looked over again. Conversation was supposed to be general — open to all. That was the reason

for the circle. Never two, seldom three, better four —
"Cliques can be destructive," Sister Mary Francine
explained.

"We're serving my package," Linda said from across the
room. We all perked up. At the end of each recreation a
snack called a collation was served. The cookies, cakes or
candy came from packages our families sent. Linda's
mother made chocolate mint chip cookies and
apricot-filled kalaches. Her packages were very highly
rated.

Nancy and I lowered our voices. We weren't supposed
to talk about the postulants who'd left. When Sister Mary
Francine announced that they had departed, she asked us
to pray for them but not to gossip or speculate.

"Belle and Alice hadn't made many friends," I said.

"They were namby-pamby," Nancy said with a shrug.
"Quitters!"

"Nancy, I wonder if June will be next." I glanced over
at Sister Mary Francine as I said this. I didn't want her to
hear me.

"Now *she*, they might kick out," Nancy said.

"Come on — she's OK."

"She's a pill."

"She's unhappy. Watch when she walks. She holds her
shoulders tight, and she always, always keeps her arms
folded under her cape. She never smiles."

"Except when we recreate with the novices," Nancy
said. "And she can sit next to her Guardian Angel, Ann
Joseph. I think she's got a crush on her."

"What do you mean, a crush?"

"Yes, a crush. Didn't girls at Ladyhill have crushes, or
were you high society types above all that?"

"Crushes on boys, yes, of course. I've had crushes on boys ever since I can remember, but crushes on girls — come on, Nancy."

"Come on yourself, Marg. I'm sure there were freshmen at Ladyhill who especially liked some junior or senior. It certainly happened at Redemption. People usually outgrow it. I guess June never did."

"But . . . "

Just at that moment Linda proudly appeared bearing her mother's pastries. "Take three," said Sister Mary Francine, "three for the Trinity." Brownies with fudge frosting and yes — toll-house cookies made with chocolate mint chips.

A few minutes later Sister Mary Francine rang her small silver hand bell.

"Good night, Sisters."

"Good night, Sisters."

Profound Silence.

I wonder if Nancy's right, I thought, as I genuflected and swung into my prie-dieu with one smooth motion. The hebdomadary intoned the first psalm of Compline.

Oh Lord, my heart is not proud, she chanted.

Oh Lord, my heart is not proud, nor are my eyes haughty, we answered.

> *I busy not myself with great things, nor with*
> *things too sublime for me.*
> *Nay, rather I have stilled and quieted my soul*
> *Like a weaned child on its mother's lap,*
> *So is my soul within me.*
> *Oh Israel, hope in the Lord.*

I knew now how to chant each phrase on one breath, to send the words out in a steady stream while making the slight head inclinations and deeper bows in unison with the rest of the Novitiate. The question my talk with Nancy turned up faded.

> *Keep us, O Lord, as the Apple of your eye*
> *Shelter us under the shadow of your wings,*

we chanted.

June will be all right, I thought.

The pace of the chanting quickened as we got to the 'Canticle of Simon'. 'Let's get upstairs,' the rhythm said. 'I want to be first into the shower and get to bed fast.'

> *Now you may dismiss your servant,*
> *According to your word, in peace.*

That night I didn't fall asleep as quickly as usual. Poor Donna and Bella and June. Funny how involved we were getting with each other and how hard that sometimes was. I'd been prepared for homesickness and difficult rules. I mean, the convent couldn't just be Ladyhill prolonged. But I thought the hard part would be, well, prayer and meditation. Yet I liked that. I wasn't about to set up as a mystic but somehow the beauty of the campus gave me a sense of God all around me. I missed boys, of course, but at least I didn't have to worry about sins against purity. Though the only time I'd really managed to break the sixth commandment, I'd been by myself and didn't even know I'd done it until the next day.

I was eleven years old and in the sixth grade. We had our heads down on our desks, eyes closed, while Sister took us through an examination of our consciences for confession later that afternoon. I already knew what I was going to say. My usual. I disobeyed my parents three times,

I fought with my sisters six times, I talked back, and so on. But then she read the Sixth Commandment, "Thou shalt not commit adultery." I squirmed a little in my seat and pushed my forehead down further. This could be trouble. "Impure thoughts," she said. Yes, impure thoughts, I did have impure thoughts. Nothing concrete, but before I went to sleep, images often passed through my mind, riding off with a cowboy with whom I was about to do something sinful, though I wasn't quite sure what that was.

But, there was a loophole. Impure thoughts were sins only if you entertained them. I relaxed. Entertain them? Offer my impure thoughts a coke and pretzels? Never. No, not me. I fought them all the way. So, no sin. But now Sister was reading a sin I'd never paid attention to before. "Touching yourself in impure places." Oh, oh. My heart had pounded wildly. "Touching in impure places in order to excite pleasure," she went on. Oh my God, I think I did that, and it's a mortal sin. Mortal — straight to hell. But how could what I had done possibly be what Sister means?

This is what had happened. I had been talking on the telephone to Alice Brady, and had taken the phone down on to the basement staircase for privacy. It was dark on the stairs and quiet there among the winter jackets that hung from hooks. I leaned back into the clothes, ready for a nice long talk. Alice went away to get some cookies. While I waited, I reached under my uniform skirt to scratch the hairs that had recently appeared between my legs. As I scratched and rubbed I began to get very strange sensations, a kind of throbbing. It was surprising but nice. At first I didn't connect the scratching and the feelings, but then I rubbed my fingers over the hairs and the sensations increased. When Alice came back on the phone, I told her I had to go and hung up.

"Margaret Mary," my mother said when I finally came out of the basement, "haven't you changed your uniform, yet? It's dinner time." But later that night in the bathtub I rubbed the same area and got the same results. I'll have to try this again, I'd thought. But now here was Sister, listing it as a mortal sin, "touching yourself for pleasure." That's just what I'd done!

On the way to confession I thought — no, I mean murder's a mortal sin, surely stirring up a few sensations is not in the same league. But those Sixth Commandment sins were tricky. Impure thoughts alone had a dozen variations. Wait, how about if what happened was accidental — like an un-entertained bad thought? Then, I'm OK. But I did touch myself, I did feel something. Confess it. But I couldn't. I mumbled through my regular sins. Got my three Hail Mary penance and went home. But now I was in real trouble. I'd made a bad confession, another mortal sin. But somehow I could not feel I had slipped so irrevocably. I prayed. It was Lent and I was going to Mass and Communion every day. Then I realised it was a mortal sin to go to Communion, if you were in mortal sin. They were multiplying. Next day, to dampen the doubts, I'd go to Communion. But then I'd start worrying again. Sins could be doubling, tripling.

Just confess, I told myself. If it wasn't a sin, well nothing lost. But I couldn't. What *words* would I use to tell my sin? It was hard enough to say "I had bad thoughts three times," but "I touched myself in an impure place for pleasure two times,"? Not to Father O'Leary who ate roast beef at our house just last Sunday. If I just said "I broke the Sixth Commandment," he might think I'd done something really terrible. I did start to explain at confession — three times. But I lost my nerve, and so made a bad confession and another mortal sin. I was going nuts. It never occurred to me to talk to my parents and I couldn't ask Sister. If only Jesus himself would come down and hear my confession. I thought I could tell him, after all, he knew already anyway.

Then one day we went back to our old parish for a Mass commemorating the first anniversary of my aunt's death. I knelt in the pew next to my mother wondering what to do about Communion. I noticed people standing in line by the confessional. There must be a priest there hearing confession during Mass, I thought, a priest I don't know who doesn't know me. Perfect. I got my mother's attention and pointed at the confessional.

Wait a minute now, I said to myself as I joined the line. What about an act of perfect contrition? If I could be sorry for my sins solely because I had offended God and not because I feared hell and punishment, then I was forgiven without confession. In other words if sorrow came from love and not fear of God, then I was OK. But this wasn't just between me and God. I needed concrete confirmation of forgiveness. So I took my imperfect contrition in hand and entered the confessional.

I knelt down in the small dark space. With a click the little door covering the grill opened. I could see the outline of the priest's face. "Bless me, father, for I have sinned. It's been one week since my last confession," I whispered. "Father, I disobeyed my mother three times, I fought with my sisters twice, I was disrespectful to my elders, and I ... I ... I ... I — the Sixth Commandment."

"Well, what, what?" he asked impatiently. "Impure thoughts?"

"No, father, I ... I ... I touched ..."

"You touched someone in an impure way?" he asked.

"No, father, I . . . I touched . . . I touched myself."

"For pleasure?"

"Well, no, not exactly. It was more, well . . ."

I was going to faint. I felt I'd been in there for hours. Oh, Lord, help me, please.

I heard the priest shift in his chair.

"Answer me. You know if you touch yourself accidentally it's not a sin. Now was that it, while cleansing?"

Cleansing, yes, I thought, yes, the second time I was in the bathtub. I was cleansing.

"Yes, father," I whispered in a miserable small voice.

But my conscience started up immediately. "Bad confession, bad confession. Lying, lying." I was terrified. I couldn't keep going through this. The priest had already begun the absolution, but I interrupted.

"Father, I . . . I wasn't exactly cleansing. I . . . I touched ..."

"How old are you?" he whispered.

"Twelve."

"Did you touch yourself in an impure manner?"

"Yes, father. "

"When did this occur?"

"About three months ago."

"And where did you touch yourself, little girl."

"Once I was in the bathtub and the other time I was on the phone."

"No, no. I mean what part of your body?"

"Oh, Father," I said in anguish.

"You did not confess this in your other confession?"

"I . . . No, father."

"Have you received Communion in this sinful state?"

"Yes, father. I have, I . . ."

"How many times?"

"Um, six?" I couldn't say 'fifty'."

"Well, this is very serious," he said. "You must never do that again. For your penance, say fifteen decades of the Rosary, and now make a good Act of Contrition."

"Oh, my God, I am heartily sorry," I began as the priest mumbled in Latin, "for having offended thee," — fifteen decades! I had never got more than three Hail Marys for penance — "and I detest all my sins," and I didn't even tell him the real number of bad Communions, "because I dread the loss of heaven and the pains of hell, but most of all because they offend thee my God, who art all good and deserving of all my love. I firmly resolve with the help of thy grace to confess my sins, to do penance, and to amend my life. Amen."

It had been hard but finally, I was free. I got up and walked out of the confessional, back to my mother. I had no sooner knelt down when my conscience started up. "Bad confession, bad confession. Another mortal sin and nothing forgiven, nothing forgiven."

Off and on over the next two years my conscience would convince me to confess it all again. Either I'd feel the priest hadn't understood or that I hadn't been honest. For long stretches I'd forget, then I'd hear a sermon about purity. Finally during my freshman year at Ladyhill, a priest from Ireland, Father Reilly, gave our retreat. He said anyone who wished could make a general confession. We wouldn't have to mention specific sins or numbers. He would simply say the number of the commandment and we would respond 'yes' or 'no'. Here was my chance. And he heard confession not in the confessional, but in the sacristy next to the chapel.

I walked into the big room. Light poured in from three windows. In the middle of the room, two chairs stood with a half screen between them. It was a Church law for priests hearing the confessions of women to have something between them. Even when my priest-uncles heard our confessions in the living room, we had to hold up a scarf in between. When he said "Any sins against the Sixth Commandment?" I said "Yes," and the whole thing was over. Father Reilly absolved me in English after the Latin.

"For these sins and the sins of your whole life I forgive you in the name of the Father, and the Son, and the Holy Spirit."

He blessed me as he said this and made the Sign of the Cross on my forehead. That was it — three minutes and the sins of my whole life — forgiven.

What a state I had worked myself into, I thought, as I turned on my stomach and settled in for sleep. Bad theology too. Why if I didn't choose to . . . but I couldn't think anymore. And now I'm going to stop worrying. Somehow Donna and Bella and June were all jumbled up in my mind. And our last thoughts are supposed to be of God — but I was really tired.

Christmas came. A beautiful liturgy — carols, Midnight Mass, all day recreation, and no rules. Novices and postulants were together and piles of packages had arrived from the family. If I just could have been home for five minutes to see Patrick open his presents.

On New Year's Eve we counted down 10, 9, 8, 7, 6, 5, 4, 3, 2, 1 and then yelled Happy New Year — at 8:00 p.m. After that, Candlemas on February 2 became the focus of all attention. On that day we would receive our religious names.

Each of us would submit three possible choices and Reverend Mother would choose one. We couldn't take the name of a living nun and there had to be a saint attached. All the postulants were pouring over Butler's *Lives of the Saints* and passing around two *Names for your Baby* books.

"We are lucky," Jacinta told me one Sunday night in late January when the novices had invited us to play bingo with them. "Years ago there was no choice at all! You just got whatever name Mother wanted you to have!"

"That explains Sister Symphrorosa," I said. She'd been our Latin teacher at Ladyhill.

"Oh, remember those pageants we had to do!" Jacinta laughed. Ladyhill came close for a moment.

"Remember? When Sister Symphrorosa restaged the chariot race from Ben Hur on the front lawn, I had to be the horse! Cars piled into each other on Ridge trying to see why forty teenage girls were in a circle screaming 'Vale' at two moving cardboard boxes."

We had been watching our bingo cards only half-heartedly but now Jacinta straightened up.

"Did she say '1-65'?"

"No," said Nancy from the next table.

"What are you two talking about?"

"Names of course."

"Actually," Jacinta said shifting her ever widening bottom on the still chair, "some of the Latin names are nice. Carita or Pieta."

"Oh please — I want something modern. Sister John for John Kennedy and Pope John or maybe Sean," I said.

"Forget that. They'd call you Seen. Plus, I heard Mother said no more Gaelic names. The previous superior, Mother Mary Kevin O'Rourke, was overly attached to her heritage and in Mother Agatha's opinion there were quite enough Deirdres, Brendans, and Colmcilles in the order already, thank you very much."

"Patrick is my first choice," I said.

"Well, forget it." Jacinta stretched. "The word is, no single masculine names this year."

I kept a piece of paper in my office book and spent most of spiritual reading writing 'Sister Patrick Lynch', 'Sister Michael Brigid Lynch', 'Sister John Marie Lynch', and so on the way I used to write, 'Kevin Sullivan', 'Mrs. Kevin Sullivan', 'Margaret Mary Sullivan' and 'MMS' and 'MMLS' in the margins of my geometry notebook. I also lined up my name on top of each religious name and crossed out the letters that were the same. I'd done the same with boys' names: the more shared letters, the more chance of a match. I added Maura to a few of my choices, Maura John, John Maura, Maura Patrick — now that was good, feminine, Irish and my Dad's name, plus the same number of letters as Margaret Mary with, wait, yes, six shared letters.

"I've been thinking of Maura Patrick," I told Jacinta.

"No. Little kids would say Sister More Patrick."

"But, I won't be teaching little kids," I said.

Nancy heard this last remark, of course.

"Didn't you know, Jacinta, Margaret's aiming for the college. Better get a name that goes with professor."

I never knew if she was teasing or not when she talked like that.

"I'm asking for Matthew, Mark and Luke," she said.

Jacinta said, "No single masculine names."

"So — I'll try."

"Say, if I got Patrick," I said, "then March 17 would be my feast day! Not only recreation at dinner, but a party."

"Well," said Nancy, "if I get an evangelist, we'd talk on my feast day too."

"Yeah? Well, Saint Mark's feast comes during Lent!"

"Just like St. Patrick's day!"

"Yes, but Bishops give dispensation from Lent on St. Patrick's Day. It's practically Church law."

"All you Micks stick together," she said, shaking her head sorrowfully.

"Bingo," someone yelled. Jacinta cleared her card.

"Do you two enjoy bickering?" she asked.

"Bicker?" I said, "Nancy and I don't bicker. We discuss."

But Nancy wasn't paying attention.

"Look," she pointed at the group of servers from the dining room who had just entered the recreation room. Trailing along last was June in animated conversation with Ann Joseph. Nancy raised her eyebrows at me. Jacinta noticed the exchange.

"What?"

"June and Ann Joseph," Nancy said.

"Are they PFs?"

"What's that?"

"Hasn't Sister Mary Francine told you about Particular Friendship yet?" She was incredulous.

"No."

"Gee, we got that the first week. You guys have no idea how much easier you have it."

This was the novices' refrain. All Sister Mary Francine was trying to do was be rational about a few things and they acted as if she was making postulant year a Caribbean cruise.

One tall stocky novice from Boston had actually backed me into a corner of the ironing room one day.

"I hear you get to iron your own collars and cuffs," she said.

"Well, yes," I gulped, "yes we do."

"We didn't," she said between clenched teeth. "Ours were put in a common heap, sent to the laundry and ironed as an employment. Half the time the cuffs came back creased and mildewed or the collar wouldn't really be flat and . . ."

"Right — that's why Sister Mary Francine lets us put our own damp collars and cuffs in plastic bags and iron them at our leisure."

"Your leisure, yeah, I heard about that!"

I guess we did have more unstructured time than they did, but really, collars and cuffs.

"Look, Terrance Anne, I hate ironing my cuffs. I'd rather go back to the old system."

"Oh, really? And would you also rather," her rounded a's took some of the menace from her tone, "not have *Newsweek* in your study hall?"

"No — I like having *Newsweek*."

"Of course you do." She spat out the words. "We would have liked it too. But we never . . ."

Suddenly I could hear myself whining to my mother. "Why do you let Michelle wear lipstick in seventh grade? I never could. And how come Brigid can take the car when she's only got a permit? You made me wait until I got my licence . . ."

The novices wanted change but they also wanted us to suffer what they had.

"What about Particular Friendship?" I knew Jacinta was dying to tell me.

"Well . . ."

As if on cue, the electric buzzer shrieked.

"Good night, Sisters," said Sister Marie Charles just as a novice across the room squealed, "Bingo."

I brought up particular friendships with Sister Mary Francine at the bi-weekly individual conferences each of us had with her. She looked at me.

"What do you think it means?"

"Having favourites?" I tried.

"Yes," she said.

June did leave — five days before Christmas. Again, no explanations, just "Sister June has returned to her family" and faster turnaround time on her shower stall. Nancy started an "I told you so analysis".

"We're not supposed to discuss it, Sister!" I said.

Name day came and we lined up in the library of the old Motherhouse — fifty of us now spread out in front of Reverend Mother. Mother called us to her in band order beginning with the postulant who had arrived first on Entrance Day, my prie-dieu partner.

"In religion you shall be known as Sister Lawrence Elizabeth," Mother said, placing a small black cap on her hair.

We all smiled. That was her first choice — her parents' names linked. As each postulant came up and got her name, the tension eased. Almost everyone got her first choice. The novices claimed Mother sometimes gave postulants a name not on her list — say, if some nun had just died, a good friend of hers, and she felt the order couldn't go on without a Sister Ignatius Loyola or Mary Thaddeus (our founder's name).

Now it was Nancy's turn. "In religion you shall be known as Sister Matthew." Nancy beamed.

She got it — a single masculine name. Have to hand it to her, I thought.

Now my turn. "In religion you shall be known as Sister Maura." I waited. Now Patrick, surely, but no. She was placing the small black cap on my head. Maura. That was Mary, OK, but I had wanted my Dad's name too — and what kind of feast day would I take for Maura?

That night at prayers, I erased the pencilled Sister Margaret Mary on the first page of my office book and wrote Sister Maura Lynch. It looked OK. Sister Maura.

"Good afternoon, Sister Maura."

"Good afternoon, girls."

And then it was March. Spring started early at the Hills. In the country, seasons changed moment by moment. At home in Chicago it seemed the trees were bare one day and then in full bloom the next. Or green one week and then red and gold and gone. But here, I could watch the hard little buds appear tree by tree and then burst open, each at its own time. A sudden shower would hurry the leaves or a cold snap slow their development. And the orchard — well, each apple, pear and cherry tree seemed to have its own shade and texture of blossom. One particularly beautiful April evening as we meandered through the orchard kicking up clouds of black dust, I felt I had to put words on the feeling inside me.

"Matthew, when I see a sunset like that," I pointed to the sky beyond the barns, "full of pink and purple clouds, I think of the Holy Spirit breathing new life into me just like the sun creates those colours and these blossoms."

I thought she'd laugh but she didn't. "I know what you mean. I'm starting to, well, think about God a lot. I mean, He doesn't seem remote anymore."

"Yeah," I said. "That's it — not remote — that's exactly it, and also not regulated to one part of our life. I've always prayed, but that was usually in order to get God to help me with my regular life. Now I pray just to, well, get closer to God I guess."

"And are you?" she asked.

"Getting closer, you mean?"

"Yes," she nodded.

"Mm hmm, I don't know. Sometimes outside alone or after Communion or on a feast when the liturgy is really beautiful, I feel this like — joy."

"I felt like that at the Easter Vigil Service, almost holy," Matthew said.

I nodded. "Holy" seemed corny to actually say, but it did describe the feeling. Holy — whole, pure, full of love, and beautiful like this white flowering orchard.

"Can you imagine reception day?" I said. "After eight days of silence during the retreat, to be part of that ceremony — the Bishop and the choir singing just for us."

"Maura," Matthew said, "at those times, you know, at prayer when I feel that closeness to God, well, I also feel that my mother is there, loving me. No words, just her presence and I feel she's pleased with me. Happy, that I'm going to receive the habit and all. I . . . does that sound silly?"

"Silly? Oh no, Matthew. Not silly at all." Her mother had died when she was fifteen and she hardly ever talked about her. "I'm sure she does know and is very proud."

"Sisters." The line had gone ahead of us.

"We better catch up," I said jogging forward on the black road that made such a perfect baseline for the beautiful mix of trees and sky.

Sometimes Matthew brought her guitar and we all sang — 'If I had a Hammer,' 'Lemon Tree,' and when Sister Mary Francine wasn't listening too closely, 'Hey Lay de Lay', and 'I knew a girl and her name was Lil, She won't but her sister will!'

It seemed the Church too was having a kind of Spring. Pope John XXIII called it aggiornamento. "We have to open the windows," he said, "Let the spirit blow outmoded traditions away and get back to the basic message of Jesus — love."

Now that Sister Mary Francine had us more or less following the rules, she spent much of our instruction time reading us Pope John's statements. I think they reassured her, for she knew the stir his innovations were creating. And here was Pope John saying, "No misfortune, no sorrow, no calamity ought to find you strangers to it, no scientific discovery, no cultural, social or political conference should be considered: 'not your concern.' The Church should find you present wherever your spiritual contribution is needed for the good of souls and for true human progress and universal peace."

Sister Mary Francine smiled. "And this, Sisters, was written to *contemplative* nuns. His mandate to us is even stronger. Remember, our primary duty is the service of God through his people. Our personal holiness will come from that, Sisters." She leaned forward as if to make us understand. At these times her round face seemed to strain her serre tete, the white linen head covering worn under the veil, and her naturally rosy complexion flushed a deeper red. "God loves the world and so must we. As Pope John says, the discoveries of scientists, artists and," I knew this was coming, "psychologists are revelations of the Divine Mind. However, if we are to use these ideas we must be prepared, be whole and centred. Freedom with responsibility, Sisters. Each of you must find your individual path."

As she continued I thought of Terrance Ann. "So you guys are big buddies with Pope John now!" But even with the doors and windows open, some things stayed the same.

"And, Sisters," Sister Mary Francine was concluding, "would you please remember to roll your blouses in towels before you hang them up to dry? I understand the puddles in the third floor drying rooms are causing consternation. Thank you, Sisters."

Embrace the world, celebrate renewal but please keep the petty rules, make sure things run smoothly. OK — I could do that. And I did. But sometimes the institutionality of it all got to me. One day I was longing for a lamp. I just wanted to spend one evening reading by soft diffused light in a cosy room away from the incessant brightness of overhead fluorescence. And then my name went up on the package list.

Sister Myrna was twittering (no other word for it) when I arrived at her office. "The post mark is Rome!"

Had my priest Uncles Father Frank or Chuck gone there without telling me, I wondered? But no, the return addressee said 'Edward J. Charles'.

"My vagabond uncle," I told Myrna as I cut the heavy twine with the scissors she handed me. That was one nice thing about the convent — supplies were always at hand. Scissors, staplers, scotch tape, pins, all the things we could never find at my house.

"Vagabond?" Myrna was saying. She frowned.

"Not literally," I said quickly. I wanted her to see my uncle cheering the Pope in St. Peter's Square, not hitchhiking on the autostrada. "He works — he has, um, stores." They were liquor stores, but why be specific? "And he loves to travel."

By this time I was well into the innards of the package. Nothing edible but wait . . . I pulled out a very carefully wrapped tube.

"I wonder . . ."

I carefully pulled the paper away to find a parchment scroll and carefully unrolled it.

Both Myrna and I gasped.

"My God!" I said.

Close enough. Uncle Ed had got me a document that said a papal blessing was bestowed on Maggie Lynch by Pope John himself.

Myrna had to sit down.

"Doesn't your uncle know your religious name?" Sister Myrna asked.

"Well . . ." Oh please — I bet the Pope's family calls him Angelo.

I dug further into the package and pulled out a square box wrapped in stiff yellow and white striped paper.

"A statue?" Myrna guessed. I carefully pulled the tape away; we saved wrapping. The box underneath was also yellow and had a furry velvet-like surface with a white embossed dove.

Myrna peered closely. Perhaps the Holy Spirit?

But the words under the dove said 'L'Air du Temps.'

"Perfume!" I said. "From Paris. Nina Ricci's 'L'Air du Temps'." I never had perfume right from Paris. I had sprayed on my mother's Chanel No. 5, but she got that from Marshall Fields. I wore Blue Grass from the Peterson Pharmacy. Thank you, Uncle Ed.

Sister Myrna sniffed at the bottle.

"A strong smell, I don't know if we can send this to the sisters in the infirmary."

That's where any scented soaps or creams or powders we received usually went. Sickness carried its own dispensation.

I gently eased the dove-shaped stopper free and inhaled the perfume. It didn't smell like flowers or fruit or anything natural. No, it was wonderfully artificial.

"It would be a shame to discard such a beautiful thing," Sister Myrna sighed. "Wait, I know. It would make a fine Christmas present for some of the secular help. Bring it to Sister Benedicta's office." She was Sister Marie Charles' assistant and did for the novices what Sister Myrna did for us.

"And Sister Maura."

"Yes?"

"You may put a little perfume on your handkerchief and use it as a sachet in your underwear drawer."

Now that was a concession.

"Thank you, Sister," I said and I meant it.

As I left her office the deep mystical connection between Pope John and L'Air du Temps dawned on me. "The air of the times", right, spirit of the times, holy spirit, dove. I rubbed the fuzzy yellow box, my own Aladdin's lamp. Here was one wish I could make come true.

I did not go directly to Sister Benedicta. Instead, I went up the stairs to the third floor without asking permission. I headed into the tub-room and turned the hot water on to full. I took the small bottle and carefully sprinkled a few drops of the essence of Paris into the tub. Clouds of fragrant steam filled the small space. In a moment I'd stripped away my layer of black uniform and slipped into the warm sweet-smelling water. I stretched out in the tub. Bliss. *If I had a hammer . . .* I sang softly. No! *Tonight, tonight, won't be just any night. . . . .* Ah. I propped my feet up on the end of the tub. My legs stretched out, surprisingly long and slim for the rest of me. I've always been secretly vain about my thin ankles, nice calves and firm thighs. Of course now, the skin I'd kept smooth and soft had disappeared under an ugly layer of hair. Nuns didn't shave legs or underarms. The perfumed water penetrated the pores of my body but could not break through the thicket under my arms and on my legs.

But secreted under my soap dish as a kind of talisman of the old days, I had one slightly rusty Gillette safety razor. What would Pope John do?

I quickly soaped up my underarms and with a few deft strokes removed the hair. Now the legs. Not so easy. But I scraped the resisting hairs away with ruthless determination. It was worth it to see my right leg reappear — smooth and clean, though very, very white. I moved onto the left too vigorously. I gashed my upper shin. In seconds, the lovely L'Air du Temps water turned an unpleasant red as blood gushed from a very deep cut.

I leaped from the tub, wrapped my black robe around my still wet body and dashed for the lavatory down the hall for some toilet paper to staunch the blood. But the thin tissue dissolved under the onslaught. Had I severed an artery or something? Why hadn't I paid attention to First Aid in Girl Scouts?

Ten minutes later, dressed neatly in my cape, blouse, skirt with undershirt, bra, regulation underpants and black lisle stockings, I handed the perfume box to Sister Benedicta. Luckily she didn't see what would have caught Sister Myrna's eye immediately. I usually turned my postulant skirt over at the waist once or twice so it hit me at the knees instead of hanging at the regulation calf length. Now I had pulled it down almost to my ankles. That was the only way I could cover the Kotex sanitary napkin I'd wrapped around my leg. My thickest pair of hose held it in place until the bleeding finally stopped.

> *Dear Uncle Ed,*
> *Thank you so much for the absolutely spectacular gifts. The blessing from Pope John is too wonderful for words. Did you actually see him! Please write and tell me all about it. And the L'Air du Temps! I'll never forget receiving it. Thank you so much.*
>
> *Love,*
> *Sister Maura (Maggie)*

I took it as a sign — bloodshed and all. Pope John never said renewal was easy.

Ironically, I was back in the tub-room the day the tower bell began the slow toll for the dead. We had the window wide open to let out the fumes from the Toni solution.

"Another nun in the infirmary died, I guess," Linda said.

"I guess," I said. I concentrated on wrapping one last little clump of hair at her neck into pink rod curlers. I'd become our band's home permanent expert in the months since name day. You needed some extra bounce in your hair to offset the constant pressure of the black cap. It flattened any natural curl. Sister Mary Francine's approval of good grooming made getting "permission for a Toni" a snap. Sometimes Nancy helped me and on a Saturday afternoon we could have as many as four perms going at once. With the hoods we rigged up for the dryers on the wall and the smell of neutralizer, the third floor tub and sink room felt like Sandy's Beauty Nook at home. School was over now, and I had appointments back-to-back during free time.

The bell kept tolling.

"My God," I said. "Did some superior die?"

Then the door swung open.

"It's Pope John," Nancy said, "He's dead!"

"No!"

"Yes — last night."

Outside the single tone continued to sound. Poor Pope John — just when he had things moving along so well. And poor us, poor everybody. The three of us stood looking at each other. Then Linda broke the silence.

Out of the depths we have cried to thee O Lord
Lord hear our prayer.

We picked up the 'De Profundis' but then the timer went off. So we continued to ask for eternal rest for Pope John while I rinsed the setting solution out of Linda's hair. I didn't think he'd mind. In fact, in the long history of the papacy, he was probably the first Pope who'd understand how really awful a frizzy Toni could be.

He died in June — just as our days as postulants were coming to an end. Pope John had protected and nurtured the reforms and reformers in the same way that first our novice guardian angels and then Sister Mary Francine had protected us from the rougher realities of religious life. Well, we were about to move on. In August we would be officially received into the community and invested in the habit. No more the indulged children of the order, now we would assume responsibilities. That bell was tolling for us too.

5

RECEPTION DAY

Why do spiritual milestones require such mammoth material preparations? Imagine fifty weddings staged simultaneously and you'll get some idea of what filled the weeks leading up to our Reception Day, August 15, 1962. On the feast of the Assumption, we would do what thousands of Sisters of Redemption had done before us, we would ask for and receive the holy habit and admission into the Congregation of the Sisters of the Redemption. In other words we'd move from the postulant sidelines into true community life as novices. Canonical novices, 'Canonical' because our next year was governed by Canon law.

This was the only period of formation that the Church hierarchy had much say in. It decreed that we study no secular subjects, receive only two family visits the whole year, write one letter home a month and increase our times of prayer and meditation.

In theory, it was a year of maximum separation from the world and stern testing of our vocation. In practice, since we didn't have school, it was a year in which we would do most of the heavy housework of the Novitiate and Motherhouse and act as nurses' aids in the infirmary. But, as Jacinta said, it was more fun talking to the old nuns while you dusted their rooms than writing term papers anyway.

Though Sister Francine spent our instruction periods reading and explaining the 'Rules and Constitutions of the Sisters of the Redemption' to us, the real command post for August 15 was in Sister Myrna's office. She was the mother of the brides. All fifty of us. On reception day, we would process up the main aisle of the Big Church to receive the habit dressed in full wedding regalia — bridal dress, veil, white satin shoes and even something old, something new, something borrowed, and something blue. Sister Mary Francine had assured us that all this did not mean that the community saw us as brides of Christ. No, that was a sentimental idea that grew out of 19th century spirituality, and was more pre-Raphaelite than theological. It was just such saccharine notions about religious women that the Sister Formation program, Vatican II and we ourselves were striving to put to rest. The wedding gowns had evolved from the simple white garment worn in the early Church, first by candidates for baptism and then by virgins consecrating themselves to the service of God through the Church. St Paul used the term 'Bride of Christ' for the Church, she explained, to symbolize the intimacy between God and his people. Paul himself got it from the Old Testament, where Israel was the bride. Did we understand?

Yes — it sounded good but why, then, was the novice choir practising 'Veni Sposa Christe' and why did Angela Taylor's parents spend $350 for a silk brocade wedding gown at Marshall Fields?

The dresses made one appearance only. After use in the ceremony, they were cut apart and used to decorate altar linens and vestments. I wondered how the Taylors felt about $350 for pearl-encrusted tabernacle veils?

Every day, two or three large dress boxes would arrive at Sister Myrna's office from Fields or Saks in Chicago or

Woodward and Latham in Washington or Ayers in Indianapolis. Some plain boxes came, too. Martha got her aunt's dress, Josie her cousin's and Amy told me her mother found hers at the "Nearly New Store" in their town. Some postulants without sisters would wear their mothers' dresses.

That wouldn't work for me. My parents were not married in an elaborate ceremony in my mother's Chicago parish, but simply, in New York, where my Dad snatched a few days leave from his Naval air station base. Pictures show them coming down the steps of St. Patrick's Cathedral under the swords held by my Dad's fellow Navy pilots, all of them decked out in their white dress uniforms. My mother moves forward holding my father's arm. In her Kelly green suit, with its swing skirt, a wide brimmed hat and slingback pumps, she looked romantic and dashing like Ginger Rogers or Jean Arthur or Gene Tierney striding confidently through a Forties movie. She never regretted not having a formal wedding, she said. How could she have wrapped herself in layers of white tulle when war was raging and my Dad's plane waited not ten miles away to take him into the thick of it? I agreed, but it meant no heirloom gown, as I explained to Sister Myrna — unless I wore kelly green, or we could alter my father's old uniform, ha ha.

I really didn't want my parents to spend a lot of money on a dress that would become a sacred remnant after one wearing. But time was getting short. Dress after dress arrived, was carefully ironed and hung in a special room. My mom felt some friend of hers must have stashed a traditional dress somewhere. But I was getting nervous.

By July 20 I'd sent out all my invitations, each neatly addressed, to aunts and uncles and cousins. We each had a limited number of tickets for the church itself, but could invite anyone we wished for the afternoon's visiting in the grove. I just assumed that all my relatives and close friends would be delighted to drive four hours in the height of an Indiana steam bath summer to sit in a circle outside and see me in my new habit. And they were. The acceptances rolled in, and so did the white nylons, shoes, gloves, handkerchief and veil I needed. But no dress.

"Does your Mother realise time is getting short?" Sister Myrna asked.

"I'm sure she does, Sister." How hard would it be to whip up a simple white cotton garment à la the early Christian catechumens, I wondered. But now I wanted a wedding dress too. And then my box arrived. "This was Mrs. Ward's dress," my mother wrote. "She went to Our Lady of the Hill College and would love for you to wear it." Sister Myrna lifted a long candlelight satin dress from the box. It was very simple and elegant with a high neck, narrow fitted bodice and long tight sleeves. Sister Myrna looked at the dress, then at me and then at the row of covered buttons that went up the back.

"Must be a size six and not much give in this material," she said shaking her head.

"So — I'll lose a few pounds and, and wear a basque like I did to the prom. I love it, it's perfect. I've got to wear it!"

"It is beautiful," Myrna agreed. She held it up. "This was the fashion in my time — late Thirties." She sighed. "Let's press it and hope for the best."

We postulants weren't the only ones looking forward to August 15th. The second year novices took their first vows, promising poverty, chastity and obedience for one year. These temporary vows would be renewed three times —

first for one year, then twice for two years. You could leave at any time during this process. Then, after eight years, final vows were taken. After that, leaving the community meant dispensations from Rome. Very rarely did anyone leave after final vows. In fact most people left during the Novitiate or not at all. Only fifteen percent of those who entered left. Some bands had even better records.

"At our Twenty-fifth Jubilee Celebration," Sister Myrna confided, "all but two of our members were there!"

Since Name Day, three more postulants had left, including Elizabeth Ann. So much for medieval history. I doubted if anyone else would go now — not if they had a wedding gown hanging in the brides' room.

On August 7th, the whole order stopped for eight days of silence and reflection — the annual retreat. Summer had brought most of the community home to the Hills. They brought all their possessions with them, because Mother announced the year's assignments on August 15th also. So no one was sure they would return to the same mission. The older nuns at home took some college classes, but for most, those weeks meant leisure and seeing old friends as well as the retreat.

After the first panicky day, I liked the quiet. The priest retreat master spoke at 10 a.m., 2 p.m. and 7:30 p.m. He was interesting, up-to-date, and it didn't hurt that he was good looking and a Jesuit. Apart from attending his talks, we were totally free. We could walk outside, nap, pray in the chapel, read, write. No one paid a bit of attention because each was within her own world, plumbing the depths of her soul or at least sloughing off the year's tension.

I spent my time outside. Of course, the weather was hot and humid but I moved slowly. I settled into the shaded lap of a wide-leafed maple tree on the far edge of the grove most afternoons with e e cummings and an apple, reading and meditating in a daydream kind of way. Sometimes I sang show tunes softly to myself. Amazing how the words could apply to God, with a twist of the lyrics. I liked especially 'It Was Always You' from *Carnival*.

> *It was always, always you.*
> *Always, always you.*
> *Though my mind might wander*
> *to and fro and yonder*
> *Still my heart's affection*
> *always led in your direction.*

I also tried -

> *I'm as corny as Kansas in August*
> *High as the flag on the fourth of July.*

But in spite of the joy I was finding in the Divine Presence, I couldn't sing

> *I'm In Love With A Wonderful Guy.*

But it wasn't God as the Bible pictures him I felt close to, or even the Jesus of the holy card with his long wavy hair and sad eyes. No, this was a more all-encompassing reality, certainly containing all my former images, and calling me to go beyond.

On those summer afternoons while the campus slept, I guess I discovered the Holy Spirit — L'Air du Temps, the breath of life. I sang the 'Veni Creator'. The first notes of the Gregorian chant aren't really sung but kind of breathed out.

> *Ve — ni Cre — a — tor Spiritu*

on one long tone that sounded very like the summer mix of insects, birds and lazy winds that filled my retreat afternoons. 'Veni Creator Spiritu' and *West Side Story*.

> *Something's coming I don't know*
> *What it is but it is gonna be great.*
> *The air is humming and something great is*
> *coming.*

Yes, I was doing the right thing. I was where I was meant to be.

And then it was the morning of August 15th.

I was awake before the rising bell. The sun was clearing the edge of the cornfield and shining in my window. I took out my brush rollers for the last time. I won't miss you, I thought, as I carefully took each out and unrolled my hair section by section. Usually I just yanked them out as the pads of toilet paper I'd wadded between the stiff brush and my scalp fell on the floor. I thought of all the fights we'd had at home over picks and rollers. There were never quite enough to go around, so the first one to bed got the best and the most. Many a night I'd had to substitute toothpicks or even Patrick's tinker toys for the pink plastic picks and then force two hanks of hair over one decrepit roller.

One night, Brigid actually re-set Michele's hair while she slept in order to get more rollers. I laughed to myself as I remembered Brigid crouched on the bed deftly unwinding and rewinding. She almost got away with it but Michele woke with a terrible roar, and charged her — literally like a bull does, while Brigid ran backwards tossing rollers at her in desperate expiation. I was laughing out loud when the rising bell rang and Sister Janice Marie yelled, "Benedicamus Domino."

"Deo Gratias," I sputtered.

I had a lot of underwear to put on. My jello and crackers diet had worked pretty well. I was down to 110 pounds, but I still wanted the basque. Smaller waist, better bust, I thought, as I struggled to fasten the wire hooks. Now the nylons — sheer and smooth. A quick trip to the sink room to brush my teeth and put vaseline on my eyebrows and lashes — it wasn't mascara, but it was something. Then the postulant uniform. We would put on our wedding dresses in the Motherhouse.

No Mass or meditation for us today. We headed right to the big old-fashioned sewing room on the third floor of the Motherhouse. Rolls of black serge material and half-finished habit skirts usually covered the long wooden tables. Now our wedding dresses and veils, white slips and heels were laid out in spaces labelled with our names. When I die, I bet Sister Maura #98 will mark my coffin. Next to the frilly white piles, our habits waited — folded into compact packages that would be given to the Bishop to present to us.

I had asked Sister Mary Rose, who had taught me in high school and was a second cousin of my great aunt's husband, to be my dresser. She would help me first into the bridal gown and then the habit. She gave me a quick smile and then looked down. Retreat silence held until after the ceremony, so we dressed in silence with guarded eyes.

I slipped out of my synthetic black skirt and cape. My habit would be all wool. I stood in my basque as Sister Mary Rose dropped the white slip over my head. The satin felt smooth and cool against my legs. We'd been allowed to shave.

"In the name of the Father and of the Son and of the Holy Spirit." Sister Mary Francine began the Rosary, the order's traditional prayer during the bride's robing. "Holy Mary, Mother of God, pray for us sinners now and at the hour of our death. Amen."

Sister Mary Rose methodically buttoned the fifty tiny satin covered buttons.

"Hail Mary, full of grace . . ." Sister Mary Francine prayed.

"Holy Mary . . ." we answered.

Almost everyone was ready. A clattering sound broke the silence as we all exchanged our rubber-heeled black shoes for white pumps. I took a tentative step. My ankles buckled slightly. I regained my balance. I know how to walk in heels, I thought, annoyed. I'm the one who came down those twenty-five marble steps in three-inch stilettos when I was a princess at the St. George Prom. Sister Mary Rose picked up my veil and carefully set it on my head, pushing the tortoiseshell combs into my hair. She shook her head "no" at me. I didn't understand. She moved her head again more vigorously.

"What?" I whispered.

"Your veil — is it secure?"

"Oh," I twisted my head back and forth. Yes, it could withstand a blast from the large fans that would try to cool the church.

"Glory be to the Father and to the Son . . ."

One by one we walked up to the full-length mirror at the front of the sewing room. Forty teenaged brides. In an hour and a half we'd be back to put on the habit. I watched each one before the mirror. Matthew barely glanced at her image, Helena Mary reached up to re-adjust her veil, Lawrence Elizabeth pushed a piece of hair back behind her ear.

Then my turn came. The tightly-fitted satin dress clung to my waist, then fell gracefully to the ground. The silk lilies of the valley at the crown of this veil were just like those that had decorated my First Communion veil. I looked at the face framed by the veil. "When I grow up I'm going to be a nun," I'd told sister on that First Communion day.

I walked down the wide wooden stairs, carefully holding up the back of my long skirt. Lift the back going down and the front going up, same as with the habit skirt.

I found my family in the hall. We had twenty minutes to visit before the ceremony. They could take pictures now, but not once we were in the habit. I hadn't talked to anyone in eight days and here were the people I loved most in the world. I grabbed up my skirt and ran to them. I kissed and hugged my Mother, my Dad, Brigid, Michele, Sally, Laurie, and picked up Patrick. My Mother realigned my veil, bringing it forward on my head. All my life she'd been pulling hats — tams, Easter bonnets, grey flannel bowlers — further forward on my head. My father took a picture of little Patrick and me, and then of my sisters grouped around me, and Brigid took a picture of my father and mother with me. My father put his arm around me and I leaned for a moment against his shoulder. "Always thought when you'd be in an outfit like this I'd be walking you up the aisle," he said.

"Yeah, but you don't have to give me away, you're not losing a daughter, you're gaining a congregation," I said.

And then the bell was ringing and the families left to take their places in the Big Church. "One last shot," my Dad said, backing up to focus. "Dad!" It was too late — he collided with Sister Marie Charles escorting Reverend Mother to church. "Excuse me, Sister and Mother," I said.

But they just smiled absent-mindedly and hurried past. The families left, silence settled over the hall, and we all quietly assembled in our assigned places for the procession into Church.

All the church bells on campus rang, and the organ began. The long swaying line of brides began to move. "Keep a wide space before and after, and small steps, Sisters, small steps," Sister Mary Francine whispered. "And stand close together on the altar."

Veni Sposa Christe, Veni Sposa Christe, sang the choir as we waited together in the back vestibule. "Click, click, click." That was Sister Myrna's signal. The shortest postulant started out in the slow step-pause gait we'd practised. One by one, my band members went off. When Nancy reached the fourth prie-dieu, I started. I kept my eyes on the main altar, where white roses and carnations and calla lilies stood in tall silver vases. Midway up the aisle, I slid my eyes to the side, looking for my family, but all the faces seemed a blur of mothers in hats and fathers in suits. The fans fluttered the edges of the white linen altar cloths and dried the film of perspiration above my lip. Sun poured through the stained glass windows outshining the lines of candles and rows of frosted lights. I reached the first step on the main altar. 'Veni Sposa Christe' ended and the organist played the distinctive single tones that began the 'Tota', an ancient almost Oriental-sounding hymn to Mary.

Tota Pulchra est Maria, Tota Pulchra est Maria. The notes were low and the choir sang them softly, but then the music swelled and their voices rose. *Tu Gloria Jerusalem, Tu Laetitia Israel. You are all beautiful O Mary*, I translated to myself as I climbed the white marble steps into the sanctuary. *You are the glory of Jerusalem, the joy of Israel.*

I pivoted on the top steps and carefully moved into my place next to Nancy.

O Maria, Maria, O Maria, Ora Pro Nobis, Ora Pro Nobis. The sopranos took this part, their high strong voices sweeping down from the choir loft. I moved into the sanctuary to join the other brides who waited with folded hands and downcast eyes. I took a few short quick breaths.

The Bishop sat on a carved wooden throne in front of the altar. As the last bride took her place, he stood. In his gold-embroidered white vestments and tall mitre, he was as dressed up as we were.

The choir stopped. The Church went silent except for the hum of the fans' motors.

"I ask," we said together, "to receive the holy habit of the Sisters of the Redemption."

He continued the ritual questions. "Were we doing this of our own free will? Did we understand the holiness of the estate we sought to enter?"

"Yes. Yes. We knew. We wanted this." And we did. I did.

Each of us stepped up to the Bishop. Sister Mary Francine stood next to him with Sister Myrna at her side. Sister Myrna passed a bundled habit to Mary Francine. She gave it to the Bishop who handed it to us. I carried mine carefully, the way the little ring bearers at a wedding carry their pillows, and walked slowly from the sanctuary.

Once outside in the hall my pace quickened. The scholastic novices would take their temporary vows and receive the black veil, the tertians would make final vows. We had to be dressed in the habit and back in the sanctuary to receive our chaplets — those long rosaries so evocative of nuns — in less than twenty minutes. I caught up to Nancy at the stairway. We picked up our wedding gowns and took the stairs two at a time.

In the sewing room, the dressers were ready. This time the Rosary was not slow and languid, but clipped.

Hail Mary ...

"Leave the basque on, there isn't time, and the sheer stockings." Long black petticoat, pocket, habit skirt, blouse, big sleeves, small sleeves. Sister Mary Rose dropped each garment over my head. I fumbled with hooks and eyes. Now the serre tete.

"Ow — No — that's OK, I want it tight."

Cap. Veil. Yes, I have white head pins. Good — shoes. Now get in line and back to church. As I slid around the table and out the door, I glanced in the mirror. A nun looked back at me — a nun with my face.

'Veni Creator Spiritu' the Choir sang as I fastened my chaplet on to my waist and the ceremony ended. All of us new novices, the first professed and those with final vows, marched in pairs down the main aisle as the organ triumphantly played the 'Te Deum'. We processed out the main doors towards the green lawn and the fountain where our families waited. The bells rang. Families called their daughters' names.

"Mag — er Sister Maura," I heard.

The rest of the day was a blur of kisses and hugs and three-minute conversations. Fifty people had travelled from Chicago to spend this day with me and I wanted each one to know how grateful I was for their coming.

"I never saw a bride so happy," I heard my Aunt Mary say. At noon our families went to eat and we entered the refectory to applause, cheers, and a fried chicken dinner. "I am so glad and happy," I said to Nancy/Matthew as we swished arm in arm back to the grove, whipping our long skirts in rhythm.

"Come and meet my Dad and brother," Matthew said.

The Thurler men seemed too big for the wooden benches; there was no place for their arms and legs. All but Johnny, the 19-year-old, had dropped their suit coats over a chair. Johnny was a Marine and kept his blue dress tunic buttoned up to his chin despite the 85° temperature and 100% humidity. That's what we talked about — the weather.

"Yes, just terrible," I said to Mr. Thurler. "Much worse than Chicago."

"You get no breeze off the lake here. That breeze off the lake does more cooling than you'd think."

"That's right," I said, looking at the exhausted trees, "This humidity's so heavy it would take a typhoon to lift it." I smiled and left. Not much to say but that was alright. Talking with the serre tete was hard anyway. The linen band cut under my chin. I kept moving my jaw at odd moments to loosen the material. Once, I caught my mother staring at me.

"It's the hair," I explained, "I've got too much under here. But I'll get a hair cut tonight — then it will fit better."

Our circle was very animated. My Dad had spent the dinner break buying a huge cooler and filling it with Pepsis and Cokes, Old Dad Root Beer and 7UPs. A few six-packs of beer rested on the bottom. My sisters and cousins were downing the icy cokes one after another.

"Maggie, er Sister Maura?" My Mom held the bottle toward me. The condensation ran down the heavy green glass making tiny cool rivers. I was so hot — the stays of the basque dug into my waist and the neck of my serre tete was wet with sweat.

"I can't Mom. You know — it's a rule . . ."

"Now Maggie." Father Frank turned from his conversation with Uncle James. "There's the letter of the law and the spirit of the law. Given this heat, I'm sure the spirit would allow you one soft drink."

"Of course, of course," Uncle James chimed in. "Rules are meant to be broken."

Maybe in the 39th Ward, where he was the assistant to the assistant Alderman, I wanted to say, but not in the convent.

"That's OK," I said, "I'm not really thirsty."

All three looked at me.

"Of course, self-control is a wonderful thing," Father Chuck volunteered.

"Absolutely necessary," James agreed quickly. "Essential." He patted my shoulder and surveyed the other family circles. "How many did you say were from Chicago?" he asked.

"About half," I replied.

"Really." He straightened his tie and headed into the crowd.

"And all registered Democrats," I said to Father Frank.

"He knows that," he replied. "So, Margaret Mary, is it what you expected?"

"Well, I'm not sure what I expected. But I'm happy, Uncle Frank — really happy! Of course it's going to be hard, with no visits until February."

Patrick was chasing our cousin Bobby in and out of the benches. Michele, Brigid and my cousin Kathy were bent over a portable radio trying to tune in a decent station. Sally and Laurie and three other cousins sat on the grass playing Monopoly.

"I'll try to come by," he said.

"Oh, would you? We're allowed to see a priest any time!"

"Maggie, Maggie," called Michele. "Look."

It was The Group. Janet and Ann looked very dressed up. I'd been with Janet when she bought that blue linen sheath and Ann had worn that red and white striped shirtwaist to the final term club dance. Susie wore bermuda shorts — convent or no — but Tommy and John wore sports jackets and ties. I looked just in case Kevin had somehow arrived from California, where he was studying on a National Science Foundation grant.

I started to run toward them but got tangled in my long skirt. Janet couldn't move too fast in her heels either so it was Susie who hugged me first.

"Maggie, I can't believe it," she said, "you look like, like .."

"I'd take Audrey Hepburn in *The Nun's Story*," I laughed.

"So would I," said Janet. We hugged.

"Sorry we missed this morning, but we were at George's wedding. He married a girl from Minnesota."

"Great party," John said. "There was a pool and they dunked the father of the bride!" Ann said.

"No!"

"Well, everyone was throwing everyone else in," Tommy explained.

"Did he laugh?" I asked.

"He had to," John said.

"You do know how to 'commote a ruskis'," I said.

They looked at me for a minute.

"Commote?" said John.

"Don't you remember last summer when you said 'commote a ruskis' instead of, well I guess, 'commence a ruckus' and we said it all summer . . .?" My voice trailed off.

"I remember," Janet said loyally.

"Kevin loves California," Susie said. "He might move there."

"Oh. Great."

"I told him we'd send him a picture." Ann already had her Brownie aimed.

"I can't, Ann," I started to say but I didn't move all that fast when she clicked the shutter. California. We did have a high school in California but it was an academy — prep school types. I hadn't entered the convent to teach rich girls.

I felt a tug on my habit skirt.

"Can we visit the soldier nuns now, Dee Dee?"

"Of course, Paddy!" I took his hand.

"See you in a minute," I said to the group.

"Dee Dee," Patrick said, as we entered the cemetery. "If I married you, could you come home?"

"Oh, honey. You marry me?"

"Well, this guy in my class, Joseph, he said you had to become a nun because nobody would marry you. So if I married . . ."

"No, Paddy. That's not why." I knelt down and hugged him. "Sweetheart, I want to be a nun. It's wonderful to get married and have a family, but somebody has to help kids who don't have good families."

"But couldn't you stay with us and still help?"

Just then the tower bells rang their melody.

"You know what the chimes say, Paddy?"

"No."

"Listen. One more ho-ur clos-er to God.

Love and serve Him with all your heart. That's what I want to do."

"Oh." But his attention was distracted by the life-sized replica of an outdoor station, 'Jesus Falls the Third Time'.

"If Jesus was God, why did he let them whip him like that?"

"Well, that's a mystery, Paddy."

I spent the rest of the day thanking relatives for coming and for their gifts.

"It's all books and holy cards," Laurie said with some disgust.

"But it's what I wanted." Mom had put out the word. Other daughters registered at Fields. She directed would-be gift-givers to the St. Thomas More Book Shop and Conception Abbey.

"These aren't old fashioned holy cards. They're silk screened and have scriptural quotes and good sayings. There's a whole section of quotes from President Kennedy and . . ."

"Yeah? I'd rather get albums," Laurie said.

"Oh, that's right. You're a teenager now." What a sappy thing to say. Pretty soon I'll be asking her what grade she was going into and what she did on her summer vacation.

I did get a few minutes with The Group. We took a quick walk into the apple orchard.

"Remember the time we climbed over the fence at Soldier's Field for the demolition derby?" I realized I was fingering the beads of my chaplet as we walked. One bead for each memory. Reciting the stories the way I now said Hail Marys.

Suddenly, it was all over. The grove emptied. The Group was gone. Then my family left.

"Goodbye, goodbye," I said, holding Patrick's hand through the open window of the station wagon. My Dad started the motor. I leaned in and kissed him one more time.

"Bye, Mom." I reached in with my other hand.

"Thank you, thank you for everything!"

"Don't forget the thank-you notes," my Mom said.

"Don't worry!"

I waved the car out of sight. Matthew was at the steps.

"Six months before I see them! Seems so long."

"Canon Law," she said.

"And letters only once a month! Gee."

"Canon Law," she repeated as we turned toward the building. "But it'll go fast."

"I don't know," I said. "I'll miss taking classes and seeing the college girls, even if we can't talk to them."

"Canon Law," Matthew said again.

"If only we could get letters more than once a month!" I said.

"Canon Law. The first year of the Novitiate, entirely passed under the direction of the Mistress of Novices, has for its object the forming of the mind of the novice by means of the study of the Constitutions, by pious meditations and prayer, by instructions on those matters which pertain to the vows and virtues. During this year, the novices must not be employed in external works of the institute, nor take regular courses of study in letters, sciences or arts."

"What is *that*?!" I said.

"Our holy rule. I'm memorizing it."

"Oh, Matthew."

"No, really," said Matthew, "I like the sense of structure, tradition."

We stood for a moment at the top of the Novitiate steps. The glass doors reflected our images back to us.

"Gosh, look at us. We're real nuns now." I pulled my cap forward a little and adjusted my veil. Matthew tightened her serre tete. "I had chills walking up the aisle this morning."

"I know," she said. "Me, too."

"I felt holy . . . like on my First Communion day."

"We're starting our lives all over," she said. "Fresh, clean, new . . . pure again."

The electric bell rang from inside.

I had a flash of a parked car in the forest. "Are you . . .?"

"No No No," and the twelve-year-old me in the confessional, trying to confess to touching myself in an impure manner.

"Come on," I said. "There's sure to be ice cream for supper . . . Canon Law!"

That night I was exhausted. It took me fifteen minutes to get out of the habit and unhook the basque. Hopefully, I'd get faster. I put on my nightgown, robe, and carrying my new nightcap, I went into the upstairs study hall where an assembly line hair-cutting operation was in full swing. Profoundly silent of course. Ann Martin had an empty chair. I sat down. With a few clips of her scissors my page boy came off. The old nuns used to shave their heads. Lucky that's over, I thought, as she moved up to the top of my head snipping away. I glanced at the other chairs. Pixie haircuts predominated. There goes Nancy's D.A. Jacinta swept up the hair — blonde curls, auburn swatches, a deep brown ponytail and light brown all mixed together into one huge pile. No more Tonis. Ann Martin touched my shoulder. She was finished. I pulled the nightcap on and walked back to my cube.

I'll have to pin the serre tete more loosely tomorrow, I thought, as I got into bed. My chin feels like it's taken ten left hooks. There was a knock on the side of my partition. A hand came through the curtains and set down a container of Vaseline on the chair. I jumped up and looked out. Ann Martin was at the end of the hand. She pantomimed rubbing vaseline into her neck. I nodded and smiled.

"Congratulations," she mouthed.

"Thank you." I rubbed the vaseline onto the raw place under my chin. Outside the clock chimed. One more hour closer to God.

But far away from home and farther still from California. No one said it would be easy.

"It was always, always you," I sang silently, as I climbed into bed.

6

THE INFIRMARY

"Why are we always the pioneers?" I whispered to Matthew as we followed Ann Martin and Jacinta over to the infirmary. Two days after Reception and we were already being plunged into one of the most fraught aspects of Canonical life — trays.

Ann Martin heard me and turned around.

"All you do is bring the trays, pick them up when the patients are finished and wash the dishes. Nothing to it. Now, come on, pin-up so you'll be ready."

We trotted up next to her.

Without breaking stride, Ann Martin took hold of her skirt and in a 'hand-is-quicker-than-the-eye' motion, reduced the voluminous habit into two neat triangles, one in front and one in back. She gave instructions: "See, put the two side seams on your hips, then pin the front fold together. While still holding your skirt, do the same in the back."

Matthew and I just looked at each other.

"Come on, come on," she said.

We reached the door of the infirmary still holding our hems with our elbows. I tried to get a pin, my grip loosened and I had to start all over.

"Here," Ann Martin said, "Jacinta." The two advanced on us, pins in their mouths. Seconds later, the skirts were swept away.

"Keeps them clean," Jacinta explained to Matthew, "and out of the way — You can move fast, which you have to do in the infirmary, between the nurses' orders and the patients' demands."

"OK," Ann Martin interrupted. "Roll up your big sleeves, take off the small ones, hitch up your cape. There are special aprons in the floor kitchens. Move — we can't be late for Vespers."

"I wonder," laughed Jacinta, "if Ann Martin and I will have to be standing next to St. Peter to show you two how to go through the proverbial pearly gates."

We heard a tap on the window above us.

A very old face frowned down. She placed a finger on her lips. Ann Martin nodded.

"They think they're supposed to help the novices keep silence," Jacinta said, "so watch it."

We were in the building now.

"But surely this comes under Charity, Necessity and Politeness," I objected.

Though I kept silence — more or less — I had learned that the Charity, Politeness and Necessity exceptions to the rule created a lot of loopholes. But now that we were novices, Sister Marie Charles was our mistress and she favoured a very strict observation. She gave us a new item, perfection beads. The ten black beads, strung on a circle of clear plastic fish line, were supposed to help us keep track of the times we broke silence — move a bead each time. She also handed each of us a small book covered in black paper — the examen book. It contained an examination of conscience that covered all possible ways we could fall short of the holy rule. Last but not least were silence slips — small papers printed with grids.

"You will receive one each week, Sisters. Fill in Monday, Tuesday, Wednesday, etc. above each small box, then in the box write the numbers of times you failed to observe silence. Your perfection beads will help you keep track easily," she smiled as if she had just made our lives much easier. "And then, every Friday, drop the slips in the box on the bookshelf in my outer office."

I had squirmed slightly in my chair. Alright. Alright. I knew 'The unexamined life is not worth living'. Sister Mary Francine had quoted that to us often enough. But did Aristotle mean we should become spiritual chartered accountants? It would be harder to dispense myself if I had to write it down. Like eating a second donut when you're keeping a food diary.

"Think of your souls as a garden," Sister Marie Charles had continued. OK, I could do that. Better than souls as pails and thimbles, the images my third grade teacher, Sister Mary Steven, had used to explain varying capacities for grace. A garden. And?

"As in every garden, weeds may appear and the sooner we uproot the weeds, the better. Now, while breaking silence is not a sin" — good, I thought, — "it is a fault and can lead to more serious failings such as gossip, uncharitable speech, idleness, as well as destroying the inner state of recollection so necessary to the development of our spiritual lives. I would also urge you to practice guarding of the eyes whenever possible."

What? This was new. During profound silence I was careful not to make eye contact but . . .

"Words are not all that can distract us, Sisters, even the beauty of nature can shatter our inner sense of contemplation."

But, but, but, my mind sputtered.

"Now, I do not expect you to accomplish all things at once or even understand why we do these things. But now you have certain material aids" — she gestured to the books and slips and beads — "to chart your progress and help me help you. The seeds have been sown. God's love will water them, but it is up to you to keep the weeds away." She stood as if to leave and then stopped. "One more thing, Sisters; as novices, you will now be able to attend the Chapter of Faults. Once a month we gather and accuse ourselves of any lapses."

Sister Marie Charles said this last in that light, perfectly modulated voice that made every announcement sound like an invitation to a tea party — a *garden* tea party. And that was it. Sister Mary Francine had always tried to explain the underlying reason for every rule and custom while showing us the hidden psychological benefit. Sister Marie Charles, with great grace and infinite politeness, simply laid down the law. This is what novices did — they obeyed the rules and kept track of times when they disobeyed. While she would, of course, check over our silence slips, examine our examen books and listen to us during the chapter of faults, she was a mere observer. We were the gardeners.

Every other Sister of the Redemption going back to Mother Thaddeus had had perfection beads and black books and chapters of faults when they were in the Novitiate. Now it was our turn. So if we needed any help keeping on the straight and narrow . . .

"Maura, stop day dreaming!" Ann Martin said as I ran up the steps. We had to take care of the third floor, 'Our

Lady's'. Other novices took care of the other four floors. Ann Martin and Jacinta would help us tonight, but after that, Matthew and I were on our own.

The square brick infirmary building was about fifty years old and jutted off the back of the Motherhouse like a poor relation. No French flourishes here. The curved corridors and polished wooden floors of the older buildings became plain straight halls covered in dark linoleum in the infirmary addition. We passed a row of open doors and I could see ancient nuns in robes and night caps sitting in high-backed naugahyde chairs. They were waiting for their suppers, with religious forbearance, I hoped. Ann Martin was 'dishing-up' — putting the food the nurses left on the stove on the plates. Mashed potatoes, Swiss steak, limp green beans. I took a tray and started off for Room 303. No one on the floor was seriously ill, just old. Well, I like old people, I told myself as I walked carefully down the hall. Would they like me?

Here it was, Room 303. Sister Barnabas Mary — Barney to the novices.

"Take hers first," Jacinta had said, "Barney's sweet and very jolly." She did look like a feminine version of Santa Claus, sitting there in the chair — all pink and scrubbed in her white nightcap.

"Good evening, Sister. Here's your dinner."

"Thank you, Sister," she beamed at me.

I smiled back. This could be fun. I removed the stainless steel cover from her plate, and unwrapped the linen napkin and handed it to her. But she shook her head, no.

"I'd rather eat in bed," she said. "This table goes up and then you can push it over for me."

I can do that, I thought, as I cranked up the tray table.

"All set, Sister."

"I can't get up. You have to help me." She stretched her arms out to me.

"Er, Sister, maybe I'd better call a nurse. I don't know ..."

"Come on, come on. No need to bother the nurses. You can do it." She clutched my arm and tried to pull herself up.

"Well . . ."

I tried to reach around her waist. But she had no waist, she had no indentations of any kind. This is like trying to get a grip on a giant beach ball, I thought, as we struggled together. I was never sure what happened next but some principle of physics must have kicked in because the two of us seemed to slide across the floor and somehow bounce. Sister Barney was in bed. Unfortunately I was in there too — under her.

"Matthew," I called weakly. "Matthew . . ."

Ann Martin came and rescued me. And of course we all had a good laugh — but the nun nurse was not amused.

"Novices are not to touch the patients."

"But Barney — I mean Sister — wanted to go to bed."

"Many patients want to go to bed," she said. "We want them up! Sister Barnabas Mary knows that, which is why," — this with a glance at a seriously defiant Barney — "they try to con some poor inexperienced novice into helping them do what they know they shouldn't. Alright Sister, what is your name?"

"Maura."

"Alright, Sister Maura." She patted my shoulder. "Don't worry — pick up the trays or you'll not only miss prayers, you'll miss your dinner."

Well, of course, it became a story.

"Are you the Canonical who ended up in bed with Barney?" a scholastic novice I hardly knew asked me at recreation the next afternoon.

"Yes."

She laughed and I forced a smile and hurried across the grove where a number of Canonicals reclined — insofar as hard wooden benches and religious decorum allowed. Matthew rested her head on the chipped green paint. Her legs stuck out in front of her.

"Watch out, you'll get your veil dirty."

"I don't care. I am so tired."

"You're supposed to be tired," Jacinta said. She was darning the toe of a pair of hose. "You're a Canonical. You'll get used to it."

"I hope so," I said plopping down next to them. I made a half-hearted attempt to pull my habit skirt off the dusty ground, but why bother? This wasn't the exquisite french serge outfit I'd been clothed in at reception. That habit hung in my closet waiting for another ceremonial occasion. Like all other Canonicals, I wore a hand-me-down 'horse blanket' — heavy and tough and patched by its two previous owners.

Ann Martin leaned across Jacinta and picked up my skirt.

"You got a real prize," she said. "This weighs a ton."

"Yeah," I said. "I pin up not to protect it but so I can move."

"How's Barney, Maura?" someone called from across the circle.

"Fine, she asked for you," I said.

Actually Sister Barnabas Mary and I got along fine now. Today she'd given me a holy card. I pulled it out of my pocket,

"The Sacred Heart."

"That is really ugly," Matthew said.

It was. Jesus had a myopic stare and a weak mouth. His heart, an indistinct red smudge pierced with thorns, shone outside his pinkish garments. Gold gilded the scalloped edges of the card.

"I know, but Barney likes the Sacred Heart. He's appeared to her."

"Oh, really? Any revelations?"

"Yes, the nurses are supposed to buy softer toilet paper. He recommends Charmin."

They laughed.

"It's not funny," I said to Matthew. "I bet the old nuns don't like these syrupy images any more than we do."

"I could give Barney one of my Sister Corita cards."

I started to put the Sacred Heart away. Matthew took the card and tore it in half.

"Hey," I protested, "it's ugly but it's mine. It was a gift."

"Bad art is blasphemous!"

"But . . ."

"Don't start, you two," said Jacinta.

"You Canonicals have to make an issue of everything!" Ann Martin said. She got up and walked over to another group.

"Nice going, Matthew," I said. "You know she hates philosophical arguments."

"Maura, all I said . . ."

Sister Benedicta, the presiding Sister, rang her bell, "A nice brisk walk before we finish, Sisters."

The Canonicals groaned, but we struggled up.

Hey La di la di da I began in a cracked voice. Matthew gave me a dirty look. I moved on to the cluster ahead.

"Hi, Frederick." She was from a farm town in southern Indiana and cleaned the infirmary with me.

"I'm still laughing about this morning, Maura."

"Oh?"

"You know, the mop!"

"You should have seen Maura," she said to the others. "She didn't know you had to squeeze a string mop. She slopped water on that floor an inch deep and then . . ."

Alright, alright, I thought. It had been mildly amusing. Me sloshing through the soapy water. Frederick sliding over the linoleum floor to claim the mop. Tall and broad-shouldered, with not an ounce of fat on her prominent bones, Frederick had whipped through postulant employments with the disdain of a racehorse forced to canter along a bridle path. But now —

"We always used sponge mops," I said trying not to be defensive.

"Sponge mops." The scorn in her voice! "They just move the dirt around! A good heavy string mop is best but you've got to really twist them." She demonstrated wringing the air until her prominent knuckles showed white.

"Give me a break, Frederick, OK?"

"A sponge mop." She shook her head giggling as the bell to end recreation rang.

The next morning I pushed my dust mop into Barney's room and handed her one of my nicest new holy cards. "Children are the world's most valuable resource and its best hope for the future. — John F. Kennedy," it said, in a child's printing. Abstract red figures held hands in a circle.

"I know you taught second grade, Sister."

"For sixty-two years," she said turning the card over. She looked puzzled.

"Made at Conception Abbey," I volunteered.

"Catholic?"

"Of course! Uh, do you like it?"

"It's nice. Thank you." She stuck it in her office book. Good, a victory for liturgical reform. I dust-mopped my way out of her room and continued down the hall humming under my breath. As I approached the patients' recreation room, I heard the sound of a television. I knew they had one, but it was for the evening news and specials like the Hallmark Hall of Fame, not morning TV viewing. I looked in. A small nun, very close to the TV, was peering at the screen. Unlike the patients, who wore nightgowns and robes, she was fully dressed.

"Come in, come in," she said. "He's just about to speak!"

I hesitated. What if someone saw me and reported back to Marie Charles? But I edged in further.

"Dr. King, he's going to speak," the old nun said.

"Has there been any trouble?" I asked. The Ku Klux Klan had threatened to attack Dr. King during his March on Washington.

"No," she said. "And look, look at all the people."

The camera switched from the speakers' platform to show the crowd gathered in front of the Lincoln Memorial.

"Gosh," I said. "Did they say how many?"

"Way over 100,000. I'm Sister Columba, by the way. Sit down, child."

"I can't. I've got to clean . . . "

"This is history. Sit down." She could still crack the whip with her voice. Must have taught boys, I thought as I sat.

Dr. King stood at the podium and began to speak. By the time he reached "I have a dream . . ." I was clutching Sister Columba's hand.

"Free at last, free at last. Thank God almighty, I'm free at last."

The camera panned the cheering crowds.

"Look, Sister Columba. Nuns!" A large group in the habits of various orders stood clapping right along with the rest of the people.

We shall overcome, We shall overcome, they sang.

"I wish I were there!"

"None of our sisters went. Mother thought it would be too dangerous."

"How do you know?"

"I asked to go."

"But you're, you're . . ."

"I'm retired, Sister, I'm not dead."

"But, well, your age . . ."

"I'm only ninety! Around here that's young, Sister."

Who was this nun? Ninety and hardly a wrinkle on her smooth thick skin. Her left eye had a cataract cloud but the right was bright and alert.

"And what's your name, child?"

"Sister Maura," I said.

"Maura what?"

"Just Maura. I wanted Maura Patrick but . . ."

"You have a family name, I presume."

"Oh yes — I do — Lynch."

"Oh," she sighed and actually grinned. "Irish. That's nice. Oh, not that I don't appreciate our German Indiana farm girls and Poles make fine nuns too. Even the occasional Italian. But, well, the Irish built our order, Sister — check the names in the graveyard."

"But weren't the first sisters French?"

"Oh they founded it, but all those buildings? Reilly Hall? The church, the college dorms — Mother Mary Michael O'Rourke engineered those, Sister. But she had a dream." Columba pointed to the TV. "That's why I wanted to go to Washington. I remember the 'No Irish' signs. People forget."

"Give an Irishman a quarter," I started.

"And he becomes a Republican," she finished. We laughed.

"Do you know the definition of a bigot?" I asked her. "An Irish Catholic who wouldn't vote for Kennedy because he didn't go to Notre Dame."

"Oh that's good," she said. "I'll have to tell . . . "

"Columba!"

"Jiggers, the nurse," she said.

"Come on, Maura," the nun nurse said, "Go."

I hurried past her.

"And Sister," the nurse said, "remember you are here to work!"

"Yes, Sister."

"Now Columba, you shouldn't distract the novices," I heard as I quickly put my mop away and rushed down the stairs. I was late and probably in trouble, but I didn't care. Ninety and wants to march. The apostolate. Once I'm out there, I'll be alright. *She* would love a Conception Abbey card!

"So you see, Sister Benedicta," I said a few days later, "we have so many holy cards, we'd like to share them with the other novices and the older, I mean, the professed Sisters in the Motherhouse and the infirmary."

"Right, Sister," Matthew continued. We were in Benedicta's office during the permission hour she held each afternoon. "We thought we'd trade old cards for new."

"If we could just use the study hall for an hour or so sometime next week."

"During recreation?" she asked.

"Of course," we said together.

"Well," she said slowly. "I can't think of any particular objection — yes, Sisters, you may."

It wasn't the apostolate but it was something, getting rid of soppy saints!

That Wednesday afternoon our study hall was jammed. We'd moved upstairs now, and this room on the first floor was close to the side entrance. Sister Columba must have really spread the word because a constant stream of old nuns shuffled in looking for bargains.

"Yes, Sister," I explained, "you give us one of yours and take two of ours."

Well, we really raked them in. After an hour we were sold out, but what a haul!

"One hundred and five, one hundred and six. Oh, Maura, look at this one!"

It was a polychrome rendering of Saint Lucy, Virgin and Martyr, holding her recently gouged out eyes on a plate. We also had treacly Virgin Marys, impossibly pious St. Josephs and a whole assortment of Sacred Hearts.

"What should we do with them? We can't just throw them away," Matthew said.

No. The cards might be ugly but they were also sacramentals and couldn't just be tossed out with the coffee grounds. Recently, the junior sisters who lived in the old Novitiate across the road had cleared their quarters of garish statues. They'd carried them very reverently out to St. Ann's Lake and dumped them. That should confuse some Twenty-second century archaeologist, I thought. Still, they couldn't just smash St. Philomena and we couldn't just rip up these cards.

"We'll burn them," I said.

So we did. Our next free period we headed for St. Ann's Lake. The trees had begun to change and spots of red and yellow showed among the green. We found some twigs. Surprisingly, Matthew had been a Girl Scout too. We didn't rub two sticks together but we only needed the one match she'd borrowed from the kitchen to get our miniature bonfire going. One by one we fed the cards into the flames.

"St. Agnes couldn't have been as simpy looking as this," Matthew said as the fire licked the gold leaf.

"Look at St. Sebastian stuck with arrows and smiling! These were real people. They deserved better," I said as the card became ash.

A woni kuni ca a woni, I sang.

"What?"

"Oh sorry — an Indian song we learned in Girl Scouts. You know, around the campfire, in the forest preserves. Didn't you have fires and make S'Mores?"

"No."

"Well, we did. And we'd sing 'A Woni kuni ca'. "

"A woni?" she finished

"Right."

I started the song again, adding the next verse. Matthew shrugged and tried to sing along.

"There was an Indian dance that went with it."

"An Indian dance??"

"Yeah, see." I demonstrated — step — step — hop.

"Oh, Maura," she started to giggle.

"Try it."

She did. There we were, chaplets clinking, veils snapping in the wind, stomping around our fire in time to an Indian chant while the saints smouldered.

For days after, all I had to say to Matthew was 'Kateri Tekakwitha' and she started to giggle.

Now, I was sure we'd been alone at St. Ann's Lake but somehow Sister Benedicta found out. She was not amused.

"I assumed they would send the cards to the foreign missions," Sister Benedicta said during the conference in Sister Marie Charles' office a few weeks later. "When the novice told me Sister Maura and Sister Matthew burned them, why I couldn't believe it . . . I . . . If the sisters who donated the cards ever heard . . ."

Usually Benedicta didn't dither. She had a straight-ahead no nonsense style. Petty enforcement didn't interest her. We knew the rules and we should obey them. Period. She wasn't going to check up. We had our examen books and Chapter. Spiritual development? Not her business. That was between the Mistress and us. No, she ordered the supplies, presided over recreation and supervised the ground keepers. Benedicta loved to be outside. She used her spare time to plant pansies and impatiens along the Novitiate walks. She had the same surefire cure for homesickness, restlessness or the dark night of the soul: "Take a nice long walk, Sister." Though the oldest of all the Novitiate staff, Benedicta was the one who'd agree to take us for a walk at night. "Come on, Sisters, otherwise we never get to see the stars!"

But now Benedicta was in uncharted territory. Novices desecrating holy cards?!

"But, Sister, we burned them out of respect! The whole idea was to replace bad art with good," I said.

"Yes," Matthew chimed in. "Those cards are desecrations."

"The old nuns gave them to us . . ."

"For the foreign missions!" Benedicta thundered.

"But if they're ugly to us why would an African or Asian want them?" I asked. Or Indian, I thought — she hadn't mentioned our pow wow, thank God! That I couldn't defend.

"I believe we are straying from the point, Sisters," Sister Marie Charles' quiet modulated tones brought us to order. "Sister Benedicta, I understand your concern. We must guard against scandalizing the professed Sisters at the Motherhouse and in the infirmary. However, there is no reason that they should know. This story need go no further. I presume the novice who informed you of this incident understands that?"

"Yes, Sister," Benedicta said.

Novice? Novice! Matthew and I glanced at each other. A novice. Someone we told . . .

"Sister Maura and Sister Matthew, you will be attending your first Chapter of Faults next week. Perhaps this," she paused as if searching for a word, "action should properly be mentioned there."

Sister Benedicta nodded in agreement.

"And Sisters," Marie Charles concluded, "In future when such a project occurs to you, please pray 'Virgin most prudent'." Then she smiled. In fact, if it weren't clinically impossible, I'd swear she even winked.

"Who told?" we asked each other during recreation that afternoon in the grove. "I mentioned it to Ann Martin," I said, "but one thing she's not is scrupulous. I don't think she'd go to Benedicta. There were a few band members I told but . . ." I looked around the grove. Frederick? I doubted it. Not Linda. Nobody from Ladyhill, surely, Lawrence Elizabeth? No, she keeps so much to herself these days. Matthew thought it meant she was getting ready to leave. "So who?"

"Stop worrying about it. We'll never know," Matthew said.

"Exactly."

Maybe someone will react during Chapter, I thought, as we lined up for the event a few afternoons later. Two scholastic novices taped brown paper over the glass panes in the door of the novices' recreation room to prevent any of the newly arrived postulants from peeking in. Though I knew a few of the Ladyhill girls who had entered, because I wasn't a guardian angel, I had only seen the postulants from a distance.

"They are even wilder than you guys were," Jacinta had reported.

"Wild? We weren't wild," I protested.

"Who's this new group, the Beatles? Ten postulants brought albums by them. All in the trunk room now."

No, these postulants wouldn't be privy to things like the Chapter for a long time. Wonder how they had reacted when they heard about silence? Beatles, huh!

The curtains had been closed too, I noticed as I took my seat. Two straight rows of chairs faced each other. Very monastic. We sat in band order, so I could forget about disguising my voice. We were very silent, happy to guard our eyes. This was like first confession all over again. I could hear myself starting out, "I disobeyed my father and mother; fought with my sisters; talked back three times." Now what I really felt bad about was the revulsion I sometimes felt when I helped the nurse slide a bed pan under the flaccid flesh of an old nun in the infirmary. Or when I teased Frederick about her accent that time or brushed Lawrence Elizabeth off at recreation. But that wasn't the kind of imperfection expected at Chapter.

"Just say you broke silence or were late for prayers," Ann Martin had advised. "Most people don't get too personal."

"Except for fraternal correction," Jacinta volunteered.

"What?"

They explained that you could accuse another novice of an offence 'for her own good'.

"Most people don't though, unless they're, like, fanatical."

Well, I'd already been fraternally corrected anonymously and I didn't like it.

Sister Marie Charles said, "Come Holy Spirit." The prayer that began the Chapter. Then the oldest scholastic novice stood.

"I accuse myself of neglecting my studies and breaking of silence. I humbly ask pardon." One by one each accused herself and humbly asked pardon. 'Humbly' was important since humility was the object of the exercise. Nothing anyone said sounded that bad to me. Nor did I think less of anyone who spoke. Yet, the sense of dread I felt since I walked into the room grew as my turn came closer. Why had we made such good time driving down on Entrance Day? Why couldn't I be number fifty instead of twenty-two? Three away, two away, one then me. I'd practised a formula.

"I um, I accuse myself of acting imprudently in a way that gave scandal." Oh no, I thought, as I listened to myself. That could cover anything from bank robbery to fornication.

"I humbly ask pardon," I mumbled and sat down. My chaplet hit the steel chair as a kind of punctuation. There. My imperfections laid on the bonfire with all the rest. Three more silence breakers, a few uncharitable thoughts, one 'I slept through meditation'. Every Canonical could accuse herself of that! Now, Matthew.

"I accuse myself," very crisp and clear, "of breaking silence and resenting fraternal correction."

Great. She cops out and leaves me holding the bag. I know Benedicta was listening. Marie Charles won't like this.

"Please pardon me, Sisters."

That evening Matthew told me she wasn't going to accuse herself of something she didn't think was wrong!

"But that was the way to calm Benedicta! Didn't you see Marie Charles wink?"

"No, I didn't. And why should perjuring myself please Sister Benedicta?"

"Oh perjure, Matthew, come on. I didn't want to say anything either but Benedicta's so nice to us and I mean, it was a minute."

"I don't see it that way."

"I suppose you're not going to do a penance either?"

"No."

"Yeah, well I'll think of you Saturday, when I'm cleaning lavs at Reilly Hall."

Older retired Sisters who didn't need the constant care of the infirmary lived there. The plumbing was older than the nuns. The toilets often backed up or wouldn't flush. The head housekeeper of the Motherhouse said that sanitation demanded that the lavs be cleaned every day. Saturday afternoons were the only really free block in the week. To spend it wiping out those toilets was penance indeed.

"You plunge, Sister, plunge," the housekeeper had demonstrated using a small string mop. She sloshed the water around the bowl until it somehow disappeared, then she scrubbed the inside with Ajax. I thought wistfully of Saniflush bubbling dirt away on its own. No need then to even look at these streaks of excrement caked into old porcelain.

Offer it up, offer it up, I told myself. There are missionaries in China being tortured right at this moment. This is nothing. Make it a project for Reverend Martin Luther King and civil rights, or John Kennedy, or that Michele gets asked to the Tulip Trot.

I moved on to the next toilet stall. An unpleasant odour lingered. Luckily, there was a round stained glass window here, part of the facade. I pushed it open. Crisp air drifted in. The top of the window framed a blue October sky. All the leaves had changed now and the campus trees flamed up in every shade of red and orange and gold. A perfect day for a football game. Then, as if my thoughts had triggered it, I heard, *Cheer, cheer for old Notre Dame* — sung by male voices.

I'll just stand here for a minute to see what's going on, I thought, as I climbed up on the narrow old window-sill. Directly below me I could see the fountain, the centrepiece of the campus. "Pick me up at the fountain", the college girls told their boyfriends. And that was what was happening. Cars carrying boys circled around to the fountain where their dates waited. While none of them wore racoon coats and waved pennants, I wouldn't have been surprised if the girls in their kilts and knee socks and the boys in letter sweaters broke into 'The Varsity Rag' and danced their way down the avenue. That could so easily be me, jumping into a car and roaring off to South Bend to cheer Her loyal sons 'onward to victory'. What am I doing scouring decrepit toilets because even more decrepit nuns can't . . . Stop — that's uncharitable. It's supposed to be hard, I told myself. It's a penance. But a penance for what? I wondered. I'm glad we burned the cards. I thought of my perfection beads and the examen book of chapter. Checks and balances, checks and balances.

The whole caravan of cars moved down the avenue. "Stop feeling sorry for yourself," I scolded. "You've been to football games. You dated. It's not like you didn't know what you were giving up. It makes the sacrifice more valuable. OK, forget it. Move." But I couldn't not watch the line of cars. The car radios blared rock 'n' roll but I didn't recognize the songs. There were new hits, new groups I didn't even know about. I must ask Brigid and Michele in February.

A hand had touched my shoulder. I jumped.

"Sister Columba, you startled me!"

Columba looked over my shoulder at the scene below.

"It gets easier, little Lynch. There are the children and their parents, outings, trips downtown. Many kindnesses," she said.

"Good. I guess I'm just getting cabin fever. I haven't been off this campus for fourteen months. I'd ask to go to the doctor but there's nothing wrong with me."

"Corns?"

"What?"

"Don't you have corns, planter's warts, bunions? Your feet, little Lynch."

"Well, yes, I do have corns on my toes and something on the bottom of my foot but everybody . . . "

"Still, the feet are the key to our vocation, Sister. Must be cared for. There is an excellent chiropodist in town."

"Oh, I see, I get it. Thanks, Sister Columba!"

She smiled and nodded graciously. Then she chuckled, "Why are you working? Isn't Saturday afternoon free?"

"Well, I . . . the lav needs, well . . . "

She sighed. "So humiliating to be old. We were all so fastidious. But now . . ." she shrugged. "Your Holy Card sale seemed very successful," she said.

"Too successful," I moved to look out into the hall. "I shouldn't really be talking to her. "We burned the old cards. Someone told. Benedicta hit the ceiling and Marie Charles . . . Well, I'm supposed to pray Virgin most prudent and ..."

"Swab out the toilet bowls . . . "

I nodded.

She started to laugh — a surprisingly full-throated sound for such a small person.

"Oh, dear," she said. "Benedicta was always such an even-tempered little thing. For her to 'hit the ceiling' must have been quite a sight."

I thought she started laughing again but then I realized she was coughing and gasping.

"Sister Columba, Sister Columba . . . "

"In my room — 310 — my pills."

I helped her around the corner and into her room. Her pills and a pitcher of water were near at hand on her night table. In a minute she stopped gasping and breathed normally.

"It's panic as much as anything," she explained. "I'm ready to die, of course, but my body wants to hold on a while. It has its own wisdom."

I looked around her room. She didn't let Rule 173 — Sisters shall not paper their rooms nor adorn them in a manner that savours of vanity — cramp her style. Two collages covered her wall. One was of Irish scenes, the other of pictures of John Kennedy taken from newspapers and magazines. A crucifix hung over her bed and a beautiful wooden Madonna stood on the dresser.

She saw me looking at the collages.

"I always decorated my classrooms for the children. Cheerful surroundings are a necessity."

I went over to the Kennedy wall. Some of the pictures I knew very well — others were new.

"That's a great one," I said. "John John under his desk. Remember when Caroline wore her mother's high heels into his press conference? Oh look — here's all of them. Bobby is handsome too, just not as spectacular as the President. Teddy and Joan, Ethel. Rose and Jackie always so serene. And you've got the pictures from his trip to Ireland!" A young woman in an Irish crowd at Shannon Airport was holding a sign "Johnny, we hardly knew you."

"The Kennedys are from Wexford, you know," she said. "Not far from where my mother's people lived."

"Really?"

"Sister." I had to tell her. I knew she wouldn't think I was bragging. "I saw him two times in person. Once after the first debate in Chicago at the Glenview Palladium. And then, Sister, I went to his Inauguration. My uncles, the priests, took us."

"How wonderful," she said.

"It was magic. We didn't have tickets but it was cold and everyone was so happy. I sat right near the Marine Band for the address. And went to the Inaugural Ball. He was, well, resplendent and Jackie so beautiful. His eyes, Sister, pictures don't really do them justice . . . "

"Hrrum." We heard a cough in the hall. Columba went to the open door.

"Zita, hello."

Sister Zita stared in at me.

"Do they recreate in the sleeping quarters at the Novitiate now, Sister?"

"No, Sister, I . . ."

"What is your name, Sister?"

"Run along dear," Columba said to me. "Thank you for your help. And we all," she underlined the word, "are grateful for the services you and the other novices do. Good-bye."

I ducked around Sister Zita down the hall.

"Columba, really, at your age," I heard Zita begin.

"Don't take that sanctimonious tone with me, Zita."

Matthew and me in sixty or seventy years!

Now — the foot doctor — I would put in a request today!

7

JOHNNY WE HARDLY KNEW YOU

"Hey Matthew, look — a belated birthday present!" I waved a slip of paper at her as I came into evening recreation three days after my nineteenth birthday.

"What is it?"

"An appointment for the foot doctor! I'm going tomorrow to get my corns cut off! I'm so happy."

"Gee, Maura," Matthew said, "I'm overwhelmed. I don't know what to say. Wow — the foot doctor!"

"Now don't be sarcastic. I get to go to town. For the first time in fourteen months I am leaving this campus. Oh the city lights, the hustle and bustle . . ."

"Of Hicksville — are you crazy Maura?"

"OK, so I won't ask to have you come as my companion. Sister Marie Charles told me to choose. Of course, after the way you finked out during chapter . . ."

"I'm going, I'm going!" Matthew said.

The next morning the 1954 black Buick which, with a 1935 hearse, made up the Motherhouse fleet, pulled up in front of the Novitiate. The Motherhouse chauffeur stepped out and opened the door. Most nuns entered with a valid driver's licence but the rule forbade us to drive.

Matthew and I settled ourselves in the roomy back seat, adjusting the black veils novices wore to go to town.

"You look like a real nun, Maura," Matthew whispered.

"You too."

The driver drove around to the front of the Motherhouse and got out. A professed nun is coming. Should have known, I thought. He returned in a few moments. A tall robust nun came out. She dragged her left leg slightly and used a thick cane which she passed into me as she climbed slowly into the back. The cane was covered in snakeskin. Who is this nun?

"Nice, isn't it?" she said. "Made specially for me by order of the mandarin of our village. Kept it with me all these years. Came in handy with this dratted fall. I'm Sister Ann Loyola, by the way."

Snakeskin? The mandarin of her village? This could be quite a day. Ann Loyola didn't seem very concerned about the rule of silence. "What high schools are you two from?"

"Ladyhill," I said.

"Redemption," Matthew answered.

"Don't think I've any pals who would have taught you. Course, I've lost touch — been in the East since '38."

"Wow, that's . . ." I started.

"Twenty-five years. Started in China and ended up in Taiwan with a lot of other people."

We'd left the campus now and turned on to the main highway.

"How did your accident happen?" Matthew asked.

"Walking in the rock garden at Sun Moon Lake — place I go during holidays. It's in the mountains, and it's beautiful — except that students who fail to get into university often kill themselves by jumping off Sun Moon peak. Loss of face, you know. Well, I slipped crossing the reflecting pool and broke my fool hip. Always had rheumatism in it too, but that wasn't the worst. It was the hospital that really did me in. Different than ours. No real nursing care. Whole families move in to bathe and feed the patient. They cook on charcoal fires in little braziers. Well, our nuns tried to help, but it's really a full-time job and there I was up in the mountains and school starting. And then I got all kinds of complications. Finally I gave up and came home. Still can't get better medical care in the world than in the United States of America."

Sun Moon Mountain, reflecting pool, charcoal braziers. I wonder how people were picked for the missions? Maybe I could volunteer.

"Must say the scenery here looks dull to me now, though. No pagodas."

Pagodas! The outskirts of town were exotic enough for me. We passed the state college. Male and female students walked across the newly built campus. There was the athletic field. I poked Matthew. The football team was drilling: twenty-five men doing jumping jacks, more boys than I'd seen in fourteen months. Sister Ann Loyola talked on, describing their school in Taipei.

"We have the biggest girls' school on the island, first grade through college. A little too ritzy, if you ask me, but you need the rich if you're to make a go of it and wealthy Chinese girls are used to servants. Two of the General's nieces are at our school. Want that Western influence, you see. Don't know if I agree with that, but the old ways and times are gone now, have to go along I guess. Some think the General will invade and get it all back, that the U.S.'ll help him. I don't. All that Quemoy and Matsu nonsense stirred things up for a little while but we've got two different countries now, like it or not."

I'd love to talk politics with her. I missed the conversations Janet and I used to have analysing the President's press conferences, making up questions we would have asked.

"Janet Gorman from *The Chicago Tribune*, Mr. President!"

"Yes Miss Gorman, but speak slowly, your questions are always thought through."

"OK girls. Here we are at the hospital. Jim'll drop me and then take you over for your feet. Here's a dollar — get yourselves some cokes on the way. See you back here around 1:30."

Matthew and I waited until she and the driver were inside the hospital, then . . .

"Yippee!" we said.

"But do you think that counts as permission?" Matthew asked.

"We can say she offered us a coke and we interpreted permission."

"Where do we get them? Should we ask the driver to buy them?" Matthew sounded worried. Silly to make a big deal about buying two cokes and maybe a candy bar. But we hadn't purchased anything in fourteen months.

"Let's wait until he drops us off at the doctor's. I'll bet there's some kind of a store nearby."

There was.

"Two cokes, a Nestlé Crunch and a Milky Way, please," I said to the old man behind the counter, who didn't try to hide his surprise. He didn't smile. I guess I expected the beaming, "Good Morning, Sisters," that would have greeted any nun who ventured out in Irish Catholic Chicago. But this was the Bible Belt of Southern Indiana where people didn't like Catholics, let alone nuns. The other customers stared silently at us.

We were the only patients in the doctor's waiting room and the nurses worked inside with the doctor. So I slowly unwrapped my Nestlé's Crunch and took the first exquisite bite.

"You know, Matthew, I actually could not have comfortably eaten this in front of anyone. And to drink from the bottle . . . " I let the implication trail out as I swigged some coke. We always had straws in the Novitiate.

She nodded. "I know what you mean. I don't think I even remember how to order in a restaurant."

"Sister Maura," the nurse called.

"Guard this," I said handing Matthew the half-eaten bar.

"Shouldn't I come in with you?" Matthew asked.

"With a charcoal brazier?"

"This will only take a moment," promised the pudgy doctor. It did. I had to elevate my bare treated foot for one hour, however.

"You should have privacy in the waiting room, I'm going to lunch. No other patients until two." This doctor dealt with the nuns frequently.

My coke waited and the Nestlé crunch, and on the coffee table, *Time*, *Newsweek* and *Life*. Matthew was reading *The Seven Storied Mountain* but I pulled the magazine over to me.

"In for a penny, in for a pound" as Grampa used to say. I opened the latest *Time*. The President was going to Dallas for a campaign stop. Pacifying Lyndon, I thought.

The doctor left. "See you in half an hour."

Now we should keep silence. But Matthew looked at me. "How is your foot?" she asked.

"Much better."

That was only politeness.

"It didn't hurt much," I volunteered.

That was charity.

"The driver will be here in about forty-five minutes," Matthew said.

"Yes, then we'll pick up Sister Ann Loyola," I replied.

That was necessity. We'd exhausted the loophole in the rule of silence. I went back to *Time*.

"Um, Maura." Good, I'll talk if she does. "Yes?"

"Would you please put my empty bottle in that waste basket."

"Oh, sure. Guess we lose our deposit."

She laughed. "Four cents gone."

"That's four cents more than we've earned since we've been here," I said, hoping she'd laugh again. She did. Then she was quiet. Neither of us wanted to be the first to break the silence rule. But if the other were willing . . . then I remembered something.

"Wait a minute, Matthew, what time is it?"

"About a quarter to one, I guess."

"And what's going on at the Novitiate right now?"

"Now? It's recreation, I suppose."

"Right. It's recreation, and shouldn't we follow the order of the day even if we're away?"

Matthew grinned. "We certainly should, Sister Maura."

"Now," I said placing a piece of the candy bar on my tongue, "tell me about . . ." As I talked the chocolate melted deliciously away, and with it the time and the place. We were just two girls drinking cokes and talking.

"Sisters." It was the doctor, back early. We straightened. I removed my bare foot from his coffee table and grabbed for my stocking and shoe.

The doctor didn't come in. He leaned against the door frame. Was he sick, I wondered.

"Doctor," I began, but then he walked quickly by us into the inner office. I heard a click and then voices. The radio. Then he came out and stared at us.

Matthew and I looked at each other.

"Doctor, what is . . . " I tried again.

"You don't know, do you? You don't know . . . The President's been shot." He sounded puzzled. "Someone shot the President in Dallas."

"Oh, God," Matthew moaned.

"No," I protested. "Well he wasn't seriously hurt, right? He's OK, isn't he?" I heard my voice climb in pitch. "Isn't he?"

"No, no," the doctor shook his head. "He's not alright. They're operating, they don't think he'll, he's . . . it's on the radio."

He walked away and we heard the radio announcer's voice louder now.

Let them say he's OK. Please God, let him live. Please. Don't take him away. Please, God, please.

At some point the driver came and then we were in the car on the way to pick up Sister Ann Loyola.

If I hold on, if I don't cry, if I don't act like he's . . . like he's . . . bad . . . then he'll be alright. If I sit straight and look ahead, stiff shoulders, lips tight — it won't happen.

He won't, won't die. We'll get back to the Novitiate and they'll tell us he's survived the operation and he'll recover — not easily, of course, a struggle, he'll need our prayers, but not dead. Please God, don't let it all be over. That grin at Glenview, his laughter at the Inaugural ball. His face, not puffy like it looked in pictures sometimes, his eyes. His energy, strength, that hurried grace. "Johnny, we hardly knew ye . . ." It can't be over so fast. Please, please.

The campus was deserted when we drove in. Ann Loyola got out at the Motherhouse. "I don't understand," she said more to herself than to us. "I'm home. This is America. This doesn't happen here."

The operation must be over, I thought. There'll be a note on the chapel door. "Let us offer our thanksgiving for the preservation of our dear President John F. Kennedy and let us pray for his swift recovery."

We'll go to Chapel.

Oh, God, we were drinking cokes and eating candy when he was shot. He lay bleeding while I unwrapped a Nestlé Crunch and broke silence. Please let him be well, Lord. Please.

But there was no one in the Chapel. There was a note on the door — a square white paper with three lines of black type:

> *Our dear President John Fitzgerald Kennedy departed this life at 1:35 p.m., Eternal rest grant unto him, O Lord, and let perpetual light shine upon him. May he rest in peace. All college classes are suspended. Vespers as usual.*

The same wording as for a nun of ninety — Rest in Peace — but he's not ready for rest!

Death for the old nuns meant beautiful funerals and an honoured place in the graveyard. Fine for them — but he was life, energy, tomorrow, the future, dead.

"Sister Maura." I was leaning against the Chapel door. It was Sister Marie Charles.

"Are you sure? That note? Is he really dead?"

"Yes, Sister, our dear President has departed this life. We must pray for him, for our country and for the President's dear family. A terrible day."

I nodded. Yes, yes, a terrible day. Dies Irae, Dies Illa.

"Sister, I was there, there at his inauguration, you know. I saw him, I heard him say his speech, you know, the Inaugural address? Remember, 'I do not shrink from responsibility, I welcome it'... 'Ask not what your country can do for you' — I heard it all and I met him at the ball. I ... He danced when I danced. He ... I stood on a chair to see him come in and he saw me. He smiled at me. Sister, he smiled ... " I knew I was babbling but I couldn't stop.

"Sister, please," she said, "control yourself. We must be strong for each other. You will find that the strength of the community supports our human weakness. We all must rise above our very natural grief and see with the eyes of faith. Now go to your cubicle, Sister, and ..."

"My cubicle?"

"Your veil." She pointed to her own head. "Sister, you are still wearing the black town veil."

"Oh, I forgot ... I ..."

"You have my permission first to go to your cubicle and change; Sister Benedicta has taken the novices on a walk to St. Ann's Lake. You may join them there." I nodded.

"Remember our Lord's words 'I am the Resurrection and the Life. Whoever believes in me, even if he dies, will live'.

157

And this President died believing. He received the last rites of the Church, the first President ever to do so."

The last rites, so what. He believed but he wasn't protected. Shot in the head, no hat, wouldn't wear a hat; that stubborn hair of his, going its own way . . . all the criticism about his haircut . . .

"Sister Maura? Did you hear?"

"Yes, Sister. Thank you, Sister."

The habit skirt seemed so heavy that I had to use the railing to pull myself up the stairs — right foot and now the left.

Our faith, no Catholic could ever be elected . . . Yet, he was proud of his religion. Those ministers in Houston didn't shake him. Look where he was on the morning of his inauguration — in the pew beside his mother for early morning Mass. "Jack!" He'd surprised her, slid in next to her after Mass started. At Communion time he stepped back to let her go first up the aisle. Just like my Dad, like thousands of Catholic men stepping back following their wives, their mothers up to the rail. And he was the President. And from Harvard, not Tammany Hall. Not the pear-shaped cigar-chomping Irish politician they imagined, painted by prejudice. The night he was elected President, my Dad said, "My father promised me a pony if Al Smith got elected." So Dad went out and bought a Ford Mustang. When Kennedy spoke on TV, we had dinner in front of the set! "Al Smith's grinning," my Dad said.

Oh, God, how can he be dead? Why didn't God save him? Why? Why? I replaced the black veil with my white one. I wish I could lie down just for a minute. Sister, I interpreted permission to go to bed to try to sleep away this nightmare.

Coming down the back stairs from my cubicle, I heard a man's voice. Coming from where? A classroom — but what class was on now?

The voice came from a television. In the classroom, Sister Mary Francine and a group of postulants and novices sat huddled around a small portable television set up on the teacher's desk. Dusk was closing in and the only illumination in the room came from the screen and the white veils. Somehow, they reflected the last of the outside light.

Someone touched my arm. "Maura," she whispered. Matthew pulled me into the room and on to the arm of a student desk. "Sister Mary Francine's letting a few of us watch the news bulletins but we have to be quiet. The others are out on a walk."

Sister Mary Francine turned in her chair and put a finger to her lips.

The voice on the television told us that his killer had been caught, Lyndon Johnson had been sworn in, Russia had not attacked us. John Fitzgerald Kennedy had been shot dead. He was dead.

I looked out the classroom window. The trees in the grove stood shadowed but still there. They looked just like they had yesterday. How was that possible? How could those trees be the same when everything had changed? John Fitzgerald Kennedy was dead.

The electric prayer bell rang. Sister Mary Francine turned off the television. I got up and went to the Chapel. We said the Rosary just as on every other evening. We prayed the De Profundis for him and asked that perpetual light shine upon him, but neither Sister Marie Charles nor Reverend Mother suspended the order of the day. It remained and I observed it: prayed, slept, ate, cleaned and recreated at the appointed hours during the next three days. But in between those times, I returned to that room to stare at the small screen, to the world where everything had changed, where what was left of John F. Kennedy lay in state at the Capitol Building and where Jack Ruby shot Lee Harvey Oswald in the Dallas County Jail. Novices came in and out of the room. Sister Mary Francine watched sometimes and Sister Marie Charles came in once.

The television was brought to the auditorium for his funeral. We sat together, 100 novices, sixty postulants, the Novitiate Sisters. When Jackie mounted the Capitol steps with Bobby and Teddy, the sobbing began. We didn't look at each other, just watched, crying silently, weeping out loud when John John saluted his father's coffin. I thought of Patrick and my family watching as we were. Sitting together on the same couch where we had watched the election returns until dawn and he was well and truly elected. "Don't worry Maggie," my Dad had said. "Daley won't let him lose."

Janet would be watching at school, thinking of the Glenview. I knew Brigid was remembering the Inaugural parade as she watched that final procession. She'd liked the horses. And now there was only one horse. And it carried an empty saddle. Boots were turned upside down in the stirrups.

Irish bagpipes played at his grave.

"Dear Jack," Cardinal Cushing said and prayed, "I am the Resurrection and the Life," in English. The same ritual for John F. Kennedy as for Sister Anastasia Marie from the third floor infirmary, as for me.

Through the rest of the dark, hard winter, I could hear the hymn the Marine band played as military pallbearers carried his coffin down the Capitol steps. 'O God of

Loveliness, O Lord of Heaven above.' A Catholic hymn.
We'd sung it in grade school. Had he? Dear Jack.

My mother sent me a memorial card, with his picture on
the front, and on the back, a poem by Emily Dickinson.

> *After great pain a formal feeling comes*
> *The nerves set ceremonies like tombs;*
> *The stiff heart questions — was it He that bore*
> *And yesterday — or centuries before.*
>
> *The feet mechanical*
> *Go round a wooden way*
> *Of ground or air or Ought, regardless grown.*
> *A quartz contentment like a stone.*
>
> *This is the hour of lead*
> *Remember if outlived*
> *As freezing persons recollect the snow*
> *First chill, then stupor, then the letting go.*

Yes that was right, that was the way it was.

I thought Christmas would lift my spirits. It didn't. All
the little holiday treats nuns prepare for each other fell flat.
Silence was suspended on Christmas Day. We could talk
anywhere in the building.

"Weren't you just thrilled at the harp solo during 'O
Holy Night'," Jacinta asked at breakfast.

"It was nice."

"I loved coming back for hot chocolate and sweet rolls
after midnight Mass," Matthew said. "Tasted good."

"My favourite was the procession that brings the infant
to the manger. All of us with our candles going through the
dark halls. The three part 'Silent Night'. Beautiful,"
Frederick sighed.

"Yes," I said.

By noon I wished for silence and I was actually glad when the bell for Compline rang. Christmas dinner had been delicious but all that rich food shocked my digestive system. Eating eighteen of Linda's mother's bourbon balls didn't help.

"She really loaded them up," Linda had giggled.

I ended Christmas bent over the toilet, vomiting.

We had our New Year's Eve party. I twisted my noisemaker and tossed confetti at 8 p.m. But I didn't applaud wildly with the others when Sister Marie Charles extended recreation to 8:30 p.m.

"So childish," I muttered to Matthew. We should be in mourning, I thought. I remembered how I hated my Uncle Gene's wake. Why were all the grown-ups talking and laughing?

All through January, the skies stayed a steel grey. I can take the cold. After all, I grew up in Chicago. But you can face down the Lake Michigan wind when it comes straight at you. Here, the chill air invaded your bones, making you hunch over, shivering.

I dreaded the daily walk through the cold to the infirmary. The patients no longer seemed so quaintly eccentric. One day Barney scolded me for over-watering her African violet. I'd seen her drown the plant and I snapped at her.

"You watered it yourself. You forget and then you blame me!"

Of course she cried.

"I'm sorry, Barney. Please forgive me," I said.

But then she told me that Our Lady had appeared to the Vestal Virgins of the temple of Diana and they became the first nuns.

"I don't think so, Sister," I said. "If that's all the cream of wheat you're going to eat I'm taking away the tray."

When I left the infirmary I'd walk across the courtyard feeling the old nuns' eyes on me, begrudging me my youth and strength. They should just be grateful to have lived so long and stop complaining!

Sleep became my greatest pleasure. I woke up in the morning counting the hours until I could go back to bed. I nodded off in Father Jakowski's theology class, and one morning during meditation, my head hit the prie-dieu in front of me, I was so sound asleep. My cap saved me. A more direct hit and I'd be rooming with Barney. Columba wasn't around. She had talked Mother into letting her spend the winter on mission — in Anaheim, California.

We had one funeral after another and after each the same prayer. "I am the Resurrection and the Life." But when you're mired in Lent, Easter seems very far away.

Then, just to put the tin hat on it, as my Great Aunt Rose would say, I was assigned to the kitchen. On the third day, Sister Wilfreda, the cook, threw the coffee urn at me. Wilfreda was a very heavy, very unhappy woman. She hated cooking, which I could certainly understand, but that wasn't my fault. Her feet preoccupied her. They had swollen to such a size that she had to cut the sides from her shoes and lean on a service cart to push herself around the kitchen. I annoyed her.

"You call this corn shucked? Didn't your mother teach you to pull the silk away from the kernels? Oh, I forgot, you Ladyhill girls probably grew up with servants."

That was her mildest criticism.

"There's a job you can't mess up. Wipe the outside of the refrigerator and freezers, Sister," Sister Wilfreda ordered.

The appliances were all stainless steel. It took special rags and an oil solution to clean them. I knelt on the floor and started on the first of the eight. Naturally there was a trick to it. The oil had to be applied evenly and wiped quickly or it streaked.

Apply. Wipe. Dry. Apply. Wipe. Dry. Eleven o'clock. One hour to go, then dinner, then recreation, class, prayers, supper, recreation, then bed.

"Sister!"

I dropped my rag and jerked around.

Wilfreda stood over me with her fists jammed onto her hips and her bare arms jutting out.

"Can't you even wipe off a door right," she screamed. "Look at them. Look at those streaks!!"

A light rainbow film covered the door where the oil still adhered — just traces of blue and red and green. Not streaks, really. Just a film.

"You are the worst I ever . . . " she started, "you . . . you . . . " She lifted her right fist. "You . . ."

I jumped up from my knees and backed towards the door. Her arm dropped and she hobbled away.

I took a step forward and bent over to retrieve the rags and the oil. BANG! One of the big forty-cup coffee urns hit the wall next to me and crashed against the tile floor. God.

"Didn't I tell you to fill this!?" Sister Wilfreda screamed. "Get out. Get out. Get out."

I did. I ran. Out of the kitchen, down the hall, I passed the Chapel . . . I'll go in there. She wouldn't dare . . .

"Sister Maura," Sister Marie Charles stood at the door of her office. "You are running!"

"I didn't do anything. Sister Wilfreda threw the coffee urn at me. She chased me and . . . "

Sister Marie Charles held up her hand.

"No need for details." She glanced quickly down the corridor to the empty kitchen. "I wonder if you realise how much pain Sister Wilfreda is in? She has many responsibilities, and she has not been blessed with an even temper."

"I can't go back in there. She hates me."

"Sister, I can assure you Sister Wilfreda does not hate you. Certain personalities do not mesh. One learns to live with this in community. You are lucky to have such a powerful lesson so early."

I'm lucky all right, lucky she missed me, I thought.

"Failure can be good for us, Sister," she went on. "It reminds us of our weakness and God's strength. You have a fine intellect and are accustomed to success. But God does not judge by the standards of the world. Menial tasks you perform this year will teach you much about the spiritual life," she paused.

"Yes, Sister, but . . ."

Sister Marie Charles stopped me with a raised finger. "Sister Maura, could it be that Sister Wilfreda senses that you have less respect for her because she lacks academic training?"

That had never occurred to me.

"Oh, no. No, no, Sister. Really, I never thought . . . I mean, her job is certainly important."

"It is, Sister, and also very difficult. However, I am sure that whatever happened between you and she was not caused by malice. Pray about the things we have discussed. Perhaps tomorrow will be better for both of you. You may go now, Sister."

Go? Go where? Not back to the kitchen. Not for 10,000 days' indulgence and an extra brownie at collation time.

I decided to go out. I got my shawl and mittens and was out the side door in minutes. Boy, Wilfreda was mad, I thought, as I ran across the grove. I wanted to get out of sight of the Novitiate. An empty field abutted the cemetery, waiting for the inevitable expansion. I'd go there. The look on her face when she really flung that pot. Made her forget her feet. What if she'd hit me? How would they explain it?

'Dear Mr. and Mrs. Lynch, your daughter, Sister Maura, was killed in the line of kitchen duty.'

Would they put a flag on my grave? I had just passed Veronica wiping the face of Jesus when the first flakes began to fall. By the time I reached the field, snow had dissolved the line between the earth and the sky. Everything was one white swirling mass. Hundreds of flakes landed on my habit. They kept their distinct feathery shapes for an instant, then melted into the black wool to be replaced by others.

I couldn't even see the Novitiate and Motherhouse buildings. The storm hid the lake below the field. It was really only a large drainage ditch, but today it reminded me of Robert Frost's 'frozen lake'. I could stand between it and the trees beyond the cemetery and watch the 'woods fill up with snow'; the only sound was 'the sweep of easy wind and downy flake'.

I started to run, kicking through the fast forming drifts. If anyone saw me . . . but no one could see me. There must be three or four inches already, I thought. The snow was totally untouched, not a footprint or a mark of any kind. Perfect for making angels. I stretched out on the ground and moved my arms and legs through the snow. I got up slowly, careful not to blur the outline. The long skirt made another angel, and then another until a whole choir sang together in the snow. Then I lay still and faced the sky, watching the endless outpouring. Infinite. Infinite. Ineffable. Omnipotent. Eternal. My thoughts are not your thoughts. My ways are not your ways. And he who believes in me, even if he dies, he shall live.

I closed my eyes and rose in my imagination high above the campus. I drifted, past Saint Ann's lake, over the barns and beyond the orchard. I watched snow soften everything, the infirmary, the Reilly building, the Big Church and the Bell Tower spire. As I floated by, I heard the bell ring, tolling the Angelus. The Angelus. The Angel of the Lord declared unto Mary. Mysteries. May it be done to me according to your will. Bong. Bong. Bong. Dinner, and I'm late. I opened my eyes. The snow had stopped. The sky was quite suddenly blue. The sun, absent for so long, made the white ground sparkle and my seven angels shine. I got up quickly and headed back to the Novitiate. The cedars in the cemetery looked like flocked Christmas trees and I started to sing 'The First Noel'. The formal feeling went. No, not death by freezing. The woods were lovely dark and deep but a promise is a promise — we'd all be asleep soon enough.

Just ask Barney. "End of the world?" she said. "2002. It's in the Fatima letter, but the Pope can't tell anyone. There'd be panic in the streets."

The snow and my habit turned to water as soon as I entered the Novitiate. Everyone was in Chapel saying the

Angelus. If I hurried I could change and get to dinner on time. I dripped along the terrazzo floor and up the stairs to my cubicle. A quick change into my Sunday clothes and down to the refectory. The hall was empty. I hurried past the kitchen, eyes averted. Good. The last novice in the line was just walking into the refectory. I slid in behind her and matched her decorous pace and got into my place. Suzanne, across from me, raised her eyebrows. I was panting. She pointed to her cap. Mine was off centre. I straightened it.

Sister Marie said Grace and then "Benedicamus Domine".

"Deo Gratias!" A near shout answered Sister Marie Charles. No one expected to talk today; it was Lent, and St. Patrick's and St. Joseph's day were the only oasis.

Sister tapped her little bell to silence us. "Sisters," she projected her light voice to all corners of the refectory. "We are recreating in honour of Sister Mary Ann, who is joining us as a Novitiate sister and teacher of theology. Sister has just received her degree in . . . " — Sister Marie Charles paused, consulted a piece of paper in her hand — "Catechetics from Loyola University."

The young professed nun who sat next to Sister Marie Charles smiled. Sister Mary Ann, tall and thin, with a serious face, dwarfed Sister Marie Charles and wore rimless glasses — she reminded me of the Bolshevik student in *Dr. Zhivago*. I didn't know how right I was.

At the meal's end Sister Marie Charles announced "Canonicals will meet with Sister Mary Ann in Room 127 immediately after recreation." Catechetics. I had a feeling we were about to begin a revolution — and that day, the revolution established its command post in the novices' study hall.

8

RENEWAL

Vatican Two was in full swing. Pope John, with his countryman's cunning, had managed to outmanoeuvre the Curia bureaucracy and open all areas of the Church's life for discussion. His successor, Paul VI, kept out of the way of the turning tide and document after document came out of the Council that scraped away the encrusted prejudices of centuries and revealed the essence of the Church as the people of God. It was a group that included Protestants, Jews, all kinds of non-Christians, in fact, anyone who tried to lead a moral life and find faith according to their conscience. And Latin, it turned out, was not the only language which God spoke. It was OK now for people to explore the centre of their spiritual life, to even look at the priest who presided over their prayer, to sing with joy, and to wish the person next to them 'peace' with a handshake and a smile. There was nothing outrageous here. Nuns could do this.

But when the superiors began to ask the sisters to implement these reforms and change convent practices, war broke out. We in the novitiate felt like Che Guevara's guerrilla force hiding out in the mountains, huddled around campfires singing 'Kumbaya'. We also read — Hans Kung, Karl Rahner and Edward Schillebeeckx. What's a revolution without European intellectuals? Question.

Examine. Believe, but as an adult, not an eight-year-old reeling off answers from the catechism.

Sister Mary Ann started the process. When she was promoted to become the Mistress of Postulants, it meant Mother herself gave the changes her stamp of approval. Sister Mary Francine moved to become Mistress of Novices. Sister Marie Charles retired and left for our convent in California, taking with her a way of training nuns that had been unchanged for generations. I imagined her shaking her head in disbelief as she left. How elastic can religious life be made anyway?

Our new theology teacher, Sister Claudette, encouraged us to see novels, poetry and movies as opportunities to learn about the workings of grace. I immediately ordered J.D. Salinger and John Updike from my mother. We read the 'Document on Religious' and were glad to see that the Church finally acknowledged that nuns were grown-ups who knew what was best for themselves and their orders. It was as if the Bishops had suddenly noticed that the 'good sisters' ran multi-million dollar enterprises very successfully. I had cleaned the bedroom of our order's treasurer, and seen the old-fashioned stock ticker busily printing out share prices under its glass globe.

"Oh yes," Columba told me, "Sister made a number of killings over the years. Xerox — of course any teacher could have predicted *that* would be successful." But now expertise didn't have to be hidden. We could emerge from the shadows and stop worrying about petty details, such as having a companion to go out with in public.

"The nuns don't like it," Columba told me one morning after she came back from California. I was hurrying through my employment so I could go home and write a poem. Oh yes, that was part of the renewal too. In Sister

Claudette's class, we read passages from the Old Testament and then found ways to express what they meant to us creatively, through poems, pictures, collages and music. Sister Giles danced her reaction to the passages in Wisdom that began 'Who shall find a valiant woman'. Matthew and I got an old blanket, put it over a piece of cardboard, propped it up in the hall, and called it the creative bulletin board. Poems and sketches and stories were pinned up for all to see. So our revolution had broadsides, graffiti, an artistic ferment.

"Don't like what, Sister?" I asked.

"All this folderol. You pull one thread and the whole garment can unravel."

"Is that what you think?"

"No, I love change. But you would be surprised how threatened people get when the way it's always been done gets overturned by a bunch of teenage know it alls."

"Columba!"

"Just giving you a sample of public opinion."

"We don't like it," Barney told me when I brought up her tray.

"Don't like what?"

"All this foolishness at the Novitiate. The altar turned around and English," she sniffed.

How do they find out these things so quickly, I wondered.

"Wouldn't you rather actually see the Consecration, watch the priest break the bread and hear and understand the words 'This is My Body'?"

"Sister!" Unfortunately, Sister Zita had come into the room with a copy of *The Sacred Heart Messenger* for Barney. "We do not bandy around sacred words."

"Barney, er Sister Barnabas, asked me about the vernacular."

"Ridiculous," Zita said. "Latin is the holy language. As for the celebrant facing me, well, I'd prefer to look at a beautifully embroidered vestment any day than the visage of most of the priests I have known."

"And St. Philomena," Barney wailed. "She's been answering my prayers for fifty years and now the Bishops say she's not in heaven! Did they send her to limbo?"

"I told you," Columba said later. "The nuns know what's going on over there. Don't think those boxes of novels don't get opened. Watch it, little Lynch."

But a momentum was building and when Mother announced that a special convention of the Sisters would be held in August as part of 'the summer of renewal', the partisans moved down from the mountains and headed for the capital. I tried to explain all this to my family during that long-awaited February visit. It had been six months since reception and it seemed like so much had happened. "See, there was a snowstorm. It came when I was so depressed after President Kennedy died, and it was like a sign, a metaphor, God's power dropping from the heavens. Just like in Isaiah. And that was the day the changes began."

"Isaiah," my mother said, "very nice, we're very pleased for you."

" Mom," Sally said, "Don't forget . . . "

"We're going to leave a half an hour early today, Maggie," my Mom said.

"You are?"

"Oh Maggie," Sally said, "The Beatles are on Ed Sullivan tonight. I've just got to get home in time to see them."

"Who are these Beatles?" I asked. My sisters just started laughing. My mother patted my hand. "Your sisters are in the grip of some uncontrollable frenzy, honey. It's bigger than all of us."

I stood at the window of the car saying goodbye. "Goodbye, Maggie," my mother said.

"Oh, Mom, by the way, when you write, could you say "Dear Sister Maura" instead of "Maggie"; it is my name now."

My mother looked at my dad and then back at me.

"Of course, if you want us to. Well, goodbye Sister Maura."

"Goodbye, enjoy the Beatles," I said as they drove away. I think I'll invite Father Chuck and Father Frank down to say Mass. We could do it outside. Easter. Yes, Easter would be perfect. I just can't believe they left early so the kids could see some pop group. Teenagers.

We set up the altar the week after Easter, under the trees by the lake behind the Novitiate, and my two uncles con-celebrated our first ever outdoor Mass. All 150 of us, novices and postulants, stood in concentric circles holding banners we had made and a huge multi-coloured kite. Matthew played 'Amen' from *Lilies of the Field* and we clapped in rhythm. Father Frank and Father Chuck looked over at me and winked. "I'm wearing the gold medal," I whispered as they were leaving.

In the following months, a lot of petty restrictions were lifted. We didn't have to ask permission to go to our rooms or to walk outside. There was talk of home visits, of nuns going on vacation and then the best news of all, Tampax would be allowed. Compared to the Declaration on Religious Liberty, permission to use tampons may seem minor, but believe me, I had been in charge of burning the Kotex and this was a much needed innovation. Except not one of us knew how to use Tampax. When we were in high school, the ads in women's magazines still presented Tampax as the 'married woman's secret' — something not quite respectable for the uninitiated.

"It's freedom," my sister Michele had written me when she sent us our first box of Tampax. The tide has turned, I thought, as I sat by the sink in the main lavatory, reading aloud from the directions. In the stalls, Matthew and four of my band members waited. We had plenty of tampons but only one set of directions. Luckily, a lot of us got our periods around the same time — though I guess in a group of 150 eighteen to twenty-two year old women, the odds were in favour of that.

"OK," I said. "Unwrap them and dip the tip in Vaseline." The jar slid from partition to partition. "Ready?"

"Yes." "Yes." "Yes." "Yes." "Yes."

"All right — now choose one of these positions for comfortable insertion," I read. "Sit on the toilet with your knees apart or stand placing one foot on the toilet seat. Got that?"

Five yes's.

"Now just relax and take your time."

"Relax? My hand is shaking," Lisa said. "Hope I can guide this thing in."

"With your thumb and middle finger, grasp the grooved centre of the applicator. The removal cord should be hanging down outside the smaller inner tube," I read. "Now, with your other hand gently spread the folds of the skin at the vaginal opening (as shown in Diagram D)."

"Only *you* have Diagram D," Matthew said.

"Insert the rounded tip of the Tampax tampon into the vaginal opening. (If you are not sure where your vaginal opening is, you may wish to use a mirror to see, referring to Diagram E.)."

"A mirror? Are you nuts?" Matthew said.

"Stop with the diagrams!" Lisa whined.

"I'm just reading. Anybody lost?"

No answers.

I read them through it, a bit like Cary Grant in *Wings* talking the pilot in. And we became modern women. My burn load dropped perceptibly.

Tampax, and outdoor Masses, the times they were a-changing. The summer went by quickly, with long evenings of picking strawberries — one for the basket, one for me — and drinking cold juice in the cannery afterwards. The strictest part of my training was over. In September, I went back to school, or rather school came to us, because we still weren't allowed to go over to the college for our classes. But I was busy, and with all my projects, the time went quickly. Family visits and letters seemed to come and go without being the huge events they had been in my first two years.

Then in March it was decided that novices should have a chance to get involved in the apostolate. Floodtown, a community of shacks on the Wabash River, had become the target of a social service effort by Father Joe, the chaplain of the prison where the fathers of most of the Floodtown families resided. He asked Sister Mary Francine for volunteers. Matthew and I got to the list first, number three was Sister Nicole, a Canonical novice who was a year behind us in community but a year older in age. She'd gone to the college for two years and had a self-possession I found intriguing.

"Sister's letting a Canonical go."

"We couldn't leave the campus," Matthew said.

"Stop," I said, "you sound like Barney and Zita. Plus, I would like to get to know Nicole to see what she thinks."

Matthew just said "Hmm".

Remember the squatter village the Joads pulled into in *Grapes of Wrath*? That's what Floodtown looked like. But this wasn't a movie set. It was home to 200 people. Dust was everywhere. No paved roads, no grass, no trees, no weeds even, just blowing dust. Our car stirred up a cloud as Father Joe drove by the two taverns and small grocery store. That was the business district. The window of the store was lined with big cans of potato chips. That and soda pop were the food staples, Father Joe explained.

Father Joe stopped in front of a stucco building that looked like a garage.

"This is it. This is the Centre. St. Christopher Centre on the banks of the Wabash. Even he couldn't carry anyone across this river. Should be St. Jude's Centre. I tried to get the kids to come here. The teenagers had a dance here. You probably don't realise this, Sisters, the dances now are obscene, literally obscene."

Oh great, a critic of popular culture — just what these people need. He led us into a square room.

"Well, anyway, you're welcome to give it a try. I'll help you with supplies as best I can but I can't be here much. My schedule is at the prison. I don't think there is much you can do with these kids. They're like little animals and the parents . . . One family keeps a retarded boy chained up behind the house. Chained just like a dog, and he runs back and forth until the chain pulls him down."

Father Joe stopped himself. Then it dawned on me. Floodtown was too much for him. That's why he wanted us. The poor guy. He found it all too depressing. Mere grinding poverty couldn't depress us, we couldn't have been happier. This wasn't serving God by keeping the bottom bedsheet taut. This was real life with real people who needed us.

"My Sisters, what do you ask?" This. This, bringing the good news to the poor. We started planning in quick whispers. We could get story books from the library and records and a record player from the Motherhouse community room. They only use it for Christmas carols and we'll return it then. Our parents would send us colouring books and crayons, we can get those big sheets of paper and finger paints from the art department. And brooms, buckets, soap — plenty of that in the Novitiate.

"Father," I said, "this will be just fine. And we can get some of the supplies."

As we walked back to the car I could imagine the eyes behind the tarpaper windows, watching us.

"But we'll need a car. Sacred Heart School got one really cheap at the auction at Fort Greene. I think it cost only 300 dollars. A station wagon would be best. And could you please remind Mother that we'd have to have our drivers' licences renewed. If we always have to wait for one of the workmen to drive us, we'll waste a lot of time." I hoped he could pull that off. The professed had just received permission to drive and if only we could too. Just to be able to get into the car and go. "And then . . ."

"Hold on, Sister." Father Joe's eyes glazed over.

"Don't worry, Father," said Matthew, "I've made a list." She handed it to him.

The car was easier to get than the permissions to drive, but hey, this was aggiornamento, so after two weeks we were back in Floodtown, unloading our 1957 army-green station wagon. It was another hot September afternoon and and there was no shade in Floodtown. Weeping willows grew alongside the river but nothing grew on the flat space above. No wonder the government had never bothered to evict these squatters, or charge taxes. Who'd want this desolate land, anyway?

We got all the stuff in and sat down for a minute inside the centre.

"Whew," said Matthew, "at least it's a little cooler in here."

"Yeah," I said, "It's the stucco and the roof. But did you see the roofs on the people's houses?"

"I know," said Nicole, "they look like sheets of tin stuck together some way. It must be 100 degrees in those houses."

Just then we saw a little face at the door — a freckled Huck Finn type face, with pale hair and pale eyes.

"Come on in," I said. He was about seven, dressed in cut-off jeans and a ragged undershirt.

"I ain't afraid. I told 'em ain't no such thing as witches, right? Least not driving cars in the middle of the day," he said.

We converged on our guest.

"Hello, I'm Sister Maura."

"I'm Sister Matthew."

"I'm Sister Nicole."

Well, that was too much. He was out of the door faster than a rabbit. We followed him out and found a miniature-sized gang waiting. There were about fifteen of them — boys and girls. All of them had that same pale look around the eyes. It was almost as if the sun that had browned and freckled them had bleached out their eyes and hair too. These weren't the regulation Catholic schoolkids I had always known, running over to hold Sister's hand and hang on her beads. There was suspicion on these little faces. A lot of them carried sticks and a few had handfuls of stones. It wasn't as if they were going to attack, but just holding these weapons seemed to make them feel better. Later, I noticed that every shack had one or two shotguns leaning against a wall or behind the door.

Matthew was the first of us who did anything. She went over to the car and got her guitar. "Try 'Old MacDonald'," I suggested.

But she knew what she was doing. She started a song I'd never heard here before.

> *If you're happy and you know it, clap your hands. /If you're happy and you know it, clap your hands. /If you're happy and you know it then your life will surely show it. /If you're happy and you know it, clap your hands.*

There was dead silence, but it did seem as if they moved closer to hear.

"OK, you guys," she said to Nicole and me, "you do the actions."

> *If you're happy and you know it, turn around.*

Nicole and I made decorous turns.

"No, no," said Matthew from between her teeth, not missing a chord, "Whirl, put something into it."

If you're happy and you know it, turn around.

We whirled. Our chaplets flew, our skirts billowed, our veils whipped around. Our audience started to giggle. Two black and white tops were spinning in front of them. They moved in closer. What was under those skirts! One more twirl might tell.

If you're happy and you know it then your life will surely show it. If you're happy and you know it, turn around.

They were making noise now.

"Look, look," said our first visitor. "They do got legs. I seen 'em."

"Clap your hands," sang Matthew. We clapped and they clapped.

Matthew picked up tempo.

If you're happy and you know it, stamp your feet.

This was too much to resist. They stamped, rather, stomped.

If you're happy and you know it then your life will surely show it./ If you're happy and you know it, stamp your feet, turn around, clap your hands.

They were right with us on every action. By the time we got to *jump up and down*, the kids were singing along and hamming up the actions.

Soon they had us by the hands or rather by the fingers and were taking us through the streets. I soon saw their hidden treasures — two dust mountains for playing soldier, paths that led down to the river and fishing, and not an adult or car in sight.

The backwoods was here, 200 yards off US 41.

Scottie was about five, the scrawniest and my immediate favourite. I couldn't help it. Maybe it was because he was the last one to drop his stones and ever since Patrick Malloy in the first grade, I'd always liked the 'bad' boys. Scottie was like a high tension wire — quivering and jumping. He wasn't about to hold anybody's hand but he stayed within three feet of me during the entire tour.

Tiny was Scottie's sister and she insisted that we come to her house to meet her mother. Theirs was a shack like the rest but it was further back and closer to the river. There was a tree in the front yard.

"Ma, ma, we got company," Tiny hollered.

Ma came out. She was thin and faded like her children, but smiling.

"Well, I never thought I'd see sisters in my own front yard. I saw some of you all once in the Five and Dime in the city but I didn't never think I'd ever speak to one personal."

We all smiled back at her. "You're speaking now. My name is Sister Maura." She stretched her hand out and we shook. "And this is Sister Matthew and Sister Nicole." She shook hands with each one, nodding as she did so. Then we all just stood there smiling at each other. What was next?

"I'd ask you in, Sisters, but the house . . ." She gestured toward the door. "Oh no, it's nice out here. You have a lovely view of the river," I said. The yard was green, too, though it was mostly weeds. There were rusting parts from cars and pieces of bicycles piled around. There was a tree stump that she pointed us toward and we three sat down on the stump. She and Tiny sat on the steps. Scottie was a little distance away playing with a broken toy car.

"You have beautiful children, Mrs. Um . . ."

"Just call me Emmie, Sister. Yeah, they are good kids. Course, poor Scottie, he's got the nerves."

"The what?" I asked.

"Nerves. See the way he shakes."

I saw. His hands were trembling and his right eye twitched. "It's the river done it," his mother said.

"Did he drink some bad water?" Nicole asked.

"No — ain't from drinking it. Little friend of his got drowned. Scottie saw him go under. Both of 'em screamed and screamed but no one got to the little boy. Scottie ran to me screaming and hollering but it was too late. Only four years old the child and dead. Scottie stood and watched the whole thing. Couldn't get him to come inside. The sirens were blowing, police boats draggin' the river. Took two whole days and nights to find the body and Scottie never slept, watching, listening the whole time. Never been the same since. Think he's shaky now? Should see him if he hears a police siren or even when the noon whistle goes off at the paper mill."

Scottie must have heard everything but he didn't react. Poor little boy.

"Yeah," Emmie was going on. I was to learn that for some people meeting a nun was the key that unlocked years of pent-up talk. People on buses would start telling me their most intimate marital troubles. Emmie was my first lesson.

I was sure that she was usually a closed-mouth woman but now she had a lot to say.

"Yeah, that river's a devil. If it don't drown you it floods you out."

Nicole was nodding. "I've heard it overflows about every two years. But I suppose it doesn't get up this far ..."

"Oh, yes it do," Emmie said, "Sister, it certainly do. Why we built this house four maybe five, yes, five times since we been livin' here. And that river sweeps something new away every time. Quite a few times it's run over the whole of Floodtown."

I knew enough not to ask the obvious question, "Why not leave?" Father Joe had told us that it wasn't only poverty's built-in passivity and a certain loyalty of place that kept the people there. There was a mark on the people of Floodtown, a mark that in that part of Indiana was more damning than race. People from there couldn't even get a job in town. And even if they gave another address there was something in their accent that gave them away to the townspeople. If you wanted to leave Floodtown you had to go very far away.

As we got the Centre going, I spent more time talking to Emmie and her friends. They told me how their grandfathers had come down from the hills to work on the barges and railroads. They'd stayed on the free riverbed land and there had always been bad blood between them and the townspeople.

"Any crime gets committed they blame us. See, the police was afraid to come in here after dark and so they said our men would rob and then run back," one lady was saying.

"They are just plain mean." That was the consensus about the town. I never asked them and they never told me whether what Father Joe had told me about the Floodtown ladies was true. He'd said that a lot of them worked as prostitutes in Linton and that the retarded boy and some of the other deformities in the children came from VD. I successfully ignored the whole argument until one day Emmie told me, "Mrs. Smithfield is terrible worried. She come up pregnant and her husband's been in Germany in the Army for the last two years. Worst of it is she swore she'd give up tricking if he went in the Army and get together enough money so as they could move out."

I went to see Mrs. Smithfield. She was upset but I never yet had seen one of those ladies really get hysterical.

"If I could just make him understand, it was only for the kids. And I just couldn't ask him to send me more money. He was saving so as we could get out of here."

"When's he coming home?" I asked.

"Not for near a year but he's gonna know, sooner or later."

"But maybe when he sees the baby." One thing everybody liked in Floodtown was a baby. I'd never even heard talk of abortion but then, where would anyone from there get one? I stopped myself, horrified. It was bad enough I was friendly with, well, I guess some of them were prostitutes, but thinking about abortion?

That night at Spiritual Reading I tried to sort out my thoughts. Was I failing in Floodtown by not being more of a moral presence? I hardly ever said anything religious. In fact it was the ladies who would throw in the Bible sayings. We mostly just talked. They were only a little older than me but they certainly had gone through more. Who was I to advise? But wasn't that what a nun was supposed to do?

Then I started to look through one of the Gospels and these words jumped out at me. 'Judge not and you shall not be judged.' Judge not, judge not. That was it. I had no responsibility to judge those ladies. 'Love your neighbour' not 'Judge your neighbour' was the Commandment. In fact there was even a bonus for not judging — I didn't get judged. Now that was very appealing! What a relief. I felt like a load had come off my shoulders. But I didn't think Mrs. Smithfield should write to him or anything. Wait till the baby comes. It's sure to be cute and that should help to soften him up. The Bell rang for the Angelus. 'The angel of the Lord declared unto Mary. And she was conceived by the Holy Ghost.' Hey, no that would never work twice. Better to tell him 'judge not'.

After Nicole and Matthew and I went every Saturday for six weeks, it was felt things were running smoothly enough so that everyone could take a turn. I didn't really like the idea of rotating.

"Why can't we keep going?" I said to Matthew. "The people are used to us, they like us."

"They'll like the others too," Matthew said.

"But it won't be the same. The superiors act like we're all interchangeable," I said.

"We're supposed to be," she said.

"But Matthew, you can't believe that! Why Anna Celia isn't going to be able to play with Scottie or talk to Mrs. Smithfield as well as, as well as . . ."

"What do you want to say? As well as you can?"

"Yes, that is what I want to say and I don't know why you're trying to make me feel ashamed of it. I'm an individual and so are you." I was mad.

"But, Maura," I wished she didn't sound so patient, "it is not we as individuals that matter but as representatives of the community reaching out. We have to be willing to sacrifice personal satisfaction for the greater good."

"Matthew, I know you're getting into humility and all but come on," I said.

"I'm serious, Maura. I've been talking to Sister Mary Ann and reading about monastic communes and . . . "

I listened, but it sounded awfully dogmatic and unnatural to me. Oh well, she'll work herself out of it. Right now I have to plan what I'm going to say to Sister Mary Francine at my conference tomorrow.

"And so, Sister," I was concluding, "that's why I think it's important that the same people go at least for the entire semester. It would be much easier for the people of Floodtown and . . ."

"Sister Maura," she said, "not to interrupt but I don't think you understand that Mother approved this project so that novices and junior sisters could have some experience of the apostolate. We can't base formation on what the people of Floodtown might or might not like."

It seemed to me that there was a rueful tone in her voice but maybe that was because I needed to hear it there. This was worse than Matthew's commune. If you took this reasoning a step further it would mean we had schools so the nuns would have some place to teach and hospitals so they'd be able to nurse. Did that mean the apostolate was only a reason to justify the existence of this institution? A reason for all these buildings and offices and stock portfolios? Something for all these women to do? But that's crazy. The order is here because of the people's needs, not the other way around. Right?

"Sister, there was something I wanted to discuss at this conference if that is alright," Sister Mary Francine said.

"Yes, Sister." Now what: breaking silence? messy cubicle? making my slip into culottes?

"I'm sure you know that you have much academic potential. Your scores on the College Boards and other tests were very high. However . . ."

Oh good, it was only my potential. I'd got this "not working up to it" speech since grade school. What I never could make anyone understand was that I had my own plans for my potential. If only I hadn't got straight A's in the first grade I'd be better off. I had tried once to explain that I'd done so well because I had Brigid helping me. I can still see her — not quite four years old, sitting cross-legged on the kitchen table cutting capital Z's out of magazines for me with those blue and yellow plastic scissors we had. I was getting the small z's, an easier job, while Brigid with the eagle eye found the capitals. Then, unfortunately for me, she started school and had her own potential to worry about. Well, this lecture was better than the neatness one.

"However," Sister was saying, "while your grades as a freshman were adequate, now you are taking courses in your major field and you must give your school work your best efforts, even at the expense of projects like Floodtown. Our order is dedicated to academic excellence, thus it is perfectly proper for us to seek the deep pleasure of study. I understand this new enthusiasm for the active apostolate but remember, Sister, learning is your primary vocation. You must be a scholar and a teacher."

A scholar? When I pictured teaching I saw myself reading Frost to my class so movingly that their faces would open up and an intense young black student would stand up to speak of the promises and the miles he had to go before he slept. Scholar sounded more like sitting alone in the library than helping a homeless family find an apartment.

"You see, Sister," she said, "My generation had to well, yes, had to *fight* to convince the more conservative elements in the community and local hierarchy that it was not worldly or irreligious for nuns to pursue higher studies. At one point the bishop accused us of pride because we wanted our college accredited and all our teaching sisters to have degrees. And as for studying on secular campuses, those 'hotbeds of sin', well, it was quite a struggle before our sisters were even allowed to accept scholarships."

I nodded. What was she trying to say?

"You have intellectual gifts, Sister, that can now be nurtured — a masters, a PhD even — social work is fine but it, well, doesn't require the same mental ability. You have great potential . . . "

Here it is.

"But if you don't cultivate it . . . Sister, we have fine academies and of course, our college. We will need young teachers . . ."

So I had to watch Saturday when three other novices climbed into a station wagon and went to Floodtown. Nicole came up. "Don't worry," she said, "after a few months the novelty will wear off and they will be glad to have us go back."

"A few months? I'll be in the Juniorate."

"Exactly," Nicole said. "And think about it, what happens in August?"

"I take temporary vows."

After three years in the novitiate you were professed and got the black veil. You vowed poverty, chastity and obedience, but only for increments of one year. For the next five years, you could leave or the order could dismiss you very easily, but then you took final vows and that was forever, only the Pope could release you from your vows then. Now the whole idea of making solemn promises subject to cancellation seemed odd, but by saying those words, I would become a full-fledged nun.

"Ah," I began to follow her. "I'll be professed, and even though I'll just move across the road to live in the Juniorate, I'll have a lot more freedom."

"Well," Nicole said, "let's just say more leeway. For now, instead of arguing with the system, try ignoring it, that's what I do."

"Really?" Of course, we were ignoring it right now by having a conversation in the driveway of the Novitiate.

"Let's go to the cemetery," I said, looking over my shoulder.

"Why?"

"I don't want to talk right here!"

Nicole shrugged and we headed off down the path of the Stations of the Cross. Jesus was having the nails hammered into the palms of his hands. Not much leeway there.

"Anyway," Nicole continued when we entered the cemetery, "don't try to beat the superiors over the head with your opinions. Just do what you think is right."

It seems so simple.

"Take the Chapter of Faults," she said. "I wish someone would," I said.

Matthew had suggested guitar music to lighten the proceedings but the humiliating process continued. Most of us just said things like, I broke silence at my employment, which was a nice non-specific minor offence but even Sister Mary Francine didn't think she could cancel this ritual of public confession. The older nuns in the order would really flip if we didn't have to do the thing everyone hated most. I couldn't figure out why it was such torture. I knew everyone. Most people just mumbled something and sat down. There were no real punishments. We always got three meals plus snacks. "It's the atmosphere," Nicole said. "It's all designed to engender guilt about nothing and that is very unpleasant. So I have just stopped going."

I couldn't believe it. "And what happened?" Nothing, she said, nobody even notices. "I couldn't, Nicole, I just couldn't not go."

"All I'm saying," she said, "is if you don't make a big deal about things around here, you can do what you want. Next year, if you want to go to Floodtown, just show up, touch your black veil and say, 'If there's room in the car, I'd like to go.' " It made sense.

"Except now," I said, "Sister Mary Francine has decided that I have to be some kind of a scholar."

"So," said Nicole "aren't there subjects you like?"

"English and don't laugh, but I want to take some drama courses. But I want to take them in the college."

"And why am I not surprised?" Nicole said. The heads of those two departments, Sister Marie Brian, English, and Sister Blanche, Drama, were the two star nuns at the college. Marie Brian's beauty alone, her white Irish skin and deep blue eyes, would have made her stand out, but in addition she was so smart that the order had sent her to Oxford to study and so independent that she drove around campus in a golf cart which one of her golf pro brothers had given her — and no one said a word. Sister Blanche — well, hers was a delayed vocation, the best kind in so many ways. I sometimes wished my vocation had delayed until I was seventy-five or eighty. Before entering, Blanche had acted on Broadway and directed regional theatre. If Margo Channing, the actress Bette Davis played in *All About Eve*, had become a nun, she'd be Sister Blanche. But the drama department was off limits for us, since the theatre, to quote the superior who was education director, was 'an occasion of sin'. Blanche was tolerated because her productions brought acclaim and money to the college. My chances of working with either of these women were not good. While intellectual formation might be the new priority, the order still wanted us to do our learning on this side of the bridge, separate from the college girls.

But Nicole had opened a new line of attack. The rebels could call a ceasefire and move into the political process. I could negotiate my way into their classes, act as if it was a matter of course.

Another novice was walking among the white gravestones. It was Matthew. The three of us met in the centre near the three elaborate tombs of the order's three priest chaplains. No simple markers here.

I couldn't just blurt out, Matthew, you won't tell that you saw us talking, will you, but I thought it. It was strange. As we got more freedom, Matthew became more scrupulous. She thought the revolution demanded a higher standard of behaviour. I also knew she was making promises to God so He would protect her Marine brother who had just shipped out to Vietnam, to a war we were just beginning to hear about. Probably keeping perfect silence was one of her bargaining chips. I hoped fraternal correction, i.e. snitching, wasn't another. She nodded at us.

"Nicole thinks we'll be able to go back to Floodtown even when we go to the Juniorate." Matthew nodded again, smiled and walked away. She hadn't spoken a word. And as we watched she began the Stations of the Cross. Matthew didn't tell, but I think that afternoon marked the first split in the central committee.

9

SPIRITUAL ADVISORS

On August 15th, 1965 I lined up with my forty band members to change my white veil to black. Only fifteen of our group had left during the Novitiate. Not bad. We might lose one or two more but most of us would probably stay sisters until our Golden Jubilee. I moved up to the bishop, trying to concentrate on my vows, petrified that the electric fan would blow my white veil off. Only one pin held it on. The bishop had to slip the black veil over the white one and then yank the white one off. Not easy for an elderly cleric. Somehow the bishop and I made the switch. Then the question, "Sisters, what do you ask?" Now we answered "We ask to take for one year the vows of poverty, chastity and obedience according to the rules and constitutions of the Sisters of Redemption." I smiled at my family and walked back to the pew.

Two days later I was in the Juniorate asking for a bed on the porch. We lived in part of the Motherhouse and everything was old, very old — the wooden floors, the plumbing and the nuns who ate with us in the refectory. Still, it was less institutional than the Novitiate. Wood was warmer than tile. The high ceilings and big leaded windows let in streams of light.

A sleeping porch opened off the smaller of the two dorms — an old-fashioned screened-in porch with six-foot-high windows and a great view of the grove and the lake beyond. It was coveted in the summer but abandoned in the winter. I must get out there, I thought, looking at the rows and rows of iron beds separated only by white muslin curtains that clogged the inside dorms.

The porch had only one line of beds. I wouldn't have to draw the curtain closed on four sides but could leave the curtain at the foot of the bed open and look out to the sky. In October, when the temperature dropped, I was allowed to move out there. The porch became my studio apartment and little by little, I became a commuter nun. My life would be classes at the college, drama department rehearsals, the Floodtown activities and the hours I spent in the library periodical room, catching up on three years of news. I had lost my conditioned response to wars and murders. The news didn't fall like blocks of type into a specially set aside section of my brain. It hit directly. *Time* and *Newsweek* and *The New York Times* seemed to be reporting events happening to my own family. The babies who screamed because the burning napalm couldn't be scraped off their skins were Patrick, Sally and Scottie in Floodtown. I wrote stories about Vietnam and the Chicago ghetto, Ireland and any place I had never been.

Our Superior was Sister Augusta. She had just received her doctorate in theology from Rome. To have such a brilliant woman as the Mistress of the Juniorate was considered great good luck. But I wondered how she felt about giving up access to the Vatican library to supervise us. Most of my encounters with her took the form of negotiating sessions. I learned to have my arguments all marshalled and to keep my real reasons to myself. "Don't argue," Nicole had said. I didn't at first. When I wanted to take drama classes and I needed Sister Blanche on my side, I went to her office, a large room off the theatre called The Green Room. It really was green, dark green, not the awful mint green that virtually every room in the Hills was painted.

A green-upholstered couch took up the whole wall. I sat down on the first yielding piece of furniture I had encountered since I entered. Straight wooden chairs in the refectory, pews in chapel, metal folding chairs in the recreation room and those awful school desk chairs in the cubicles — to think I once took cushions for granted. And she's got real pictures on the wall, not just portraits of saints or the Sacred Heart. And lamps — at last, a dimly lit room. It's fluorescence or darkness in the convent. A tea set. I longed for a cup of tea — sipped here on the sofa from a porcelain cup, not those heavy white china things made in Syracuse we used.

"I hope you are comfortable, Sister."

Sister Blanche stood at the door. I wasn't sure how she was going to react. Her unpredictability was legendary in the college and made everyone a little afraid of her. During the years I knew her, her prickliness increased and became 'premature senility'. Then one day she lost consciousness and couldn't be revived. At the hospital they found that her 'premature senility' was really a large tumour on the brain, the size of a golf ball, according to the story. The doctors were able to remove it and it was like Lazarus come back. "I felt as if I'd been living at the bottom of a well with darkness between me and the people I wanted to communicate with. I kept shouting up and never quite getting through," she told me much later. But today, I only knew of her by legend, and I was nervous.

"Sister Blanche, excuse me but I very much want to study with you. If I could have your permission to take the stagecraft class. Then I could work on the permission from the other side."

"And to think Chinese theatre is said to be too stylised for audiences here. Yes, Sister, you have my permission to try to get permission."

"Thank you, Sister. I can't thank you enough. This was so easy. It wasn't at all what . . ."

"What you'd been led to expect? Well, now you know my awful secret. I'm a nice person. But please don't let it get out or I'll never have another rehearsal start exactly on time with the entire cast present."

"So you see, Sister Augusta," I was saying the next day, "Sister Blanche thinks it would be sensible if I learned some technical skills since most of our high schools have auditoriums with machines that we should understand."

Sister Blanche had also pointed out to the powers to be that having a nun direct the annual school play in high school meant not having to pay seculars to do the job. It worked. I was officially in the drama department.

And then I was in stagecraft class. I was taught by Mr. Wilson, a short, neat competent man, half aesthetic and half carpenter. He was really polite to me until he yelled at me for nailing a screw into a flat. He started to apologize but I thanked him. It made me feel like a normal person. We became friends; I had an ally.

Matthew was worried about me and stopped me for earnest talks, but she was busy with school and we each went our own way. The year went fast and then Nicole was over in the Juniorate with us. When rehearsals ran late she was the one who left the first floor window unlocked so I could climb in and tiptoe my way to bed. Augusta never said much to me. Most of our conversations were about permissions. By this time I'd learned to dress up my requests in worthy motives.

"Sister Augusta, may I have permission to take Rabbi Bloom's Jewish History Class at the college? We're so lucky to have the only Jewish Rabbi in the country who is teaching at a Catholic College and we should take advantage of it."

I prattled along all the time thinking "Why do I have to stand here mouthing all these reasons? Why wouldn't I want to take a fascinating course from the first Rabbi ever to teach on a Catholic campus anywhere? He talks 10,000 words a minute and tells great stories and makes every class a drama."

Of course if I had said any of that aloud I'd never be able to take the course. Better to stick to the theological benefits, the sociological benefits, and any other worthy reasons I could think of.

And then it was, "Sister Augusta, may I please have permission to take part in a series of ecumenical dialogues with students from the State University? The Rabbi has invited me to come and they are under the sponsorship of Sister Mary Joan. In addition, Sister, I would be a witness to our order's commitment to ecumenism as urged by the Vatican Council . . . "

What I wanted to say was, "Hey, Sister, it's going to be so much fun to talk to other kids my age but who are Lutheran and Methodist and Greek Orthodox and Jewish. They have probably never even talked to a nun. Some of them are probably involved in the Civil Rights movement and anti-war protests . . ." But I didn't.

And of course the drama department brought the need for larger and larger permissions.

"May I please speak to you, Sister Augusta? As you may know, one of the requirements for credit for the directing class is to direct a play. Now I was wondering if since I am a junior sister it wouldn't make more sense to direct a play with the junior sisters instead of using college girls. After all we have just as much talent here as they have over there and . . ."

"Listen," the inner voice said. "We can act, sing and dance rings around the college girls. Let them watch us for a change. We'll do an adaptation of *Twelfth Night* with medieval-style costumes that can accommodate the habit. We can have contemporary music and Sister Giles can choreograph the dances. We'll put it on in May, a Spring festival when all the magnolias bloom."

"Yes, Sister, well I realise the play is getting a little out of hand — it's larger than I anticipated. But so many of the sisters wanted to be in it, I added a chorus and dancers. But don't you think it is beneficial for so many to be exposed to Shakespeare and . . ."

"And we're having such a good time!" I wanted to say. "All of us are really working together. All the little petty differences and separations are over when we're rehearsing and making the scenery and sewing the costumes. Why, Sister Samuel Mary, who I've never said more than three words to, turns out to be an electronic whiz. She's taped all the music and sound effects, designed the lighting. And who would have thought that Josepha, so serious and intent and seemingly rigid, would turn out to be a comic genius. Her Andrew Aguecheek is brilliant and when she dances with Sir Toby Belch my stomach hurts from laughing. And Gertrude who I was afraid would freeze — she's so shy usually — makes Sir Toby a wonderful ham. Look at the beautiful costumes Mary Raphael made out of Sister Blanche's odds and ends. And the sets — Chloe is a real artist."

"Please, Sister" I said out loud, "nobody minds missing recreation and this is our dress rehearsal. No, I really don't feel that any of the junior sisters feel I'm imposing on them. No one said that, did they? Why, it's everybody's project."

"Listen," I thought, "you're not going to make me feel guilty. I know everyone is having a good time."

Four days later I was back there trying to not smile all over the place.

"Sister, I'm sorry you didn't feel well enough to attend a performance but Sister Blanche asked me to ask you for permission for the junior sisters to give another performance. It seems that there was no room at the last performance for everyone who wanted to attend. Sister Blanche said she had already spoken to Mother about it so if it is all right with you then . . ."

"Sister," I nearly said out loud, "we were a hit, a hit, a standing room only hit. Everyone loved it, the old nuns, the novices and postulants and the college girls went crazy, I guess they didn't think nuns could do things like sing and dance. And my whole family came and do you know that my Dad even brought fifty-seven McDonald's milk shakes and we had a wonderful cast party afterward. The Rabbi and his wife Ruth and the kids came too and they loved it. It was such a happy day. Sister Alan, the housekeeper for the Motherhouse, sent us a wonderful thank-you card."

Are you starting to feel sympathy for Sister Augusta? As I'm writing this and remembering, I am too. But I was twenty-one years old, living with 100 other twenty-one and twenty-two year olds with untapped reservoirs of energy. I wanted to write petitions to Congress and march against the Vietnam war, direct impassioned off-Broadway plays, but that was totally out. So I did all I could, though I hated asking the permissions. But I had to. One, because I was living within this system and two, I knew Augusta would find out anyway and kill me.

"My life is very full," I wrote to my mother. "I'm happy and looking forward to next year on mission. Love, love to all! Sister Maura."

Now with Sister Marie Brian in the English department, I had a very different relationship. Not so much skullduggery. After all, teaching literature was sanctioned. It was what I was supposed to be doing. So it was alright to be enthusiastic about Wallace Stevens and Dante, and to turn *Twelfth Night* into a musical. But of course, I couldn't leave well enough alone. So when it came time to start my senior thesis I went to see Sister Marie Brian with some trepidation, because what I wanted to write about was film. Now I knew there was no way I could make movies my sole subject, but I had just discovered James Joyce. *There* was someone who understood bobbing and weaving through Catholic doctrine. Couldn't I do a comparison between a work of his and that of a film director?

"You could," said Marie Brian when I went to her office. "But how will you get materials? Last time I looked we had very few film books in our library."

"One," I said, "*The Making of the Ten Commandments.* But I have made a list of places and people I could write to for help. Except it would mean sending out twenty letters and we get two stamps a month."

"I see," said Sister Marie Brian. She got the stamps and even had her assistant type the letters. I began meeting with her once a week in her office in the college residence hall where she lived.

"She is so noble to give up community life," one of the older nuns said about Marie Brian. But I knew she liked the privacy. She commuted to prayers and meals on her golf cart. Before, while she'd been a great teacher to me in my classes, she always drew a line. Small talk was not her style. But as we met in her tiny study, I heard her story. Irish family, lots of brothers. She was 'Sis', the only girl and much loved. Her father was a police lieutenant in Indianapolis. Her mother had been born on an island off County Kerry.

"She had great stories," Marie Brian told me. "At the age of ten, she faced a wild sea and rowed to the mainland to bring a doctor for her mother. 'If you are brave in a boat,' she told me, they'll tell great stories about you.'"

"Then," she continued in a matter of fact tone, "when she was dying I was denied permission to go home. In those days, you could only go once, so if they weren't sure your parent would really die, you could waste the visit and of course, then not be at the funeral. Four of my brothers came and spoke to Mother in her office. I went home. We were all with her when she died. I stayed home three weeks with my father and the boys."

Three weeks, I thought, at home, thirty years ago. "And Mother let you?"

"I didn't ask."

Brave in a boat, I thought. The next day, I set up a room of my own in the utility closet under the stairs where they stored the mops, put a plywood board on the window sill and waited to see if the world I had written to would write back to me. It did.

"Look, Sister Marie Brian, look." I pushed the seventeen-page letter into her hands. It was from a student film maker I had read about in an article I had found in Sister Blanche's Green Room. He was twenty-five, a graduate student at NYU Film School. The article was about how he had won an award for his student film, a parody of a gangster movie. I had sent him a note care of NYU and this was his reply.

"Look," I said to Marie Brian, "look at the holes in the paper." He had typed the letter with such intensity, his periods pierced the paper. He used capitals, exclamation points, anything to force mere words to express his thoughts. No wonder he turned to the pictures and faces and music and the rhythm of movies. Marks on page just weren't language enough for him. Over the next months I got more letters. It was like taking a specialised course. He wrote about the movies he loved and the stories he wanted to tell. I had to see *Hiroshima Mon Amour* and Bergman and try to find a theatre that showed John Ford's *The Searchers* on a big screen. Marie Brian laughed when I told her this. "I know, I know," I said, *"Hiroshima Mon Amour,* when I could barely get permission to go out the front gate. And look at the list of books he recommended."

"Hmm," she said, "I just got an allotment of grant money. Give me that list."

The Gotham Book Mart must have been surprised at the order they got from our Lady of the Hills English/Cinema Studies Department. I wrote back to him from the Mop Room. He'd been in the seminary briefly and so understood the struggles of our revolution. When his student film arrived, Marie Brian and I rushed to watch it in the basement on a rickety 16mm projector. "He has the making of a genius," she said. She was right. He became one of

America's greatest directors, and a year after we started our correspondence, I went to see his first feature film dressed in full habit at The Playboy Theatre in Chicago.

For now, I was content to spend my last few months in the Juniorate forging my conscience in the mop room and filling my days with pursuits. The drama department, Floodtown, the Rabbi's course, the stories I was publishing in the college magazine, I was so busy I didn't explore my soul or bother to question my vocation. That's why I was so surprised when one Spring night I came very close to killing myself. I guess I was not chugging along as happily as I thought.

10

CHOOSE LIFE

It was Easter vacation and the order of the day was suspended. We had no classes and extra recreation every afternoon — no need to rush from duty to duty. It was almost too much free time. One night we were invited to a special showing of the movie *Becket* in the college auditorium. With the girls on vacation, we had it all to ourselves. It was solid nuns — the Novitiate, the Juniorate and the professed Sisters from the Motherhouse and from the college. It wasn't every day that Hollywood made a high budget film about a saint with two major stars, and we Sisters of the Redemption were going to give our support.

After the movie, as we walked back through the quiet darkness, I kept seeing the scene on the beach where Peter O'Toole as King Henry leans from his saddle and calls out to Richard Burton, "Thomas, Thomas." Becket looks at him for a long moment, and then turns and rides away. The image stayed with me across campus and into the big church. We all stopped in for the quick visit before bed that was customary. Some people didn't even go to their prie-dieux but nodded at the tabernacle from the doorway and then headed upstairs. It was almost ll p.m. — very late for us. The church was dark. The only light came from the candles that flickered through red glass vigil lights on the side altar and the tabernacle lamp's glow. I felt drawn to my prie-dieu. I wasn't ready to plunge into the getting-ready-for-bed rush going on upstairs.

"Thomas, Thomas."

"I carry the honour of God," Becket had told Henry when he turned away.

Throughout the movie Henry had hated the cold. Now, there he was in that freezing wind, on that empty beach. I was surprised to feel tears start. Poor Peter O'Toole, isolated as Lawrence of Arabia and now alone again. Becket had to go, of course, but what did he feel as he rode away with Henry screaming his name? The tears came faster. It was a silent disconnected weeping. I didn't sniffle or even breathe hard. But I couldn't stop.

"Thomas, Thomas." Henry wasn't begging exactly, after all, he was king. But they'd been heroes together, friends until Henry wanted to control the Church. Then Becket had to fight him. After all, as a Cardinal, Becket carried the honour of God.

Stop this now, stop, I told myself, but the tears continued. I knelt down and said a sketchy night prayer, genuflected and left the church.

The hall was empty. Good. No lights except the large candle in front of the Sacred Heart. The clock chimed eleven thirty. I had been in church for half an hour. If anyone sees me down here this late . . . I ran on my toes, my chaplet muffled in my skirt, into the Juniorate and up the long flight of wide wooden stairs. By keeping to the middle and avoiding the third step, I got to the third floor in silence. Everyone was already in bed. Even breathing punctuated by occasional snores came from the dormitory. I tiptoed past the curtained beds and out to the porch.

Soon I'll have to leave the porch, I thought as I undressed. Everyone wants to be out here in the summer. But where were they last January when the snow blew in the windows and I found a small drift at the foot of my bed? "Thomas, Thomas." Henry had seemed almost afraid of being cold. He'd bathed in a huge tub suspended over a bonfire. Becket would wait, holding a large towel ready.

I swung open the four French windows in front of my bed and the three on the side. There were more windows than walls out here. The screens had been taken off to be cleaned. Nothing separated the porch from the spring night. I was so tired I felt like just falling into bed. But I didn't. I laid my habit out for the next morning and picked up my dirty clothes and tiptoed into the sink room. Rinse the stockings in cold water, roll them in a towel so no drips. Then find a place on the over-burdened drying racks. I tossed my underpants and bra into the large white laundry bag in the corner. I could take my bath in the morning if I woke up before the rising bell . . . But I won't. Better do it now but fast. The water sputtered into the tub. I'd never realised how much noise this old plumbing made, I thought as I quickly turned it off. There was enough water for a quick wash. At least I have myself under control, I thought, as I bent over the tub to rinse away the ring. But then the tears started again.

He shouldn't have left Peter O'Toole. He should have found some way, some compromise. But to just leave Henry shivering on the beach. And now I was sobbing loudly. Oh, what if some one wakes up and finds me crying into the tub. I put my towel over my face and ran out to the porch. OK, I said to myself, let it out. A good cry at the movies is fine. After *Long Grey Line* I'd stayed in the theatre weeping so hard a lady came over to say, "It's only a story, little girl." But it wasn't, it was true and so was *Becket*. Stop. Stop.

I'm not homesick, school's fine, it's fun in Floodtown, Sister Blanche says I can help her with the next play. Everything is fine. Stop crying. Midnight. Five empty hours before rising. Nothing to slice the time into. In the day it's classes, then Vespers, then dinner, then recreation, but night goes on and on. I looked out into the darkness. The trees in the grove made one solid mass, the stars far above the trees. The lights over the hall entrance shone on the paved courtyard below me. I sat on the window-sill and leaned my back against the open window frame. I could feel the ridges that enclosed each pane against my spine. The wide concrete slabs below, like a lit stage in a dark theatre, seemed to await some action. I wondered how a body would look stretched out there. A junior sister in a white nightgown, half covered by a black bathrobe, or maybe face down, a black heap on the sidewalk. I leaned out to look at that body. Why would a junior sister, a temporarily professed nun with everything ahead of her, do that? "Thomas, Thomas." Henry didn't want Becket, he called for Thomas. And yet later, "Who will rid me of this troublesome priest?"

It would take only seconds to fall from this window-sill down to the courtyard — seconds. I leaned out further.

The wind must have shifted just then because I heard the trees stir and felt cold air on my face. I put that flannel nightgown away too soon, I thought. It would be warm in bed. I looked at the brown army blankets with their neat hospital corners. I shivered and turned back to the courtyard. The body was gone. Stupid to sit here freezing. My daytime voice said, "Go to bed." I did. But I was afraid.

The tower bell clanged at 5:15.

"Benedicamus Domine," I heard from inside.

"Deo Gratias," I said with the rest.

I picked up my cigar box of toilet articles. The contact paper cover was flaking on the corner. Have to replace it. The sink room was full with the usual morning rush. I brushed my teeth, took a sip of water, swirled it around in my mouth and spat into the sink. Frederick on one side of me and Eileen on the other, also brushed, sipped, swirled and spat. Toilets flushed and heels hit the wood floors. The stairs creaked as we hurried down to church, habits dragging on the steps, chaplets clinking against the rail. The order of the day took over and night receded.

I had exactly one and a half minutes to get into the Big Church and up to my prie-dieu before Mother started the Morning Offering. I hurried past the Sacred Heart statue in the hall. I could still see stars through the hall window but the sky had lightened. The sun would rise soon. Into the Church and up the aisle. I tucked my chaplet into my skirt and dropped on to one knee. I slid past three prie-dieux in one motion, swung my right knee on to the kneeler and pulled the rest of my body in just as the big bell pealed.

"I've never seen anyone cover so much ground with one genuflection," Sister Blanche told me once.

"Oh Jesus through the Immaculate Heart of Mary I offer you all my prayer, works and thoughts of this day . . ."

The Church was bright; the early morning sun pushed colours through the stained glass windows. Mass, breakfast, and my employment, then I would talk to Augusta. I could still see that dead figure on the ground. I mean I'm not going to dramatise myself and call it a pull toward, well, toward . . . I wouldn't say suicide to her. It would seem like showing off, but there were underlying issues . . .

"And so, Sister, after the movie, I started thinking. How much does that story reflect a medieval attitude about the Church and God. I mean . . . "

She doesn't understand. She's following everything I say very politely and waiting for me to get to the point. But what is the point?

"I guess what I'm asking is, do personal relations have to be sacrificed for the good of the Church. I mean," I gulped, "isn't human love important too?"

"Of course it is, Sister," she said. "As long as it is correctly ordered."

Ordered?

"For example, I have a close friend who was married to a very difficult man and divorced him. She has fallen in love again with a fine man."

Good.

"But naturally there can be no relationship."

Naturally?

"She may be legally divorced but in the eyes of the Church she is still married therefore . . . "

She looked at me as if all should be clear.

"But isn't love the greatest good?" I ventured.

"In the proper order!" Order didn't help when I found myself staring from the porch window to the lit courtyard below.

"Enough philosophical discourse, Sister," Augusta said. "This is vacation and we have a generous invitation from the theatre owner in town. He has invited the sisters to come and see *My Fair Lady!*" She waited for my enthusiastic response.

All I could think was, "Another movie?" I don't know if I could take a love story that ends happily. 'I've grown accustomed to your face — you almost make the day begin?' No, I don't think so. "I just don't feel up to it, Sister. Sister Marie Brian wants another chapter of my thesis by Friday, and I would like to be ready . . . "

"Very well, Sister, you have my permission to stay home."

"Yes, Sister. Thank you, Sister."

I spent the afternoon sitting in the orchard hearing the last words Henry had flung at Becket. "I loved you, Thomas. I loved you. "

Loved you. That was the dilemma. Ever since the day I entered I'd been trying to have it both ways. To be a nun, yet remain a woman, to leave my family, but stay the eldest daughter, the big sister. To separate from the world while being part of it. All well and good to quote 'in Christ all paradoxes are resolved' and talk about the Omega point where opposites converge. I could struggle to be all these things as long as the fight was between me and 'them'. 'Them' could be silly rules or Augusta's short-sightedness or Marie Charles' strict interpretation. If they would just leave me alone I knew I could be chaste, creative but ascetic, obedient and independent, simple while intelligent. But now I was fighting something within myself.

I always counted on my natural buoyancy. I could bounce back, ignore contradictions, concentrate on the good things. But on that April day, I knew something in me had broken down. I had no schemes, no brainstorms, no ideas, no rationalisations. Here was Spring in all its glory, and I had no desire to write about apple blossoms or baby birds hatching from their shells.

Then on the last day of April, Augusta walked into evening recreation and called me over. I'd been ill at ease with Augusta since the morning of our talk. She had asked me if I wanted to consult another spiritual advisor, but I didn't.

"You wanted me, Sister?"

"Yes, Sister. You have visitors in the parlour."

I have what? Who could it be? I wasn't expecting anyone, and the only people who could get in would be Father Chuck or Father Frank.

"Barbara Tierney and her brother," Augusta went on.

"But he was just ordained . . ."

"Exactly. He wishes to give you a first blessing. You may have thirty minutes."

"I can?" I said, startled.

"You may, Sister."

"Now?"

"Yes, Sister."

"Well, thank you, Sister."

I rushed out to change my dirty serre tete and put on my Sunday habit. Barbara had been a year ahead of me at Ladyhill. Her sisters and my sisters were friends, and now their brother Tom was a priest. She must have gone to Tom's Ordination and he must have driven her back to the college. A blessing from a newly ordained priest was not to be sneezed at, bless Augusta's little liturgical heart.

It took me only one minute to pull off my cap and veil, wash my face and brush my teeth, put on my best synthetic collar and cap, and pull my serre tete extra tight. Two minutes later, with Vaseline on my eyebrows and my Sunday veil sharply creased, I entered the parlour.

The windows were open. The smell of the pine trees outside helped relieve the stuffiness of the stiff Victorian room. Barbara was her usual bubbly self and ran up, threw her arms around me, and kissed me on the cheek. We had never been that close at Ladyhill, but now that she was in the college we were good friends. Sister Augusta liked Barbara and encouraged our friendship. "Because she thinks Barbara will cross the bridge," Matthew said.

"Maybe, though she never said she wanted to enter."

After Barbara let go of me, Tom stepped toward me and stopped.

"Hi," he said. We both smiled. Then there was total silence. Even Barbara wasn't chattering. I could hear the crickets in the grove, and then the chimes of the tower clock. It was 8 p.m. — recreation was over. The others would be going in to night prayers.

"Don't you want my first blessing?"

"Oh, sorry. Yes, of course I do. Yes, I do, very much. Yes."

I started to kneel down to receive it, but Tom reached out and stopped me.

"No, stand . . ."

I stood there, my eyes level with his new Roman collar, waiting. He raised his hands and extended them in front of me, palms facing each other.

"May the blessing of God,

"Father — "

He raised his right hand higher and began to trace the cross.

"Son — "

He brought his hand down in a slow definite line and then moved it halfway up and finished the cross.

"and the Holy Spirit —"

He brought his palms together, and now his hands were level with my eyes.

During the ordination ceremony they'd been wrapped in white silk, consecrated hands now, sacramental.

"Descend upon you."

He moved toward me and placed his hands on my head. I could feel them through the veil and cap and serre tete, feel them on my hair.

"And remain with you forever."

He rested his hands on my head. I stood very still.

"Well, that's it," Barbara said. "That's worth more than a thousand Hail Mary's."

Her laugh broke the silence in the parlour, and then we all were laughing. The party after Tom's first Mass was great, they said. The Tierney girls sang show tunes for everybody and their mother cried. Tom gave me one of his ordination holy cards. An abstract design in blues and greens represented living water. The quote was from St. Paul.

"Yes, to me this grace was given," I read aloud, "to announce the good news of the unfathomable riches of Christ. And to enlighten all men as to what is the wonderful plan of God."

"Nice."

"Yeah, I think that says it," he said.

Then Barbara said she was tired and wanted to get to the dorm. "I'll walk back with you," I said.

"Can you?" Barbara knew enough of the rules to be surprised. "Yes," I said. "I can." I needed to prolong the visit.

We walked through the quiet campus to Moureau Hall, Barbara paused at the entrance. "Can you . . .?"

"No, I'd better go back."

"I'll walk you," said Tom.

"Oh, she's not allowed to," Barbara began.

"Thanks Tom," I said, "That would be nice."

"OK." Barbara shrugged. "See you back here, Tom."

She went inside. We started back toward the convent. I could still feel Tom's blessing, his hands on my head. We crossed the bridge. So dark and still on this side. I glanced sideways at Tom. For once I didn't want to break the silence that enclosed us. This wasn't 'not talking', it was . . . Well it was . . . I'd better say something, I decided.

"Beautiful night," I said.

"No moon, too bad."

"Nice stars though."

A floodlight shone on the statue of the Immaculate Conception in front of the Church. We walked toward it. At the massive doorway, Tom stopped and tilted his head back to look at the rose window.

"Looks like the churches in Paris," he said.

"Our order started in France," I said. "You've been to Paris?"

"Yeah, four years ago. For the summer..."

"Fun?"

"Fantastic."

"I'd love to go," I said.

"Hope you do."

214

"Tom, did you see the movie *Becket* — you know, Peter O'Toole and Richard Burton?"

"Yeah, I saw it."

"Did you like it?"

"Sure. What made you think . . . Oh, you were thinking of the scenes in France. Yeah, those were *good.*" He stepped back to take in the Church. "My new parish has old Gothic buildings. Except it's surrounded by projects and ratty apartments. The ghetto — it's going to be great. What an apostolate."

He was full of enthusiasm. There was an active civil rights group in his parish already and he had a lot of ideas about how to make the liturgy more meaningful. And the school — he'd start a teen club and a basketball team. That's it, that's what I want too, I thought — the apostolate, the struggle for justice, civil rights. If I can just get out there . . .

'I carry the honor of God . . . '. Thomas. Father Thomas. I wish I were as sure as you are.

We reached the back of the Juniorate. 9:30, the door would be locked. I reached behind my back and jiggled the ground floor window. Open. Good. Thank you, Nicole.

"Well, goodbye, Tom." I wasn't going to climb in while he was standing there.

"I'll write and let you know how it goes," he said.

"Great." My throat was dry. I tried to swallow. "Good luck — I'll . . . we'll be praying for you."

I waved until he was out of sight. Then I tucked my skirts up, found a toehold in the bottom brick, and climbed through the window. I tiptoed upstairs holding my breath as I passed Augusta's door. I joined the last stragglers, who were still getting ready for bed. That's where it all comes together, I thought — in the apostolate. If I see the body tonight I'll just remember standing in the parlour looking at Tom's collar. Oh, who was I kidding? I'll probably never see Tom again. I'll be assigned to some little town or a high school in a suburb and he'll be too busy fighting real battles to think of me.

The next day I felt as draggy as ever. I didn't tell Augusta I'd been late and she didn't ask. In fact, she was very pleasant to me, smiling when we passed in the hall. The next Saturday afternoon, she called me up to the front of the line during our walk. Would I like to take a group into town tomorrow for an experimental folk Mass at St. Joseph's Parish?

Sister Mary Matilda, the principal, wanted some singers in the congregation so the liturgy would go well. Their conservative pastor was predicting disaster.

"Sure," I said. "Matthew could play the guitar. I'll get Nicole, Ann Phyllis, Gabriel, and Mary Rose."

The Mass began at 5:30 p.m., another innovation. The Church was crowded and with us to pep it up, the singing went pretty well, once the congregation adjusted to singing out in the Church. Catholics weren't accustomed to participating and usually did it in the same tinny tones they had learned as children. But Matthew got everyone going. Nice to be at a parish Mass again with a mix of people. There were babies, teenagers whispering in the back, young couples, old people. At the kiss of peace I turned around and shook hands with an elderly man, a four-year-old boy and his mother. I noticed a man was waving at me from the back. Rabbi Bloom — now what was he doing here?

They were waiting on the church steps after Mass.

"Rabbi — Mrs. Bloom — how great that you're here."

"Sister, Sister," he said. "How nice to see you. A lovely service. Quite a change from the Latin and chanting. Very interesting. Where are the other girls?" He saw the knot of nuns waiting over to the side. "Come over, come over, girls. Meet my sons."

Rabbi Bloom did not allow reluctance. Also, he had somehow become the host of the guitar mass, and was now introducing all of us to his wife Ruth and his sons Jonathan, Alexander and David. The two older boys, aged 13 and 11, kept their poise as habits clustered around them. But David was only five, and had a thousand blunt questions. "What do you wear under those? Do you have hair? Did you have a mother?"

The Rabbi answered David's questions. "None of your business, none of your business, and yes." He shrugged his shoulders and rolled his eyes. We were all giggling as the last of the St. Joseph's parishioners left. A few looked over at us, but didn't smile.

"Now," said the Rabbi, "we're all going to my house."

That stopped the laughing. We were not allowed to go into other people's houses. We couldn't go into our own family's house. In the course of apostolic duties we could visit the sick and the needy. But we could not visit the well and the happy. The Blooms were definitely out.

"No, I'm sorry. We have to go back. We . . ."

But the Rabbi held up his hand.

"Please. You're coming over. It's a class assignment. I want to show you all my Chagall and Ben Shan. And for those of you not in my class, it's a pre-assignment because some day you'll surely enroll."

"But, Rabbi, see, we're not allowed to . . . " I was really embarrassed. All he wanted to do was be hospitable.

217

"Not allowed? Why, Sister Mary Anna and Sister Augusta were at our house just last Wednesday. I'll speak to Sister Augusta if there is any problem."

Oh, sure, I thought. She'll be very nice to you and make us feel like criminals.

But she wouldn't be looking for us until at least 7 p.m. Maybe we could just stop by — it would be ecumenical. He did say class assignment. There was no sit-down supper on Sunday or recreation, so we wouldn't be missed . . .

As I was going through all of this in my mind, Mrs. Bloom drew me aside. "It's his birthday, Sister. He wants you all to come and celebrate it with us. In New York we always had a lot of people for his birthday. Here the people are more, well, formal and . . . "

The Rabbi, in the meantime, was heaping promises on the others. "Alexander will play the violin and Jonathan the piano, and David sings . . . "

I looked over at Matthew, and she shrugged her shoulders. I knew Mary Rose and Nicole wanted to go, I thought, and if Matthew has no objections . . Gabriel and Ann Phyllis would enjoy it and I . . . I just couldn't say no again.

"We'd love to come, Rabbi. Thank you for asking us."

Mrs. Bloom got in the car with us, to show the way. In order to drive I had to pull up my skirt. I watched her take in my knee socks, home made culotte slip and black penny loafers. She smiled, but she didn't say anything. Instead she launched into a description of how they found their house and its good and bad points. Just as if I were a regular person.

Their house was on a street with State university fraternity and sorority houses. A party was going on at the lawn of one. Every Junior sister turned for a moment to watch a group of college boys throwing frisbees with one hand and holding cans of beer with the other.

The Blooms' house was old and comfortable. Paintings, not prints, not reproductions, but real paintings covered the walls. Most of them were modern and abstract, but two representational pieces were already familiar to me. Rabbi Bloom had described them to us in class. One was a painting and one a pencil sketch. Both were portraits. The painting was of a Hasidic boy living in Israel. He had apple cheeks and was whistling. The painter, an Israeli artist, had given him great vitality. Rabbi Bloom had found the pencil sketch in an ash can in Brooklyn. This sad-eyed boy lived in the Warsaw ghetto at the turn of the century. He didn't whistle. He studied and was quiet and afraid. He was the Israeli boy's grandfather.

I guess I had been standing before the pictures for a noticeable amount of time, because the Rabbi came over.

"You remember the story, Sister?"

"Yes," I said . . . 'I carry the honour of God'.

"I'm afraid the children are going to insist on playing," Mrs. Bloom said. "They're so excited to have this many sisters in the house."

"Ruth, wait. First, how about a drink, Sisters? Scotch, bourbon, cherry brandy, wine. We have altar wine." The Rabbi was on his feet, pulling bottles out of a buffet in the dining room that adjoined the living room.

"Mark," said Mrs. Bloom, "I don't think the sisters drink."

"No, of course not. And they shouldn't drink. Not in public, but this is private. The law is set up so the sisters will not give scandal by drinking. But here there is no one to give scandal to, so therefore the law does not . . . "

Mrs. Bloom interrupted. "Sisters, would you like a coke, Seven-up, fruit juice?"

"No, thank you," we chorused.

"You see, Ruth. They would prefer a drink. Now we have Kahlua and creme de menthe and . . ."

Well, between the two of them they listed everything in the bar and in the kitchen. I kept saying, "No," but I just couldn't tell them that we were not allowed to eat in front of people. It seemed too ridiculous. She brought out a box of home-made fudge and said, "Eat it — a favour. Passover is coming!" I shook my head. "Would you like to take it home?" Finally manners pushed away scruples. I mean, there is such a thing as insulting people by refusing.

"Thank you. I'd love to have a piece."

Pretty soon we were all chomping on the fudge, asking who made it and how, and happily forgetting that we were collectively breaking seven major rules. Then Jonathan played piano and Alexander played the violin and David sang and danced. The Blooms kept apologising, but for us it was wonderful. We all came from big families and had brothers and sisters and cousins who performed at family parties. It was home. I was sitting between the Rabbi and Mrs. Bloom, and during a pause in the entertainment we started talking about movies. The Rabbi had shown *The Shop on Main Street* in class for us, and he said that for him, seeing that story about the destruction of the Jews of one village somehow made the Holocaust more real.

"Millions. How can the human brain comprehend the murder of millions? It goes beyond our powers of imagination. But one child, one two-year-old boy half asleep in his mother's arms, being carried into a gas chamber, that we can picture, that brings home the horror." We sat silent. "But enough — this isn't a time for sad thoughts. But film is very powerful, very powerful."

"Did you see *Becket*?" I asked.

"*Becket, Becket*, yes I saw *Becket*. A silly story — Hollywood cannot deal with religious subjects. They over-simplify."

"But the performances, Mark," Mrs. Bloom said. "Peter O'Toole was brilliant."

"Oh, brilliant. What's brilliant? So he's a great actor. But the story, they made it a fairytale."

"But Rabbi," I said, "Becket's conflict was real. He had to choose God or man. He . . ."

"Sister," the Rabbi said, "in our religion God commands us to choose life. We don't set up these false dichotomies between God and man. The struggle in *Becket* was political, between two great powers, church and state, over who was going to control whom. To drag in spiritual significance to disguise the truth of the struggle is to misrepresent its true nature. You see, Sister, I don't believe acquisition and materialistic empire building should be a part of religion. I think . . . "

"Relax, Mark. This is one of his favourite topics, Sister."

"Don't stop me, Ruth. I'm not referring to Catholicism only, even in Judaism it can happen. We have no Pope or hierarchy, but we do have buildings, plants — what a horrendous word — and a congregation can become so enamoured of itself as an institution, it forgets its mission."

"And what is that mission, Rabbi?" I asked.

"Sister, I think it is best said in the Book of Micah: 'You have been told, O Man, what the Lord requires of thee —

Only to do justly, to love mercy, and to walk humbly with your God.' "

"Yes," I said, "that is it, isn't it?"

"I think the sisters want to get back now." Ruth had noticed the other nuns were getting nervous. Not Nicole, she had moved over on the couch with us and had taken in every one of the Rabbi's words. The others had been playing with the kids, but it was late, and they had started to think of possible consequences. In a flurry of handshakes and goodbyes, we were off.

My stomach sank slightly as I got into the car. I really didn't know what the reaction of the Juniorate would be. At first it looked like everything would work out. Augusta hadn't come down to dinner and had retired early, so unless someone got carried away by the spirit of fraternal correction and told on us, we were alright. In a way I didn't care. I knew I would sleep tonight and that the body wouldn't be there. Choose life — simple.

"I don't care if Augusta finds out," I told Nicole. "It was worth it."

11

EXAMINATION OF CONSCIENCE

When the 5:15 a.m. bell sounded, I got up eagerly. In the apostolate there would be lots of evenings like last night's, with students, their parents, community leaders, lay faculty, priests. Maybe Father Tom will invite me to Mass at his parish. I needed to do useful things for real people. In one week I'll get my obedience, I thought, then I can really start planning. Five years in one place is just naturally depressing.

We sang one of my favourite psalms during Communion.

> *Happy those whose strength you are! Their hearts are set upon the pilgrimage. When they pass through the arid valley, they make a spring of it.*

I hummed to myself as we walked to breakfast and then sang aloud while I cleaned the bathtubs.

As I settled down in the study hall for instructions, I resolved to listen to Augusta with an open mind. She was an intellectual and a scholar with 100 twenty and twenty-one year olds looking to her for emotional and spiritual guidance. Why not appreciate her for her brilliance? There, listen she's quoting Emily Dickinson. Instructions ended. Augusta had just reached the study hall door when she turned.

"Will the sisters who attended Mass at St. Joseph's Church last night assemble in my office immediately."

My stomach knotted. I knew that tone. That's how my grade school principal said, "Will the girl who came to school out of uniform please see me," and how Sister Carlotta at Ladyhill announced, "Will the girl or girls who placed a sign on the school library door announcing, incorrectly, that it would be closed for George Washington's birthday, please report to my office immediately," and my mother asked, "What time did you get home last night?" It was trouble.

The six of us lined up in two rows in front of Augusta's desk and waited. I tried to catch Matthew's eyes, but her head was bowed and her eyes focused on the polished wooden floor. Behind her Ann Phyllis shifted her weight from one foot to the other, making the floor creak with each move. Gabriel fiddled with her chaplet. Mary Rose had her eyes closed, and her hands hung slack at her sides. Only Nicole stood naturally. She was looking at the reproduction of Byzantine texts that hung on Augusta's wall. I started to pick at my fingernails.

Augusta sat down at her desk and put the binder that held her instruction notes into her right hand drawer. She looked up at us and smiled slightly. "Good morning, Sisters."

"Good morning, Sister." Every head but Matthew's came up. Our serge habit skirts made a sighing sound as the bodies within them relaxed a little. It might not be as bad as we thought. But it was.

"Sisters," she said, "you betrayed the trust I placed in you." She said this in quiet, modulated tones. "You had permission to go to St. Joseph's Church in town, to assist in the singing at their evening Mass, and to return to campus. Instead, you took it upon yourselves to visit a home — which we do not do — to eat and drink in that home — which we do not do — and to return the car many hours after it was expected. There can be no possible excuse or explanation for this," she concluded.

No one said anything. Nicole looked at me. I took a half step forward.

"Excuse me, Sister, perhaps you should speak directly to me. I was driving, and I accepted the Rabbi's invitation."

Silence followed this, then Matthew spoke up.

"Sister Augusta, I feel we all share responsibility."

Thanks, Matthew.

"After all, we could have refused to go with Maura and pointed out her error in the spirit of fraternal correction. We..."

Nicole interrupted her. "Sister Augusta, this whole discussion is absolutely senseless," she said, looking through her rimless glasses at Augusta. "We all wanted to go to the Rabbi's house. We went. We had a good time. The fact that Maura was driving is just coincidental. We all wanted to, and we all enjoyed it."

Augusta listened intently. I moved close to her desk.

"And Sister," I said. "there was absolutely nothing wrong in what we did. If Sister Matthew feels she was coerced," I glanced over at Matthew, "well, I'm sorry. But as Nicole said, we had a very nice time with very nice people."

Now Matthew moved. She took my elbow and looked at me with great earnestness.

"No, Maura, I didn't tell her that anything bad happened. I just said that we went and . . ."

I pulled my elbow away and whirled on her, my chaplet swinging.

"You had to tell, didn't you? Couldn't just enjoy it and leave well enough alone. You . . ."

"Sister Maura. Please." The force of Augusta's voice pushed me back. "Sister Matthew is not to be criticised for having a more informed conscience than you do."

"Sister Augusta, are you trying to say we did something wrong or sinful in going to the Rabbi's?"

"No, Sister," Augusta's tone dropped back to reasoned persuasion, "it was not wrong, but you should not have done it. Do you understand?"

"No."

"Sister, there are many things that Holy Rule forbids that are not wrong per se, but which we simply do not do. Now with a little thought I think you will be able to see the distinction and understand . . ."

"Sister, I do not want to think up some way to see the distinction or to understand." My voice sounded loud and forceful. God damn it. Some things were just true. "It was right to visit the Blooms and I'm glad I did." I had no more to say to her. "May I be excused, Sister?" I didn't even pretend to wait for her nod. I turned on my heel and stomped out the door as loudly as I could with soft rubber heels. Outside in the hall I paused. I was late for Shakespeare class. Forget it. I'm too mad to go.

Someone touched me on the shoulder. It was Nicole.

"Let's get out of here for a while. Go for a walk in the orchard or something," I said.

"OK."

We started down the wide middle stairs. I banged my chaplet against each rung of the banister. We had just opened the side door when I heard someone running up to us.

"Maura, Nicole, wait a minute!" It was Matthew.

Nicole moved toward the open door, but I stopped.

"Don't be mad, Maura," Matthew panted. "It was just that, well, I couldn't sleep last night. It bothered my conscience. And then all during meditation and Mass I . . .we broke the rules . . . I had to tell her, I . . ."

I looked into her face. What had happened to Nancy Thurler? Where was the girl with a D.A. haircut who destroyed ugly art, sang protest songs and talked back?

"Oh, Matthew", I said. "For Christ's sake, relax, forget it. You had to do it. Alright."

Now Matthew smiled. "I'm glad you realise that I did it for all of us. We learned. And now if a similar situation arose, I'd . . ."

"Matthew," Nicole said, "look at me. You wanted to go to the Rabbi's too. And you enjoyed it."

"Well, at the time but afterwards I . . ."

I couldn't bear it anymore. "Look, if we stand here talking, she's going to hear us and come down yelling. We were going for a walk in the orchard. Do you want to come, Matthew?"

"You got permission?" she asked, surprised.

"No," I said, "I did not get permission, nor am I interpreting permission, or telling on myself afterward."

"We're simply going for a walk in the orchard," said Nicole, and moved out the open door. "Are you coming, Sister Matthew?"

"Oh, Maura. I can't. I just can't."

"OK."

I left Matthew standing there and walked out to join Nicole.

"She's just..." I started, then stopped. There didn't seem to be any point. I was furious — but felt good too. I had told Augusta what I felt directly and truly, had refused to be infected by Matthew's scruples, and now I was going for a walk in the orchard with a friend. So sue me.

"Look at those colours," I said to Nicole. "I bet Tokyo has nothing on our cherry blossoms."

So that was it — my revolt. Augusta never mentioned that evening again but I'd turned a corner. I was going to make my own decisions from now on. I was a professed Sister of the Redemption. I was twenty-two years old — women my age were mothers. Men my age were fighting in Vietnam — enough of this nonsense. Choose life! I was going to, whether the rules liked it or not.

One week later I got my obedience. Redemption High School on the West side of Chicago, the heart of the ghetto. Exactly what I wanted. I was exultant. This confirmed it. There was a plan for me — a providence shaping my life. Nobody, not Augusta, not Matthew, not Reverend Mother herself could get in the way. I had been called. I had a vocation and now I had my mission — Redemption High School. Martin Luther King had preached in a Baptist Church directly across the street!

I finished my thesis with a flourish, ending with the last words of *Portrait of the Artist*.

'Welcome, O life! I go to encounter for the millionth time the reality of experience and to forge in the smithy of my soul the uncreated conscience of my race.'

Please welcome me, Redemption, 'cause here I come.

12

THE APOSTOLATE

A convoy of buses waited in front of the Motherhouse on August 16, departure day. Of course the weather was perfect. The humidity fell below 120% for the first time all summer. The grove was sun dappled, birds sang their hearts out and I could not wait to get away from all this bucolic bliss. I stood near my bus and sniffed exhaust fumes. It seemed to bring the city closer. Three hours, I would be there in only three hours.

A massive leavetaking was happening around me. Most of these 1,000 nuns would not see each other for a year. A buzz of conversation came from the milling group. Figures darted from bus to bus.

"Where's Mary Kathleen, I've got her book."

"Kevin Ann, paging Sister Kevin Ann."

"Oh the summer went too fast! I hate to leave."

"Wait, will you please, driver? I'll be right back. Forgot something."

This last was from a sister on my bus. Wait??? I'd been ready to go since 6 a.m., I'd said goodbye to Nicole and the junior sisters who were staying. There'd been a band going away party last night, but no real sadness. Oh, we'd miss each other but after five years of getting ready, this was finally it. Mission, the apostolate. Each of us could see herself standing in front of shiny-faced children in an artfully decorated classroom. Or bringing joy and cheer to a close-knit group of dedicated sisters. We also pictured the shopping trips, visits to parishioners with swimming pools and late night TV sessions we'd heard about on mission. But those were fringe benefits. It was truly the desire to get out there and serve God's people that propelled us on to those buses with hardly a backward glance. Except I'd had a very strange conversation with Mrs. Bloom yesterday. She'd driven out alone to say goodbye but it was obvious she wanted to do more than wish me luck.

"I've been a Rabbi's wife for fourteen years. Mark's had three congregations and in each place there's been, well, some resistance from certain people. And well, I . . . " She seemed to be stuck.

"Mrs. Bloom, I know the apostolate won't be easy. And I know Redemption is in a rough area but I'm willing to work hard to win over my students . . . "

"It's not your students I'm talking about, Sister."

"Oh. You mean all the prejudice. But see that's why Chicago's the perfect place for the Civil Rights movement to fight northern racism. And I understand the city. Political pressure works there and if the Church really gets behind the movement and pushes, well . . . "

Mrs. Bloom touched my arm. "OK, I see you've got it figured out. So I'll just give you a hug and say goodbye."

"Love to Rabbi and the boys. If you ever get to Chicago . . ."

I hope she's not another one worried about my safety, I thought, as the nuns finally started filing into all the buses. A lot of the older nuns who'd planned to finish out their lives at Redemption had come home because they were convinced a Mau Mau-type attack would wipe out the convent at any moment. I knew, because they had sought me out to tell me.

"Not our girls," they always began. "Many of them come from lovely coloured families, doctors, lawyers. But the neighbourhood, Sister! The dirt, the noise. One can just imagine . . . " And I'm sure one did.

At last, I could see the nun we were waiting for running up the road. Good. I got on the bus.

Our caravan drove through the wrought iron gates and out onto the highway. About half of the buses turned south to head for Indianapolis or Evansville and all the tiny Indiana towns in between. Well, there goes Matthew, I thought. I hope mission loosens her up a little. At least she took her guitar. She wanted to leave it as some kind of a mortification. "You're nuts", I said. I'd actually appealed to Augusta, who told her to bring it along. "Music is a gift, Sister," she'd told Matthew.

Augusta and I had maintained a polite truce throughout the summer. Of course, I'd been at the Floodville Bible school most of the time. I must say she'd been pretty good about all the flak we got over the float in the 4th of July parade. Alright, it was only an old pickup truck, but the kids had worked hard covering it with red, white and blue crepe paper. I thought it looked great and the kids were so cute, all bunched together in the truck waving their flags and hollering at the crowd. Except the townspeople went in more for riders on palominos with polished hooves and floral arrangements from the garden club mounted on tractor beds. The mayor called Mother to complain but Augusta hadn't turned a hair — figuratively speaking.

You could never predict her reaction.

"Hi, Maura," the nun next to me said.

She was a few years older and I knew her — but from where? An employment? Class — yes — last summer. Ann Stephen, Mary Stephen, Marie . . . She kept smiling. Oh please don't say, "I bet you don't remember me."

"I bet you don't remember me."

"Of course I do — Catholic Victorian Writers last summer — Stev — Stephanie Marie! So you're going to Chicago?"

Obviously.

"Yes," she said. "St. Jude's. I'll be right near you. Of course Redemption isn't what it was!"

How did she know where I was going?

"It used to be a plum assignment," she went on, "but now . . . "

"I'm happy I'm going to Redemption. It's just what I wanted. I think the Civil Rights Movement is the most important . . . "

"Whoa — I agree with you. I'm happy at St. Jude's. The kids are great. It's just . . . Well, at least you've got Grace."

We made the ritual rest stop at Kentland. Stephanie shared her lunch with me. I'd got an envelope with $1.50 in it like everyone else but Nicole and I had spent it in the college vending machines.

"You have really become a daredevil," she had laughed.

We drank our Pepsis and ate the candy bars in the orchard on the last day of retreat. "The Sabbath was made for man, not man for the Sabbath," I told her. "And nobody will see us out here."

Finally, finally I saw the sign. "Welcome to Chicago, Richard J. Daley, Mayor."

Chicago, Chicago, that toddlin' town I was singing before I knew it. *Chicago, Chicago, I'll show you around, I love it.* Stephanie and some of the younger nuns joined in. The older ones smiled benignly at us. *Bet your bottom dollar you'll lose the blues in Chicago, Chicago.* There it was: the skyline. The John Hancock Center, which I had never seen, dominated the old familiar buildings and made a huge black X against the sky.

The bus turned on to the Eisenhower Expressway. We joined the stream of traffic going under the post office. Uncle James loved to tell the story of how city planners came to Daley and pointed out that his new expressway was blocked by the main post office. "Go through it," he'd said. They had. The cars moved steadily. Traffic was already heavy as commuters rushed from the loop to their homes in the western suburbs. The neighbourhoods bordering the expressway were to be avoided at all costs. Everyone had a terrifying story about a friend forced off the Eisenhower by car problems. While no one claimed any actual murders occurred, the mere picture of a white suburbanite alone in the urban jungle of Homan Avenue or Jackson Boulevard or West Madison Street raised communal hackles. Ironically, most of the people driving this corridor grew up on this same West Side and loved to reminisce about picnics in Garfield Park or going to the show on Madison.

We turned off onto Homan. This was it. I pressed my face against the window. Knots of men stood talking on the corners. Little kids ran up and down, loosely attached to slow-walking mothers. Every woman carried something, groceries, laundry, a baby, two babies, something. It all seemed a blur of motion. Bright coloured summer shirts against brown arms; long dark legs in shorts; faces under hats and headscarves. I opened my window a crack, music

233

rushed in. I couldn't hear separate melodies or words, but a deep insistent beat came from Enda's Soul Food Kitchen or the Six Brothers Record and Novelty Shop. I noticed that some storefronts like the Cathedral of Eternal Truth had hand-lettered wooden signs. Others like King Williams Barbecue had fancy painted letters on plate glass. All the buildings were two storeys, dilapidated and seemed to lean against each other for support. The bus stopped at a light. A man in a patterned smock-like top with hair that sprang straight out from his head looked up at the bus. His eyes caught mine. "Buga, Buga," he shouted, waving his arms. I sat back in my seat and closed my window. This is not a zoo, I told myself.

"First time you've ever been in this neighbourhood, I'll bet," Stephanie Marie said.

"Not exactly, I am from Chicago and I . . . "

"I know," she said. "And you've driven through with the doors locked. I'm from Indiana."

"Well," I said, "my mother grew up in Austin just west of here. She went to tea dances at that hotel, the Graymere." The grey brick building still rose elegantly from the street higher than its neighbours, but the paint on the window frames was peeling and some panes were broken.

"Yeah." Stephanie Marie was not impressed. "Not much tea dancing there now. That's where the prostitutes live . . . and work."

"Oh."

The bus had turned onto a quiet tree-lined boulevard. We had gone through the looking glass. On one side of the street was Garfield Park, twenty-five acres of green grass and ornamental bushes. I glimpsed stone lions and columns in the distance. I knew there was a conservatory and the fanciest park field house in the city — The Golden Dome. The Chicago Park District was a sovereign state within city government and maintained its property. How else to justify the hundreds of patronage jobs and thousands of hours of overtime?

The bus slowed in front of six blacktop basketball courts. They were jammed. Boys swarmed around each hoop. They'd shoot, dribble, push each other and run to the opposite basket, all in less than ten seconds. The driver made an easy U-turn in the wide avenue and stopped. There it was. Five storeys of golden yellow brick and shiny windows that covered an entire city block. Gothic arches crowned every door and window. A stone scroll, carved with ornate letters, proclaimed, 'Redemption High School' over the main entrance. The convent attached to the school had stained glass windows along the ground floor.

I'm sure I said goodbye to Stephanie Marie, and the bus driver must have helped me down with my suitcase and trunk, but the bus seemed to just vanish. I was alone in front of the wood and iron door. A block away, children played double-dutch and in the park the games continued; but right here where I stood was very quiet.

Then the door burst open. "Welcome, Sister Maura. Welcome to Redemption. I'm Sister Grace." If there is a hero in this story, here she is, Sister Grace, tall and athletic, expansive in her movements yet neat and precise too. She had what my great-aunt called 'the map of Ireland' on her face — but this was no sweet nun with a musical brogue. This was a girl from Chicago, a Westsider who'd made her way up the rungs of authority in the order and never made an enemy. Those who might privately mutter about Grace's worldliness could never resist her in person. Charm's too lightweight a word. She just loved everyone –

unsentimentally, even impersonally, but love it was and everyone knew it. She would save my sanity and perhaps my life.

Right now she just wanted to get my trunk inside and keep her chocolate chip cookies from burning. She patted me vigorously on the back. Chicago politician blood here, I guessed. "I'll take this," she said, grabbing my suitcase. "We'll carry the trunk together. So, good trip? Where'd you stop? Burger Palace or Grandma's Kitchen?"

"Burger Palace, I think."

"Then you'll be hungry. I just put a batch of chocolate chip cookies into the oven."

I tried to open the door with my free hand, but her hip was faster and we half tumbled into the small dark vestibule. The doors shut, leaving the heat behind. It was cool in the hall.

"Do you have air-conditioning?" I asked.

"No, no," she said. "Just thick old-fashioned walls, plus high ceilings, and a breeze from the Park. This building was built in the Twenties. Let's leave this here," she said, dropping my suitcase on to the shiny tiles. "While we get the cookies out." She took off down a long hall, with me trailing behind.

"Recreation room," she said, pointing to her right.

"It's big," I said, glancing into the large dark room.

"Twenty-two of us," she said. She switched on the light. I saw easy chairs and a few couches.

"I robbed the parlours," she said.

I laughed. The visitor parlours were the only really comfortable rooms in any convent. And they were reserved for seculars. But though recreation rooms might be sparse there was no stinting on the kitchen — always the latest ovens, freezers and stoves. Redemption was no exception.

"It's not just the army that travels on its stomach," Grace said as she gestured at the appliances and pulled out the tray of cookies.

"Umm," I said. "They look good."

"Take one," she said. "They're best when the chocolate's hot and melting."

"Great," I said.

"My mother's recipe," she explained. Grace poured us each a cup of coffee and pulled two kitchen stools up to the counter.

"She was a terrific cook. Had to be. My father was a fireman. He'd bring the entire engine company home for dinner at the drop of a hat. She'd feed them Irish chop suey. And baking powder biscuits. We lived just west of here. Near Humboldt Park. I'll tell you a secret," she said, flipping me a cookie with her spatula.

"When we prayed in the first grade, 'Jesus Meek and Humble of Heart', I thought Sister was saying, 'Jesus meet me in Humboldt Park.' And every afternoon on the way home, I'd look for him. I went to high school right here. Have another cookie."

This is my superior, I thought. I have really lucked out!

"Excuse me, Sister Grace." Another nun stood in the doorway, her hands clasped under her cape. "I tried to find you in your office, but . . . " She let the sentence hang.

"Sister Maura," Grace said, "I would like you to meet your principal, Sister Alberta."

Sister Alberta kept her hands under her cape and nodded at me. Alberta was short and dumpy, but aggressively well-groomed. I could tell that both her collar and cape were the latest in synthetic material and they were too white to be her only pair. I bet she has five sets, I thought. And washes them in Wisk every day. Junior sisters had one synthetic set saved for only the most solemn occasions, and Wisk was passed out in thimblefuls once a month.

"Sister Alberta went to Redemption too — much after me, of course."

"Not that much, Sister," Sister Alberta said. "Certainly long before . . . "

"I'm trying to give you a compliment, tell her that you're younger than I am," Grace laughed. Alberta's lips hardened in what I supposed was a smile. "Yes," she said. "I did come after you. But the neighbourhood was still beautiful then." Alberta's right hand came up to smooth her serre tete. I caught a glimpse of polish on her short stubby nails. She must buff them; I thought, she wouldn't dare use polish. God, she must have to pull her serre tete tight, I thought as I watched her smooth away a tiny wrinkle on the neck. Her bone structure's all wrong; her jaw's too wide and her forehead's too narrow. It's got to gap, unless she wraps it like a tourniquet. Her skin was mottled. Patches of bright red alternated with blotches of maroon. She'll burst a blood vessel one day, I thought. Even her eyes seemed to pop out.

"Could we meet in thirty minutes, Sister?" she asked Grace.

"Sure," Grace said, adding a last cookie to the pile. Alberta departed. We had not exchanged one word.

"Come on, Maura." Grace had dropped the 'Sister' already. "I want to show you your room." We pulled my things into a small elevator and she pushed number five. "This elevator," she said, "is the reason we have so many elderly sisters. They have the rooms on the park, so you won't have much of a view, Maura, still, I found a cute rocking chair in the attic, and gave you a bed lamp in case you like to read in bed."

Read in bed? And a rocking chair . . . my own room . . .?

Grace didn't even lower her voice as we stepped out on to the sleeping floor. We dragged my trunk and suitcase into a small room at the end of the hall. "Sister Carita in the art room will give you some prints to make the room cosier," Grace said.

Cosy? This was too good to be true.

"See you at dinner, Maura," Grace said. "No formal prayers today. Say your office on the roof, if you'd like. Just don't be late for dinner. We're having a wonderful meal. I should know, I'm cooking."

My room, I thought. My own room. I opened the window. Nothing to see except the convent courtyard, but music floated up from somewhere driven by that same steady beat. Dunh-dadadada, da da. This came, not from the street, but from the door. I jumped up. Who could it be? Nuns knocked, they didn't rap frivolously. I opened the door to a tall, lanky young nun whose rimless glasses and Grant Wood face reminded me of pioneer women and covered wagons.

"Hi," she said, "I'm Marie Nicholas. Welcome to the ghetto."

"Hi. I'm Maura."

Marie Nicholas. I knew that name: she had published poems and stories in the college literary magazine during her last two years in the Juniorate — good, spare, complicated stories.

"Come on in," I said.

She walked in and sat down in my rocker and started to rock. It completed my pioneer picture of her. From the open window we heard chimes.

"That signal— Is it really . . . ?"

"Used by drug sellers to call their clients to come and get their heroin? No — it's the Mr. Frostee truck."

I started laughing. " Sister Anselm in the infirmary told me about the dealers — and I believed her!"

"Sister Rita told me when I arrived here last week, and I believed her, too. But then she said we were being watched and she mentioned roof-top telescopes!"

"Sister Anselm had the same theory!"

"Well, I know a way we can test it," she said, getting up. "Come on."

I followed her out to the hall into the old elevator that creaked its way up to the top floor. Marie Nicholas pulled back the gate. We faced a large steel plated door.

"Watch this," she said and pushed it open. We were in a garden. Pots of geraniums, lawn chairs, and a long steel couch swing transformed Redemption's big roof into our own secret garden.

"This is great," I said.

But Marie Nicholas had walked straight over to the yellow brick wall which rimmed the roof. The wall was about chest high, and the two of us leaned against it, propping our elbows on the top. There, five storeys below us, was the West Side. We watched the jammed-together energy of the neighbourhood break through in patches of movement where cars or kids rushed down the streets, and then retreated into still knots of people sitting on stoops, groups standing on the corners. The West Side — Chicago always said the words in hushed tones. I could see the

Eisenhower Expressway one half mile to the south. The evening rush hour was at its height, and all six west-bound lanes were bumper to bumper. But thanks to Chicago's city plan, the white drivers were safe from the surrounding jungle, their only contact with it the names on the exit signs: Western, California, Homan, Pulaski — almost out, and then Austin Boulevard, a beginning sigh of relief, and Oak Park Avenue, a total exhalation of breath, and then River Forest, Elmwood Park, La Grange, the suburbs, thank God. Let the blacks have the West Side of the city. It's a wreck anyway. We've got the suburbs and Eisenhower Expressway to whisk us safely out here.

But Marie Nicholas was talking to me. "Over there, on Jackson Boulevard, Martin Luther King held a big rally," she said. "Just a few weeks ago too. A shame we missed it, but SCLC has their headquarters there and maybe he'll come back."

"I hope, I hope," I said. "Maybe he'll come and speak to the students."

"Speak here?" Marie Nicholas looked at me quizzically. "Not with Alberta as principal."

"But Sister Grace would ask him."

"Sure," she said, "and serve him the best meal of his life. But Alberta's in full charge of the school, and she's been principal for ten years. Grace's just starting as superior of the Convent."

"But isn't she over Alberta?" I said.

Marie Nicholas turned her palm up and down, her way of saying yes and no at the same time. It wasn't only her stories that were spare and allusive.

"Well, I'm just going to concentrate on my students. I'm not going to worry about the nuns. This is what I came for!"

I pointed out beyond the wall. "And I can't wait to get into the middle of it. We're so lucky."

Marie Nicholas just nodded. We stood there looking out for a few more minutes, then from inside we heard a bell.

"Supper," I said.

"Dinner," she said. "The main meal is at night when you're on mission."

On mission. I was on mission at Redemption High School on the West Side of Chicago — at last.

The next morning after prayers, Mass and breakfast, I found my way into the great main hall of the school. My footsteps — though muffled by my orthodox soft rubber heels — sounded loud on the gleaming terrazzo floor, the sound bouncing up to the ornate moulding that rimmed the ceilings. Polished wooden doors opened off the hall into classrooms. Behind one door I could hear sounds of activity.

Somebody's getting her classroom ready. Could I go in and say hello, I wondered, or would that be breaking silence? The nuns had been nice last night at dinner and on the roof, but I'd better not chance offending anyone. The hall clock said 9:00. There was not a thing I had to do until 12:00. I couldn't remember the last time I had three unbroken hours to myself.

At the end of the hall I found the executive suite. 'Office of the Principal' said the gothic gilt letters, and underneath in small black print, 'Sister Alberta, S.R.' Two doors with frosted glass, one with 'Registrar' and the other 'Secretary to the Principal' written on them, flanked the first. I could hear a typewriter going. I held my chaplet quiet against my side and tiptoed past.

Across from the offices were big double doors. Oh, I thought, the auditorium. I pushed one of the doors open and walked in. It was gigantic. There were at least 1,500 seats here on the first floor and another 500 up above in the balcony. In the dimness I could just barely make out the stage with a heavy red velvet curtain, fringed in gold, draped across it.

I walked closer, guiding myself by the backs of the seats on the centre aisle. The only light came from the space left between the edge of the shades and the sills of the great arched windows along the side. Even that light was muted, because the auditorium was enclosed by the school's courtyard.

I felt my way down to the front and along the railings of an orchestra pit. An orchestra pit! Even the Gregorian Auditorium at the Hills didn't have an orchestra pit. I climbed the three narrow steps on to the stage and edged along next to the curtain until I found the centre opening. I pulled the curtains apart, and particles of dust rose out of the faded folds. I coughed and waved the dust away.

Behind the curtains the stage went back twenty feet. God, this stage is bigger than Greg's. There's the curtain rope. I took the hold of the rope and pulled with the smooth hand-over-hand motion Sister Blanche taught me. The curtains parted easily, and the stage lay open. Near the curtain pull was the light box and dimmer boards. I opened the board and looked over the black-handled levers.

There were spotlights in the balcony and the overhead grids, footlights and sidebars. This is a professional theatre, I thought, as I pulled a lever and a splash of light hit the centre of the stage.

I tried a few switches. The other balcony lights flooded the stage, and harsh white circles intersected each other on the floor. Amber and pink gels on those lights, maybe one lavender, I thought, switching on the footlights. Now blue and red light shone up from below and scattered on the brick wall.

I walked into the centre of the stage.

Curtain up, light the lights, we've got nothing to hit but the heights,

Ethel Merman sang in my head.

> *Some people can thrive and bloom*
> *Living life in the living room,*
> *That's okay for some people of one hundred and*
> *five,*
> *But I at least gotta try,*

The spotlight glare made the auditorium disappear. I was alone in the light. I sang the words softly.

> *When I think of all the places I gotta go yet*
> *All the places I gotta play*
> *All the people I gotta met yet*
> *Da da dee da da dee da da dee...*
> *Some people sit on their butts*
> *They got the dreams, yeah, but not the guts.*
> *Well, that's okay for some people*
> *For some humdrum people I suppose*
> *Well, they can stay and rot, but not Rose.*
> *Not Rose, Not me either.*
> *That lucky star I talk about is due*
> *And everything's coming up roses and*
> *lollipops,*
> *Everything's . . .*

I'll fill these seats, fill this stage! I did a little time step and sang aloud.

Everything's coming up bright lights and Santa
  Claus
Everything's coming up roses for me and for
  you...

From the back of the auditorium I heard applause. Oh, no. All my muscles tightened, and I stood paralyzed in the light. One of the Novitiate Sisters had complained because I led a bunny hop. She said I did "bizarre things" at recreation. This is an even worse offence! If that's Alberta it's all over. I'll . . .

But it was Grace. Grace calling my name and clapping. "Not much of a voice, but you have a lot of energy and know the words." She smiled at me.

My shoulders relaxed. "That's my curse. I know all the words but can't carry a tune."

Grace came around now and walked up the steps. "Let Sister Joan handle the tunes. Best music teacher in the order."

Sister Joan, she was the tall one with that strange walk — as if she had to hurry her feet to keep up with the forward momentum of her body. I knew she and Grace were band members.

Grace was gazing around the auditorium. She had just left a modern high school in the suburbs with the biggest enrolment of all the order's schools, lots of energetic nuns and gung-ho parents. Here 500 students attended a school designed for 1,000.

"*H.M.S. Pinafore*," said Grace.

"What?" I said, startled.

I polished up the handle of the big front door. That was my song in *H.M.S. Pinafore* on this very stage, Maura. I wasn't much of a singer either, but I was tall and loud —

very loud. Good for the men's parts. Yes, this auditorium was packed that day. Standing room only. I'd like to see it like that again, full of people and music."

"You would?"

"Yes, I would," she replied.

"That's just what I was thinking. We could do wonderful productions here."

Grace looked around. "Of course, that's Sister Alberta's province — the school — but I don't see why not. Always were big plays at Redemption. Made money on them too, and had a lot of fun besides. It's a good way to bring the parents into the school."

"Yes, Sister. A wonderful way."

"Well, plenty of time for that. Have you found your classroom yet?"

"No, not yet, Sister. This is as far as I've gotten."

"Go up and look it over. Lots of cleaning to do. It's next to Marie Nicholas. She'll help you out."

"Thank you, Sister."

Grace started down the stairs. "Oh, Maria, the girl who helps out on the switchboard, one of our students, brought her sister Carmen with her. Poor little girl's bored to tears. I'll send her up." She was halfway up the centre aisle. "Oh, and Sister," Grace said from somewhere in the house, "Take a break around 11a.m. You and Marie Nicholas and Carmen go down to the cafeteria and have a Pepsi."

"Thank you, Sister," I said in the dark.

"The key's in the kitchen behind the third cabinet door, in case Sister Andrea's not there. If she is, just say I sent you. See you at lunch."

"OK. Thanks."

But she was gone. Now the auditorium wasn't empty. People filled it; they clapped for the doorhandle polished so carefully and sweet soul music. The back exit of the auditorium led to the other side of the school. I found the stairway that led to my classroom, Room 204.

The second floor sounded just as hollowly empty as the first — again the long halls and silent wooden doors. It was clean though. The floors, the lines of lockers along the wall, all were clean. As I passed Room 208 I thought I heard music — a radio. Must be from outside, I thought. These rooms face the side street. Then the hall came to a right angle, but instead of following it I went to the left. One room was back there off the main hall, my room, 204. I opened the door and went in.

The teacher's desk sat on a raised platform. The wooden swivel chair behind it was just like the chair of every nun teacher I'd ever had. And there before it were the students' desks, nailed down to the floor in inflexible rows. A blackboard covered the front wall — not a green innovation, but a real slate blackboard.

On each side of the blackboard, cork bulletin boards waited for the clever pictures and sayings which the grade school nuns called 'projects'. They collected and traded cardboard rabbits and frogs and flower buds which held letters or numbers, or the names of state capitals, spending many recreations cutting out squirrels and puppies from patterns borrowed from older sisters. Well, you don't need that in high school. I could put some magazine pictures up — Martin Luther King, Bobby Kennedy — especially Bobby, Jack too, but maybe the focus should be on living heroes. I'd love to move these desks in a circle or something, but . . . Well, at least there are a lot of windows to let the sun in.

I went over and looked out into the broken panes of an abandoned building. If I'd opened the window, I could have touched the crumbling brick. What an eyesore, I thought. The buildings on the opposite street didn't look much better. They seemed to be about to cave in too, and boards covered many windows. Must be inhabited, because the stoops were full. All the people on the stoop directly across from me were men. They lounged against the sides of the bannisters, drinking from cans or bottles in paper bags. I opened the window a crack and could hear their music and a jumble of talk.

Further down the street children were running through the water that poured from a hydrant. I saw one little boy get knocked down by the water and start to cry. Scottie. How was Scottie? Nicole would keep an eye on him. Scottie and Tiny and all of those Floodtown kids, what would they think of this crowded, busy neighbourhood and all these children? Is it better or worse to be poor in the city? Is it easier to . . .

"Sister."

I jumped. It was such a little voice. I turned to the door and saw a honey-colored girl standing there.

"Sister. I'm Carmen. Sister Grace said come here and help you." She held onto the doorknob with both hands as she spoke. It was just level with her eyes — bright dark eyes. I thought of the bleached-out Floodtown kids and compared them to this vivid little girl.

"Please come in, Carmen. Thanks — I really need your help."

She came in then and walked over to see what I was looking at.

"Oh, you see the sissy house, Sister?"

"The what?"

"That house there." She pointed to the one where the men were gathered. "Sissies live there."

"Sissies?" I didn't get it.

"You know — men that go with men — sissies." She also said a word in Spanish which I didn't understand. "Make love with each other."

"Oh, I see. Well, let's start on the room." Can't let a nine -year-old see she knows more than I do. Sissies — I had only learned about homosexuality when I read *Advise and Consent* in my junior year of high school. She was looking at me the way I must have looked at my first grade teacher, Sister Mary Jane, when I stood waiting for my orders.

Only now I was in Sister Mary Jane's place. And my helper spoke Spanish and could point out the neighbourhood homosexuals. Still, the setting was familiar and all the classroom smells were the same. The red sawdust compound used to sweep the floor combined with the smells of special types of furniture oil and of ammonia that schools bought in bulk. As Carmen and I filled our buckets and got the rags out, I repeated the cleaning rule I learned in first grade — "No soap on the blackboards, Just clear water or else it streaks," I said wiping the board with an up-and-down motion. "And now dry it in the same way," I continued. I turned and smiled at Carmen. She pointed at the board. "It's streaky, Sister." It was. I started laughing. Carmen stared at me a minute and then giggled. "All streaks," she said, giggling more. I didn't recall ever laughing at Sister Mary Jane but then she never streaked her boards. Carmen and I worked along happily until she tried to lug the statue of Mary Immaculate out of the closet and put it up on the pedestal in front of the room.

"Oh, Carmen, that statue's so ugly. Leave it in the closet," I said. No glassy eyes and sickly plaster smiles in my classroom.

"But, Sister . . . "

"Sister's going to find a big picture of St. Carmen," said a voice from the door, "and put it in that poor cross-eyed statue's place." It was Marie Nicholas.

"Hi, Sister," said Carmen, giggling. "Sister always teases," she explained to me.

"Sister is also 'always' easily tired. Time for a break."

"Grace even told me . . ." I began.

"To go and get some Pepsi," Marie Nicholas finished.

Minutes later we sat around a table in the cafeteria, sipping Pepsis. Carmen left to take one to Maria. I leaned back in my chair and looked at Marie Nicholas.

"God, I feel so normal. We could be two friends in the student lounge of some college," I said. The Pepsi machine glowed, humming its own electric music.

"The school seemed so big and empty this morning. Where are the nuns?"

"You'll see them at lunch, but then most of them wander off to their rooms or to work in their classrooms or to go shopping."

We both heard the far-off tinkling of a bell. "Right on cue," Marie Nicholas said.

The dining room wasn't full. Only ten of the twenty-two nuns were there, because many were still at summer school and others were using the days before school started for home visits.

I must ask Grace if I can go home for a day, I thought. I bet she'll let me.

After lunch we went up to the roof garden for recreation. But fifteen minutes after recreation began, Alberta left, followed by Angelica, Marie Ralph, who was the business teacher and Alberta's closest friend, and then Sister Evangeline went, and Sister Rita and Sister Francis. Soon only Sister Grace, Sister Joan, Marie Nicholas and I were still on the roof.

"Sister Paula arrives tomorrow," Grace said. "She'll be living with us but working for the Archdiocese."

Paula was a community star. She had achieved highest academic honours in graduate school but everyone said she was down to earth. She had taught ten of my band members at their Indiana High School. They had entered the convent to be just like her.

Now Grace was laughing with Joan over a Novitiate memory. A few nuns who want to be together. Good. Here's my community — Grace, Joan, Marie Nicholas, Carmen and the Pepsis. The girls' laughter and chatter will bring life to the empty halls. The students, my students. That's who's important. As for the others, damn, I'd rather have Carmen as my sister any day.

On the first day of school I found my throat strangely dry as I stood at my desk waiting for the students of my first class.

"Try to be organized," Marie Nicholas had told me. "Tell the students they need a certain sized paper, that they have to write in ink, and have a seating chart. Do it alphabetically and put it on the board."

"Oh, but Nicholas, I don't want to be so rigid and structured! I don't care what size paper they use, or if it's in pencil. And a seating chart, I'll feel like a Nazi!"

"It's something to hold on to — for the students. They'll feel secure."

She was right. As the freshmen filed into my home room, silent and shy and lost, I would point to the seating chart on the board. I saw their-relief. My name, thank God, there's my name! And miraculously, a seat to go with it.

At two minutes to nine, the room was filled. Desk tops creaked open, coughs and giggles were stifled.

I smiled at a girl in the second row, June Johnson according to my chart. She half-smiled back and quickly looked down. They are so scared, I thought. That girl in the last row with the single braid sticking up like an African princess's, she's so nervous she's going to bite through that pencil she's chewing on. And the heavyset girl with the solemn face looks like Mahalia Jackson; she keeps twisting the ring around on her finger. And that very light-skinned girl in the back, how many times can she pull the same sock up? These kids are scared. But of what? Of me, I guess. And of a new school, different people, a new bus ride, new books to buy. On my first day as a freshman, it took me ten tries to make my locker combination work. But did I look this young at fourteen? I guess to the teacher I did. And now, the teacher's me.

I wanted to touch each one on the shoulder, and say, "Relax, don't worry, no one's going to hurt you. Don't be afraid. It's going to be fun." But if a teacher had done that to me, I would have died. No, if I can just not embarrass them, not ask questions they can't answer, or intrude on the shy privacy that protects each one right now, I'll be doing well.

The bell rang. I smiled, breaking the cardinal rule given me in my college educational psychology class. Never smile until Thanksgiving. I began to tell them in general terms what we would be doing. I saw them carefully write in their notebooks, '8 1/2" x 11 1/2"' paper, and no homework in pencil'. Thirty fourteen-year-old girls looked at me — twenty were black, eight Spanish and two were white. I could almost hear their thoughts: maybe this year this teacher will like me, maybe I'll bring home A's, or be elected to a class office, make a friend for life, be popular. Were these the tough ghetto teenagers I'd been led to expect?

I sensed that the faces could go blank or hostile if I disappointed them or patronised them or underestimated them. But today anything was possible. Today was the first day of school.

"I don't really see myself *teaching* you," I said. "I see us *exploring* together." I looked straight at June. She looked out the window. "We will have the deepest parts of the human experience to study."

Now June stood up and took a step toward the window.

"Sister! Sister! There's a man over there and he's doin' something nasty!" She took another step.

"June," I said, "Please sit down."

The entire class rose and rushed toward the window.

"Girls! Please."

June, the scout, shouted the news. "He's waving his *thing* at us."

He was. Human experience.

It was June who came back at the end of the day. I had taught my six classes. I sat slumped at my desk, the window shades drawn. Was she here to discuss the trauma of the morning? No.

"I know all my prepositions. About, above, before, behind . . . " As she spoke she wandered down the aisle and into the back closet, "between, beyond," muffled now.

She stopped and then loud and clear, "Sister, look what I found. Why did you hide her?" June carried the Blessed Mother and set her on the window-sill.

"Not that window. Please, June," I said.

"OK," she said and carried the statue up to my desk. "Sister Mary Stanislaus had an infant of Prague we dressed," June said. "Where's Prague?"

"It's in Czechoslovakia, June, and Mary's not a Barbie doll."

"Oh," she said.

That was cheap. "I mean that statue is so — well, I'm sorry. Mary didn't look so stupid."

June looked at the statue, turned it. "She looks a little like the mother in the Brady Bunch."

Before I could answer June started to clean the board. "See, you go up . . . and down . . . " she said. "No streaks. Sister Mary Stanislaus . . . "

"June, I just talked for six straight hours. No one answered a question or raised a hand. That guy next door got the only animated reaction."

"Oh, Sister, you should be glad that we didn't act up. You being young and all. How old are you, anyway?"

"June, I can't tell you that." Imagine someone at Ladyhill daring to ask any nun her age. June had stopped cleaning the board and she looked at me in the way she had stared at the statue right before she saw Florence Henderson's features in the Blessed Mother. "I'm twenty-two, twenty-three in November," I said.

June nodded. She just wanted to know, I thought. I hope she doesn't tell anyone.

"I'd better go. Mama doesn't allow me on the street after dark."

I pushed myself up from the desk and started walking her to the classroom door. She had come to the party, been a good guest, even helped clean up. She was telling me about her brother who went to St. Aidan's High School near by. As we approached the office, we stopped talking. I wrapped my habit skirt around my chaplet and we both tiptoed by Alberta's open door. What am I doing? I am a nun, I don't have to sneak by the principal's office. Let those beads jangle, I told myself. Speak to your student, Maura.

"Thank you very much, June, for all your help," I said loudly. Now June will really think I'm crazy. I stood with June in the doorway of the school. The basketball courts and all of the activity of the street continued against the sky beyond the park. It had started to go pink. Not the dramatic sunsets of the Hills, maybe, but a nice softening of the autumn light.

"I know 'em backwards, too. Without, within, with, until, unless . . . " June said as she walked away.

I watched her head for the bus stop on Washington Boulevard. June would go east — most of our kids still lived east of school, though the ghetto moved further westward each day, up to Pulaski, heading for Austin Boulevard and maybe for Oak Park, but not River Forest, or the other white suburbs, the blessed isles where the sun was going now along with all the other commuters. It was time for me to go to church. Vespers, then dinner, then recreation — about, above, before, beyond — that's as far as I can go.

"Television did it. A mistake." Grace was watching the nuns pull their Lazy Boy rockers into a circle around the set. Tonight was 'The FBI'.

"It's relaxing," Joan said.

"So is conversation," Grace said. "And it builds community. This, this," she gestured toward the group at the other end of the room, "is communal isolation." Indeed they did look very separate, like passengers on a cruise ship bundled into chairs and staring straight ahead toward some horizon or in this case, Efrem Zimbalist, Jr.

I was glad they were watching TV. My tries at recreating with Sister Alberta and her friends had gone like this:

"Good evening, Sister," I said, standing in front of their circle. "Nice weather, isn't it?" They would smile at me — kind of — but nobody urged me to sit down and tell them all about my day. But I had Marie Nicholas for that and Paula when she was around, which wasn't too often. She would hurry in from her day's work at the Archdiocese for prayer and dinner, then go out again. She was involved with anything progressive going on — anti-war, civil rights. She knew the Berrigans, had met Hans Kung. Grace gave her the room behind the chapel built for some long ago resident chaplain so she could come and go without comment. "I'd be coming in with the rising bell," she told me later. "I'd throw some water on my face and slide into the prie-dieu." Sometimes she tried to bring me along to meetings or lectures but Grace felt responsible for me. As a Junior Sister I was supposed to stay close to home, apostolate or no.

"How about charades?" Marie Nicholas said, keeping her face expressionless. Grace and Joan stared at her. I burst out laughing.

"Only a suggestion."

"Does Sister Alberta know 'sounds like'," I asked, putting my hand up to my ear.

"Don't be smart, Maura," Grace said but then she started laughing.

"At Nolan," Joan said wistfully, "we played Bridge, Bingo . . . "

Sister Alice came into the room. She managed to straddle both camps. As a contemporary of Alberta's and head of the English department, she could have made things hard for me, asking for lesson plans and monitoring my class. Instead, she looked over what I planned to do, approved it and left me alone. Sometimes she watched TV. Sometimes she talked with us, but she seemed to live in her own thoughts and I imagined her reading Trollope or George Eliot far into the night while Paula plotted for Cardinal Cody's overthrow and I tried to figure out how to make *Lad, A Dog* interesting to students profoundly uninterested in the Highlands of Scotland. This was our text: short stories set in various times and places — 'A Boy of Ancient Greece' or 'of Merrie England' and so on. Never, of course, 'A Girl of . . . ' and nothing set anywhere near the West Side of Chicago in 1967.

"Have them write their own stories," Marie Nicholas had suggested.

How could I when they wouldn't even really talk to me except in those 'this is for school' voices, so unlike the quick run of talk I'd hear as they tumbled into class. There had to be other stories, but what? I read *Return of the Native* in my freshman year and I understood not one word — I never got beyond picturing heaths.

"Sister Alice," I said, "I've got to find something else to teach my kids."

"Something else?" She looked at Grace.

"Nothing I say has any real relevance."

"Relevance!!!" This was Joan, with more energy than I'd ever heard in her voice. "That word! All summer at the Woods that young nun who teaches at the Novitiate . . . "

"Sister Mary Anne?" I asked.

"Right, she was after me to make the music for Mass relevant. Relevant to what? There's good music and bad music — music the nuns can sing and songs they can't."

"Well, she just wants to get rid of the bad sentimental songs — 'O Lord I am not worthy' — stuff like that," I said.

"But 'O Lord I am not worthy' is relevant to some people, though I agree it's drippy . . . "

"Drippy? — it's inane," I said. "And the words . . . "

"Bridegroom of my soul? Fly thy sweet control? You don't like poetry, Maura?" Marie Nicholas asked.

"Do you have to make a joke of everything?" I snapped.

"Sisters," Grace said in her rarely-heard superior's voice, "not at recreation."

"See why TV's a good idea?" Joan said.

"Anyone want a Pepsi?" Grace called out to the other group. A few hands went up. Marie Nicholas and I were up and on our way before she finished counting. "There's a fresh batch of peanut butter cookies in the tin," Grace called out after us. "I made them this morning."

Food can't smooth away my problems, I thought. I need, I need . . . what? Some kind of guidance. Some key to unlock these kids. A few days later it came in the mail — the key. But could I use it? It would depend on Grace.

Grace's bedroom was on the second floor near the chapel. By custom, the superior had the best bedroom.

Huge leaded bay windows faced Garfield Park. Heavy velvet draperies, too frayed for the parlour but too good to give away, hung at the windows, making a little alcove. The door was open. I looked in and saw Grace sitting on the window-sill looking out at the park. I coughed.

"Come on in, Maura," she said. "You know how the nuns used to punish me when I was here at Redemption? They wouldn't let me stay after school. I remember talking in Geometry one day and Sister Helen made me go right home. I sat in the park and waited for Marjorie Quinn, my best friend, to finish cleaning Sister Helen's room. Do our kids want to stay after school?"

"Joan's kids in the glee club do and Marie Nicholas' paper staff — and . . . "

"Good."

"Sister Grace, look at this." I handed her the flyer from the University of Chicago addressed to 'Teachers — English Department'. "In-service training," I said. "Look, here's a class designed for inner-city teachers, given by a well known linguist. My linguistics background needs help and . . . "

"Maura," Grace said, handing me back the flyer, "you've been 'in-service' for exactly one week. Tell me what you want right out. I hate being conned."

"Conned?"

"Look," she said, "conning the Superior is a way to get through the community, but it demeans both sides. If you want to take a course at the University of Chicago, just ask."

"I want to take a course at the University of Chicago," I said.

"No."

259

"Oh, come on."

"Don't Loyola, DePaul or Mundelein have any 'in-service' courses?" she asked.

"Oh, Grace, I'm so sick of Catholic education. Chicago's one of the great universities of the world. Saul Bellow is there. Saul Alinsky . . . " I could see she was weakening.

"When is this class?"

"Well, at first that was a little bit of a problem. But, then I realised . . . "

"When?"

"Wednesday nights, six to nine," I said quickly.

"Impossible," she said. "You'd be travelling through some of the roughest neighbourhoods in the city. To ride the 'L' at that time of night alone . . . "

I walked over and sat down next to her on the window-sill. "No, no, not the 'L' — the bus. I'll sit right behind the driver on the bus. The safe CTA bus. I called and they told me it would take one hour and fifteen minutes, door to door. I'll be in the door by 10:17. Even in the Novitiate, we got to stay up till 10:00 if we were good."

"Don't be a smart aleck, Maura," she said. "I'll think about it." Grace walked over to her dresser, took out a small bottle of scented cream, and rubbed it into her hands. She looked out the window again.

I pressed on. "Tuition's half for teachers . . . credit toward my Master's . . . a chance to make some converts for the faith . . . "

"Maura!"

"Just thought I'd throw that in."

"I don't like the idea of your missing recreation — not to mention Vespers and Compline," she said.

"But on the other hand, we are a teaching order," I said. "And the pursuit of knowledge is a point of rule. Think of Aquinas, St. Augustine and St. Teresa . . . the big one."

"Spare me the litany." Grace held her hands to her face and inhaled the fragrant cream. "I'll do time in Purgatory for my love of good smells. Go on — do a lesson plan or something."

"I have to register by Friday," I said.

"No time for me to write home to Reverend Mother."

"Technically speaking, the local Superior can give permission."

"You really want to do this course — you think it'll help you with your class?"

"Yes I do, I really do."

"And you'll be careful?"

"Yes, I will, I really will."

"OK."

"Yippee!" I said. I couldn't help it — of course Alberta would be going into the chapel just at that moment. She whirled around and saw me jumping up and down in the doorway of the superior's bedroom. I didn't care. I was going to the University of Chicago.

1 3

THE WORLD

The easy fast way to get to the campus was on the 'L' but the 'L' was feared. The station was four blocks from the convent and considered dangerous. The walk to the station was also dangerous. Really, anything beyond our front door was dangerous. The bus stop was in sight of the convent only a half a block away. The nuns trusted the bus. Seated there behind a solid uniformed driver they felt safe, secure. The fact that the trip to the University of Chicago on the Washington Boulevard bus and the Cottage Grove line took almost twice as long as going on the 'L' could not outweigh the sense of relief Grace had, knowing I was encased in the green and yellow steel bus going slowly along Washington Boulevard while right above, the Lake Street 'L' sped downtown. What heinous acts were being committed in the sealed metal cars? None probably. Yet not only nuns, but most of white Chicago would have bet the other way.

I would travel twice as long, I thought as I walked up the Midway. One of the great universities of the world. I am entering one of the great universities of the world, I told myself as I passed the Gothic buildings and entered Martin

Hall and my class with Raven I. MacDavid. No one teaching at the Hills had a name like that. Nor had any of the teachers I'd ever had worn just that exact combination of tweed sports coat and striped tie that said academic major league to me. His vest and South Carolina accent didn't hurt either. He sounded as I imagined John Crowe Ransom must. But it seemed it was his own southern speech that had inspired his study and class. Here he was, a truly great linguist who had crash taught foreign languages to OSS operatives during World War II. But when he had taped his own speech and played it for a cross-section of Chicagoans, they had guessed his education at "less than eighth grade".

"In the South," he told us that first night, "there are certain usages that are perfectly correct. All the most educated people say 'two mile' and 'might ought' and 'done did'. You'll find some of these same usages among black people in Chicago, many of whom were born in the South. Only here, southern speech is taken as a sign of ignorance."

He went on to explain how many people who speak a dialect of English could also speak the standard version, but often, their own inner sense of inadequacy prevents them from doing so. He said the worst thing to do was to belittle the dialect or to be continually correcting 'incorrect forms.' This just made the person more self-conscious and ill at ease.

He suggested that students be made aware of the fact that they were in a sense, bilingual, and that teachers start encouraging them to use language appropriate to different situations and become aware of the difference.

"Ask your students," he said that night, "you'll see that they have very effective ways of getting their message across on their block."

It was almost 10 p.m. when I stood at Randolph and Michigan waiting for the second bus to take me home. The Loop was empty, with shoppers and workers long gone home. I was alone at the bus stop. One car slowed. The driver stared at me. An incipient kidnapper? He sped away. Just someone surprised to see one nun downtown. I over-did my smile at the bus driver and happily took the seat closest to him. There were only a few other people on the bus – a woman in a nurse's uniform, two men in work clothes. They rode with their eyes closed. The woman seemed asleep but held the purse in her lap tightly. When the bus turned her body automatically followed its motion. The bus moved through a no man's land of empty warehouses and blocks marked for urban clearance and renewal, of buildings torn down and lots cleared but never renewed. Just as the bus approached Racine, the nurse opened her eyes, stood up and walked to the front. A veteran. I rode with my eyes wide open, my shoulders tight. Then we passed under a viaduct advertising 'WGRT — The Voice of the West Side'. I was back in the neighbourhood. We passed St. Malachy's, June's parish and home of the famous Sister Stanislaus. Then Jude's, where Stephanie Marie taught. Why don't we ever see the Jude's nuns, I wondered. Marie Nicholas explained to me, "The big social divide between grade school and high school teachers keeps us apart." The blocks were quiet and dark. I must tell Sister Helen that most people in the West Side go to bed early. She thinks the whole neighbourhood dissolves into nocturnal orgies.

Raven MacDavid had said to ask the kids how they communicate with friends on their blocks. Here were those blocks — the square high rises of the projects backed against the 'L' tracks, the old limestone mansions divided and subdivided again and again into smaller and smaller apartments, and the stalwart mainstay of Chicago neighbourhoods, the yellow brick buildings with six apartments that had identical layouts — living room, dining room, a hall with two bedrooms and a kitchen in the back. We had lived in one like that on St. Louis Ave. and Kedzie, just a little north from where the bus was right now. Except now, the six apartments were turned into twelve or even twenty-four 'studios'.

"Garfield Park," the bus driver said as he slowed at the corner.

"Oh, thanks," I said, grabbing the back of my skirt and wrapping it around me. The driver worked the doors with a quick rhythm. I'd seen the nurse disembark quickly and gracefully. I didn't want to catch my skirt in the door and slow the driver down. I was off in seconds but not before the light changed to red. The bus revved up waiting to head west. I was alone at Garfield Park and Madison at 10:30 on a windy, cold September night. This was the point in the movie when you want to yell at the movie screen, "Get back on the bus, get back on the bus. He's waiting in that doorway. Get back on the bus." How often had I said, "It's silly. No one would walk alone from safety into a dangerous neighbourhood." The bus pulled away. Only half the street lights from Madison to the door of the convent worked. So patches of absolute dark alternated with murk. And the sidewalk was twice as long as it had been that afternoon. I started out. Get past the abandoned buildings and I'll feel better, I told myself.

Why don't I have hard heels now? The click, click would be comforting. Except that would be a tip off — a victim coming. Across the street the trees and bushes in the park were dark masses hiding who knows what? Sister Helen swore she saw nocturnal prowlers. Probably not true, but I didn't look over. 'Woo-woo', this is where the frightening music swells and you yell, "Run, run." I did, I'm ashamed to say. I dashed down that dark block, my skirt up and my chaplet bouncing against my side. I pounded up to the convent entrance, my key clutched in my hand. A loud squeal turned me around. One burst from a police siren. Across the street a police car was parked at the curb. The cop at the wheel waved at me. I lifted my hand. So they had sat there watching me all along — damn. I could imagine what the cops thought about nuns loose on the West Side at night. "Stupid. Just askin' for it. A naive do-gooder." And I had shown I was afraid. I had run. How could I face my students? And yet Grace had probably called the precinct and asked them to watch for me. Probably told them not to make a big deal about it. Thanks, I thought, letting myself in — thanks, but next time, well, next time, we'll see.

Maybe it was because I felt I had to make up for being scared in their — our — neighbourhood, but next day I was on fire. And the kids really seemed to listen as I explained about Raven MacDavid's class. I told them how he'd gone from teaching spies like James Bond to liberating Southern speech from bigots. They nodded when I repeated his examples. "Two mile", they said, "two mile", and they weren't surprised that Southern speech was judged uneducated.

"This teacher's not a cracker, is he?" June wanted to know.

"No, no — just the opposite. He said, 'Ask your class. They know a rich and powerful language you've never heard — African English'."

"African?" a few said.

"Well, American African. The way you talk in your neighbourhood."

"You mean you want us to tell you expressions we use at home but not at school?" Cherise, the light-skinned girl in back, asked. She rolled her eyes at the row next to her. The class laughed.

"Well, not *all* the expressions," I said. "But, you know, sayings that are . . . Like, I've heard you say, 'all up in here.' What does that mean?

"Sister, we don't say, 'all up in here'. We say, 'awlupinheah'," said Wanda, the princess with the pony tail.

"Oh, 'all up in heah'," I tried.

They laughed out loud. "You say it so funny, Sister," June said. "Put the words all together, 'allupinheah'."

"But what does it mean?" I asked.

"Oh, when things are good, people are happy, and you're partying and eating, and having fun, then it's 'awlupinheah'."

"Aha," I said. "Awl up in heah."

"I don't know, Sister," June said. "I guess it takes a lot of years of eating chitlins and greens to say it right." But they didn't need me — they had too much to say. Lenore and June and Wanda and Charlotte took chalk, and covered the blackboard with the expressions used on their block. The sayings *their* grandmother told them. Some words were country, I found out, and looked down on. Some styles of speech were "sidity" or affected. Some were hip, and some, the kind they used in school, were proper.

"You know 'rap', Sister? they asked me.

"Knocking at the door?" I asked.

Gales of laughter.

"No, dudes rap to you, about deuce-and-a-quarters, or hogs."

"That's a Buick and a Cadillac," June translated.

They told me the different terms for skin colour. You could be 'light' or 'bright', brown, yellow, or red. And hair was 'nappy' or 'good'. When the wind blew it was 'the hawk', and 'the eagle flew on Friday', that is, the pay cheque came.

Hands waved wildly. When the bell rang for the end of class everyone in the room groaned. As each one left, she had one more word to tell me. The next class coming in saw the group crowded around my desk, and the expressions printed on the board. And so the floodgates opened. In the words of that great educator, "It's a very ancient saying, but a true and honest thought, that when you become a teacher, by your students you'll be taught."

The next day it was more of the same. And it continued. Religion classes changed too.

Brenda *had* been shy in the distant past of two months ago on the first day of school. Now, she sprang out of her seat at every opportunity. Energy vibrated through her skinny five-foot body, and out through her carefully processed curls.

"This is a gospel song," she said, putting a record on the portable I'd borrowed from Sister Grace." See, Sister, I'm not really Catholic, I mean I've been going to Catholic schools and all, but my family, we're Baptist."

"Baptist!" June snorted from the back. "Your family goes. to the Holiness Church."

"We do not!"

"Do too."

"Well, only sometimes."

"What difference would it make?" I said. "If Brenda went to the Holiness Church . . . What is a Holiness Church anyway?"

Charlotte raised her hand and began talking — saving me the trouble of calling her. "They're Holy Rollers, Sister," she explained. "They jump up and scream and holler, and act the fool. My grandmother always wants me to go, but I don't go. I been going to the Catholic Church all my life."

"Well, I hate the boring old Catholic Church," Brenda came to her own defence. "You just sit there listenin' to the priest, whispering and sing those dead old songs."

"Yeah, Sister," Lenore was puzzled. "Why is everything so dull with the Catholics? The Baptists got the spirit, and the Holiness people . . ." she rolled her eyes.

"The Church is trying," I said. "There are some new songs. The Latin's gone, at least."

That was June's cue.

"Credoinunumdeiomnipotentemfactoremcoeliaetern am". She was off again, reeling off the Credo in her preposition rhythm.

"OK, June, OK," I said. "Could you tell me that in English?"

"When in the course of human events it becomes necessary for one nation . . . "

"June! All right! Stop! . . . OK, Brenda, let's hear your song."

Brenda and the record began at the same moment. "I've been cheated, lied to, kicked at, talked about, sure as you're born," she sang with the West Side Radio Choir, "but as long as I've got you, Jesus, as long as I've got you, Jesus, don't need nobody else." Now she took off in a hopping dance across the room, arms flailing.

Don't need no mother, she sang loudly. *Father.*

The class answered her back. *Father.*

Sister. . . .

Sister, they shouted.

Mother, father, sister, brother, as long as I got you, Jesus, don't need nobody else.

Up jumped Linda "Big" Billips. And June. Doris, and Charlotte. Beverly and Margaret, Judy and Brigitte. *Talked about,* they sang together. *Talked about just like a dog. But as long as I got you, Jesus . . .*

Now I was clapping with them. *As long as I got you, Jesus, don't need nobody else.* We sang — together and awlupinheah — *don't need nobody else.*

"Sister, you should come over to Jude's for choir practice. At Jude's, sometimes Father lets us do a real gospel song," June said when lack of breath finally stopped Brenda and the bell ended the class.

"I'd like to, June, that would be great," I said, following her into the hall. The classes were changing and nuns and students filled the hall. Sister Alberta stood at the head of the stairs. She gestured for me to come over to her.

"What was that hideous noise coming from your classroom?"

"Singing, Sister."

"Singing?" she said. Her voice rose.

"Watch the vein on her right temple," Marie Nicholas had told me. "If it starts pulsing, run."

"That wasn't singing," she said, "that was screeching."

270

"That was a hymn," I said. It was starting, the vein — I saw blue coming up under her skin. But I couldn't stop. "A Baptist hymn, Sister. Quite beautiful."

"Beautiful??!! I heard those words. How dare you call that beautiful. The language — it's not even English."

Where was Raven MacDavid when I needed him? The students had stopped to stare. "Sister's getting in trouble," I heard June say to Lenore.

"Please, Sister Alberta, can't we talk about this later?" The bell rang. "I have a class," I said, "and the students ..." Her rage ebbed enough to let her see the girls standing stiller than I'd thought possible, watching us. She turned away and walked down the stairs.

June was behind me. "Maybe we better forget about choir practice," she said.

"I will be there," I said too loudly. "Next period, girls, go into your classroom."

I expected trouble, but Alberta simply stopped speaking to me. "I could not care less," I told Marie Nicholas, and I couldn't, especially after Grace decided we could be part of the St. Jude's choir.

Once, St. Jude's had been the centre of the neighbourhood. The first basilica in Chicago. "We used to go to the novena service every Wednesday," Sister Grace said . . . The Church would be full. People from all over the city came. Why, during the war, they ran special CTA buses with destination signs: St Jude. You could catch them at any bus stop in the Loop.

Now Jude's itself — a school, church, rectory, convent and boys' high school, St Aidan's — was a three block square island in a decaying neighbourhood. There were still parishioners but they were black and poor and more interested in the school as an alternative to the public school than in attending novena services or keeping up the huge church. The choir lofts and whole sections of the main floor were boarded up.

But it was one step closer to the people in the neighbourhood than Redemption was, and a second night out every week. The stretch of Jackson Boulevard between Garfield Park, our street, and Kedzie, the street the church was on, was one of the worst on the West Side. The transient hotels and studio buildings had mostly male and mostly alcoholic residents who used the street as their living room.

"Grace probably has an unmarked car following us," I said to Marie Nicholas the first Thursday we set out for choir practice. "I wouldn't mind," she said as we approached the first knot of men. But the group watched us in complete silence.

A man carrying a small brown bag rushed toward us. "You will find, Maura," Marie Nicholas said "that drunks and children are irresistibly drawn to nuns."

She was right.

"Sisters," he said, "I wanna tell you that, I wanna tell you that I'm a churchgoing man, I'm a man who, I wanna tell you, I'm a — and God hasn't, He hasn't, God hasn't. . . ."

He fell into Marie Nicholas. Marie Nicholas reached out and steadied him.

"Now what?" she said to me holding the unsteady man by arm and elbow.

"Excuse me, Sir," I said, "we really have to be going. We have to, well, to be in church. We'll pray for you."

He nodded and straightened up. He patted his hair and bowed to us. "Thank you, Sisters, thank you."

"Damn," I said to Marie Nicholas. "Did you hear me? My first chance to talk to someone who has problems and I come out with, 'We'll pray for you'."

As we turned the corner toward the church, two little boys about eight years old came running, trying to catch up with us. The braver of the two grabbed the other one's arm — to make sure of his ally, I guess — and looked up at us.

The man sent them, I thought. He's sick. He needed me and I ran again.

But then the little boy spoke.

"Which one of you all," he asked, looking hard from one to the other, "which one is the flying nun?"

Marie Nicholas pointed at me, I pointed at her. "She is," we said together, and started laughing.

"I told you," the other boy shouted, and they both ran.

"Nuns must not walk along Jackson Boulevard much, Nicholas," I said.

"No," she said, "it's not that. You really do look like the flying nun."

I was still trying to get her to take it back when we entered the church basement where practice had already begun. A priest stood before eight ladies and two nuns who sat on folding chairs. He was singing a solo.

Here was *the* new Church priest, handsome with black curly hair and very blue eyes. He wore the habit of his order, but I suspected modifications. I knew pleats, and no robe fell like that without a tailor's hand.

His beautiful tenor rose in the folk song he had adapted for Mass. Here is my natural ally, part of me said. What a phony, the other half responded.

He waved Marie Nicholas and me into our seats without missing a note. Now stop, that's not fair, I reasoned with myself as I sat down and got out a hymn book. He's just trying to work up enthusiasm. Look, the black ladies love him. The two nuns from Jude's love him. Marie Nicholas probably . . .

I stole a look at Marie Nicholas. The hymn book covered her face, blocking out Father. She turned to me and raised both eyebrows. Marie Nicholas didn't love him.

"Welcome, Sisters. I am Father Glenn. As I was telling the group, I wish to form you into a wonderful choir, but you will not be a choir in the traditional sense. No — you will be the leaven in the Congregation, the core of light which radiates into the entire . . ."

The ladies hung on every word. Baptists in their souls, they were greedy for anyone promising to inject life into the Catholic liturgy. "I've been lied to, cheated on, talked about, sure as you're born," I heard in my mind. "But as long as I got you, Jesus . . . "

Father Glenn singing 'I've Been a Rover' just wasn't the same. Plus, it had a tricky tune. Now why not start with an easier song?

But Father Glenn didn't mind our faltering efforts. He liked singing alone. He half-closed his eyes and extended his arms until the full sleeves of his habit became wings. Quite a performance.

Just then a teenaged boy came down the basement stairs. He didn't look like the kind of kid who joined choirs; he looked more like a quarterback, star basketball player, the guy with the most girlfriends, or all three. Tall, brown skinned, as the kids would say, and confident. He smiled at Marie Nicholas and me and sat next to us on the bench.

Father Glenn finished his song and opened his eyes. "Yes, young man, may I help you?" Very sternly.

"Hi, I'm John Wakefield," he said to us. "Brother Sean, the glee club director at school, asked me to come."

"Very well," Father Glenn actually sighed — exasperated at competition? "Sit down. Sit down."

John took the empty seat next to me.

Father Glenn started talking again about the emotional demands of the liturgy. He went on and on. I lifted my hymn book up over my face and yawned.

"Sister." It was John, whispering from behind his hymn book. "Do you teach at Jude's?"

"No, at Redemption," I whispered back.

"Oh. Do you know June Johnson?"

"Very well!"

"She's my cousin," he whispered.

"I'm Sister Maura. June is one of my most interesting..."

"Interesting," he interrupted, "that's June all right."

"Sister!" Father Glenn's voice startled me. "We are here to learn. John, please, your attention. Now I'd like to sing Hymn Number 73, and then we'll try it together. Hmm . .." He hummed a pitch for himself. 'Kumbaya, my Lord' . . .

I practically dived into my book. All the ladies looked at me, and I looked at Marie Nicholas. She was fixing Father Glenn with one of her amused stares, and John had his hymn book in front of his face, too.

"Sorry," he whispered to me.

"Forget it," I said from behind mine.

Father Glenn's a self-important little twerp, I said to myself. I peeked over my book. Glenn had closed his eyes again. "Someone's crying, Lord," he sang.

I allowed myself a slight wince and then caught John looking at me from behind his book. He was wincing too, suppressed giggles came next. Marie Nicholas had put her handkerchief to her mouth. If Father Glenn opens his eyes now we're all through, I thought. But he didn't. "Any soloists?" he finally asked. John raised his hand. He sang 'Go Tell It On the Mountain' in a rich baritone voice that made Father Glenn's tenor sound, well, like Father Glenn's tenor. Glenn had the grace to compliment John but he didn't recover his grand manner until after practice when the ladies and nuns from Jude's clustered around him. Marie Nicholas and I headed for the door. John came up to us.

"Can I walk you Sisters home? You really shouldn't go alone at this time of night." It was 9:30.

"But is it out of your way?" I asked.

"No problem," he said. After a semester, I had mastered the dash from Madison to our door on my University of Chicago night, but Jackson Boulevard was another story.

On the way home John pointed out local landmarks. "That corner, most of the drug dealing goes down there." Four men stood in a huddle. I speeded up. "It's safe," he said. "See that guy — the raggedest one?" We nodded. "He's the undercover cop."

We passed the Umoja Record Store. "All the black nationalists hang out in there," John said. "They buy dashikis, let their hair grow natural, and call each other African names. My cousin George is Jamal X now."

We walked through the aroma that poured out of King Henry's Barbecue. "His ribs are just OK. Prince William has the best." He hurried us past the Graymere Hotel with one succinct word: "Hookers."

As we turned on to our block I pointed to the tenement second from the end.

"That's the sissie house," I said.

"Good, Sister," John said, "you're learning."

At the door, the normal thing would have been to invite him in for, what, hot chocolate and cookies? A Pepsi? But of course we couldn't.

"Good night," John. "Thanks!" I said.

"Thank you," added Marie Nicholas.

"I'll tell June we met you," I said.

"Do that."

"And John, when we have our Spring musical, please come and try out. You're a great singer."

"I will," he said walking off.

"Spring musical?" Marie Nicholas said. "We're having a Spring musical, since when?"

"Since now — Grace is dying to see the auditorium full. She did *HMS Pinafore* and . . . "

"Please, Maura, our kids would find Gilbert and Sullivan . . . "

"Sidity?"

"Exactly."

"I'll find something contemporary and believe me, no more girls playing boys — not when we have a school full of John Wakefields right down the street. Good night, Sister." I bowed.

"Good night."

I was making a nice life for myself. I had the students, my class at the University of Chicago and choir practice. On the next walk home, John and I weighed the pros and cons of *Stop the World I Want to Get Off* and *Bye Bye Birdie* for the Spring musical. Sister Joan said she would do the music for anything but *Hair*. "Even with body suits?" I asked. "Especially with body suits!" she answered.

Redemption was fun. Of course Alberta was there hovering, watching me. But she made no moves. Nothing was said when I asked Sister Alice, head of the English department, to order sixty copies of the *Autobiography of Malcolm X*. "That's what the third and fourth period want to read," I explained. "June said her uncle Jamal X would come as a guest speaker. "Let's wait on that one," Alice said.

But the books came and Alberta said nothing. "Because I didn't tell her," Alice said. Didn't tell her — like Nicole just not going to Chapter. No fights. Just do it.

On the last Indian summer-type day of the year, all the windows in Room 204 were opened. I was really trying hard to explain exactly what a noun is. Charlotte rested her head on her arm looking at the blue sky. "Could we go out and play baseball?" she asked. They laughed. I laughed. Let's see Father Glenn sing to these kids.

"OK, enough — now look. There's another way to identify a noun — through words called 'markers'." I carefully wrote sentences on the blackboard pointing out the way each word worked. Now they were listening, listening hard. "Get it?" I asked. But there was silence.

"No, Sister," one girl said. She must have seen the disappointment on my face. She hurried to add, "But your handwriting's getting better."

If all this sounds idyllic and naive, well it was. But remember, they were thirteen and I was twenty-two, and we were high up in a yellow brick castle in our own little room. It was 1967 and the walls had yet to come tumbling down.

So we listened to Moms Mabley and Pig Meat Markam and analyzed the lyrics of current hits by The Temptations and Gladys Knight and the Pips. We read *Manchild in the Promised Land* and the *Autobiography of Malcolm X*.

"It's wonderful here and I'm really happy," I wrote on the communal Thanksgiving card I sent to the Juniorate. I would have liked to send a personal note to Nicole asking how Floodtown was and what was happening at the college, but in spite of my classroom and my access to the CTA and Jackson Boulevard, letter writing was restricted. A Christmas card or Feast day wishes were all I was supposed to send to my band members and the junior nuns at the Hills. I'm sure if I asked Grace she would have given me permission but I was too busy with my new life to want to look back. When I was a child I thought like a child . . . Now I was a professed sister with my own students and bus fare.

On the last Sunday in November Marie Nicholas and I headed toward Jude's and the nine o'clock Mass. It was three minutes to nine. Just as we reached the third of the dilapidated row houses (which, according to Sister Helen, contained black revolutionaries, heroin addicts, and welfare mothers who produced babies every nine and a half months) a man I'd seen at St. Jude's Sunday Mass came down the steps.

"Good morning, Sisters," he said.

"Good morning," we replied.

"Sisters, I don't want to be forward or anything, but I know you all are going to Jude's and so am I. Like a ride?"

Marie Nicholas and I consulted each other silently. If one of the old nuns saw us getting into a car with a 'coloured man', they would have a stroke, real or feigned. On the other hand, it was freezing. And we were late. And he had a nice smile that showed three gold front teeth. So, with a quick look back at the stained glass windows of Redemption, we followed him into his red Chevrolet.

"My name is Benton, Sisters", he said.

"Glad to meet you, Mr. Benton," I replied. "I've seen you at Church."

"So have I," said Marie Nicholas.

That was it — no one could think of anything else to say. We drove three blocks in silence.

"I have two boys who go to Jude's. One's in first, the other's in second," he volunteered.

"Lovely," I smiled. We were almost there. Two more pleasantries should take care of it. "Father Glenn has done a lot for the liturgy, hasn't he?" I said, in the Sister-meets-the-parents voice that came on me unbidden now.

Mr. Benton didn't reply, but nodded politely.

Every Sunday after that, Mr. Benton drove us to Mass and every Sunday we went through the same sort of dialogue.

"I feel like we're reciting phrases from an 'English as a Second Language' text," I said to Marie Nicholas. I was dying to ask him where he worked, what he thought of Martin Luther King, of Jesse Jackson, and a thousand other things. After all, this was the only adult black male we'd met.

But the wall of politeness we erected together precluded any such chit chat. "And how are the boys, Mr. Benton?"

"Fine. Just fine," he said.

"Only two weeks to Christmas," Marie Nicholas piped up.

"That's right, Sister," he replied. "Only two weeks, yeah."

"We're practising a special programme for Midnight Mass," I said. "John Wakefield's singing a solo, it should be beautiful."

"Oh, that will be very nice," he said.

One more block.

"You must have a wonderfully strong faith, Mr. Benton, you never miss church."

"At first it was hard," he replied. "I didn't know when to sit or to stand. And you see, we don't kneel in the Baptist Church."

"The Baptist Church?" I said, startled. "I didn't know you were a convert."

"Oh, I'm not Catholic, Sister," he said, laughing. "Lordy, no."

"But you go to church every Sunday?"

"Well, you see, Sisters, I don't want my boys to go to public school, they don't care about 'em in public school. The Sisters, they teach them good. But Father has a rule, that parents have to go to Mass every Sunday and put an offering in an envelope, or their kids can't go to the school. So . . ."

"But that's . . ." I stopped myself from saying, "that's awful." Marie Nicholas wasn't surprised.

"Yes," she said. "I hear many of the parishes do that."

"Suppose so, Sisters," he said. "Here we are . . ."

During Mass I thought about the choir. Mrs. Brown, who sang so enthusiastically, was she Catholic? Mrs. Jones? Claire Williams?

"It's about fifty/fifty, " Sister Stephanie Marie told me after Mass.

"And do you think it's okay to *require* the non-Catholics to attend Mass?" I asked.

"How else will Father get support for the church? The collections are small enough anyway."

"But Stephanie, to force people, to require it — I don't understand."

"Look, Maura, if we don't have a certain amount in the collection each week, the archdiocese withdraws their funds. And if they do that, there's no heat, no hot water, and no St. Jude's. How many closed down churches and schools have you seen in the neighbourhood? Do you think the archdiocese keeps places open indefinitely if they don't produce something?"

"You mean they would take the money away and let Jude's close?"

"Of course," she said.

"Oh, Stephanie, I just can't believe that. I mean, my God, this is a mission of the Church. And the archdiocese has plenty of money," I said. "The archbishop's spending three million dollars to renovate the cathedral."

"People will give money to renovate the cathedral but not to keep some decrepit buildings open to serve the 'coloureds' who aren't even Catholic."

"Maybe some of the parishes in Cicero feel that way, but the people in my parish. . . . "

"Don't be so sure, Maura. Do you think the order's happy about all the money they've got to pour into Redemption?"

"But our kids pay tuition."

"How many kids are there? 500 in a building designed for 1,000. The order's used to making money on Redemption. Now they're losing. And the forecast is for more losses, with. . ."

"But the apostolate isn't a business where we have to show a profit! The church and the order only exist to serve the poor. How can you . . . "

Behind me I heard a tentative 'toot toot' from Mr. Benton's horn. In the car on the way home, I tried to open the subject again with Mr. Benton. He just smiled, his gold teeth winking out at us.

"Am I over-reacting?" I asked Marie Nicholas in front of the Pepsi machine later.

"Naive is the word that comes to mind," said Marie Nicholas.

"Well, I'm going to bring it up at the community discussion this afternoon."

"That should be interesting," she said.

"Marie Nicholas, do you always have to be so damn low key about everything?"

"You mean you don't see through my cool exterior to my even colder heart?"

"This isn't funny."

"But it is. You're getting excited about something that's been going on since the Middle Ages."

"Making Baptists go to church so that their kids can stay in school?"

"Paris is worth a Mass."

"What?"

"Some king said that."

Sister Paula entered the cafeteria. "I thought I'd find you here," she said. "Maura, give me a sip." I passed her the bottle. She took a long swig. "Let's go, the meeting's starting. I need you two."

"Paula," asked Marie Nicholas, "is it true you eat pepperoni pizzas and drink beer in your office downtown?"

"What?"

"Helen told me that in tones of utter shock and amazement."

"She's completely wrong. I hate pepperoni. Come on upstairs."

The weekly community meeting was part of the order's renewal effort. We would discuss our spirituality, our ideas, our "concerns" — usually we skipped right to "concerns" which reminded me a lot of, "Will the sister who is not wringing her blouse out properly before she hangs it up, please remedy the situation." But Paula was our renewal officer. She never gave up.

"I thought we could talk about the Eucharist as communal celebration tonight."

She tried. She was brilliant. The Cardinal used her as a theological consultant but "a prophet is not without honour except in his own country." She never got beyond suggesting that sometimes we have Mass at 5:30 p.m. instead of 6:00 a.m.

"Father is willing," she was saying when Alberta ripped into her.

"Are we to violate our holy rule to accommodate Father's schedule? Never. We are meant to begin our days with Mass. Begin them, not defer the sacred moment like, like, like . . ."

"A frozen TV dinner?" Marie Nicholas volunteered.

"But Sister," Paula said, "surely we are all more alert, more relaxed, more able to interact with each other in the evening."

"I am perfectly alert in the morning," Alberta spat the words out. "As are all those who keep sensible hours."

She hears Paula coming in too, I thought. I said nothing. Paula looked at me. But I wasn't going to stick my neck out for a schedule change.

"We fill our souls each morning and that sustains us. To wait until evening would mean . . . would mean . . . " Alberta went on.

"Running out of gas?" That was me. Shut up, Maura. But I didn't. "Really, Sister, prayer doesn't run out. And at night we wouldn't be so rushed. We could experiment more. In the Novitiate we had dialogue homilies where every one spoke."

"It'd be easier to do some decent singing in the evening," Joan chimed in. But Alberta didn't seem to hear her. She turned to look straight at me.

"The Novitiate — you dare to mention the Novitiate. That's where all this trouble started. The Novitiate — spoiled brats with big ideas." She stood up and shook her finger at me. "You're ruining it. You're ruining everything — everything."

"All right, Alberta." Grace's voice was low but had the tone of the superior. "Sit down, please."

I looked down at the floor studying the brown tiles. Nuns didn't yell — not at each other — barbed comments, a laugh that wounded and "fraternal correction," yes, but an out-and-out confrontation in front of other people — Never.

"Alberta hates me." The thought formed on its own. Flat and there. My rational voice tried. "She's threatened by young nuns, challenged, neurotic, uncomfortable with the changes," I told myself. But those bare words stayed. "Sister Alberta hates me. Watch out."

That ended our community meetings. Back to 'The FBI' and 'The Flying Nun'.

"Do your job and avoid Sister Alberta." This was Grace's advice when we discussed it the next day. But the outburst at recreation had disturbed even her smooth exterior.

"You know, Grace reminds me of an old-style Irish American politician. She has that same easy persuasive style, a word here, a squeeze on the elbow there and the troubled waters happily calm down," I said to Marie Nicholas as we walked to our last choir practice before Christmas. "But she's out of her depth now."

"Oh," said Marie Nicholas, "I hope that was an unintended pun."

"Come on, Marie Nicholas. Be serious. If Alberta really goes after us and Grace can't keep the peace . . ."

"Listen, Maura, the nuns like Grace — they're just afraid of Alberta. Love casts out fear, right?"

"I hope so."

That very minute we were confirming that love casts out fear. Our weekly walk to Jude's was familiar now and fun. Weather had driven most of the 'brown bag' gentlemen inside but we had one wino who blessed us faithfully. The little kids called out from windows. It wasn't *The Bells of St Mary's* but instead of seeming like a corridor of crime, Jackson Boulevard was now part of our lives. I didn't dash from the bus after my class anymore, though the 'L' was still off limits. But I slept on the bus just like the nurse who got off at Racine. I even sometimes caught a quick nap in class. Years of practice during meditation had taught me how to keep my head up — I sat on my veil. Yes, love or at least familiarity, made teaching and the neighbourhood and my class less fearsome. But the nuns . . .

"I would just hate to put Grace in the middle," I said as we entered the rectory basement.

"Grace can take care of herself," Marie Nicholas said.

Father Glenn hardly nodded at us now. I wouldn't go as far as saying he sulked but he didn't like the way John had replaced him in our hearts and in the hearts of the ladies.

"Sing it again, honey," Mrs Walker was saying to him. "Sing it for the Sisters." She hit a few dramatic chords on the piano. The song was calypso, 'Mary 's Boychild' and believe me, Harry Belafonte never hit the notes as effortlessly as John did. Next we did 'Go Tell it On the Mountain' with bongo drums. I was trying to give Mr. Benton his money's worth.

On the way home that night John told us that he had applied for college — St. Louis University. "Good," I said, "the Jesuits."

"And a basketball team that will consider a 5'11" guard," he said. "Hope you two can come to some St. Aidan's games during the season."

"Of course. Sure. We'd love to," I said.

I ritually invited John in for hot chocolate and he ritually refused — knowing, I think, that I couldn't really deliver.

"Go to St. Aidan's basketball games?" Marie Nicholas said as we made ourselves hot chocolate. "You think your superior will give permission?"

"Well, I couldn't say 'no'. Besides, when Grace hears John at Midnight Mass and Brenda and June want to stand behind him in angels' costumes and . . . "

"Angels?" It was Grace herself. Now in the Novitiate or Juniorate, if the superior had walked into the kitchen and found two sisters talking at 9 p.m. she would have had to deliver a major reprimand. Grace simply pulled a chair up to the table.

"There are fresh chocolate chip cookies in the tin," she said. "So how was it?" she asked.

"Great," I said opening the tin and passing the cookies. "Wait until you hear John Wakefield sing 'Mary's Boychild' at Midnight Mass."

"Midnight Mass?" she said. "You invited him to our chapel? That's impossible. Maura, you should have asked me. The nuns . . . "

I laughed. "No — not our chapel — Midnight Mass at Jude's. Some of the girls from my religion class are coming. Marie Nicholas and I and the choir . . . "

"Maura, you're not going to St. Jude's for Midnight Mass."

"But, but — the choir, that's why . . . We have to."

"You have to be here, with the community. My God, if we can't be a family on Christmas when can we be?"

"But, but, but," I started.

"They are expecting us," Marie Nicholas said.

"Well, they can just unexpect you," Grace said, "Father will say Mass at 9 p.m., then we'll have to decorate the tree and . . ."

"But Sister, really, they are counting on us," I said.

"So am I."

"Fine, Sister," Marie Nicholas said.

"Fine?"

"It is fine with us — right, Maura?"

"Yes, OK," I said.

"That's settled then," Grace said. "Let's have another hot chocolate. There are marshmallows somewhere."

Marie Nicholas looked at me in her plains woman way, so I smiled. I couldn't believe it. A family. Grace was dreaming.

"If you would like to visit your family on Christmas afternoon, Maura, that would be fine," Grace said, stirring her hot chocolate.

The politician. The Lord giveth and the Lord taketh away.

"Thank you, Sister," I said. But how would I explain to June?

The convent Christmas Eve Mass was bearable — mostly because of Joan and Paula. Joan sang and Paula had written a really beautiful homily. At 10 p.m. we were all assembled in the community room ready to wish each other a Merry Christmas.

"Here, Alberta — you and Marie Ralph can start the tinsel," said Grace. She handed a box of shiny silver strands to Alberta. She didn't take it.

"Grace, is this activity a matter of obedience?" Alberta said.

"Obedience? It's Christmas, Alberta."

"It's just I'm extremely tired and I would like permission to retire."

"Oh," Grace said.

"I'm exhausted, Grace," Sister Gerard chirped. "I was correcting papers all day."

One by one all of Alberta's friends told Grace how weary they were and would she mind . . .

And so there we were again. Grace said nothing as she climbed the ladder next to the tall tree she had ordered specially.

"Hand me the lights, Maura. Have to get the lights on first. Joan, come on, start us off. How about 'God Rest Ye Merry Gentlemen'?"

God rest ye merry gentlemen, Joan began, *Let nothing you dismay.* She picked up the tempo, *Remember Christ the Saviour was born on Christmas day.*

Marie Nicholas and I joined in, then Paula and Alice. *To Save us all from Satan's power when we had gone astray, O-oh, tidings of comfort and joy, comfort and Joy, O-oh tidings of comfort and joy.* There was some comfort and joy in that big room, but not family, not when most of the members had retired. At 11:30 p.m. I handed Grace the papier maché angel. Even she had to stretch to reach the top branch. 'Peace on Earth' said the angel's scroll. Peace.

"Now," she said climbing down. "I have some champagne chilling. We can pop it right at midnight."

"No," I said. "No, please, let's just put on our shawls and walk out the front door."

"What?"

I ran to the community room cloakroom and took shawls off their hooks. "Here," I said coming out. "Here." I draped Grace's over her shoulders and gave Marie Nicholas and Joan theirs. "Here, come on."

"What is this, a scavenger hunt?" Joan asked.

There was no snow but the cold had frosted the streets and they shone in the moonlight. They did follow me out.

"Maura, what is this?"

As I hoped, Mr. Benton was just getting into his car. I hurried down the block.

"Maura," I heard Grace say, "Enough!"

"Can you fit four?" I asked, out of breath.

And so we all went to Midnight Mass. John sang, June and Charlotte looked angelic. During the kiss of peace, Grace found herself hugged by two little girls at once. Mass ended with a rousing 'He's Got the Whole World in His Hands.' That night I even liked Father Glenn. We stood on the church steps saying Merry Christmas and visiting until Mr. Benton's horn tentatively called us home. It started to snow. Big soft flakes, that covered the park and the tenements and the sissie house. "Covering all the living and the dead," I said to Marie Nicholas, squashed against me in the back seat.

She smiled. Grace chatted away to Mr. Benton in the front seat. When we got home, he took her by the arm and escorted her to the front door. As we all muffled our chaplets as we went up the stairs, Grace gave me a thumbs up sign. Merry Christmas.

But Christmas Day was not a success. Grace had crossed Alberta's line by going to Midnight Mass with us. Alberta was not speaking. Christmas dinner was delicious but silent. Grace had cooked it herself.

"These candied sweet potatoes," she told us, "once saved a marriage. My mother's sister invented the recipe and her husband, Uncle Johnny, had a terrible thirst. One Christmas they fought about his drinking. The whole family was there. He stormed out. Well, we waited dinner and waited dinner."

She told her story with great animation. Classic, of course, Uncle on a tear. She was scandalous enough to get our interest, not shocking enough to offend even the most hidebound. Marie Nicholas, Joan, Paula, Alice and I were smiling, already poised to laugh at the punchline. But the other nuns would not even look up from their food. I slid my eyes over to Alberta, sitting right next to Grace, She was pushing her knife back and forth through her turkey, scraping the plate with every stroke. The turkey was tender enough to cut with a fork but she was decimating it, turning the slices into square white pieces.

"So finally we hear the key and in comes Uncle Johnny, tipsy, with tears in his eyes. 'Jesus, Kate,' he said (she put on a brogue) 'I was drinking Powers but I was tasting those sweet potatoes.' He never took another drop. They have six children (then the pièce de résistance): one of them is pastor at St. Gerard's and the other is a provincial in the BVMS."

I laughed. Marie Nicholas laughed. Joan laughed. Paula and Alice laughed. But the other nuns did not. I saw Marie Ralph look over at Alberta who was now impaling her little pieces and forking them into her mouth in precise movements.

"This turkey's quite dry," she said to no one in particular.

"Slightly overcooked," Marie Ralph contributed.

"My mother always put cheesecloth over our turkey," Helen chimed in.

A general discussion of "my mother's turkey" began.

"Must have set the oven too high," Grace laughed.

How could she, I wondered, let Alberta insult her that way.

"How can you take it?" I asked her after dinner. The others had trailed off to the community room but I was helping her carry in two punch bowls of eggnog — one spiked, the other not.

"Take what?"

"You know, Grace. The way Alberta acts."

Grace laughed. "Maura, our nuns in China had bamboo slats stuck under their finger nails. I'm not going to get upset because somebody doesn't laugh at my stories."

"It's because you went to Mass with us. It's . . ." I stopped, sloshing the eggnog from the bowl to the floor.

"Damn," I said watching the thick yellow splat spread over the dark brown tile.

"Watch your language, Maura," Grace said automatically.

"I'll go clean it up," I started.

"Forget it — it's easier to get up when it hardens."

I laughed.

Now if Alberta heard that she would really be horrified.

"Don't let Alberta know," I said. "A mess in the hallowed halls of Redemption. That's much worse than going to St. Jude's or. . . "

"Look, Maura," Grace said, "I'm going to make a very long story short because we're standing here holding heavy punch bowls. Alberta was a year behind me in high school here at Redemption. She'd had an awful childhood — mother dead, father, well, unstable. She worked for her tuition here . . . "

"Then why doesn't she have more sympathy for our kids, they have hard times."

Grace wasn't listening. "She worked as a maid here in the convent. She cleaned toilets and served the nuns in the dining room. In those days there were 'housekeeper students' who lived in special servants' quarters."

"That's awful!" I said.

"Awful? She loved it. A room of her own, peace, the nuns were kind. We regular students were jealous. She was the ultimate teacher's pet. She couldn't wait to enter the order. When she was assigned to Redemption as principal; well ..."

Grace started walking toward the community. I guess she assumed, enough said. OK, it was a sad story but a lot of people had hard early lives. They don't take it out on everyone else. I stood still for a moment. Grace turned around. "Come on, Maura."

"Grace, Alberta wants to be principal of the Redemption High School of 1937 or 1947 or even 1957 but not of 1967!"

"How old are you, Maura?"

"Twenty-three."

"I'm fifty-three, Alberta's fifty-two," she said. "I can't hold this bowl much longer. Come on."

"Once more into the breach," I said under my breath. Two hours and I would be on my way home for my first Christmas with my family for five years. I can smile at anybody for two hours.

My Dad picked me up at 5 p.m. I could have taken a cab or the bus or even the, dare I say it, 'L'. But it didn't seem odd to anyone, least of all my Dad, that he should leave in the middle of his Christmas dinner and come to pick me up. That's just how nuns were treated. He presented Sister Grace with five pounds of Fanny May candy and a quart of Johnny Walker Black — "for the eggnog," he said.

"Thank you, Mr Lynch," Grace said — and winked.

And then we were on our way. The usually quiet streets of Sauganash had bumper-to-bumper cars moving slowly along the snowy streets. Our neighbourhood had the best display of Christmas lights in the city. Some houses like ours did the respectable minimum — coloured lights on the shrubs in front of the house, a spotlight on the Christmas tree in the window and a wreath on the door. Other houses seemed inspired by Disneyland — Santa and his sleigh landed on at least one roof per block and there were many life-size nativity scenes.

Some decorations were awful, some beautiful but all of them glowed with Christmas and all said, "Welcome home, Maggie. You made it! Welcome Home."

"This must cost a lot," I said to my Dad. "You'd feed a family in our neighbourhood for a week on one day's electricity bill."

"Probably," he said pulling in front of our house. "But don't mention that inside, Mag, John and Marie are here."

"Oh no. I thought it would be just us."

They weren't really relatives, just old friends who had kind of adopted our family.

"Well, they wanted to see you."

"OK."

"Maggie, Maggie!" It was Patrick running out of the front door down the walk and into my arms. "I got a cowboy suit and an electric train."

I hugged him and hugged him and hugged him.

My first time at home in five years. My first Christmas back. Forget about Uncle John and Aunt Marie. Forget about Alberta, forget even about poverty and Black Power and the truth. I'm home. I'm home.

Michele, Brigid, Sally and Laura had stayed inside and their hugs were more reserved but we were all together again. "It'll look small to you," Marie Nicholas warned. And it did, especially the staircase — such nice narrow steps, not the long wide flights I'd had to clean every morning. My presents were still under the tree. I unwrapped a pair of black gloves, a black cardigan, the new Hans Kung and a pen. "Thank you, thank you," I said and then admired Sally's roller skates and Brigid's Beatles albums, Michele's new portable hairdryer, Sally's stereo and all the sweaters and hats that were standard for Christmas. "And the Brooks Brothers shirts?" I asked. There they were, the familiar navy and yellow boxes my Dad tossed to each girl every Christmas morning. Identical turtleneck sweaters or blouses in almost the right sizes — his personal shopping for each of us.

"You know, I went to Redemption," Uncle John's wife said. They had been more or less observers. "Of course, that was before, I guess I wouldn't recognize it now."

"Oh, I don't know, Aunt Marie. I think it looks pretty much the same."

"But don't you have, I mean isn't it all — well, coloured people have taken over that neighbourhood, haven't they?"

"Yes, Aunt Marie, we do have a lot of black girls, especially in the freshman and sophomore classes. And . . ."

"*Black* girls?" Uncle John repeated. "That's the new thing to call them, right, black?"

"Well," I said, and caught my mother's glance from across the room, "some of my students feel that terms like 'Negro' or 'coloured' are, well, a little bit demeaning. They believe black is beautiful," I said, imitating the kids' cadences and giving my most charming smile.

"Beautiful!" He snorted. "Beautiful! They're ruining our city. All our tax money goes to support these people. Babies born, fathers taking off, nobody working . . . and that *used* to be a beautiful neighbourhood."

"But Uncle John, it's really not like that. The people aren't all on welfare. And the ones who are can't find jobs, they . . . . "

"Well, what about my family? We hustled, we worked. We weren't afraid to get our hands dirty, nobody gave us anything. It wasn't easy for us. And the Church wasn't worried about us, either. Now they're taking our collection money and sending it to the people who won't work. Well, I won't have it. We told our pastor . . . "

"John," my mother interrupted. "Come on. This is a family holiday, let's enjoy each other."

"You see," Aunt Marie went on, "there's this new young priest at our parish, every sermon's about racial justice. And John feels the priests and nuns should stick to spiritual things. There's plenty of things we could do in our own parish. The pastor is always talking about building a swimming pool in the recreation hall for the kids."

"A swimming pool? But Aunt Marie, people in our neighbourhood need food, clothing . . . "

"Margaret," my mother said, "we're not going to talk politics anymore. That's it."

"But mother, this isn't politics, this is . . . "

"Margaret!!"

I couldn't believe she was stopping me. I had heard my uncles get into bigger arguments than this over who should be the next Democratic alderman with no hard feelings afterwards. Yet Uncle John was clenching and unclenching his fist, and gripping the arm of his chair. He's really mad, I thought, and he's mad at me!

Later, in the kitchen, I tried to explain to my mother why I'd felt it was so important to answer Uncle John. "I know things, now, Mother, I've seen things," I said. "People have these prejudices, and they're not based on facts. Why don't they get mad at the government or the economy or the things that cause these problems, not at the people who are the victims of them?"

"Honey, that's probably all true and I want you to tell me more sometime. But just be sure before you leave that you say a little something to your Uncle John. He's always been so good and generous with you and the kids."

"I know that, Mom, I love him. Uncle John would like the kids that I teach. They're funny, they're fun to be with, they're kids. Ma, have you ever heard Aretha Franklin? You'd love . . . "

But my mother had stopped listening. She was loading the dishwasher with dishes from the Christmas dinner I couldn't eat. Grace's sweet potatoes, Alberta and Uncle John — the Christmas combination. "We raised our children not to be prejudiced," my Mom was saying, "and I'm sure you're doing a lot of good for those poor young girls."

"That's just it. I'm not — I mean, it's at least equal and really, I think I'm getting more from them than they are from me."

"Good, Mag." My mother hugged me. "But don't be surprised if you can't convince other people to see things your way."

"But, Mom it's not *my* way, it's just the way it is. Oh, I wish you could know these kids. The play — you'll see when you come to the play."

"What play?"

"The Spring play, our musical."

"What will you do?"

"I think *Stop the World I Want to Get Off* — John wants to sing 'What Kind of Fool Am I'."

"John?"

"You know, the young man I told you about — the choir practice kid."

"Oh, right. Well — tell you what. When you put on your play, I'll make sure Uncle John and Aunt Marie come."

"Thanks a lot, Mom."

Uncle John and Aunt Marie left early — smiles covering all. We had an hour — my sisters, Patrick, Mom and Dad and I.

"Quick, quick," I said. "Tell me everything." But it's hard in an hour to hear about Brigid and Michelle at college.

"I hate the papers — my English teacher is fixated on John Donne," Michele said.

"John Donne," I said, "But John Donne is great — 'No Man is an Island', 'The Bell tolls for you and the fleas.'"

"Yeah, what is it with that flea?" Michelle said. "Professor Stevens is crazy about that flea."

"Why don't you come over some afternoon and I'll help you with your paper. Maybe this week. I'm on vacation and I'll ask Grace."

"Please, Mag — I'm not thinking about school during vacation. Everybody's home. If I'm not out every night, I'll be a social failure."

"Oh," I said. "Right, Christmas parties, New Year's Eve. Why don't you come by, Brigid?"

"Can't. I'm going skiing in Wisconsin."

"Skiing — that sounds rich and glamorous."

"Not in Wisconsin," she laughed.

But in the five years since I'd left our family had got richer. The girls had a car — a pink mustang convertible — that Sally and Laura drove to Ladyhill every day, unless Brigid and Michele were home from college. My Dad had given my Mom a fur stole for Christmas. There were new carpets in the living room. Even little Patrick had got his new blue blazer and a suit, of course, from Brooks Brothers. "All my best clothes come from Brooks Brothers."

Not that this new wealth went very deep. "We may live like millionaires," my Dad would say, "but we'll die in debt." But all the neighbours seemed to have, well, moved up. Janet's whole family had gone to Florida for Christmas. She herself was making enough at her first job to rent an apartment in Old Town and buy a car!

"Did you get a raise or something, Dad?" I asked him on the way back to Redemption.

"I'm a vice-president now, Mag, the economy's good. People are buying so. . . . "

"So advertising prospers," I said.

"That's right." He started to explain to me about market share and demographics but once we got off the expressway and started through the neighbourhood near Redemption, he got quiet.

The brown bag contingent was on Jackson despite the snowy street and a temperature of 15 degrees. They stood around an oil drum fire. The flame shot up in the dark, spotlighting a face or part of a hunched form. We stopped at the traffic light.

I rolled down the window, "Merry Christmas, Mr. Dayton," I called out.

He looked up, surprised to hear his name from a car.

"It's me. Sister . . . . "

"Oh, yeah. Merry Christmas, Sister."

We pulled away.

"You know him?" my Dad asked.

"Visit him every Thursday night."

"What?"

"On our way to choir practice."

We turned on to Central Park Boulevard.

"Where does he live?"

"He has one room in this hotel that's so awful, he told us he can only go in when he's too drunk to care." I pointed at the buildings we passed. Many boarded up, full of debris.

"I could have done something about this," he said.

"What?"

"I had ideas, plans after the Navy. A new kind of politics for Chicago. But Uncle James said, 'No. It's a dirty business. We don't need it anymore.' "

"We?"

"The Irish. And he didn't think I could take the corruption that went with the territory."

"You couldn't."

"Maybe not but, well, Mag, it's nice to be able to pay college tuition and buy your sisters a car but I didn't think I'd spend my life making people want things they probably don't need."

We were parked in front of Redemption. I made no move to go in. I'd never heard my Dad talk like this before. I mean, he'd joke about the office and how business was all a con — like the sign he had, "Irish diplomacy: Telling a guy to go to hell so he looks forward to the trip." But he was serious.

He had just turned fifty — was that part of it?

"What's being fifty like, Dad?"

"It's like being thirty-five, only no one believes you. We've got this young guy at the office. He's going to revolutionise the business."

"He actually said 'revolutionise'?"

"Revolutionise. My God, on one hand I have a board that wants me to measure the sideburns on every new ad salesmen and on the other this kid who wants only to do informational ads . . ." he stopped.

"Do what?" I asked. *Talk, Daddy, talk.*

"Well," he said, "we should list each brand's merits and drawbacks and let the consumer decide."

"Sounds good to me," I said.

He sighed. He patted my hand. "Not on Christmas." He kissed me on the cheek. "I'm just glad you're so happy. And you were right to stand up to John." He got out and came around the car and opened my door.

"Dad," I said, "would you be terribly disappointed if I, if I ever left the convent?"

Now where had that come from — the words had just come out! Dad would be shocked.

But he didn't hesitate. "I'd be delighted!" he said.

"Of course it's just an abstract question; I mean hypothetical," I started.

"Of course."

We were at the door.

"I'd say come in but it's 10 p.m. and . . ."

"It's OK. I need to get home. Goodnight, honey, Merry Christmas."

"Thanks, Dad and thanks for all the presents." He turned and started down the walk.

"Daddy, wait," I called out. "Dad, you would have been good in politics. You would have been honest. You would have made a difference."

He just smiled, waved and was gone.

I watched his car drive away and remembered my dad at thirty. I must have been five or six. I was the only one in school. My mother, Brigid, Michele and the new baby would be asleep in the early morning. But I would hear him get up and go into the bathroom.

"Dad, Dad, can I come in while you shave?"

I would sit on the rim of the bathtub and watch him pull the razor through the white cream. He was such a good shaver. Definite straight strokes and a quick curve under his nose. Just another indication of what a superior father I had. Then it was time for his shower and I had to leave.

"Please, please, please," I'd beg, "I'll stand in the corner and cover my eyes."

After all, my mother let us in when she bathed. Brigid, Michele and I took turns washing her back but as she explained to me, "your father's a man." I suppose that was obvious but I didn't really place him in that category, "men", which sounded so separate from our world of duplex houses bought on the GI plan and filled with children just my age.

In order to keep me busy while he took his shower, my father gave me a job. I could make the coffee or rather wait for the water to boil and let him know when it was ready. We had no kettle so he would fill a pan and put it on the electric burner. He'd pull a kitchen chair over for me so I could stand and watch. The bliss, the sense of importance I felt as I stared down at the water. No soldier kept watch with more attention than I did staring at the surface. I wanted it to boil as fast as possible so I could run up and get my Dad. Of course, it took forever. "Come on," I'd say, staring at the inert water in the pan. "Move."

I'd look away hoping that when I'd turn back the water would be bubbling. But I couldn't distract myself long enough. Sometimes I'd pick up the coffee can from the counter and stare at the Hills Brothers. They were two men dressed like the wise men in the Nativity scene who sipped coffee from ornate cups. They wore turbans and painted robes and I imagined them at the manger offering Mary a cup of strong black coffee ten times better than Frankincense or Myrrh after what she'd been through. They couldn't stay at the stable because Herod was after them, so I moved my father's packet of Camel cigarettes close in case they needed a ride through the desert on their way home from Christmas.

Finally, the first little pinprick bubbles would start moving on the bottom of the pan, scuba divers launching themselves from the floor of the ocean.

"Jump up," I'd urge them. "Come on, break through." The first two or three hit the top of the water and broke apart but then others came propelling themselves up popping out of the water. This was the crucial moment. At first I would have run for my Dad now, yelling, "it's boiling, it's boiling" knocking on the bathroom door. He'd come down in his robe and look at the water. "It's *not* boiling yet, Maggie."

"Oh."

But now we had our routine. When the water was really boiling, wild waves of it dashing against the sides of the pan, tumbling the divers and shaking on the stove I'd go get him. He'd measure the spoonfuls of coffee into the little basket that fit onto the coffee pot.

"Let me," I'd say.

"OK, but make them heaping," he'd say, handing me the spoon.

How steady I'd make my hand as I put the spoon into the centre of the Hills Brothers can and brought out a tiny mountain of good smelling coffee grains and then pile them into the basket.

The top of the coffee pot fit onto the basket and then when we knew it was secure my Dad poured in the boiling water. He'd go back upstairs to dress while I'd wait for the water to drip through the grains. This was a hidden process and I'd have a bowl of cereal while I waited. But finally it was ready. He'd hurry down and drink a cup standing up.

"You make the best coffee, Maggie," he'd say. Then he was gone off to work and I'd go up, dress for school, wake up my mother and say goodbye.

"You make the best coffee, Maggie."

I never even wondered if he liked the job he'd done all his life. He took care of us and that was all we knew.

"I'd be delighted," he had said.

14

SHOW BUSINESS

The discussions would just start.

One January day in the middle of English, Charlotte looked up at me and said, "Yazoo, Mississippi, Sister, what kind of a name is Yazoo? Think it's real? My Mama said she comes from Yazoo, Mississippi."

"Shit, it's real all right," said Lenore. "I got to spend every summer down there with my Grandma. It's scary down there," she said. "You go in a store you got to wait 'til all the white people get served. My Grandma's always saying, 'Don't act smart, don't act smart.' Shit, you can't even act alive."

In February, Janice began, "Sister, you think it's right all these boys should go and fight? My cousin wants to run away to Canada. My uncle whipped him, said, 'You're an American.' But why's being an American always about fighting?"

"No Viet Cong ever called me nigger," Belinda said. "That's what my brother said."

"Your brother's a Black Power!" June said.

"So what if he is," said Belinda, "So what!"

"Nothing wrong with Black Power," Lenore said. "Black Power's right. Hey, we got some Black Panthers on our block give out free breakfast."

"Well, the Conservative Vice Lords in my neighbourhood," Charlotte said, "they got a boutique."

This was too much.

"A street gang runs a clothing store?" I asked.

"Sure do, Sister. Sell Dashikis and all kinds of fly clothes."

"Fly?"

"Fly, yeah, cool. You know."

"Nice clothes," June said.

"Sister's still got lots to learn."

"Let's teach her Z talk," Brenda said. "Like 'get out of tizown clizown'. That's 'Get out of town, clown'."

And then there were more personal topics.

"Yep, she came up pregnant," Charlotte told us one day in Religion. We'd been following the saga of her cousin's life as the daughter of very strict parents. "Wouldn't let her off the porch," Charlotte had told us.

"What about goin' under the porch," Lenore said.

"Stricter they be more she'll find a way."

One day they came in fuming from their history class.

"Sister Helen said soul kissing is a sin," June announced.

"Yeah, just because it's soul it's wrong. What you think, Sister?"

"Well, I mean, I wouldn't say wrong," I began, "but you get your emotions stirred up and common sense goes out the window." Under the porch, I thought. "You have to be ready for, well, the consequences."

"She means a baby," Brenda volunteered. "Hey, Sister, we don't want to get babies yet. That's why my Mama sends me to Catholic school."

"But kissing — if you don't put some tongue into it," Charlotte said, "it's like kissing some old brick wall."

So. I ordered a set of books that combined *Romeo and Juliet* and *West Side Story* in one edition. It allowed us to discuss love in broader terms but Charlotte's point about brick versus flesh kept coming up. One Sunday afternoon I borrowed St Jude's school bus and June's father drove us all to a dinner theatre production of *West Side Story*. Forty girls went. The theatre was on the far south side, in a white enclave full of people who had fled the coloured invasion. I knew that, but it was a public place and this was Chicago, not Yazoo, Mississippi. The other patrons were surprised. There were looks, whispers, pursed lips. But the waiters, most of them from our neighbourhood, were nice to us. The girls, all dressed up in their going to church clothes, were having so much fun, they were hard to resist. The tight atmosphere dissolved during the balcony scene when Charlotte in a very carrying whisper said, "Kiss him girl, and put some tongue into it."

We rode home singing 'Tonight' and 'Somewhere'. 'There's a place for us, Somewhere a place for us', they sang as the Dan Ryan drew us back into the city. 'Peace and quiet and open air wait for us somewhere'.

But not out here, I thought. Still, in the throes of a common artistic experience, prejudice had been forgotten. There — I'd worked that sentence out for my meeting with Alberta about the play. She had postponed it several times. But that was how she dealt with me — I just wasn't there. After her Christmas flare-up at Grace, she pulled back into silence. I was supposed to feel angst at being shunned but really, it was a relief. With no specific battles being fought, the others of her set were pleasant enough on a superficial level — after all, a junior nun like me was useful for errands, shoe shines and washing habits.

At times I felt a little sorry for Alberta. She was fighting a losing battle. Black people were never going to retreat to being the kind of stereotypic Uncle Tom figures she might have been able to accept. The Church and convent weren't going to turn back into the safe, ordered institutions she'd lived in most of her life. I could sympathise with her fears and insecurities. But then something would happen. Like June's sister coming to me in tears.

"Sister Alberta won't let me take chemistry. She said, 'LaBelle, face facts, the medical profession would be much too difficult for you. You'll do very nicely in the secretarial course.' But I want to become a doctor."

How dare she! I wanted to bluster and yell, instead I patted LaBelle's hand and said, "Take it in summer school at Marshall."

"What kind of fool am I . . . " I sang one Saturday morning as I polished the stairs. I heard three gongs, then two, over the convent PA system. That was me.

I picked up the intercom phone in the linen room. It was Joan. "Maura, get down here. Alberta's nephew is here, and they've got the whole play planned out."

"What!" I yelled. "That's impossible."

"Alberta said she told you about the meeting and you must have forgotten."

"That's a goddamn lie! Where are they?" I said.

"In the parlour," replied Joan.

I slammed the phone and pounded down the stairs, breathing fire. I was charging toward the parlour when a voice stopped me.

"Wait a minute, wait a minute." It was Grace. "Relax."

"But she, she . . . "

"I know, I know. But don't you see, if you run in there and sound off you'll be playing into Alberta's hands, by acting like a rude, impetuous young nun with no respect."

"But she can't do this to me," I sputtered.

"What do you want?" she said, putting her hands on my shoulders, "to prove Sister Alberta wrong, or to direct the play the way you want? Now calm down."

Just then Sister Joan came out of the parlour. "Maura, at last!"

"Be very calm, dignified," Grace said, "and stand up for yourself. You want to do a good play for the students and you can, so don't let yourself be demeaned. I'll be right out here."

I followed Joan into the parlour, outwardly calm, but inside I was mad and a little afraid. Alberta and her nephew/director were on the couch. She is not happy to see me, I thought, as her usually burnt sienna face deepened to Chinese red.

"Sorry to be late, Sister," I said to her. The nephew was about twenty-five. He wore a three piece suit and a sense of his own importance. But I smiled my best at him. "Hello. I'm Sister Maura. I'll be directing the play. I'm so looking forward to working with you."

"First, that play you submitted is totally unacceptable," Alberta said. "What was its title?"

"You mean *Stop the World, I Want to Get Off* ?"

"Yes, I am surprised, Sister, you wasted my time with it. On the second page the word virgin appears."

I looked at her, amazed. The *word* virgin . . . ?

"Now, Albert thought perhaps one of these." She handed me three playbooks. None of the three were musicals, and the only title I recognized was "An Abridged Annie Get Your Gun, without music, for all-female cast."

"But Sister Joan and I had planned to do a musical."

"You and Sister Joan have such heavy schedules that Albert will do the actual directing," Alberta said.

"Oh, really. Albert, have you done much directing?" I asked him.

"Uh." This was Albert's first contribution to the discussion. "Uh, I directed the play last year here."

"That's all?"

He nodded.

"And where did you study, Albert? Were you a Drama major, or have you worked in the professional theatre?"

"Well, no, I didn't, I . . . "

"I must say that I admire your courage in undertaking a big production. I studied with Sister Blanche at our college and directed quite a few plays, and I still feel a little apprehensive." I looked at Sister Alberta.

Certain parts of her red face had come out in purple blotches. Albert cowered in a corner of the sofa, and Joan averted her eyes. I'm not afraid, I thought, surprised. I'm not going to let her replace me. I'll get Sister Blanche to go to Reverend Mother if I have to.

"Perhaps Albert could help with lights and scenery, Sister," I said. "We could call him technical director."

"Yes, Aunt Bertie, I mean Sister Alberta," Albert said eagerly. "I liked that part best anyway last year. The girls on the stage crew were so nice."

Poor guy, I thought. Alberta's only using him as a pawn, he'd be willing to do anything.

"Well, good, Albert," I said before Alberta could reply. I turned to her. "And, Sister, as Albert or anyone in the theatre knows, there has to be one person in charge. If that's to be me, I'll have to know you're behind me and will ... "

She was still staring at me in silence. Purple mottled her whole face. The two veins framing her forehead started to twitch. Uh, oh, I thought, here it comes. Hold on.

There was a knock at the parlour door. Grace was there.

"Telephone, Sister Maura."

Was this a ploy so she could talk to Alberta, I wondered as I left and Grace entered. But no — there was a call. It was John Wakefield. What timing. I had a thought. Maybe I could offer Alberta a compromise.

"Listen, John," I said, "do you think *Annie Get Your Gu'* would just be too corny to do for our play?"

"Let's see - *Annie Get Your Gun.* Isn't 'There's No Business like Show Business' in that play? I like that. What are the other songs?" he said.

"There's 'The Girl That I Marry', 'Anything You Can Do I Can Do Better', 'They Say Falling in Love is Wonderful'. Great songs, but old-fashioned ones. *Stop the World* would be so much more modern."

"Don't worry about that," he said. "Hey, I always wanted to dress like a cowboy . . ."

I went back into the parlour. Grace was making cheerful conversation. Alberta had faded back to a rust colour.

"Sister Alberta, I was thinking. Let's go with your suggestion. *Annie Get Your Gun,* but the regular musical version."

"I have time to do the music," Joan said. "Truly."

Grace looked at Alberta and smiled. I smiled, and then so did Joan. Even Albert spread his lips apart. Finally Alberta grimaced.

"I just hope your school work will not suffer," she said to me. It was settled. She got up and walked out, leaving poor Albert alone on the couch.

"Give me your number, Albert. I'll call you when I need you," I told him.

After he left, Grace came over to me. "See, it wasn't so hard. Alberta does want the best for the school. Now, just make sure you do a good job."

But I knew that was only the opening skirmish. Full battle came when I showed Alberta the list of cast members.

"Sister Alberta, excuse me, um . . ." I said from the door of her office. We hadn't spoken since that day in the parlour.

"Yes, Sister," she said. She stopped writing and looked up. For a moment our eyes met. My God, I thought, why does this woman hate me so? For liking my students, for enjoying my job? Because I am young and part of changes she resents. And she has power over me. She could curtail our use of the auditorium for rehearsals, or undercut ticket sale efforts. Traditionally the entire school supported the play. In fact, a free day was given to all students who sold at least four tickets to the play and one ad in the programme. All through grade school and high school, I had participated in the ritual of the 'school play'. It didn't matter that the show's main purpose was to raise money and that aesthetics often bowed to the necessity of having every child in the school march across the stage so that their parents could applaud them. The play was a celebration of the school, an affirmation of the students. Why couldn't our play be a communal celebration of our students too?

The students were willing. Over two hundred, both black and white, had come to the tryouts. Though only seniors were eligible for main parts, the other classes could take smaller parts and dance and sing in the production numbers. How exciting it had been, I thought, to see the kids up there singing and dancing. And so much talent and energy! What had one group sung? "To be young, gifted and black, oh what a lovely, blessed feeling?" That song defined the energy, the pride in being young, gifted and black that gave such punch to their performance. These girls were tired of being treated as uninvited guests or invaders. Redemption was their school too, and they wanted to add their particular talents.

Deep down Alberta must want Redemption to provide education and opportunity for all. She was a nun. She'd promised to follow the new direction of the Church in obedience, to identify with the deprived in poverty and to love universally in chastity. Certainly with this basis we could find common ground. I'd try. I took a deep breath.

"Sister, I brought you a list of the students who will be in the cast. Um . . . I was . . . um, very gratified with the students' response, and . . . um . . . Sister Corita in the art department said she'll have the art students help with scenery, and I um, believe Sister Mark Ann headed the play ticket and ad drive last year. I asked her, and she said if you wanted her to, she'd be glad to do it again."

Alberta hadn't changed her expression, but at least her face was still a normal hue. I went on.

"Sister Joan has already begun with the music. She'll have the glee club do the overture, and we've found . . . "

Alberta lifted her hand, palm out, a traffic cop's signal to stop.

"Sister Maura, you know I view this whole undertaking with scepticism," she said.

Well, I thought, better that than outright condemnation.

"However," she continued — good, some hope — "I know my duty. I am even now sending instructions for all teachers on the organisation of the ticket and ad drive, as well as informing them to urge their students to participate in the play itself."

Better than I'd hoped.

"Thank you, Sister," I said. "And you'll be glad to know the participation has already begun. We had a wonderful turnout at auditions, and here is the list of those I've selected. I also . . . um . . . included the volunteers for the stage crew, which I'll pass on to Mr. Slotsky — um, to Albert."

"Very well, Sister. Leave them on my desk. Good afternoon, Sister."

Well, I thought as I left, that wasn't so bad. Reason could still prevail.

But the next morning I saw how wrong I'd been. I was just at the doorway between the convent and the school when Alberta appeared in front of me. She stood there blocking my way. One hand held a crumpled paper. The other clutched her chaplet. Her face was flushed, and the veins in her forehead strained so that I doubted whether they could hold the blood in much longer.

"Sister," she hissed the word, "the names, this list, these girls — they are all coloured."

"Well, yes."

"The main parts, the stars. Florence Martin, Sylvia Ford, Shirley Waters, Helen Brooks — all coloured. We have white seniors. Where are they . . . ?"

"I gave roles to the ones who tried out, but I had to pick the best." I tried to keep my voice low and reasonable. Hysteria seemed very close. Be calm, I told myself.

"I want a white cast! Alumnae come to this play."

"But, Sister Alberta, most of our students are black."

"All right, have a coloured cast. They can perform the second weekend."

Oh my God. She can't know what she's saying.

"Sister Alberta," I spoke very quietly now, as I had done to Patrick when he was throwing one of his year-old tantrums. "You know we can't do something like that. We need to show black and white students together, and . . . "

"No," she shouted this now. "I will never turn this school over to the coloureds. I will never give up the heritage that . . . "

"Sister," I shouted back, "They're our girls, they're Redemption's seniors."

She reached out and grabbed my cape. Her face was bunched together into a purple fist. "Never. They are not taking this school. They took the neighbourhood I grew up in and turned it into a pig sty. They took my father's job, took his savings when he had to sell the house for nothing. Now they want to take my school — my school! Our stage will not be a showcase for their obscene dancing and barbaric music!"

I stepped back, pulling my cape out of her fist, and mustered up my coldest tones.

"Sister, if you want those names changed, you'll have to see Sister Grace."

Sister Alberta seemed to have regained some control.

"Perhaps a Mexican for the lead then, or a light-skinned coloured girl, but these . . . " she waved the list, her voice and colour rising again. "They're so dumb. They'll never be able to remember the lines, you'll see, you'll see. You'll be sorry you let these niggers . . . "

"Sister." Grace's voice cut through. "Sister, please."

I turned to see her standing behind me. She was looking at Alberta with the same expression I'd seen on her face at Christmas — not anger, but a great sadness. She walked past me and took Alberta's arm. "Come into my office, Sister. Maura, wait for me in the community room."

I paced up and down in the community room, pounding my feet as I walked. Alberta is crazy and dangerous and evil, I thought. Her words swirled through my head.

"Maura," Grace came in.

"Sister, I can't believe . . . I mean, what a . . . " I started.

"Maura, Sister Alberta and I have decided that you will get any permissions you need about the play directly from me. As superior I am responsible for any large events — and I have a feeling this will be an extremely large event!" She smiled at me.

I was recovering. Grace always made it better.

"Quite a large event, Sister," I agreed.

"In fact, from what Sister Joan has told me, it will be an extravaganza."

The rest of that winter, the auditorium was my home. I couldn't believe it had once seemed dead and empty.

Only the principal actors — John Wakefield as Frank Butler, Florence as Annie, Sylvia as Dolly, Helen as Honey, the ingenue, and John's friends, Leo, Mark and Leon, who played the male leads, Charlie, Buffalo Bill and Sitting Bull — were at the early rehearsals. Later I'd add the other actors and the dancers in the different production numbers. But Sister Blanche had taught me to take the main scenes and work with the principals first. We sketched out those first scenes on the bare stage. I thought how wrong Alberta was — the lines, the lyrics, the kids knew them the first week. Then we started to talk about motivation. They knew about motivation. John saw his character, Frank, as a street dude.

"See, Frank's big on the street, got an image to maintain," he explained to us. "A front. He's cool and everybody's got to know it. Now he can't act like he wants anything or needs anybody, or that'll blow his thing. So he has to act like he's doing the others a big favour by being in their monkey-assed Wild West Show. He says he'll leave the show when Annie crowds him. But all the time he's just waiting and praying for the others to coax him, so he can come back and still be cool. Like this. Come on."

He gestured to the others, Florence, Leo and Mark, and they jumped up on stage. Florence — Annie now — let John, as Frank, get halfway down the stairs into the auditorium, and then started singing softly. *The costumes, the scenery, the make-up, the props, the audience that lifts you when you're down* . . . On the stairs John stopped and on his face I saw Frank Butler's memories. He was listening to past applause. Now Leo — Charlie the advance man — moved downstage. *The headaches, the heartaches, the backaches, the flops, the sheriff who escorts you out of town.* Now Frank was half smiling. He knew those sheriffs.

Mark, my football tackle Buffalo Bill, added his deep voice. *The opening when your heart beats like a drum, the closing when the customers won't come.* Frank half turned to them. They were his people and being cool isn't everything. *There's no business like show business,* the three on the stage sang to him. *Like no business I know* . . . *Everything about it is appealing, everything the traffic will*

*allow. Nowhere do you get that happy feeling, when you
are stealing that extra bow . . .*

John let us see that they had Frank now. His tall, supple
body moved to the stage almost against his will. And now
he sang with them.

> *There's no people like show people*
> *They smile when they are low . . .*

There they were happy, young, invincible and together.
Their strong voices united in the last verse and scattered
the last of the dust that still hung in the air of that old
auditorium. Let any ghosts of those Good Old Redemption
Days still up there in the balcony hear this.

> *Yesterday they told you you would not go far*
> *Last night you opened and there you are*
> *Next day on your dressing room they've hung*
> *a star*
> *Let's go*
> *On with the show.*

And we did go on with it. Near the end I felt more like
General Patton than Joshua Logan, but somehow all the
elements — Indian dancers, cowboys, townspeople, chorus
(totalling one hundred and twenty-seven students), plus
costumes, scenery, lights — coalesced. I knew the music
would be great, Joan was fantastic. She could take a song,
transpose it, arrange it and play it, five minutes after
looking at the music for the first time. Once I walked in
when she was teaching 'I've Got the Sun in the Morning
and the Moon at Night' to the chorus. Her veil was pushed
way back, and her big sleeves were rolled up. She stood at
the piano, playing the tune one-handed without looking at
the keys, all her attention was on the chorus. An electric

charge ran from her to the singers and the chorus became alive, expressive, a character in the play.

Opening night was a sellout. "It's jammed," I told the kids as I ran from one classroom to the other, dabbing on make-up, lining up little kids in Indian costumes, brothers and sisters of the cast. I was proud of how well everybody looked in the home-made costumes. Only Frank and Annie had the real thing. We'd rented a blue satin cowboy suit for John, complete with fringe and glitter and pearl-handled revolvers. Florence as Annie wore a white leather cowgirl outfit encrusted with rhinestones and sparkling gems. Sitting Bull had a floor-length headdress. I'd used mission money. After all, art was an apostolate.

"You look wonderful! Good luck!"

"It's all up to you now," I said and headed for my seat in the back of the auditorium. I waved to my parents, sisters, brother. I whispered, "Dim the house, light the lights," into the intercom that connected me with Albert backstage. As the pink and amber glow came on, I saw Joan signal the band. The music started, the chorus marched smartly in and sang the overture. They swung off, and I whispered into the phone, "Curtain up."

And then for me it was all magic. I was carried right along with the audience as they cheered Annie, swooned over Frank, and laughed at Sitting Bull and Dolly. Thunderous applause greeted the first act curtain. A young voice said, "Oh, Ma, is it over so soon?"

No, little girl, I wanted to say, it's not over yet. When the second act began with a grand march of the whole cast up through the audience onto the stage I realised I never wanted it to be over. But the last scene came, as it had to. I picked up the intercom phone to instruct Albert on curtain calls when I heard a loud "Ahhh" come up from the entire audience. Frank Butler was making his last entrance, resplendent in a complete dress suit — top hat, white tie and tails. We'd wanted a tux for the last scene but we had no money left to rent one. So he rented it himself. Fantastic. The audience stood and clapped in rhythm to 'There's No Business Like Show Business', the last song. We got fifteen curtain calls, and by the end, most of the audience had gathered in the orchestra pit to sing along with Sister Joan who just kept playing.

All four performances were like that. We played to 6,000 people and made $15,000. The NBC station in Chicago even came out to film part of it as a feature on their news. At the last performance, the whole audience had seen it before, so they laughed before the punch lines. Buffalo Bill and Sitting Bull came down into the auditorium and escorted me onto the stage. John presented me with a bouquet of two dozen red roses. Florence brought a similar bouquet to Joan at the piano, and for an exhilarating minute both cast and audience cheered us. Surrounded by my students, with their cheering parents in front of me, all my dreams had come true.

Just a few months ago I'd stood in a dead auditorium isolated from the people of the neighbourhood. And now this.

> *Yesterday they told you you would not go far,*
> *last night you opened and there you are ... next*
> *day on your dresssing room they've hung a star.*
> *Let's go on with the show.*

> *And they who instruct the many to justice shall*
> *shine like stars for all eternity.*

I spent the next few days reliving our triumph. We've won, won, I kept thinking. Look what those kids did — the discipline, the talent. Let Alberta tell one of them they're too dumb for Chemistry, I thought as I packed the costumes away and cleaned up backstage. The others were at recreation and I was glad to be alone. The stage only seemed empty. To me the play was still going on. WGRT was on the transistor radio Grace had given me. Redemption just couldn't be isolated anymore. The kids had become accustomed to dropping in after school and on weekends. During rehearsals we'd made a classroom into a green room with a phonograph where those waiting to come on stage could dance and visit. I had talked to Grace about making this permanent.

"The Stagedoor Canteen?" she'd said. But she had agreed to talk to Alberta about it. Alberta had definitely lost ground with the play. She attended only one performance and left with no comment. But the other nuns in her coterie had enjoyed the play. Sister Helen even sent me a congratulation card. Well, it was actually a birthday card she'd received with Birthday crossed out and Play written in — 'Happy Play' — but I appreciated the thought.

I'm going to try harder to get along with the other nuns, I promised myself. After all, my situation here just mirrors what's going on in the country. Look at the anti-war demonstrations, the civil rights marches — and they were working. On the last night of the play, Lyndon Johnson had said he wasn't going to run again.

"Do you realize what this means, girls?" I had said in class. "Bobby Kennedy will be elected now, the war will end and we'll start spending money here on our own people — our poor people."

"King's leadin' a Poor People's March on Washington," Brenda told me. "Our whole church's going — want to come?"

"I'd love to," I had said.

And I would go. Then I could get some of the kids to work with me on Bobby Kennedy's campaign. I'm not going to spend a whole summer at the Hills with so much going on. Funny, I'd rather be here than back at the Hills with the Band. Do I miss them? I hadn't written much but has anybody else? Postcard from Matthew — just "I'm busy and happy." Busy and happy. So was I.

I'd been afraid my father would bring up our Christmas conversation when they came for the play. Just like him to say something like, "So should we move another bed into the girls' room? Delighted, I'd be delighted." Well, he'll be delighted when he sees the difference I'm going to make at Redemption. Next year — *West Side Story* : The Conservative Vice Lords v. The Latin Kings. John for Tony of course and maybe Leo as Riff. *There's a place for us,* I hummed to myself, *A time and place for us.* On the radio the Temptations wished it would rain. Just then they were cut off in mid-note. "Listen, listen," the announcer shouted. "Dr. King is dead. They shot Dr. King. He's gone. He's dead. Martin Luther King Jr. is dead!"

I grabbed the radio and just held it — the announcer kept repeating "DEAD, HE'S DEAD, DEAD, DEAD." I ran down the stage steps through the auditorium to the nun's recreation room. They were all there. Sister Grace and Sister Joan were playing double solitaire. Sister Alberta was sitting there sewing. Marie Nicholas and Paula were talking with Alice. I looked at them and realised once I spoke nothing would ever be the same again. Just like John Kennedy. Like Kennedy all over again.

"They've killed King, they've killed Dr. King . . . I just heard it on the radio news. He's dead."

All conversation in the community room stopped. Marie Nicholas said, "Our poor kids, our poor kids."

"What happened?" Grace asked me.

"He was shot in Memphis."

"Do they know who did it?" Paula asked. "I don't think so," I said.

"Oh God, this is so terrible. I just can't believe it," said Joan.

"Have riots started yet?" It was Alberta.

"What?" I said.

"That'll be next. They'll use this as an excuse to run wild."

"My God, Alberta, have you no feelings at all?"

"The man was a Communist agitator. He stirred up trouble. There are consequences . . . " She said this calmly, darning a sock as she spoke. We all just looked at her.

"What about tomorrow?" Paula said. "We have to have a memorial Mass. I'll ask Father Pete from our office to come to say it."

"Good," said Grace. "Maybe Father Egan would give the sermon."

"Perfect," I said. "He was at Selma."

Alberta stopped sewing. "Is it really necessary to disrupt classes? If some of our students wish to um, mourn this man, let them do it privately but to *impose* it on the whole school . . . ?"

"We are awfully close to Easter vacation and I have a whole unit to cover," Sister Anselm chimed in.

"Martin Luther King is dead. What is wrong with you?" I shouted.

"Sisters," said Grace, "Let us stand and pray."

Out of the depths I have cried to thee, O Lord, she began. One by one the nuns stood and joined in.

Lord, hear my prayer. Let thine ears be attentive to my voice in supplication, we said together. *If you, O Lord, will mark iniquities, Lord who can stand it,* we prayed.

Alberta stood with her head bowed, but her lips were held tightly together.

The next day was among the saddest I had ever known. I had wondered if the kids would even bother to come to school. They had. They wanted to be together in grief and in anger. Over all the feelings was this sense of disbelief. Martin Luther King was non-violent — a man of peace. Why? Why? Why?

"The white man just lost his best friend," Lenore said. "The fire next time, the fire next time."

"Oh Lenore, just let us be sad," June said. "You know he's got three little kids. Oh Sister, why, why are white people so hateful to black people?"

"Did you see Bobby Kennedy last night?" Pat Shaw, one of our few white students, said. "He understands, he said his brother was killed too and was killed by a white man."

"All the good ones, they only kill the good ones," Charlotte said.

"Malcolm X," Lenore said.

"The little girls at church in Birmingham."

"What's God got to say about all this," Brenda wanted to know. "I thought He's supposed to be good and all."

"Oh Brenda, God seems awfully far away right now. I guess we have to find God in each other. Mass will help. We'll be all together . . ".

"Oh shit," Charlotte said. "I can't go to communion!"

"Charlotte, don't worry about fasting. Nothing should keep you from communion on a day like this."

"Yeah, what about mortal sin?"

"I doubt if you . . . " I started.

"You're wrong, Sister," June said. "We all got sins."

"Only real serious sins keep you from communion, not just, well — you know — 'putting some tongue in it.' You all love God, don't you?"

They nodded.

"You're good to others, right?"

They nodded.

"Well?"

"See, Sister . . . " Charlotte said.

"Please. Dr. King is dead. Do you think God wants you left out of the most important part of Mass because of soul kissing or making out or . . . ?"

June just shook her head. "Sister Stanislaus said you go to hell if you take the host with a sin in you."

"Oh June," I started and then I remembered how I'd been at thirteen, confessing my one big sin over and over, afraid that every time I swallowed the host I was damning myself. "OK, look — I'll get Father to give you general absolution. I'll be right back."

I found Father Pete with Sister Paula in the sacristy vesting for Mass.

"Pete." I knew him — he had taken Paula, Marie Nicholas and me to a lecture by a Vietnamese monk who belonged to the order who were immolating themselves to protest the war. It had made my conflicts with Alberta seem pretty insignificant. "Pete, would you give a general absolution?" I asked.

"General absolution!" he said.

"Paula, they're afraid to go to communion," I said.

"So," Paula said to him, "Do it!"

"I can't. General absolution is only for soldiers going battle."

"Pete," Paula said. "I can't believe you said that."

I left them discussing it and went back to my room.

I'd never seen Father Pete celebrate Mass before. When he read from the scriptures he looked at us. And when he spoke the words of consecration I heard separate words, not just that familiar pattern of sound so many priests make. But there was nothing showy.

Father Egan stepped forward to give the homily. He reminisced about Selma and Dr. King, then read quotes from Dr. King's speeches. Right before communion Pete stopped and coughed and said, "I'm now going to give General Absolution. Just think of whatever you are sorry for. I absolve you in the name of the Father and of the Son and of the Holy Spirit. There, you're all, um, absolved."

Absolve them, I thought. Absolve us. Absolve this country. June looked over at me. I nodded, she poked Lenore. All my freshman stood up and headed for the altar. *We shall overcome*, they sang, *We shall overcome. Deep in my heart I do believe, we shall overcome* . . .

After communion, Florence stepped up to the podium. A few days ago she had sung and danced on the stage as Annie Oakley. Now she stood there as Senior Class president. "I'm going to read from Dr. King's August 1963 speech," she said. *I have a dream,* she began. Her voice didn't crack until the end. *Let us all pray that some day all God's children, white and black, may say in the words of the old Negro spiritual, 'Free at last, free at last.'* Sobs broke through, and tears fell with the final words. *Thank God Almighty, we're free at last.*

Then everybody was crying. I was crying — the grief was uncontained. We're falling apart, I thought, we're falling apart.

Then Joan stood up and gestured to the members of the glee club. "Stand up girls," she said. She walked to the piano in the orchestra pit and played a series of notes. The glee club recognized their Graduation concert piece. She repeated the phrase and they began to sing.

> *This is my quest, to follow that star*
> *No matter how hopeless*
> *No matter how far*
> *To be willing to fight without question or pause*
> *To be willing to march into hell for a heavenly*
> *cause*

And then the whole school joined in.

> *And the world will be better for this.*
> *That one man scorned and covered with scars*
> *Still fought with his last drop of courage*
> *To reach the unreachable star.*

It did what the Mass hadn't, what even Dr. King's words hadn't. It joined our pain and sadness and made us one. We all stopped weeping for ourselves and remembered the man who had fought with his last drop of courage to reach the unreachable star.

We were still singing when Alberta hurried down the centre aisle. She stopped at the front row and motioned to four white seniors seated in the middle of the row. At first they didn't understand. "Come, come," she said. They got up from their seats and left the auditorium. Alberta worked her way back calling only the white girls, and sending them hurrying up the aisle.

I cut through the rows and caught up with her near the back of the auditorium. Florence and Sylvia were close behind me.

"What are you doing?" I asked.

"We must get our girls out quickly," she said. She was holding a puzzled Lisa Cyswenski's arm. "Go — your brother is waiting in the office to take you home."

"Go — go."

The black girls in the row stood up. "Sister, what?" asked one.

"Sit down," Alberta said. From the back of the auditorium she turned to the school, rang the hand bell two, three, four times. The last of the singing trailed away.

"Regular lunch periods, regular lunch periods," she bellowed. "Everyone to the cafeteria." To me she said, "Keep them down there until our girls get away."

Alberta turned and left.

"What in the hell," Sylvia began.

"Go downstairs," I said. "Let's get everyone to the cafeteria." The students stumbled out — puzzled — only the black and Latino students were left. What now?

In the cafeteria, I stood with my freshman trying to say something comforting. Florence and Sylvia came up to me furious.

"I heard her, I heard her," Sylvia fumed. "Does she really believe we'd jump our own classmates?"

"No, no, she's just nervous," I said. "She'll dismiss us all soon. I'm sure."

But these weren't my willing freshmen. These were almost women, only a few years younger than I was. Friends, as well as students. And they were mad and were right to be mad. I thought of everything I'd pushed down — Mr. Benton paying his way into the apostolate, the racism of the nuns. The world outside our yellow castle was erupting. I didn't know what to do.

"Here, Sister. Want a sip?" Florence offered me her Pepsi bottle, and I took a long drink.

"Thank you, Florence. Thanks a lot." It helped — that long cold swallow helped. Get through this hour, then face the rest. Remember this moment — remember that Pepsi bottle.

Marie Nicholas came over to the table. "Florence, your brother is here. He says there's trouble in the park between the police and kids from Marshall. The students were holding some kind of memorial service in the park because they couldn't at school and the cops broke it up. Now the kids are headed for the stores on Pulaski and Madison."

"We've got to go to Alberta," I said. I looked at the crowded cafeteria. "She's got to let these kids go home before things get out of hand."

The stores on Pulaski were ghetto furniture stores where shoddy merchandise was sold 'on time' and food stores with artificially coloured meat and rotten produce. There had never been a riot on the West Side, but there were plenty of targets. The loudspeaker switched on, and the panic in

Alberta's voice cut through the murmur of talk in the cafeteria.

"Girls, I can only hope you will not answer violence with violence."

A loud groan went up from the group. "Did you hear that, Sister?" June said. "She just don't understand it."

"All students may leave the building," Alberta went on. "You are dismissed. Leave the building. Leave the building."

"What is it?" "What's happening?"

"A riot? There's a riot."

"A riot?" The whole lunchroom rose and ran for the exits. Some students went to their lockers for books and jackets. Others just ran out the door, some to get home to be safe from any disturbance, others to join in whatever would happen.

"Wait, wait," Marie Nicholas called.

Grace and Paula stood at the doors. "Slow down — take care, now. Be careful. Go home," we shouted after them.

The school emptied in minutes. An eerie silence filled the halls. Nicholas and I went up to Grace's bedroom to listen for news on her radio. At 4 p.m. the reports of violence started.

"Groups of teenagers are breaking windows in the Pulaski Madison shopping area," the announcer said. "Similar outbreaks are reported on Roosevelt Road and on Homan and Kedzie Avenue. All disturbances are on the West Side. The South Side black community is quiet."

Marie Nicholas and I looked out the window. We could see groups in the park, but they seemed to be milling around, not doing anything. My gong rang, and I went to the phone. It was John Wakefield, calling from a pay phone on Madison Street. In the background I could hear shouting and the sound of glass breaking.

"Sister, you and the others better stay inside. It's crazy out here. They've broken all the windows out of Steinberg's, and people are rushing in, just taking things. It's amazing!" He sounded excited, almost gleeful.

"John, go home; The police will . . . "

"The police!" he said, "Hell, the police are loading colour TV's into squad cars themselves. Stay inside. It's going to get wilder."

Sylvia called then with the same news, and two of Marie Nicholas' students called her. It was almost five o'clock and getting dark.

"We better go down and tell Grace," I said.

But she knew. She stood in front of the TV, watching the news. Rioting had broken out — they were calling it rioting now — all over the West Side. Pictures of stores being looted in a square that extended along Madison Street and Roosevelt Road from Ashland to Pulaski were on the screen. Redemption stood in the middle of that square. On television, teenagers ran down Madison, hurling rocks at windows and laughing. When the vespers bell rang, Grace turned to me.

"Tell the sisters to assemble in the community room, Maura. Right away."

I ran up to the Chapel and caught the nuns as they came up. Most of them didn't know that anything was going on and were surprised to see me waving them down.

"Sister Grace wants everyone in the community room, now. Everybody to the community room."

"What is this about?" asked Sister Ethel. She was a visiting Superior from the Motherhouse, one of Mother's counsellors, who had just arrived here to do Redemption's annual inspection. She'll remember this visit, I thought.

In the community room Grace stood next to the television, facing the assembled nuns seated in front of her. She had turned the sound down but the pictures continued.

Somewhere high above us a helicopter camera crew recorded billowing black smoke and leaping flames. "The rioters have begun setting fire to buildings," the announcer said. Grace began to speak, but the nuns were mesmerised by the fire on the screen. I looked at Alberta. Her choleric face was pale for once.

I hope you're scared to death, I thought. Feel like screaming for a light-skinned coloured girl now, Sister? Do you want to pace the auditorium balcony now, Sister, to glare down at the students, and dare them to talk or laugh or swing their arms? I remembered Florence, Sylvia and myself pressed against a wall, hiding, as Alberta rampaged down the hall after a rehearsal. How humiliated I felt, how cowardly. You're good at inspiring fear, Sister. Well now, are you afraid? Good!

"We're next," Helen cried out. "we're next."

"Come on, Sister Helen. No one wants to do anything to us," I said.

"How do you know? They'll break in, they'll burn us out."

"They'll . . . "

"Sister, please. All of you listen to me," Grace said in that voice of command she used so rarely. We all looked at her. "I am sure we are all safe here, but there are those among you who would feel better going to other missions. So I have arranged for cars to take you to St. Andrew's convent and St. Jean's. Please get your things together."

Most of the nuns stood up and started for the door. Sister Paula remained seated, as did Marie Nicholas and Joan and Alice. Alberta didn't move either, and after a few whispered words with her, Mary Ralph sat down again. God, please let Alberta leave so I can enjoy the riot in peace.

"Maura," Grace called. "would you go up and do Sister Helen's packing for her, and bring her walker down too?"

"My nightgown's under the pillow," Sister Helen said, "and the other things are in the top drawer."

I ran up the stairs. Sister Helen's room faced the park. What a beautiful sunset, I thought as I lifted her pillow and got the nightgown. Then I realized I was looking north. Fire! The whole sky was alight with it, not only to the north, but to the south, east and west too. On TV, the flames seemed evil, but from up here they made only a rosy glow that marked off the ghetto from the rest of the city, enclosing us in a square of pink light. Martin Luther King was dead. In the rest of the city, it might be business as usual, but not here — water no more, the fire next time.

I gathered Sister Helen's things together and hurried down the stairs. The nuns had been amazingly quick. They stood in the hall with their overnight bags and shopping bags.

"Sister," I motioned Grace aside. "Fires have broken out near us."

"Near us?" she asked.

"Yes, I saw them. Roosevelt, Madison, Homan too, I think."

"Well, in that case, get your things, you're going too. Marie Nicholas, the young nuns should go. We don't need many here."

"But Sister," I started. The doorbell rang. Somebody opened it, and there stood three nuns from St. Andrew's.

"We've got two station wagons and a car — plenty of room for you all," one said. In the bustle of getting the nuns out Grace didn't notice me run up the stairs. I went into her room, got up on the wide window-sill and pulled the drapes together. I can't leave, even Grace can't make me. I have to stay.

I watched the others hurry into the cars, glancing around all the time. I curled up into the window sill and looked out over the park. In the gathering dark, the fire's glow deepened and reddened the sky. The street lights flickered on and then went dead. Then the school and convent went dark, and even the traffic lights went out. A black-out! Was it an accident, or had the city done it on purpose?

I've got to go down and see what's happening. I found Grace.

"I wondered when you'd come out," she said. "Okay, come on."

The other seven stood in the hall.

"First, Joan and Alice, go to Chapel and bring down all the candles and candlesticks," Grace directed. "Put them in the front hall. Then, Alberta, go get that portable radio you keep hidden. Maura, Paula, and Marie Nicholas, bring the easy chairs from the community room here."

We hurried up, and soon set up camp in the wide entrance hall, a circle of easy chairs around the telephone switchboard, our link with the outside. Hour after hour we listened, eating sandwiches Grace made.

"Thank God I baked yesterday," she said handing out cookies.

The radio announcer described what he called the "devastation of the West Side." The only stores saved were those on which black owners had hastily painted "Soul Brother". Madison, Roosevelt Road, Homan, Pulaski, were aflame, looting was widespread and the police were staying out of it. Women wheeled baskets through the supermarkets, filled them up, then pushed them out the empty plate glass window frames and home.

At 10:30 p.m. we got a call from the city asking if we'd be willing to shelter burned-out families. We said, "yes," but to my disappointment none came. The only apartments burned were those over stores. Miraculously there were no injuries. The police continued to act with restraint, waiting for the people to wear themselves out and go home. Last summer the riots in Watts and Detroit had shown that police action could increase violence, not quell it.

"Sister, maybe we should go upstairs and check the roof?" Marie Nicholas and I asked Grace.

"Yes, do," she said.

Marie Nicholas and I took a candle and went up to the fifth floor of the school. It was quiet and still. We opened the door that led to the roof and stood for a moment. From this height we could see flames and smoke in all directions. We stood fascinated, until the wind blew a spark on to the roof. "Finally these clunky shoes are good for something," I said as Marie Nicholas and I stomped out the spark.

"What do you do with a dream deferred," I quoted. "Does it shrivel up and die like a raisin in the sun, or does it explode."

"Maura," she asked, "are you scared at all?"

"No," I said, "Excited but not afraid. Are you?"

"Not at all," she said, "and it surprises me."

A few more sparks landed. We jumped on them, hopping from one to the next, until we reached the wall. We leaned over and looked down. The breeze that brought the sparks lifted our veils. I looked at Marie Nicholas leaning casually against the wall and thought of the first time we'd come up here together. How strange the neighbourhood seemed then — seething with people and pressed down feelings.

"Look," she said to me, and pointed down to the street. A sectional couch walked across the park, each section balanced on the head of a different family member. Alongside it, people strolled home laden with clothing and food, TV sets and easy chairs.

We both laughed. "Direct action," I said.

"Redistribution of wealth," she agreed.

"Instant urban renewal," we said together.

People were going home now, and we went down to reassure Grace that the riot would end soon.

We said Compline at 3 a.m., chanting the psalm from our circle of armchairs. The two gold candelabra used at Benediction held only stubs of candles now, eight flickering lights in each. Just a few more hours and the sun will come up, I thought. The rage will be spent, and only the mourning for Dr. King will be left.

Grace intoned the last psalm, the De Profundis, the prayer for the dead we had said the night before.

> *Out of the depths I cry to you, O Lord;*
> *Lord, hear my voice!*
> *Let your ears be attentive to my voice in*
> *supplication:*
> *If you, O Lord, mark iniquities, Lord, who can*
> *stand?*
> *But with you is forgiveness, that you may be*

revered.
I trust in the Lord; My soul trusts in his word.
My soul waits for the Lord more than sentinels
wait for the dawn,
More than sentinels wait for the dawn let Israel
wait for the Lord,
For with the Lord is kindness and with him is
plenteous redemption;
And he will redeem Israel from all their
iniquities.

Grace came to the end of the prayers, and said, "And for the repose of the soul of Martin Luther King."

"Eternal rest grant unto him, O Lord," Sister Joan, Paula, Marie Nicholas, Alice and I answered. "And let perpetual light shine upon him."

Sister Alberta and Mary Ralph sat silent. Grace looked at them.

I saw Alberta's lips tighten; she said nothing.

More than sentinels wait for the dawn.

The dawn. I must have closed my eyes because I dreamt of the dawn, only it was the sky I'd seen from Grace's bedroom, red with flames that were burning the West Side.

Then a loud pounding started and a bell ringing loud and insistent. Mary Ralph screamed. She stood up. "Run for the basement."

"Sister, please," Grace said. She got up, straightened her habit and walked to the front door. I followed her into the vestibule. Through the glass of the door we could see the circling red light of a fire truck and the outline of a fireman knocking at the door. Grace let him in. He was dressed in a long slicker and smelled of smoke. Soot covered his face.

"I'm Captain Bach," he said. "My daughter is one of your nuns. I couldn't believe it when I heard you were still here. Are you crazy? We can take you out in the truck."

"Are we on fire?" Grace asked.

"No, but the circle is closing."

"But Captain, we're not in any danger," I said.

"Danger? The whole city could go up," he said."The Mayor just ordered the cops to shoot to kill any looters."

"Kill?" I said. "Killed for carrying a couch?"

"That seems rather extreme," Grace began.

"Extreme? You want us to turn the city over to animals? There's going to be a curfew. We're sealing this neighbourhood off, so it's now or never."

I looked at Grace. I could imagine her thoughts. The other nuns, were they in real danger? But to leave would be to say to the people in the neighbourhood, "We're afraid of you. We think you're what Captain Bach said, animals." And what if refugee families did show up?

"Grace, what about food?"

"Food?"

"Yes, for the people. They won't be able to get groceries in the neighbourhood. Right, Captain?"

"The stores are being boarded up. Double coupon day is over."

"So how will people eat? Our storeroom is jammed with canned goods, powdered milk."

I watched Grace — a picture was forming in her mind. Families locked in. The neighbourhood children crying for milk. We were staying.

Captain Bach just didn't get it. "I just don't get it," he kept repeating.

I tried. "Look, we're not afraid and if we leave, well, when we came back it would just never be the same. The kids would always know we ran."

"Nuts, you're all nuts," he said and stomped out.

Grace closed the door behind Captain Bach and turned to see Alberta.

"You have no right . . . " she said to Grace. "We must listen to that man."

Grace started to open the door. "You wish to leave, Sister. I'll call him back. You can go."

"And you?" Alberta asked.

"Staying here," Grace said quietly.

Alberta, you're afraid, terrified, I thought. Why won't you just go? Alberta took a breath, straightened her collar and turned on a flash light from her pocket. "Good night, Sisters," she said and headed up the stairs. We watched the pinpoint of light disappear.

"Well," said Grace to me. "She never was a coward. Let's go to bed, Maura. I hope I made the right decision. Tomorrow we'll make up grocery bags." I followed her and her candle up. At the chapel she stopped.

"Come on." We went in. The tabernacle lamp was suddenly practical — the only place in the convent that wasn't pitch dark.

All day I'd been saying, "Oh, God, no", or "Dear God, why?" But now here I was, face to face with the Infinite. My spiritual life at Redemption was simple. I was doing what I always wanted to do as a nun. I was working where I wanted to be, so prayer became a mutual plotting — how to help June, or make grammar interesting or the play good. I prayed to be sensitive to the kids and more charitable to the nuns and then of course to stop the war and to get Bobby

Kennedy elected. But those hard nights I'd had in the Juniorate were gone. I was having too much fun to spare time for a dark night of the soul.

But now with Grace, sitting here in silence, prayer was different. Why did the evil prosper? Why were the good struck down? "I had a dream". Why couldn't he be allowed to live out that dream? We hadn't seen the footage from his last speech in Memphis yet, hadn't heard him tell the crowd in that Memphis church, "I've seen the promised land. I may not get there with you, but I've seen the promised land." But that night in the chapel at Redemption I wasn't praying to see the promised land but just that this night would end with no one killed or hurt or arrested. I heard Grace get up — I stood up too and followed her out.

Early light came in from the window in the hall. "And with the dawn rejoicing," I said pointing out the window. "At least we'll be able to see," and I blew out my candle.

Grace's bedroom door was opened. She started in, then turned.

"Good night, Maura."

"Good night, Grace — um, listen. I was there in your window seat when the nuns left."

"You hid in my bedroom?"

"Sorry."

She laughed, shook her head and went to bed. It was 5:30 a.m.

"Maura, Maura! Wake up, Maura." It was Marie Nicholas knocking her way through my dreams. I got up and went to the door. Marie Nicholas stood there, a black robe closed over her long white cotton nightgown. Habitless and without her nightcap or glasses, she lost her

341

pioneer woman look. "Come and look. Look out Helen's window. The whole park is full of soldiers!"

I followed her across the hall. She was right. Garfield Park looked like TV footage of Da Nang, full of pup tents and soldiers, walking guard.

"But the riot's over," I said.

"They probably think black guerrilla bands are organising to march on Wilmette and Bridgeport," she said.

Two tanks rumbled by. "Tanks, Maura," Marie Nicholas said, "tanks on our street! Look!"

The turret revolved and now the long gun pointed at the first floor window of an apartment. Soldiers with rifles held ready accompanied the tanks walking slowly along each side of the street.

"What are they doing?" I said. "Who are they?"

"The National Guard," Marie Nicholas told me.

"Great," I said, "just what we need. Suburban kids who joined the National Guard to stay out of Vietnam. Wonderful — this is their chance to play war, and only a short commute. The boys from the West Side get to hack their way through the jungles and these jerks patrol Madison, M16 rifles cocked and ready."

"I just can't believe it, Maura."

"Let's go up to the roof," I said.

From the roof we could hear the tanks and see the soldiers as they stood with guns poised, guarding the empty basketball courts. But guarding from what? A Viet Cong raid? They wore the same gear as the soldiers we saw on the news — heavy green khaki jackets, high black boots, combat helmets. There were about twenty facing us from across the street. Some had beer bellies, and a few stood awkwardly with all their weight on one foot. All twenty held their rifles straight out, pointed at the street. Bayonets shining in the sun, fixed. But against what enemy? Dear God, don't let these guys get trigger happy. God, please don't let anything happen.

Just then a nine-year-old black boy ran out from a gangway into the middle of the street.

"Draft dodgers, draft dodgers!" he screamed out, and then turned and ran.

We heard the rifles click as the guardsmen lowered and aimed them towards the direction the little boy had run in.

"Stop! Stop!" Marie Nicholas and I screamed, leaning over the wall, forgetting that we were in robes and night caps. But the boy was gone. The soldiers lowered their guns.

"Jesus Christ," I said. "Everyone better stay in today."

Was revolutionary rhetoric, which I'd always taken as an elevated jive, true? Black frustration, violence and white overreaction, then civil war. That was the extremist prediction. But no one had mentioned the obvious. One side had the bombers, the bayonets, the tanks. An army invasion of the ghetto had seemed impossible even to the most radical, yet here it was. Dear God, please let it stay quiet.

That Saturday night there were no new fires, no more looting, but 400 people were arrested for breaking the 6 p.m. curfew, and seven black men were killed resisting arrest.

Sunday was Palm Sunday. Marie Nicholas and I insisted on going to St. Jude's for Mass. Mr. Benton drove us as usual. Along Madison the devastation was startling.

"Roosevelt Road is even worse," Mr. Benton said. "Can't buy food either — no stores open around here, and the soldiers stop any cars that try to leave. Sister Jane at

Lisieux House got food shipments in somehow, so people's going there. Really something."

"Yeah," I said, "we've got food too — but nobody came."

"I know some folks in pretty bad shape. I'll tell 'em." At church a small group, including John Wakefield and most of the other choir members, had gathered in the vestibule. Sister Jane, a tall, sixty-year-old Sister of Charity from Lisieux House, was arguing with Father Glenn.

"But, Father, it's more important than ever that we have our procession of palms," she insisted.

"What, parade past those guardsmen and tanks, carrying those banners?" He pointed at three placards saying 'Free at Last, Free at Last, Thank God Almighty I'm Free at Last.' Another had a picture of Dr. King, and on the third a large central cross and two smaller ones. Drawn under these were purple letters saying, 'Greater Love than this has no man, that he give up his life for his friends.'

"They'll see it as an overt act against them, as . . . " he stopped.

"Nonsense," said Sister Jane. "I'm sure the families of many of those boys out there have worshipped in this very church."

"We're ready," I said to, her, taking a palm from the bunch she held. She smiled at me and at Marie Nicholas. John Wakefield came and got his palm and stood next to us.

Should he go? If the guardsmen were jumpy . . .

"John," I whispered, "don't go . . . "

"Those guys won't do anything. Besides, my brother is a Green Beret and . . ." He made a few karate moves.

"Oh, great, that's all we need."

"Just kidding, Sister," he said.

By this time Father Glenn had accepted the inevitable. We started out, led by our three banner bearers, singing.

> *Holy, Holy, Holy*
> *Lord God Almighty*
> *Early in the morning my soul shall turn to*
> *you . . .*

We were on Jackson Boulevard now, approaching the corner of Kedzie. All of Kedzie had been hit, and the smell of smoke was still in the air. Tanks sat on each corner of the intersection, and as we approached, guardsmen appeared out of the turrets. On one side of the street stood the Chicago Transit Authority terminal, the 'barns' where hundreds of buses were garaged. A two-deep detachment of guards was stationed around it. More than 200 soldiers and the four tanks were out in the street, watching our small contingent processing among them.

> *Holy, Holy, merciful and mighty*
> *God in three persons*
> *Blessed Trinity.*

When we reached the CTA barns we stopped. Sister Jane left her place in front of me and walked up to the tank surrounded by guardsmen. As she approached, I saw them tense and grip their rifles. But she took no notice. They were just boys. She'd taught so many like them. She stopped before the soldier who stood closest to the gigantic rubber tracks that stretched over the wheels of the tank.

"Here, son," she said, handing him a palm.

I stopped directly across from him. I was close enough to see his face and eyes. He stared into space not even looking at the nun before him. But then he took the palm.

It's okay. He's . . . he held it a minute, then dropped it on the ground and kicked it under the wheels of the tank.

Sister Jane said nothing. She looked at him and the others and then rejoined us as we marched back to St. Jude's. Inside we shut the tanks and soldiers out, and prayed and mourned together. At communion Mrs. Wilkes, the ex-Baptist lady from choir practice, stood and sang alone. Not a Father Glenn special or a Catholic hymn. "This was Dr. King's favourite," she said.

> *Take my hand, Precious Lord, lead me on, let*
> * me stand . . .*
> *I am tired, I am weak, I am worn*
> *Through the storm, through the night*
> *Lead me on to the light.*
> *Take my hand, precious Lord,*
> *Lead me home.*

15

CONFRONTATION

We lived surrounded by an armed camp. They actually blocked the neighbourhood with police barricades. No one came in. No one went out. People came to us for groceries. Others called. Marie Nicholas and I made deliveries. The first was to a woman who lived in a terrible building with falling plaster and broken down stairs. She had three kids in one room with just a bed and a few folding chairs. I think that was the first really poor apartment I'd seen. We weren't allowed to go into homes, so I hadn't visited any of my students. I had only seen the outside of the poverty. As the days wore on I saw that how a place looked depended a lot on the individual family. Some were very neat with one grand touch like illuminated statues, and some were really luxurious, though all the furniture was covered in plastic. A few were a mess. Adjoining apartments would be totally different. We made a delivery in June's building so I knocked on her door. A nicely dressed woman answered. She was astounded to see me.

"Hello, I'm June's teacher."

"Well, come in. I'm June's mother. Kind of a strange time for a home visit. June's not here. I sent the kids to my mother's in Maywood."

"No — I won't come in. I was just dropping off groceries to the Walkers."

"Good," she said. "Those poor people."

"Are you all right?" I asked.

"Fine," she said. "Come on in, Sister. Tea, coffee, sherry?" She opened the door wider. I saw a long hall with an Oriental runner and beyond it a crystal chandelier.

"Thanks, Mrs. Johnson, but I'd better go. Best to June. She's a very good student and a . . . "

"Character? She's my mother reborn. Don't let her boss you."

"Goodbye."

The day of Dr. King's funeral the National Guard pulled out. The police lifted the barriers between us and the rest of the city. The nuns came back home. Marie Nicholas and I sat in the community room watching the funeral. Paula had gone back to work. Grace was to come in but she hadn't yet.

"It's the nightmare we can't wake up from," I said to Marie Nicholas as we watched yet another dignified widow soothe her small children. Coretta King took her daughter Yolanda's hand during the eulogy. *And someday all God's children may sing in the words of that old Negro spiritual, 'Free at last, free at last, Thank God Almighty, I'm free at last'*. Well he was free now.

Bong, Bong, Bong. My gong. "I must have a telephone call," I told Marie Nicholas, "probably my Mom." She and my Dad were on their first trip to Europe when the riots began. Brigid had called me. They were frantic. The Rome papers said that Chicago was burning, there was fighting in the streets. She'd reassured them. Maybe they were calling me.

Grace sat at the switchboard.

"Which line?" I asked.

"It's not a phone call, Maura. Sister Ethel wants to see you."

"Oh, Sister, couldn't she wait? The funeral's on.."

"Maura," Grace said, "she's a home superior."

"But ... "

"I'm afraid it's important." Grace looked grave.

Oh God, what now? I thought as I went into the parlour, where Sister Ethel waited for me on the blue velvet couch, under the gold-framed painting of the Assumption. Even the Blessed Mother seemed to be rolling her eyes as I sat down.

"Sister," she said, "I am very upset." Dramatic pause.

What did she want me to say? "Well, it has certainly been a trying time, Sister Ethel," I tried.

She didn't pick up on this remark, but rather repeated, "I am very, very upset. It has been brought to my attention that you were seen drinking out of a Pepsi bottle in the cafeteria on the final day of school last week." She frowned.

"A Pepsi bottle in the cafeteria?"

"Exactly, Sister. To think that you, clothed in our holy habit, would actually lift a bottle to your lips and drink from it in front of students. Sister, I ... I ... can find no words."

A Pepsi bottle in the cafeteria? Yes, that day someone had passed me a bottle and I had taken a sip.

This was right after the memorial Mass where Florence had sobbed out, "I have a dream," and Father Pete had absolved the whole school. And we had all cried together. I had drunk from a Pepsi bottle, while Alberta called out the white girls, and before the fires came, and the tanks. Before six men died. And the National Guardsmen refused Sister Jane's palm branch.

"Sister," I began, "I did drink, yes, I remember now. Please believe that I do respect the holy habit, and there are certain things like . . . well, like chewing gum that I would never do in . . . "

I couldn't look at her. I kept my eyes on the toes of her black oxfords. She was Augusta, Marie Charles, all the superiors. Once again my mind sought phrases, justifications, rationalisations, some words to bridge the gap between us, to explain that my position and her position were in some way joined. I had to stave her off so that I could continue my work. This woman had power over me, she could take me from this mission, from the people in the neighbourhood.

"If you remember, Sister, that day was very tragic, and the students were so grief-stricken, that I felt by being with them, that . . . and when the, er, the student, offered me, well I . . . "

"I could perhaps overlook this slip, Sister, but it seems to be part of a pattern. Do you know, Sister, that almost every single Sister in this House has mentioned some complaint about you to me? You are offending your Sisters with your virulent pro-Negro sentiments. Sister, Mother herself has received letters about you. One of which raised a very important point, which you perhaps in your naivety have missed, how many . . . " she hesitated for a minute, "pregnancies" — she forced the word out — "do you think resulted from the mixture of sexes you in your play encouraged?"

"Pregnancies? Sister, they just sang and danced together."

She shook her head sadly. "And now drinking from bottles in public."

She's crazy, a voice inside me said, and you're crazy to try to pacify her. But she'll transfer me, I thought. They'll send me away from here. But I could not go on. First the tears came and then I started to laugh — a Pepsi bottle. After all this, to be undone by a Pepsi bottle! I laughed and laughed and then I started to cry.

"You are excused," said the stunned Sister Ethel.

Grace found me in my room. I was sitting on the bed — that was against the rules too, but now that I'd broken the Pepsi bottle taboo, anything was possible. "They're going to transfer me, aren't they?" I said to Grace.

"I want you here," she said. "I've written to Mother."

"You knew!" I said. "Grace knew about these complaints to the Motherhouse. Why didn't she tell me?"

"We have a week before the obediences come out," Grace went on. "Mother's in the city next week, I want you to write her a letter. Explain your side of things. I'll get it to her, and maybe . . . "

"My side of things?" I said. "What, that I've tried to be a good teacher and help the kids? Isn't that obvious? What can I write?"

"It doesn't matter so much what you write but that you write — I'm not saying you should apologise but maybe admit you've been, well, over-eager and perhaps insensitive to your sisters . . . " she stopped and made a 'what can I do' gesture.

"Do you think I've been over-enthusiastic? Insensitive?"

"What I think is not the point."

"Will you write to Mother and tell her Alberta's a racist and shouldn't be allowed near black children? Will you write that?"

"No."

"Why? It's true!"

"It's not that simple, Maura."

"Grace, you were the one who told me not to con the superior — you said be direct, honest."

"Yes."

"Well, get her out of here."

"Alberta has friends in the community, on the council. It will look like I'm accusing her to save you. Later in my own way I'll let Mother know about Alberta. Maura, please — Mother needs a document — something from you to show the others who don't know you."

"OK," I said. "OK."

Paula helped me. So did Marie Nicholas. We spent three days on the letter. We had plenty of time. School had stayed closed since the riots through Easter vacation and now this week. It was quite a document — the *perite* at Vatican II would have been impressed. We quoted Council documents, the Old and New Testaments, Martin Luther King, Gandhi, Robert Emmet. We even brought Mother Taddeus, the order's founder, who at one point had been excommunicated by a bishop for refusing to turn over the title to the order's property to him. If she came back from that, surely Mother could overlook one tiny gulp from a Pepsi bottle.

"I wouldn't keep coming back to the Pepsi bottle, Maura," Paula said. "This is not about drinking out of a Pepsi bottle."

"I know, it's Alberta."

"More than her, too."

"What? What?"

"Look, the chapter is this summer, right?"

"So?"

"It's going to be a real battle — the nuns who want change versus those who don't."

"I know."

"You don't know. They — we — want a new Mother General, an entire new council, a complete revision of the rule book, and a modified habit."

"Dream on, Paula."

"We will get it," she said. "There are petitions circulating within the community. We've spoken to pastors, bishops, members of other orders. Maura, the time is now. Mother is very nervous and you, well you're just the kind of new nun they are afraid of."

"Afraid — come on, Paula, you're making this all too complicated."

"Grace is doing everything she can for you. But she has to be careful. She's our candidate. She's who we want for Mother."

"Grace? But why didn't she tell me?"

"She doesn't know. We don't want anyone accusing her of campaigning . . . "

Grace as Mother — boy, that would be something.

"Here," she gave me back the letter, "put in something about hope and patience and then it's fine."

School resumed Monday, May 1. June insisted on a May altar and so she and Charlotte and Denoris stayed after school to try to do something with the poor plaster Mary. June had her own view of the riot. "I think the worst was stealing from the dry cleaners," she said. "After all, those're people's clothes. A lady from my building says this boy had the nerve to come to the door and try to sell her one of her own dresses! She cursed him up one side and down the other."

They carried the statue to the front of the class and sat it on my desk.

"Salem Aliechim, Mary," Lenore said, tying a turban on to the statue.

It wasn't Mary We Crown Thee, but Our Lady didn't seem to mind.

"Sister." June pointed to the classroom door.

Alberta? No. I relaxed, it was Grace. Uh, oh — she looked so serious.

"Sister Ann Pierre is here to see you," she said.

Sister Ann Pierre was the regional superior. Well, this was it.

I took a breath. "Do you know what ... ?" I asked Grace.

"She just asked to see you."

"OK." Better hurry. I prayed as I walked — nothing modern or liturgical, but the old standards I'd used for exams and trying to make the phone ring. "Sacred Heart of Jesus I place my trust in thee. Little Flower/In this hour/Show thy power. Not my will but thine." If I'd had time I'd have turned the statue of St. Joseph to the wall.

Sister Ann Pierre was a heavyset nun, usually described by the community as "jolly." She didn't look jolly today, sitting there alone in the parlour. I went in.

"Sit down, please, Sister Maura."

I sat.

"Sister Grace asked me to come. She wanted you to be informed of your obedience personally." The obediences would be in the envelopes in everyone's prie-dieu that

Sunday morning. "Yours will be in your prie-dieu also. However, . . ."

Oh, why didn't she get to the point.

"Sister, your assignment for next year will be Marydale Academy in Indianapolis."

Marydale! The order's fanciest school, housed on a huge estate donated by a millionaire, run for the daughters of other millionaires. Most of the students were boarders.

"Sister Maura," she said using the formal phrase from the rule, "I ask you to accept this assignment in the spirit of Holy Obedience."

"No." Just like that — flat — NO. Was that me talking? "Sister Ann Pierre, I can't. I don't want to leave this neighbourhood."

"But Sister, you don't have that choice."

"Not as a Sister of the Redemption. But I can stay as myself. As Margaret Mary Lynch."

Sister Ann Pierre sighed and settled down further into the cushions of the couch. "Well, to be honest, Sister, I thought you might say that."

"You did?"

"And perhaps it is for the best," Ann Pierre went on. "I wish you luck, Sister."

"Thank you, Sister," I said and smiled — smiled so widely I stretched my serre tete. I had said I was going to leave! I had made the decision.

"Can I get you something to eat, Sister?" I asked. "Cookies, coffee?" I jumped up and headed for the door. Grace stood there.

"Marydale," I told her, "but I'm not going. I'm staying but not as, not . . . Grace, it's time for me to go."

"You're sure?"

"I am — It's so funny. I can't explain it. I didn't know what I was going to do, but now, it's like having weights fall off my shoulders. And this way, I won't really have to leave you, I mean, I plan to stay close, we'll see each other, I . . . "

Sister Ann Pierre was stirring on the sofa.

"Maura, go get some ice-cold Pepsis, and I left a tray of cookies in the kitchen. Bring them here," Grace said.

"Oh, sure, Sister," I said. "Sure." I ran down the hall and almost collided with Sister Ralph.

"Sister, my goodness . . . " she started.

"Sorry, sorry," I said as I ran by.

Down in the basement I opened the machine and took out three icy Pepsis. When I get my apartment, I'm going to keep the refrigerator stocked with Pepsis for Marie Nicholas, I thought. Paula will visit a lot, and Grace and Joan. Wait until I tell my family. "Delighted" my Dad said. Maybe I can go to the cottage in Wisconsin the week before I join the March on Washington organised by Dr King, and go to his Resurrection City campground. Free at last; free at last.

I tucked one cold bottle under my arm and ran up to the kitchen. The cookies were still warm as I shovelled them on to the plate, which I balanced on my wrist as I had learned in the Novitiate. Back in the parlour I was a smiling, chattering hostess, handing out cookies and Pepsi, and glasses of course. "Can't ask you to drink out of the bottle," I joked.

They both looked at me a little strangely. Was my giddiness some kind of nervous reaction? Were hysterics next?

I told my freshmen I had been transferred to another school, but nothing more.

"Well," said June, "you wouldn't have been our teacher anyway."

Sylvia and Florence came to me after school. "What's all this about going?" Florence asked.

"Come on," Sylvia said, "John's outside."

"Let's walk over to the park." The yellow green of early Spring covered the park. "So what can we do, Sister," John asked. "Picket, petition? Just tell us. We don't want you to go."

I was tempted. A long line of students marching around the building, chanting, "Hell, no, she won't go." Very dramatic. What would be accomplished? I could hear the nuns taunting Sister Grace. "See, that Sister Maura is a rabble-rouser, an egomaniac, a sensation seeker, a . . .see how necessary our letters were," they'd say. "Good we complained." Grace would have to listen to enough "I told you so's."

"Well, Sister?" John brought me back.

"No," I said. "No. I don't want to cause a lot of confusion."

"You're just going to go teach at some boarding school in the sticks?"

"Well, I could . . .I could . . . . " I stopped and looked at him dead in the eyes, as Charlotte would say.

"Yes, Sister," John said slowly, "you could."

"And stay here."

"And you will, won't you, Sister?"

"Yes, I will," I said.

Sylvia and Florence exchanged an annoyed look. "What are you two talking about?" Sylvia asked. "Yes," he said, "there are apartments in the neighbourhood, and jobs," John said.

"Jobs?" The other three said.

"Yes, if Sister wants to make a change."

"But Sister Alberta and the others would never let you live outside the convent!" Florence said.

"No, they never would," I said.

"So how . . . "

"Oh, I get it," Sylvia interrupted. "You're leaving. You're leaving the convent!"

"Yes I am, but I hope you don't think I'm deserting you or anything."

"Deserting? This is great! You could still put on plays with us."

"There's a stage at St. Jude's and another one at Lisieux House that I bet we could use," I said.

"Remember that play I told you about, Sister? The white kid and black kid who get killed. I've got the script," John said.

"But I, I won't be a nun."

"So what?" Florence said.

So what? That was it? So what? I thought they'd be shocked. My God, if a nun at Ladyhill had ever told me she was leaving, I would have fainted. So what!

Well, that high subsided. There were serious things to do and see to. Leaving the convent wasn't all that simple. But what shocked me was how easy the decision had been. I knew it was right. I could never go to Marydale. Just let me out. I remembered a dream I'd had in the Novitiate. I was home in my bedroom looking into the mirror and I was sobbing. I knew, in that emotional way you know things in dreams, that I had left the convent and was home and miserable. I was glad when I woke up and realised it was only a dream and that I was still in the Novitiate. I didn't want to be miserable now. But I wasn't miserable. I was sure and happy. Then I got sick, with a a hacking cough.

"Psychosomatic," Marie Nicholas said.

"Then you're part of the reason — I'll miss you so much."

"Maura — come on — you'll see me more this way than if you were in Indianapolis."

"True," I said and started hacking.

Grace gave me some cough medicine and I spent the next week in a codeine haze.

My cough and I went to the Motherhouse for the formalities. I was still swigging codeine on the bench waiting to go into Mother's office, taking it straight from the bottle.

"Reverend Mother will see you now." I followed the secretary into the office. This was the first time I'd ever spoken to Reverend Mother alone.

"Sit down, Sister," she said.

I sat, but the coughing began again. "Excuse me," I gasped, and walked over to the window. Turning my back, I took a quick sip of medicine. I waited for my breath. Same old grove, I thought, same old cedar trees; same grass, same blue sky, same quiet hanging over everything. But not the same me.

"Are you all right, Sister?" Reverend Mother asked.

"I'm sorry, Mother," I said. "I seem to have developed this cough."

"Yes." She was uncomfortable. She kept twisting the last bead on her chaplet with her left hand. She began to talk to me about my letter, and the religious life. She felt I'd missed an essential point, suffering. "Sister, we must expect to suffer. We follow the flagellated Jesus. Your transfer is an opportunity to suffer. Life within community occasions suffering."

"But, Mother," I said, "I'm willing to suffer, if need be, from fighting evil and injustice. But how can suffering itself be a goal? I expected support from the community. Flagellation shouldn't come from our sisters."

"The ones closest to us always bring the greatest pain," she said. "Jesus suffered most from his own disciples."

"But they didn't crucify him! And Mother, he did rise. What about the Resurrection, Mother?"

"Of course, Sister," she said impatiently. "We all believe in the Resurrection. But glory and fulfilment must wait for the next world. I do believe you are sincere in your commitment to help coloured people. Therefore I would be willing . . . "

I sat up straighter. Could she possibly reconsider it? Was I going to win? My stomach contracted and I felt my heart beat faster. Six staccato coughs ripped open my throat. If she says yes, there'll be no Resurrection City, no Wisconsin, no summer production for the kids, unless I could possibly get permission. And Alberta all over again. But I could stay — stay at Redemption.

She continued. " . . . to arrange for you to reside at St. Brigid's Parish."

"St. Brigid's?" I said. "And do what, teach at the grade school?"

"Well, no, Sister, we couldn't permit that. However, you could help out around the convent, study, and . . . " her voice trailed off.

"Well, I don't know, Mother, this is totally unexpected. I . . . "

"Well, don't feel you must give me a decision right now, Sister. Pray about it. You may return here . . . " she reached under her cape and pulled out the small steel watch I'd seen nuns consult since my early childhood, "in one hour, Sister. Perhaps you would like to consult with Sister Augusta or Sister Mary Francine. In fact, I must insist that you speak to Sister Augusta. As a Junior Sister, she is your official superior."

Nicole was waiting for me on a bench outside the office. We walked together down Parquet Hall, past the big church, to the Juniorate. I looked up and saw the same pictures and mottos overhead that I'd seen as I processed down the hall in my bridal gown to receive the habit, and then in my white veil to take my vows. "My dear Sisters, what do you ask?" the bishop had said. What I asked was to live out those passages painted so carefully in gilt on the walls. I read each one as we walked beneath them.

> *My soul magnifies the Lord*
> *My spirit rejoices in God my saviour*
> *Blessed are the meek*
> *Blessed are the peacemakers*
> *Blessed are they who hunger and thirst after*
> *righteousness, for they shall see God.*

And then my favourite, because it was so strange.

> *Keep me as the apple of your eye*
> *Shelter me under the shadow of your wings.*

I heard again the choir sing the 'Tota'. "You are all beautiful, O Mary."

And the 'Veni Sposa Christi', 'Come Spouse of Christ.'

"My dear Sister, what do you ask?"

We turned into the corridor leading to the big church. I could see through the doorway the flickering tabernacle light and the sheen of the white marble altar, gleaming in the darkness.

Nicole and I went in, walked up the aisle and slipped into my old prie-dieu. Here I am, Lord, what the hell should I do?

We walked out the door of the church and started towards the juniorate.

"I hated one nun on my mission, Nicole, really hated her. I never hated anyone before, but when I see her I feel hate. And sometimes that hate would spill over onto the other nuns who'd complain or give me a hard time about things. They drive Grace crazy with their backbiting and gossiping. And these were my judges, Nicole, the ones who wrote home to Mother about me."

Nicole stopped. "You know, Maura, a year ago you wouldn't have said any of that, even if you'd felt it. You'd say, well, Sister so-and-so yelled at me, but of course she has arthritis, or I wanted to do this project but I understand why Sister said no. You defended everyone."

"Especially myself," I said. "Mother offered me residency at St. Brigid's."

"And you'd teach at Redemption," she said.

"No," I said.

"Where then, at St. Brigid's?"

"No, I'd have my own ministry — within the walls of the convent."

"And what are you going to do?"

"I don't know. St Brigid's is in the neighbourhood."

We were at the top of the Juniorate stairs now. "Would you wait for me?" I whispered. "I don't think I'll be long." Sister Augusta's door was open. Most of the other juniors were at class; her office was empty. I knocked on the open door.

"Come in," she said without looking up from the book she was reading. "Good afternoon, Sister," I said.

"Oh, Sister Maura, I've been expecting you."

"You know about . . . "

"Oh yes, I've heard about your adventures. Prudence never was a virtue of yours, Sister."

"I guess not, Sister. But I only wanted . . . " I began.

She held up her hand. "Mother told me she has offered you a compromise. You know of course, Sister, that's most unusual. Our vow of obedience does not include any options."

"I realise that, Sister," I said. "And I appreciate what Mother . . . "

"Sister Maura," she interrupted me. "I have no doubt that you'll consider Mother's offer. You are too kind a person and too polite to simply ignore it. But, Sister, let me tell you, you may go through the process of considering it, but you will leave."

How like Augusta to follow up the first compliment she ever gave me with something that sounded very much like an effort to get rid of me. But instead of the anger and frustration I used to feel standing in this worn spot in front of her desk, I felt again that lightness of spirit I'd experienced when Ann Pierre told me I was changed to Marydale. I was leaving. I had tried my hardest, but I was trying to be something I wasn't. They knew it, and now I did too. They weren't going to change to fit my needs. Why should they? They were the Congregation of the Sisters of the Redemption. Founded 1840, and under no authority but that of the Holy See. And I was Margaret Mary Lynch. 'My dear Sister, what do you ask?'

I was back in Mother's office an hour later. Mother hadn't seemed very surprised when I told her that I had decided to leave. "Well, Sister, if that's what you wish, if you feel prepared to make an immediate transition, that probably is for the best."

Mother opened her drawer and took out a file. "We have your separation papers here, Sister." I looked them over.

"I agree to renounce any pay for services rendered to the Sisters of the Redemption, and further state that I have no claim in any manner or form on said institution. I further acknowledge that the Congregation of the Sisters of the Redemption bears no responsibility for any medical, dental, or other expenses I may incur from this day forward."

Medieval ritual on the way in, all business on the way out. I signed the sheet. Mother's secretary, a bird-like creature I hadn't even realised was standing in the corner, moved over to sign as a witness. Then Reverend Mother signed. There it was. Though my vows wouldn't expire officially until August 15th, for all practical purposes I was no longer a Sister of the Redemption.

I stood up, shook hands with Mother, with Mother's secretary. "I'm glad you're feeling better, Sister Maura," Mother's secretary said.

"Pardon me?" I didn't know what she meant.

"Your cough seems to have disappeared."

"Well, yes, I guess it has."

"I presume you intend to finish out your last week of teaching?" Mother said.

"Oh, yes," I said.

"I need not tell you that your decision should be kept confidential," she said. "You will of course refrain from discussing this with the students or the other sisters. And your plans?"

"I'm not sure. I'll be working in the neighbourhood — teaching, I guess or social work."

"And do you intend," Mother began leaning forward, "to um, marry into the Negro race?"

"Mmmmmarry?" I stuttered.

"Yes — to uplift it."

Was I hearing right? I looked at her. She and Sister Secretary were all polite attention — What had those nuns written? Uplift it – what, make more light-skinned coloured girls? What could I possibly say? I smiled and actually said, "God bless you, Mother." I left.

Grace took me shopping. We went to the Daisy Shop on Madison.

"Bright colours," the black woman who waited on us suggested. "A change."

"No more madras?" I said.

That night I snuck Florence and Sylvia up the back stairs to show them the new dresses, which they approved.

"But aren't the skirts kind of short?" I asked.

"Shit," Florence said. "Even old ladies wear them above the knee. And how old are you, Sister?"

"Twenty-three," I said.

"Shit, take it up another inch."

"You girls are getting very free and easy with your language, I notice," I said. They giggled. "Well, Sister . . . hey wait a minute," said Sylvia. "What are we going to call you now?"

"You can call me Margaret Mary," I said. "But not one minute before your graduation and mine."

"When are you going to tell your freshmen?"

"Tomorrow," I said. "I hope they understand."

"Oh, they're glad, Sister. Everybody's glad for you!"

"Everybody?" I said.

"Oh yes," Sylvia went on. "We don't know how you stood Alberta and those other biddies for as long as you did. And we all hope you meet a real handsome guy and get married and have lots of kids."

"Sylvia, please," I said.

"Oh, sorry, Sister. But we knew you weren't no lezzie or anything."

"No what?"

"You know, Sister, no homosexual. We figure that some of the nuns are but we didn't think you . . . "

"Enough, enough," I said, "let me get through these last few days before you get me a husband."

Two mornings later at breakfast, Grace took a spoon and clinked it against her glass. "I have an announcement to make. Sister Maura will return to her family tomorrow. I'm sure you all join with me in wishing her well. God bless you, Sister." Marie Nicholas squeezed my hand. Last night she and Joan, Paula and Alice had had a going away party for me in Joan's music room. But this was the first official announcement. Alberta didn't even look up from her breakfast.

At this point I had planned to make a speech. I'd written it out and read it to my mother on the phone last night. "Don't do it, Margaret Mary," she'd said. "After all, you're not the Pope abdicating."

"But I want to explain," I'd said.

"You've explained enough, just come home."

So I said nothing, and neither did anyone else. Didn't any of the other nuns want to say goodbye or wish me luck or anything?

I guess no one did. I walked with the others down the hall in a silent file. We stood in front of the elevator. When it came, six of us got in. Still there was silence. Then Sister Martin Claire, who I characterised to myself as traditional but good-hearted, spoke up.

"Maura," she said. I waited. Good, at least someone was going to acknowledge me. "Maura, I was wondering. since . . . well, I mean . . . could I have your fused caps?"

Then Sister Hilda chimed in. "And could I have your synthetic collars?"

First I was stunned and then, thinking of my mother, I started to laugh. Oh Mom, how right you were. Not the Pope abdicating. Only caps and collars to be given away. I laughed harder.

Everyone in the elevator looked at me, horrified. Their worst suspicions confirmed. Leaving the order and laughing!

"Certainly, of course, Sisters." Right there in the elevator I took off cap and collar and handed one to each. "I'll drop off my spares in your rooms," I said.

The elevator door opened. I got out first, bareheaded and bare-necked. I skipped — my feet did it on their own — skipped back to my room.

16

OH FREEDOM

The day I left Redemption, Bobby Kennedy was killed. Gone in a minute. Murdered in a kitchen.

Again the children left behind. The dream deferred. The funeral. 'God of loveliness. Take my hand Precious Lord'.

Bobby. Announcing his candidacy surrounded by his children. Knowing the risk of course, knowing the risk and doing what was right. If he can, I can, I had thought and now, now . . . DEAD. DEAD.

At least I could suffer through this with my own family. Sally and Laura had been canvassing for Bobby's campaign on the weekends. "He was going to win. People loved him," Sally said.

"I'm going to the March on Washington," I told everyone almost as soon as I unpacked my Daisy Shop outfits.

"You are not actually going to wear those?" Laura had said.

"I really just need a pair of jeans and some blouses," I said.

"Blouses, nobody wears blouses. T-shirts. Here. Try one."

I pulled it over my head. "I can't wear this!"

"Why?"

"Look," I said, pointing to the mirror.

"What?"

"My, my breasts!"

"What's the problem?" Laura said. "You're no Jayne Mansfield but . . . "

"You can see them. Look."

"Maggie, you've got a bra on, don't you?"

"Of course I have. We weren't that backward."

"Well?" She shrugged and walked away.

I hadn't seen my body in years and now there I was, legs and boobs for all the world to look at . . . or not. You'll get used to it, I told myself as I pulled the cotton T-shirt away from my chest. And I did, after a few months. My hardest moment came at the beach, not over wearing a bathing suit, but over relaxing in public. I'd gone to hear a concert at the lake and I could not lie down on the blanket. My body just would not let itself stretch out in public. I sat with my arms wrapped around my knees for the first part, then leaned back on my hands, then eased my legs out straight. Finally my head went down and just as the band reached its crescendo, my muscles relaxed and I flung my arms out. I felt the sand under the blanket and the stars dipped down — and I was home.

But that was to come. Now I had to go to Resurrection City. My mother wasn't thrilled. "Mag, don't rush off. Stay. We've missed you. Relax. Get used to, well, being out."

"I can't, Mom. The march is next week."

"That's what I mean. Skip the march."

"Skip it? Oh no. Especially not now, not after Bobby too. Mom, I left so I could do things like go on this march."

"Maggie, you may find that you left for reasons you don't even know."

"I know why, Mom. If it was just to be home, well, I mean that would have been giving up. But . . . " I stopped.

"OK, honey. But there's no shame in choosing what's good for you just because it is good for you."

"Mom, I didn't leave for selfish reasons," I said. What did she think?

"Sweetheart, be just a little selfish. It puts other people at ease." She kissed me and walked out.

Sometimes I don't understand my mother. I'll be home in a week and then Resurrection City — the March. Free at last, free at last.

And so I was on my way again, in my jeans, T-shirt, denim jacket, and backpack.

"Margaret," my dad said as I was leaving. "Do me a favour — take the bus, not the 'L'."

"But Dad, the 'L' takes forty-five minutes, and the bus takes over two hours."

"The bus is safer."

"But Dad, you have to consider." Wait a minute. Was I trying to get permission? "OK, Dad," I said. I took 'L'.

This little light of mine, I'm going to let it shine, I sang, walking with hundreds of thousands of others. *Like a tree that's standing by the water, I shall not be moved . . . We Shall Overcome*, of course, and *If you look for me in the back of the bus, and you can't find me nowhere, Come on over to Washington, and you will find me there, In the morning. You will find me there.*

Marching with hundreds of thousands, doing it for once, not watching, wishing, putting my money where my mouth is. Well, my Dad's money actually and Laura's T-shirt.

Before I'd be a slave, I'd be buried in my grave,
and go home to my Lord and be free.

After the march I found a place in one of the A -frame huts that made up Resurrection City. There was a lot of music-making in the camp, communal meals of greens and beans, and many, many speeches. There were camp marshals to keep things moving smoothly, but there were no real problems. Sometimes a kid would stray from its mother, or someone would get too drunk on Ripple wine. Yet all in all, it was calm. On one side my neighbours were Crow Indians, on the other, Quakers, and across the way lived a family of six kids, a mother and grandmother who'd travelled up from Mississippi on the Poor People's Mule Train. Reverend Jesse Jackson and Dr. Ralph David Abernathy were there. Dr. Abernathy always used all three names when making an announcement over the camp loudspeaker.

"This is Dr. Ralph David Abernathy. You asked for fat back in your beans tonight. The cooks have put fat back in your beans."

Bible revival was the camp style.

My roommate was Johnnie Smith, a girl my age from Akron, Ohio. She taught me to carry a toothbrush at all times in case we got arrested during a demonstration.

"Charge you five dollars in jail," she said.

The second night we were there, I joined Johnnie and her friends who were sitting in all night at the Agriculture Department to protest at the way food stamps were administered. There were a lot of cops around, and many were black. Johnnie and I liked to skip by them, singing:

"Which side are you on, boy, which side are you on."

"It makes me so mad," Johnnie said, as we sat on the cool marble steps of the main entrance to the Agriculture building. "Do you know poor people in Sunflower County, Mississippi, get nine dollars a month to feed their families, while white farmers get paid thousands of dollars not to plant crops? It doesn't make sense."

"No, it does not," I agreed.

"You ladies want a taste?" It was the one of the 'medical officers' calling out to us. He came over, an older black man with a white rag tied around his arm. A red cross was painted on the rag. He carried a large jug and some paper cups.

"Oh good," I said. "I'm thirsty, I could do with a drink of water." But what he filled our cups with was Ripple wine.

"Mmm, this tastes good," Johnnie said, as we sipped under the stars. "I feel so free here," she went on. "See, I've been going to this little evangelical college, on a scholarship. I was the token nigger. The people were nice I guess, but I always felt like I was on display. What they really wanted me to do was to become like them. Jesus, at first I tried. All I wanted was straight hair and a husband who worked hard. I'd gotten myself out of the ghetto. Let the others get their own selves out.

"Then when they killed King, I got so mad, I mean, Margaret, he was a good man, there was no hate in that man. No evil, only dreams and hopes, and a lot of faith. They were real sorry at my college when he died, but then when Detroit went up in smoke, and Chicago, they weren't so sympathetic anymore." She readjusted the red kerchief she wore around her hair, and took a long drink from her Ripple.

"So I said to myself, what the hell, I let my hair go nappy, put my hat on backwards, and took off."

We laughed together. I took a slow pull on my wine. My first real drink.

"And where you been, Margaret?"

"What do you mean, where have I been?"

"You've been someplace," she said.

"Well, college and then teaching and . . ." Johnnie looked away. She knew I was, well, bullshitting. "The convent," I said in a rush. "I just left two weeks ago."

"You were a Sister — I'm not surprised."

"You're not?" DAMN.

So much for jeans and T-shirts and Michele's eye make-up lessons.

Sitting here resting my bones/And this loneliness won't leave me alone/ 2,000 miles I roamed/Just to make this dock my home . . . Johnnie began to vamp softly. Thank God the kids thought it was essential to learn Otis Redding. *Sitting on the dock of the bay, wasting time*, the brother with the wine joined in, *Looks like nothing's gonna be the same.* No, nothing will.

"Why did you leave?" she asked.

"I started to feel that they didn't really need me. Anybody would do — Any body."

"Yeah," she said. "Felt the same way and we ain't anybody — right?"

"Right!"

The last night, the festival feeling in the camp changed drastically. At 3 a.m. with no warning, the D.C. police shot canister after canister of tear gas into the camp. It hung in the Washington summer night air and turned our camp into a suffocating nightmare. Babies screamed, children ran through the gas crying. Old people fainted and were almost trampled.

I joined some women in a central tent where we collected wandering children, bathed their eyes and put Vaseline on their faces to keep the skin from blistering. They were terrified. Tear gas is terrifying. When the gas pushed down into my lungs I would have run anywhere, done anything to breathe. And these kids had been gassed in their sleep.

By five a.m. most of the children had been claimed, except for a three-year-old girl and a four-year-old boy, brother and sister. A woman carrying two babies, one six-months-old and the other eighteen months, came up

"Those are mine," she said.

She had no more arms, so I picked up the two kids and followed her. She was big, but with more muscle than fat. Her hair was cut very short, and her skin was dark. I can't remember exchanging any words as we plodded through the thick mud, coughing at the gas that still lingered. Then after a few steps, she told me to put the four-year-old down.

"He's too old for carrying. Can't let him get used to it."

"But the mud . . . " I objected. Constant rain had kept the camp sunk in swampy Washington mud. "Wade in the water," we'd sung. No more singing now . . .

"Set him down," she ordered.

I did. He started to cry. From behind a tent a man stepped forward. He had on denims and a straw hat, the uniform of the camp security guards, and the patch on his jacket said 'Blackstone Ranger'. He picked up the crying boy and joined our procession through the camp that was quiet now, with the smell of tear gas almost gone.

"Here," the kids' mother said, and we handed her children into her shack.

The ranger walked me back to the main street of the camp where my A-frame was. "Want to go around the world?" he asked.

"What? Er, well, I would love to travel someday but . . ."

He looked at me for a long moment. "Night," he said and left.

"You got propositioned, girl," Johnnie said when I told her about his strange question. She laughed. "Missed your chance, girl."

"Yeah — well, one thing at a time."

The next morning the army, National Guard and the D.C. police came to drive us out of the camp — a force of 15,000 to displace 300. It reminded me of the riots, but at least this time I could do something to express my beliefs. I could be with the people who believed as I did.

Two groups were formed, one to march with Dr. Abernathy to the Capitol building, and one with Jesse Jackson to the Agriculture Building. Demonstrating on the Capitol grounds is a federal offence. If you went you would surely be jailed. I didn't go. The kids were waiting for me to put on John's play. Johnnie and I planned to march at the Democratic Convention in Chicago. I had too much to do to go to jail.

I sat on the steps of the Agriculture building with one hundred others, listening to Jesse Jackson preach. Thousands of soldiers and police ringed the block.

"The water's broke," he said, "and you all know what it means when the water breaks — the baby has got to be born. And it will be born. Freedom will ring. We will be free."

He is my age, my generation, I thought. So are most of the others here, black or white, poor or not poor, women and men. Trying to turn it all around. Trying.

Now Jesse Jackson was asking us to join him, to repeat his phrases.

"I am Somebody," he cried.

"I am Somebody," we roared back.

"I may be black . . . "

"I may be black."

"But I am Somebody."

"I am Somebody."

"I may be white or yellow or red . . . "

We all repeated it.

"But I am Somebody."

"I am Somebody," I shouted, along with the rest, as loud as my voice would go. "I am Somebody."

"I may be poor . . . "

"I may be poor . . . "

"But I am Somebody."

"I am Somebody."

I'd been a child in my family, a student at school, a nun in the convent, a Catholic in the Church, and now I was, well, Somebody — whatever that was. Whatever that would be.

"Soul Power," he finished.

"Soul Power," we said.

Soul Power.

Soul Power.

I am somebody.
Somebody.
Somebody.
Me.

EPILOGUE

So that's the story. Putting it down I can see every face, hear June's voice and Matthew's. I can close my eyes and those six years unroll like a familiar movie. Six years. It wasn't long, really. Now, six years go by faster than it took to get from Christmas to Christmas when I was a kid. Is this how it is if you spent those years in the army or in college or nurse's training? Is the experience imbedded forever because you're young and *every* experience is so intense? I don't know.

One thing this weekend taught me was that Alberta and the other authorities who made my life miserable are the least important part of my memories now. The key to all was us — the band members, my friends and my students. The experience was each other. All weekend, we never stopped talking to each other. There were moments I met the authorities. Mother Mary Placid and I used a full ten seconds of eye contact to decide we both forgot her final question to me. But I couldn't resist telling her my husband was born in Ireland. "Uplifting mongrel Irish Americans!" I said. She smiled quickly. And Alberta? Gone — died peacefully. She paid, though. The year after I left Redemption, the raisin in the sun exploded.

"We're not taking it any more," the girls told her.

They even took over the building briefly. Grace kept them supplied with milk and cookies. Alberta left. But

Grace, well, in March of that year, 1969, she found out that she had cancer of the colon.

"I felt no pain, Margaret," she'd told me. "I just went for the check-up because the diocese was giving it free, and I wanted to encourage the other nuns to go." I visited her a lot that summer. "I'll come back and teach," I told her. I was working and living in the neighbourhood, in an apartment she helped me furnish, complete with the Virgin Mary statue from my classroom closet.

"No, Maura," she said, "never look back."

"Something may be gaining on you," I finished.

By September, she was extremely thin and in terrible pain. The injections of pain killers hurt as much as they helped. She had no flesh on her bones. "There's just no place to stick a needle," she said to me one day.

I stopped another day after work to see her. She was very weak. She held my hand, breathing heavily. I had brought L'Air du Temps and sprayed it behind her ears. "Don't worry," I said, "Vatican II said perfume was OK." I saw her gather her strength to say something to me. "Give my love to your mother." That exhausted her. And it was five minutes before she opened her eyes again. Then with a terrible effort, she said, "And to your father, too."

That was Friday. On Sunday I went to St. Jude's, and right after communion I felt gripped by fear. I ran the six blocks down Jackson. The front door was open. I ran up the steps to her room. The nuns were standing outside. Grace was dead. She was fifty-five years old.

My last visit of the weekend is to her grave — one round, white headstone among so many others — where she would want to be with her sisters. But too young, too young.

Take my Hand Precious Lord, Oh God of Loveliness.

Marie Nicholas stood with me and Paula. Both had left the convent. Paula was married with two kids, Marie Nicholas was writing and teaching.

Matthew had left too. She was married with two boys. "Doing social work," she explained. "Still really in Floodtown," she laughed. Laughed a lot and played her guitar and teased. She had become Nancy Thurler-plus again.

Paula had a bottle of champagne and three paper cups.

"Bye, Grace. We love you." We drank and Paula poured the champagne over the grave. The bubbles foamed on the grass and caught the light. Love you.

Love.

It was something about love, those years.

"We should say a prayer," said Paula. "Ask for something special, this is a powerful place."

Hmm, what did I need?

Grace would not appreciate being asked to intercede for something selfish or material. But a vague petition for world peace or the end of world hunger seemed a cop-out.

Ah, but there was a phrase we used in prayers when we didn't want to tell what it was we wanted, or when we weren't sure ourselves what we needed — a blanket that covered the present, the future, and even the past.

"Let's pray for our intentions, our Special Intentions."

The others smiled and nodded. "For our Special Intentions," they said.

"Amen."